THE GIBRALTAR AFFAIR

GEORGE WALLACE

DON KEITH

SEVERN RIVER

PUBLISHING

Severn River Publishing
www.SevernRiverBooks.com

ISBN:978-1-64875-635-1 (Paperback)

ALSO BY THE AUTHORS

The Hunter Killer Series

Final Bearing

Dangerous Grounds

Cuban Deep

Fast Attack

Arabian Storm

Warshot

Silent Running

Snapshot

Southern Cross

The Gibraltar Affair

The Tides of War Series

Argentia Station

Also by George Wallace

Operation Golden Dawn

Cold is the Deep

Also by Don Keith

A Call to War Series

Never miss a new release! Sign up to receive exclusive updates from authors Wallace and Keith.

severnriverbooks.com

This final book in The Hunter Killer Series is dedicated to our loyal readers, and especially those who have reached out to tell us how much they enjoyed our stories or had questions and suggestions. That also includes those who took the time and effort to leave reviews and ratings wherever such input is welcomed. We write these books to be read by you, and we are humbled and happy that you have accepted them so positively.

1

Ali Hakim Sherif stepped out of the *bayt al-shar*—the traditional Bedouin black wool tent, one that had become a distinctive icon in his thrust for power—and into the harsh noontime desert sun. His loose-fitting, long white *thawb* fluttered in the hot, dry wind, while his red-checkered *keffiyeh* helped to shield his sharply chiseled face from a relentless sun.

He stretched, allowed his eyes to adjust to the glare, then looked out over the barren landscape. The place was utterly devoid of life for as far as he could see. This time of year, the black volcanic rock of the Aswad al Haruj, the most inhospitable region of the Libyan Desert, absorbed the sunlight and radiated it back as unbearable heat. Any living thing foolish enough to venture out into this remote and remorseless land placed its life at the direst risk. The only reason to be in this environment was a desire to avoid people and to be unseen. And that was exactly why Ali Hakim Sherif had chosen this spot.

Further to the south and east, over near the Sudanese border, a smattering of Bedouins somehow found enough vegetation in the valleys to graze a few scrawny cattle and carve out a paltry existence, despite the area getting less than an inch of rain per year. The Bedouins were a people who took great pride in doing whatever was necessary to make the most of the life Allah had granted them.

They had learned the desert's secrets and managed to survive where no one and nothing else could or would. The closely woven camel wool tents were one good example of their methods and skill. The black wool absorbed the sun's heat, causing the air inside to rise through the weaving while drawing air in from under the tent walls. The resulting convective breeze cooled the inside of the tent, providing a form of natural air conditioning.

Ali Hakim Sherif knew that he needed these resourceful Bedouin tribes to be his allies in his fight to rule Wilayat Tarabulus Althaania, the Second Regency of Tripoli. Or what most of the world insisted on calling Libya. Just as his ancestor, Suleiman the Magnificent, had so successfully done when he called on the Bedouins to help him build the First Regency of Tripoli five hundred years before. That bit of history had great bearing on the meeting about to take place in this isolated spot. It would be one that would ensure even more assistance from another entity, but one a great distance from this dry, hot region. And a conference that would one day be covered in history books and studied by scholars the world over.

"Come back into the *bayt al-shar*," suggested a deep male voice from inside the shadowy recesses of the tent. "The shade is much more comfortable, and we can better discuss your proposal."

In the near darkness inside the tent, Bahri Dawoud Kahir ad-Din Misurata reclined on a pile of cushions as he sipped from a small glass of highly spiced, hot, sweet tea. The elderly man was the leader of the Misuratas, one of the major tribes in the eastern part of the Second Regency. He was also one of the most powerful influences in determining who would rule this land. In keeping with age-old Bedouin tradition, Bahri was the name he was given at birth, Dawoud was his father's name, and Kahir ad-Din was his grandfather. Each had served in his own time as chieftain of the Misurata tribe, and each was venerated for his bravery and sage guidance. As with his ancestors, Bahri's leadership and decisions were unquestioned.

"Bahri, my friend," Ali Hakim replied. "I am merely relishing my rare bit of quiet time here in our desert home, far from the din of Benghazi traffic."

"I understand. Still, we have much to discuss before your Chinese friends arrive," Bahri countered. "And your tea is growing cold."

Ali Hakim chuckled. "Nothing can truly be cold out here in the desert summer. The sun and the sand see to that." He re-entered the tent and resumed his position on the pile of carpets.

The other men in the *bayt al-shar*, the Misuratas' tribal elders who had been gathered to hear and advise in these discussions, remained quiet as they shifted back so that the two leaders could continue their conversation.

With stunning abruptness, an explosion erupted just outside the tent, shredding the walls with flying shrapnel. Machine gun fire ripped through the fabric, slashing down two of the men seated inside. The rest, the quicker ones, rolled to the floor and grabbed their weapons. Ali Hakim tackled Bahri and threw him to the ground just as a burst of fire chewed up the carpet where Bahri had been reclining. The pair rolled toward the back of the tent, searching for a clear way out.

Ali Hakim's Russian-made AK-74M assault rifle was never more than an arm's reach away. Dragging his weapon, he slithered out from beneath the back of the tent. He saw at once that Bahri's Bedouin warriors were already caught up in a firefight. Someone had eluded the outlying guards and managed to sneak up on and attack the small encampment. They were throwing down withering fire from up on the bluff that formed the near edge of the *wadi*. The tribesmen were doing their best to return fire, to try to discourage the attackers on higher ground, but they were in a losing position. Someone would have to figure out another way to take out the shooters if there was to be any hope of defending themselves.

Ali Hakim sensed someone crawling up beside him. It was Bahri, slipping a fresh magazine into his own AK before rolling over and spraying the ridgeline with a torrent of bullets.

"We must get behind them or they will slaughter us," the Bedouin chief announced with surprising calm, echoing Ali Hakim's own thoughts. Then he pointed toward the bluff. "Over there! There we will find our only way up."

He pointed to a small fissure in the volcanic-rock bluff that led upward. It was barely wider than their shoulders. The older man made a quick dash across the open ground to try to reach it. Ali Hakim followed close behind as bullets tore through their *thawbs* and spattered up rock shards, turning them into shrapnel that zinged all around them. Once they were in the narrow crevice in the rock, hidden from the attackers, they climbed up the steep fissure to the crest above.

When they emerged, they saw the ambushers were concentrating on the Bedouins in the valley below, rising just high enough to fire or launch another grenade, then dropping back down behind cover as their onslaught attracted return fire. The gunshots and explosions echoed piercingly off the canyon walls. A dozen or more men lined the top of the *wadi* shooting down at the encampment below, but none appeared to be aware that Ali Hakim and Bahri were now behind them.

The pair, slipping into cover behind the black volcanic rock, took careful aim before firing their first shots, picking off a pair of the attackers, and then quickly getting off another couple of shots, taking out two more. Sensing an attack from behind them, the shooters realized that roles had switched. They were the ones in the most vulnerable position. Turning, firing bursts from their own automatic weapons, the shooters fled at a full run down the back side of the bluff, quickly disappearing into the maze of ancient lava flows and tumuli that was so typical of the Aswad al Haruj.

Ali Hakim, hot with the bloodlust of combat, jumped up and was about to chase after the escapees. Bahri grabbed him by his shoulder.

"Let them go, Ali," he quietly counseled. "There are a thousand caves and lava tubes for them to hide and pick off any pursuer. You will surely end up another casualty of this cowardly attack. We need to secure the camp, treat our wounded, and bury the dead. Send out men to reinforce our outer guards and make certain the perimeter is secure. It is important that we be ready when your Chinese friends arrive this evening. And that our meeting with them is not interrupted in such a violent way."

A furious Ali Hakim tried to shrug off Bahri's grip, but the Bedouin chief only strengthened it.

"You are right, of course," Ali Hakim finally grunted. "There will be opportunity for vengeance at a later time."

Before climbing back down the fissure, they quickly checked the bodies of the four attackers they had taken down. Bahri rolled one of them over onto his back. Most of his skull was gone, but they could see what they needed to see. The body, clad in traditional long, loose blue *boubou* and similarly colored *tagelmusts* wrapped as a turban, was pale skinned with red-blonde hair, a common trait of the rural Berber tribes.

"Berber!" the Bedouin said and spat into the dirt in disgust. "Just as I suspected."

Berbers and Bedouins had fought over the desert sands for generations, even back to the days of Suleiman the Magnificent. The Berber tribes were a major obstacle for Ali Hakim and his plans. Somehow, they had discovered his meeting place and had attempted a deadly interruption.

The two men stood there for only a moment before turning and beginning their descent, back down to the tent. And to prepare for the meeting with key representatives who would help to ultimately set Ali Hakim Sherif's grand plan in motion.

A plan with a bold first step that would soon fill the void left by the elimination of Muammar Muhammad Abu Minyar al-Gaddafi as Libya's leader almost half a century before. One that would bring to a close the endless years of chaos and the worldwide disrespect that had afflicted Libya since that event.

Five centuries ago, Suleiman the Magnificent built a great empire stretching from Persia to the east all the way across the Maghreb of northern Africa to the west. For three hundred years, Ottoman rule was feared and revered. The tribal leaders of the Maghreb, pledging fealty to Ottoman rule, created rich and much-feared kingdoms. But rot from within combined with treachery and disrespect from the Western world led to the fall of the vast and powerful Ottoman Empire. The North African kingdoms became pawns for the West. Gaddafi had been spectacularly unsuccessful in his effort to restore Libya. Now it was Sherif's turn to put his plan into play. A plan that would one day have Ali Hakim Sherif become the sultan of a new and vast Mediterranean empire, just as his famous and revered ancestor had done half a millennium before.

And his first act? Inform the world that the rightful name of his homeland was not Libya. That it was henceforth Wilayat Tarabulus Althaania, the Second Regency of Tripoli. And that the sovereign nation and the empire it hosted would soon become a major player, not only on the southern shores of the Mediterranean Sea but on the world stage.

Ψ

Dawn was little more than a promising glimmer on the eastern horizon when a pair of Avicopter AC352s—the licensed Chinese version of the Airbus H175 super-medium helicopter—lifted off from the Chinese People's Liberation Army Support Base Djibouti. The command pilot for this mission, Huang Zhou, had filed a flight plan with the Djiboutian Direction de l'Aviation Civile et de la Meteorologie that showed a direct flight to Khartoum, the capitol of Sudan. Although as a Chinese military flight, no manifest was required, he had helpfully reported that the helicopters carried a cargo of diplomatic pouches and ten rotational personnel bound for the Chinese Embassy in Khartoum.

In other words, it was a routine flight.

Zhou ordered the radar transponders energized before he headed out toward the northwest. He followed air traffic control routing until they were clear of Djibouti airspace and well into northern Ethiopia.

In the back of Zhou's helicopter, Li Chung Sheng sat comfortably with the other passengers. He was not just the leader of this particular delegation; he was also Chinese President Tan Yong's principal expert on North African affairs. And Li Chung was officially the President's ambassador, even if he was without portfolio. In the convoluted reality of Chinese governmental structure, Li Chung was the head of the Ministry for State Security's African Office. That meant his secret police and intelligence agents directed a vast web of operations across the huge continent.

Once they were well underway, he unbuckled his seat belt and carefully made his way up to the pilots. Sitting in the rear of the chopper, watching the gray-brown landscape scrolling along and disappearing behind them proved to be boring for a man of action. He needed to know what was happening in any situation, to be in charge. Otherwise, he would not be in control, and that was intolerable for someone like Li Chung Sheng.

Sensing the movement behind him, Huang Zhou looked over his shoulder and saw they had a visitor. The pilot waved toward the fold-down jump seat and said, "Minister Li, it would be safer if you were seated and strapped in. The thermals can cause unanticipated turbulence."

"I appreciate your concern," Li Chung replied, "but I want to see what is going on. Where are we now?"

Zhou pointed to the GPS display. "We are well within Ethiopian air space." He pointed out to a large lake they were flying over. "That is the Tekeze hydroelectric facility. This project was before your tenure, one of the very earliest of what became our nation's 'Belt and Roads Initiative.' It is now providing electricity and irrigation to Ethiopia and its people."

Li Chung smiled ruefully. "I am quite aware. Electricity without customers and irrigation that evaporates before it reaches agriculture. But the project is serving its purpose. The Ethiopian government is deeply in debt to the People's Republic, and that obligation will be called due when necessary."

He settled into the jump seat and looked out the large cockpit windows as the view of the lake and river was once again replaced with dry desert sand and stone. High mountain peaks loomed ahead. Zhou guided the helicopters around the peaks and then across a region of hills and valleys. The occasional small village or isolated farm flitted past.

This part of Ethiopia was so deserted that there was no air traffic control for any aircraft flying below five thousand meters. The twin Avicopters had the sky to themselves, no other air traffic to worry about. The same was true when they crossed the invisible border into Sudan. At that point, Zhou reported in, requesting routing and landing instructions when they were two hundred kilometers from New Khartoum International Airport. This leg of their flight had taken two and a half hours. Even with extended-range fuel tanks attached, the helicopters were perilously low on fuel when they finally touched down in the Sudanese capital city.

Li Chung climbed down from the helicopter while the fliers refueled. The Chinese embassy in Khartoum had been informed of his trip. As a show of respect, the ambassador had made it a point to drive out to meet him. It would be unthinkable for someone with Li Chung Sheng's power, prestige, and reputation to pass through Khartoum without his country's chief representative coming out to pay his respects.

Li Chung sauntered over to where the ambassador stood waiting beside his Honqui H9 limousine. The diplomat made a respectful bow to the senior Chinese envoy and spymaster. "Ambassador Li, welcome to Khartoum," he said. "I trust that your journey so far has been comfortable. If there is any way that I can be of service during your short stay, you have only to ask."

Li Chung offered a slight nod. "I only request that our passing through be with as little notice as possible and that my presence be treated with the utmost secrecy."

"But, of course, the embassy diary won't even show that you were here," the ambassador assured. Further conversation was cut off by Huang Zhou waving Li Chung back to the helicopter. They were ready to depart.

Fully fueled, the two birds were back in the air and once more heading to the northwest. Once they were thirty kilometers out of Khartoum, Zhou dropped down to a hundred meters altitude before he turned off the radar and the transponder. The helicopters promptly disappeared from the screens of anyone who might be tracking them. But there was little to no chance anyone would have been. This time they stayed low, below the radar horizon, in the unlikely event anyone was searching.

This stretch of sand and rock was even more desolate than before. Along the eight-hundred-kilometer stretch only a couple of goatherds looked up into the clear blue sky, surprised by the low, loud helicopters thundering overhead, then quickly disappearing before those on the ground could even question what they saw.

Huang Zhou was worried most about this leg of the flight. Wasat an Nukhaylah was an exceedingly small oasis, barely more than a spring with only a puddle of water. It was surrounded by hundreds of miles of vacant desert. Had it not been for the radio beacon planted there exclusively for this mission, the Chinese helicopters could have spent hours searching for the tiny sliver of life in the vast nothingness. What if a camel had pissed on the beacon, shorting its circuits? Or shoddy workmanship by a corrupt manufacturer back in China caused it to fail? Running out of fuel would necessitate an emergency landing. That would mean death. There would be no way they could trek out of this wilderness. Or that anyone might come to their rescue.

Zhou was mightily relieved when his receiver picked up the weak pulse from the transponder, allowing him to finally home in on the tiny oasis. His passengers never had any idea how close to the edge this flight was, or how worried Zhou had been over the dire possibilities. They never saw the relief on his face as he flared out to land the AC352. They calmly deplaned and enjoyed a picnic lunch of steamed buns, spring rolls, and scallion pancakes with hot tea served in the meager shade of a date palm by the edge of the muddy pool.

While the birds were refueled from cached fuel bladders that had been delivered to the oasis, Zhou directed an even more impressive operation: a dramatic physical transformation of the helicopters. The red-and-yellow People's Liberation Army star was covered over with the green roundel of the Libyan Air Force. The cargo doors on either side of both choppers slid back, out of the way, and pintle-mounted 12.7mm heavy machine guns were swung out. The peaceful Chinese diplomatic aircraft had quickly become a pair of armed Libyan warbirds.

Huang Zhou noted that it was almost exactly noon when he signaled Xiao Chen, pilot of the second helicopter, to spool up his twin turbines. They were precisely on schedule. Huang Zhou intended to remain so. It was time for the next leg of the journey.

This segment was very much like the last one. More trackless sand and endless rock. There was no sign to indicate when they left Sudan and entered Libyan airspace. Then another oasis appeared ahead of them. Harat Zuwayyah lacked the pool of water that made Wasat an Nukhaylah seem more like what an oasis was supposed to look like. But its deep well, dug by Bedouins sometime in the distant past, had been used to quench the thirst of their herds for generations.

Zhou and Chen settled down beside the fuel bladders and proceeded to once again refuel their helicopters. The few Bedouin tribesmen that now called this tiny bit of misplaced greenery home were doing their best to stay out of the midafternoon sun and remain hidden from their visitors.

Zhou's orders were to arrive at his destination just before sunset, giving them just enough time to land before it became too dark but not enough time for anyone to find the aircraft before darkness hid them. He decided that a diversion might be needed to eat up some time and to give a feint to anyone watching them take off. As the AC352s took to the air, he spun them around and headed due north. Buzaymah, the next nearest oasis, lay sixty miles away in that direction. If anyone should inquire about the unexpected airborne visitors, the Bedouin natives would dutifully point to the north.

But after dropping below the horizon, well beyond the sight of the Bedouins, Zhou swung the flight around to the west, flying directly into the sun. That orb was low on the horizon when the two aircraft landed in a veil of thick dust near the black wool tents of Ali Hakim Sherif at Aswad al Haruj.

2

Ali Hakim watched from deep in the shadows inside the *bayt al-shar* as the helicopters settled down nearby. Bahri Dawoud stood by his side.

"Ali, do we truly trust these Chinese and are we willing to accept whatever bounty they place on offering us their assistance?" the older man asked.

"Bahri, we have little choice," Ali Hakim answered dourly. "We totally trust no one. But they have the weapons and the money that we require to accomplish our goals. And multiple incentives to offer them to us. Without the Chinese, we have no way to take on our enemies, especially when the Americans become involved, as they inevitably will. Let us go out and meet our new fast friends."

Ali Hakim waited until there was no more blowing sand being whipped up by the rotors, the lead helicopter's passenger door had slid open, and Li Chung Sheng had stepped out into the cooling desert evening. Then the Libyan exited his tent and crossed the short expanse of sand, aware all the time of the many sets of eyes—and gun barrels—looking down at them from the rocks and cliffs surrounding the oasis. Ali expected no trouble from this entourage, but he knew it was always preferable to be prepared.

He grasped Li Chung's extended hand, smiled, and told him, "*As-salaam 'alaykum*. May peace be upon you. We have waited long for this meeting. Welcome."

Li Chung responded, "And peace be upon you, my friend. May our discussions be fruitful and result in millennia of friendship and prosperity for our peoples."

A taller, bearded man in Western dress broke away from the other passengers and joined the pair. As he approached, Li Chung said, "This is *Âghâ-ye* Bijan Salemi. As you are already aware, he is joining us to represent the Islamic Republic of Iran in our discussions. He shares our desires for cooperation and success in your endeavors."

Ali Hakim waved toward the tent. "Most excellent! Come, let us sit and enjoy some tea. Your journey has been long and arduous."

He led the Chinese and Iranian envoys under the woolen cloth where Bahri waited. Hot, sweetened tea and trays of *diblah*, the honey-soaked, fried Libyan pastry, had been laid out for them.

The four sat back, enjoyed the tea and pastries while they made small talk for a few minutes. Most of the discussion was about their countries' soccer and basketball teams.

Meanwhile, outside the tent, Huang Zhou directed his men in throwing camouflage netting over the helicopters and setting up a security perimeter around them, employing the platoon of Chinese troops who had come in aboard one of the aircraft. He noted that there were a few armed Bedouin guards surrounding the tent and was certain there were many more out there in the darkness. He ordered his warriors to set up their own perimeter around the aircraft. Then, satisfied, he joined the others inside.

Li Chung glanced up and saw Zhou seat himself back in a corner. That was the cue to begin the discussions that had brought him and the Iranian representative to this remote point in the desert.

Turning to Ali Hakim, he said, "President Tan Yong sends his most sincere greetings and best wishes. He wants me to relay to you directly that he fully supports your cause. The Chinese people are most interested in the details of your proposals and in assisting you in establishing a strong, free Second Regency here on the shores of the Mediterranean Sea. In addition to having *Âghâ-ye* Bijan and myself here, Colonel Zhou" —he pointed toward the only man beneath the tent who wore military garb, and the colonel gave him a slight acknowledging nod—"will be leading a team of the People's Liberation Army Air Force Special Operations Brigade soldiers to train and assist your brave men to best accomplish their mission's requirements. I am sure you observed them unloading their weapons and communications equipment. It is, of course, only the first of the assets we will be able to provide you with. But by the time we finish here this evening, they will have set up a secure satellite comms link with Beijing." Li Chung waved in the general direction of the two helicopters. "Note that Colonel Zhou has already added to your small air force as well. The helicopters will remain with you when we depart."

The Iranian, Bijan Salemi, chimed in then. "And you can depend on the Islamic Revolutionary Guard Corp in Tehran to assist as well. With the weapons, expertise, and intelligence that we propose to provide, you should have all the tools you need to defeat your challengers and establish your Second Regency of Tripoli, all with minimal disruption or loss of life."

Ali Hakim smiled slyly. "Of course, all this kind generosity toward my people on the part of your two nations is truly from the concern in your heart for the world's downtrodden and for the cause of freedom."

Li Chung chuckled at the abundant sarcasm riding on the words of his host. "There is an ancient Arabian proverb that applies. It says, 'The enemy of my enemy is my friend.' There may be some reciprocation that we ask of our friends that will benefit us, but in all cases, it will also serve to further your own ends."

Bahri replied, "This new alliance we discuss will certainly bring each of us many new friends. We already have plenty of enemies, what with the Berbers, the so-called Government of National Unity, the Libyan Arab Armed Forces, and maybe a dozen other groups who have similar desires for the future control of our nation. Then mix in the British MI6 and the American CIA and the others who will never understand our sacred ties to the sands of North Africa, our long history, our borders based on ancient tribal territories, not on rivers or mountains or the political whims of interlopers and blood-spilling conquerors."

Bijan nodded vigorously. "All are enemies of Allah and His followers, as they have so often proved to the world. Together, we will return to the days of the Pasha and the Caliph, as our long-suffering people so desperately desire."

Ali Hakim abruptly stood. "Now, if Colonel Zhou would be so kind as to fly us, I would like to give you a quick tour of our forces that we have already assembled. Li Chung, I understand that you are meeting with your currant ambassador in Tripoli tomorrow morning. It is important that both of you are able to confidently report to your nation's leaders that we are prepared for victory. And your assistance will only hasten and assure it is a quick, glorious, and final triumph."

Ψ

When Bill Langley was studying for his geology degree at the Colorado School of Mines, he had pictured himself trekking across the Sahara Desert, maybe astride a camel, discovering vast deposits of petroleum that had been hidden from mankind beneath the sands for millions of years. Using his deep knowledge of the earth's crust and his intuitive feel for the rocky mantle's early formation, he would uncover vast oil reserves where no one had thought to look before. He would be rich and famous, operating his own oil exploration company when he felt like it and allowing his minions to run things when he wanted to jet-set with the beautiful people. Either way, he would realize his dream of tasting life's splendors before he reached the age of thirty.

The reality was he ended up spending more than thirty years driving a beat-up old Land Rover, mostly bouncing across the high rocky plateaus of Egypt's Western Desert. That historic discovery, the gusher that would change everything about his mundane life, was always just around the corner, an inch or two beyond his grasp. Oh, he had almost made it, once when they hit oil in the Alamein Basin in the northwest desert, and again when they found those huge deposits in the Ras Qattara Development Area. But each time, someone got there just ahead of him, stepping in to snatch the prize away. Never mind that it confirmed his unique ability, his intuition in ferreting out big deposits hidden from the average explorer. He could not buy yachts or jets with that unique talent alone.

Now here he was, deep in the Western Desert, hard against the Libyan border. Once again, he had discerned that the geology looked promising, at least from the satellite and aerial images, the printouts which cluttered the seats and floorboards of his Land Rover. There were also the big data predictive models that screamed at him that this was an unusually promising spot. And so far as he knew, nobody else had even come close to finding it.

More importantly to Bill Langley, his sixth sense about such things had him convinced that there was an ocean of oil hidden under these rocks. And he had more than enough evidence—without sharing too much—to convince those with the money and equipment to invest in the possibilities.

That meant it was time for field work. The dirty work. Getting out there and crawling across the sand and rock to determine for certain what was buried underneath. The heavy thumper truck toiled along behind the Land Rover as it made its own road across the flat plain. His team of Egyptian technicians had already been planting acoustic geophones at very precise locations as the little caravan lumbered across the desert. Once they were up on the rocky escarpment, they would set up the thumper truck so that its massive vibrator sent seismic waves deep into the earth's crust. The waves would then be reflected back to the geophone sensors, giving Langley a telling picture of the geology underneath. Maybe, despite the geography and Langley's intuition, it would only show more sand and rock. But hopefully, it would point toward oil captured there, longing to be set free to feed the world's hunger for fossil fuel–generated energy and products.

The desert sun was high overhead by the time the thumper truck was set up, its heavy metal platen firmly settled onto the rock and its electro-hydraulically driven reaction mass ready to quite literally shake the earth. The technicians launched their drones to orbit out over the geophones, their mission to relay the data back to Langley's waiting computer at his cramped workstation in the Land Rover.

He checked his GPS to make sure that they were exactly where his calculation predicted the best location was. With the Libyan border only ten kilometers to the west, Langley wanted to be very careful with his search. The Libyan government was unstable enough right now. There was no telling what might happen if they caught wind that Langley was uncovering buried treasure just on the east side of that imaginary line drawn through the sand.

Two hours later, as he reviewed the initial results, Langley could hardly control his excitement. At least based on this first shot, it looked like they might be on top of a very large salt dome, a promising indicator for hydrocarbons below. He ordered a second round of shots before he repositioned the thumper truck by a couple of kilometers.

Not wanting to be aced out again by someone faster or better connected politically than his team, Langley radioed back to his base camp at Abu Minqar, instructing them to send the exploratory drill rig out immediately while he continued the seismic work. It would take several days for the heavy equipment to ponderously cross over 150 miles of desert sand. In the meantime, he would complete the seismic mapping and confirm his initial opinion.

By the time the sun had slipped below the western horizon, Bill Langley's little team had finished "shaking" from three locations. Each shot was more promising than the last. He sent all the data back to base camp for the big computers and eggheads to really dig into, but he already knew one thing for certain.

He was sitting on the largest new oil field anyone had discovered in his lifetime. The exploratory wells would be proof positive, but his hand was already shaking with excitement when he hit the send key on his keyboard.

Ψ

Henrietta Foster forced herself to remain quiet, sit back, and watch. Lieutenant Dale Miller was attempting to explain to Ensign Scott Nielson the procedure for bringing the US Navy submarine *Gato* to periscope depth. He was doing so even as the operation was actually taking place. Nielson was the newest officer onboard the *Virginia*-class submarine, fresh out of Submarine Officer Basic Course. He had joined the boat just a couple of days before and was still wandering around with what Commander Foster liked to call "the newbie stun stare." But, as an experienced submarine officer, she also understood what a shock it was for someone to step from the classroom and introductory training into duty aboard a working and very sophisticated warship.

That look on the young officer's face was very much like another expression Foster often observed. The one when the newcomer realized his or her skipper was a Black female, among the Navy's very first. Henrietta had long since gotten used to it. So did the new crew members, once they realized she had earned—and deserved—her stripes. That her command was not just the result of any diversity or equity initiative.

"Scott, the whole process is really pretty simple," Miller was patiently explaining. "First, we clear baffles at one hundred and fifty feet. That's just a very careful sonar search to make sure no one is anywhere close to us when we go up to PD."

"PD?" the Ensign questioned.

Miller shook his head. This kid was really green. Did they not even teach them the basic acronyms back in Groton?

"Yep," Miller answered. "Periscope depth. The keel depth where the periscope is just above the surface. For the *Gato*, that's about sixty-two feet. As you probably know, though, it's not a periscope anymore. Not like in the old movies. It's a photonics mast. A pole up in the sail that supports cameras, antennas, and stuff. But we still call it 'PD,' periscope depth."

Miller had already resolved to keep this explanation very simple. Ensign Green would get plenty of time and experience to learn more detail as his qualifications progressed on this, his assigned submarine. This operation would be his first taste of driving the big boat.

Miller pointed to a row of computer workstations lining the port bulkhead of the control room. Operators sat at each station, busily doing functions that left Ensign Nielson even more confused.

"That's sonar," Miller explained. "We'd better tell them we're clearing baffles." In a louder voice, he said, "Sonar, clearing baffles to the right."

ST1 Jed Durham, the sonar supervisor, replied in a thick North Carolina–mountains accent, "Clearing baffles, aye, sir. Sonar's ready." Miller often used Durham as an example for new crew members like Nielson. The guy had never seen salt water or a vessel bigger than a bass fishing boat until he got to sub school. He was now, in the opinion of the officers on *Gato*, one of the finest sonarmen in the Navy.

"Pilot, right five degrees rudder, steady course zero-six-zero," Miller ordered.

Senior Chief Jim Stumpf, standing watch as the pilot, confirmed by repeating, "Right five degrees rudder, steady zero-six-zero, aye," as he reached to his panel and dialed in the rudder order and new course. The ship's computerized command and control system smoothly guided the boat as it circled around to the new course.

Miller made a couple of clicks at the command console. The large screen hanging above it changed images, as if he was switching channels on a TV.

"That's the passive sonar display," he explained as he landed on an odd-looking screenful. "We are seeing whatever the LAB array picks up. The LAB. Large aperture bow array." He looked over at Nielson, who was now even more lost. "Damn, didn't you pay any attention at SOBC?" Miller growled. "The LAB array is an array of passive hydrophones that are wrapped around the bow. It replaces the sphere they used to have on the older boats." He pointed at the screen. It showed a constantly changing confusion of dots and flashes. "This is called a 'waterfall display.' That's because it sorta looks like a waterfall. That's bearing across the horizontal axis and time down the vertical. Current time—right now—is at the top and the data gets older as it progresses down the screen and then scrolls off. Each white speck is a bit of sound energy that the LAB array heard on that bearing. Most of what we're seeing is just random sea noise. Bet you didn't know the ocean was so loud. But in waters like these, with lots of traffic and all the biologics—fish and stuff—there's plenty of racket to see on the display." Miller pointed to a trace where the dots were just a confused mess. Then to a spot over to the left where the dots were forming into a bright white line that curved down the full height of the screen. "That looks like a contact. See how it forms a continuous line over time."

"Yes, I do," Ensign Nielson replied, now showing just a hint of understanding. The young man had not become a naval officer by being a dolt. He was just ignorant, not dumb. Miller knew his job was to make the guy less ignorant.

Miller raised his voice. "Sonar, what you got at bearing three-four-two?"

Jed Durham looked over the passive broadband operator's shoulder for a couple of seconds before he called out, "Officer-of-the-Deck, new sonar contact, Sierra Two-Seven, bearing three-four-two on the LAB array, left point-two-degree-per-minute bearing rate." He smacked the operator on the back of his head and had some choice words with him for allowing the OOD to find the sonar contact before he did. Then Durham pulled a set of earphones down over his ears and listened intently. "Probable deep draft merchant based on nature of sound." A few seconds later, he added, "Gained Sierra Two-Seven on the wide aperture array, bearing three-four-zero, range one-six-thousand yards."

Jim Stumpf announced, "Steady course zero-six-zero."

No reason to react to the newly acquired trace on the screen, representing a very big merchant ship. It was eight nautical miles away. But they would need to keep an eye on it.

Jed Durham reported, "Completed sonar search of previously baffled area. One sonar contact, Sierra Two-Seven, bearing three-three-nine, classified deep draft merch, range sixteen thousand yards, past CPA and opening."

Dale Miller turned to where Henrietta Foster sat, still quietly observing but trying to appear not to be. He reported the sonar contact to her and then requested permission to proceed to periscope depth. When Foster gave him the go-ahead, Miller ordered the *Gato* up to six-two feet. Jim Stumpf, the pilot, dialed in six-two feet as the ordered depth and sat back to watch as the system drove the boat up toward the surface.

Dale Miller raised the number-two photonics mast and used his Xbox controller to rotate it around as they came up closer to the sea surface. The deep cobalt color on the large screen display gradually became a lighter robin's-egg blue before the mast broke through the surface to reveal a cloudless sky, a stretch of azure water, and a brilliant Mediterranean Sea afternoon. He carefully searched all around, but the only other ship in sight was the large orange-yellow merchant, just visible on the horizon on their port beam. To demonstrate to Nielson the capability of the system, Miller shifted the photonics camera to zoom in on the distant vessel.

"Interesting," he said, under his breath, as the big vessel came into closer view. The first thing he noticed was the bright red flag with gold stars that hung from the stern. That announced to anyone interested that the ship was registered in China.

Miller fiddled with the controller just a bit more. What he could then see, just visible through what looked like some type of oil rig structure riding on the main deck, was even more engrossing.

Henrietta Foster stepped up next to him and took a closer look at the screen. There was a frown on her face.

"Dale, are you seeing what I'm seeing?"

"Yes, ma'am, I think I am. That sure as hell looks like a submarine under all that stuff. And judging from the flag that thing is flying, it would most likely be a Chinese boat. Out here in the Mediterranean bathtub, too."

Foster rubbed her chin and thought for a moment. Then she said, "Let's get in closer and get a good look. That's what we're here for. I want photographic evidence before I start ringing the bells back at Sub Group Eight."

3

Ali Hakim Sherif watched intently from the hastily erected command center tent high up on Jebel Akhdar—the Green Mountain—as Bahir Dawoud's Bedouin fighters moved deliberately through the streets of the city of Derna down below. History had not been kind to this little coastal Libyan town nestled between the green-forested mountains—about the only tree-covered area in the country—and the blue Mediterranean Sea. It was that bit of geography that had made the town important to armies marching east into Egypt or west toward Tripoli. It was a way-stop on the Libyan Coastal Highway and a key gateway to controlling the Cyrenaica region of eastern Libya. The Romans had fought here. So had the Ottomans and the Egyptians. The Americans, too, in 1805, the first time US troops had battled on foreign soil, winning the Battle of Derna early in the Barbary Wars. Even the Italians had fought and died here. More recently, Derna had seen major fighting during the upheaval following the inglorious downfall of Muammar Gaddafi.

Far out on the calm blue sea, ships steamed peacefully by, the scene contrasting markedly with the fighting going on in the streets of Derna.

This time it was Ali Hakim's turn to attempt to rip the dusty village from the control of those who would deny him the power he sought. If he could win a resounding victory here, he would be able to control all of eastern

Libya. However, General Ja'far ou Said's Libyan Arab Armed Forces were putting up unexpectedly strong resistance. Ali Hakim's lieutenants were reporting house-to-house fighting through the ancient streets below. It was easy to trace the slow progress simply by plotting the smoke billowing up from the neighborhoods.

Huang Zhou's two Chinese helicopters danced around above the battle, their heavy machine guns and air-to-ground missiles adding to the death, destruction, and chaos. One of the birds suddenly swooped down, almost to ground level, before opening brutal fire on a truck trying to escape toward the waterfront. The unfortunate vehicle exploded in a ball of fire as the helicopter quickly climbed back up to a safe altitude to seek out more prey.

A pair of T-55 main battle tanks—relics of Brotherly Leader Gaddafi's Soviet-era buying spree—rumbled down the town's main drag, dishing out their own specialized brand of mayhem. What they did not shoot they ran over and crushed. As Ali Hakim watched through his binoculars, the lead tank's turret traversed a few degrees off from directly ahead and its 100mm main gun spat once. Five hundred meters down the street, the mud-brick wall of a building disintegrated into a dusty fog. Men fleeing from what had been their cover were mowed down by the tank's 12.7mm heavy machine gun. Without slowing, the MBTs continued their lumbering charge down the street, their wide tracks driving right over the bodies of the fallen, mashing them into the bloody dirt.

A pair of rocket-propelled grenades exploded harmlessly on the tanks' frontal armor, leaving only black smudges on the desert-brown paint. The tank turret quickly rotated to sight in the direction of the annoying RPG launcher. The main gun spat again.

Ali Hakim watched a squad of his men, bent over, duck-walking behind the tanks, progressing forward, returning rifle fire as they went. Maybe, he thought, the T-55s would make the difference in what had become a virtual and disappointing stalemate. The tanks might be what it would take to break the back of Said's LAAF troops.

Just then, a battery of Vasilek 82mm mortars—more Soviet-era relics thanks to Gaddafi—opened fire from the slopes just below Ali Hakim's position. The rounds arced high over the town before crashing down and exploding a couple of blocks beyond the battle line that had formed.

Ali Hakim smiled. Perhaps these weapons would ultimately give him the advantage. Thanks be to Allah, Bahri Dawoud's Misurata fighters had captured much of the former Libyan leader's heavy firepower, hidden in their storage depots deep in the desert. Some had laughed at him as he and his men lugged the ponderously heavy armament across the desert, even pulling some of the artillery with camels. But the Bedouin's foresight would surely give them a decisive edge in this fight.

Just as he was feeling better about the turn the assault had taken, Ali Hakim caught the flash of a rocket racing down the narrow street, heading directly toward the two tanks. A second flash immediately followed after the initial one. The first rocket slammed into the lead tank, easily penetrating its armor and blowing the turret upward, spinning it off the chassis. The second tank suffered an almost identical fate.

No one emerged from either vehicle. The burning, smoking hulks blocked the street. The men who had been trailing the tanks and had survived the force of the blasts and flying shrapnel from the explosions quickly disappeared into nearby buildings.

Heavy artillery fire erupted from behind buildings down by the waterfront. Thick clouds of dirt and smoke rose from the hillside where Ali Hakim had positioned his mortar teams for the final victorious assault on the port. The mortars fell silent under the artillery barrage.

Said's men would not be defeated so easily. They were fighting back and taking a toll. For the first time, the possibility of losing this important showdown, of having to withdraw, sullied Ali Hakim's thoughts.

The Iranian military advisor, Bijan Salemi, had remained quiet so far during the operation. He walked over to stand beside Ali Hakim, his hawklike gaze locked onto the faltering battle below.

"Ali Hakim, that building at the end of the pier is their command center," he said. "My Niruye Vizheh troops have just now managed to triangulate Said's LAAF radio signals. They are coming from there. You must take out that building. Once the command center, the nerve center of their defense, is destroyed, the resistance will fall apart, and you will have your victory."

Bijan was pointing to the largest cement building among several that lined the street along the waterfront. Ali Hakim noticed at once that the structure was only a block from the much-revered Assayedah Khadijah Mosque.

"Âghâ-ye Bijan, how do you propose I do that?" Ali Hakim retorted. "My tanks are gone. And besides, that command center is much too close to the mosque. The faithful will never forgive me if I destroy it just to win this battle."

Bijan Salemi smiled as he pulled a cell phone from his robes. "Please allow the Islamic Republic of Iran to assist you, our valiant allies."

He punched in some numbers and then mumbled into the phone something Ali Hakim could not hear.

Out on the far horizon, there was a brilliant yellow flash from one of the merchant ships that had been slowly steaming by, seemingly staying well clear of the trouble ashore. That was immediately followed by a second flash. The bright flare-ups lasted only a second before they appeared to have been swallowed up by the sea.

The Iranian picked up a pair of binoculars and looked out toward the ships. "Now, if you watch closely, you may see the solution to your problem."

Ali Hakim pulled up his own binoculars and looked in the direction that Bijan was now pointing. "I see nothing!" he said. "What foolishness is this that you are trying?"

"Patience, my friend. Patience," Bijan urged. "Remember, the holy Quran says, 'Do not quarrel with one another, lest you should lose courage and your power depart. Be tolerant. Allah is with those who remain patient.'"

As the Iranian finished quoting the Quran, Ali Hakim spied something odd. There were two small delta-winged aircraft flying down low, almost at the wave tops. They did not appear to be traveling very fast. Certainly not rocket speed. But they followed an unerring course straight toward the center of Derna.

"What are...?" Ali Hakim started to ask.

"Shahed-136 drones," Bijan answered. "Iranian technology at work. They fly at a speed of less than two hundred kilometers per hour, but they do not miss the targets they seek. And they arrive bearing a disastrous punch."

As if demonstrating Bijan's claim, the two drones barely cleared the rooftops along the shoreline before crashing directly into what Bijan had identified as the command center. The building immediately disappeared in a shroud of smoke, flames, and whirling debris. When it all cleared enough to see, there was nothing but a crater where the cement building had stood only moments before. The Assayedah Khadijah Mosque stood unscathed, not even sullied by smoke from the nearby explosions.

Bijan smiled. "As the holy *Quran* also records, 'Those who are patient shall receive their rewards.'"

He set his binoculars down on a folding table nearby, once again pointed out toward the seemingly benign ships, and then suggested, "It would be best if you quickly completed the process of mopping up. Those ships out there need to off-load their cargo. That chore should be accomplished as quickly as possible. I assure you we will soon become the target for much surveillance."

Ψ

Matteo Brunelli sat back and sipped his cup of cappuccino, relishing the peaceful view from his seat on the bridge wing of the massive ship he commanded. It was especially good to be back in the Mediterranean Sea once again after a stressful voyage from the Persian Gulf. Finally, he could fully enjoy such a fine, peaceful evening. The sun was setting off the bow, painting the limitless horizon with brilliant shades of gold, red, and purple. A few stars were just starting to glimmer in the twilight. To the south, the air was so dry and clear that he could make out the headlights of vehicles, flickering in the distance like fireflies, coming out of the city of Tobruk, driving the Libyan Coastal Highway toward Egypt to the east or Derna to the west.

As he lit his pipe and savored the first puffs of the sweet smoke, Matteo felt truly relaxed for the first time in more than a week. It had been eight days since he first guided the Very Large Crude Carrier tanker *Cygnet Dawn*, with its full load of crude, away from the Iraqi island that hosted the

Al Basrah Oil Terminal. The *Cygnet Dawn* was the pride of Swan Maritime Holdings, a New Jersey–based shipping company that specialized in contracting with large petroleum companies to transport crude for them. Matteo Brunelli and his ship were regulars on the run from Basrah to Rotterdam, carrying Royal Dutch Shell oil to feed the energy needs of western Europe.

At more than two hundred thousand tons deadweight and a length of over a thousand feet, the mammoth ship presented an impressive sight—and provided a huge target—as it plowed straight down the Persian Gulf and out through the Straits of Hormuz into the Arabian Sea. Of course, they were under the watchful eye of a US Navy destroyer escort the entire way. Even so, the Iranian Revolutionary Guard mirrored their progress with several gunboats pacing the *Cygnet Dawn* as they made their way right along the invisible boundary of Iranian waters, as if daring the tanker to stray and suffer the consequences.

Exiting the Straits of Hormuz, Brunelli turned the tanker southward. He could breathe a little easier for just a bit as they steamed through the Gulf of Oman and out into the broad waters of the Arabian Sea. But once they turned northwestward, there was a new threat from ruthless pirates who might wish to hijack his ship for its load of black gold, either to steal it or, more likely, to ransom the ship and crew. That was what kept the skipper on the bridge for most of twelve hundred miles, down past Oman and into the Gulf of Aden. The entire time, Brunelli drove the massive tanker as fast as it could churn through the sea. Hopefully, that would be fast enough to discourage or outrun any pirates.

Then, heading north through the Bab al-Mandab Straits, a different menace commanded his attention. Missiles fired from terrorist positions along the coast of Yemen were not only possible but likely. There was no way he could duck or dodge should one of those weapons come out seeking the *Cygnet Dawn*. A burning, sinking VLCC in the narrow Red Sea would be a monumental disaster.

By the time he was in the northern Red Sea, Matteo Brunelli was exhausted, but the hazardous part of the journey was behind them. He had earned his rest. From this point on, they only needed to avoid fishermen, freighters, and ocean liners. He gratefully turned the *Cygnet Dawn* over to his First Mate and the Suez Canal pilot. They would steam routinely down "the big ditch through the desert" while he slept. Brunelli collapsed onto the bunk in his stateroom and slept through the entire eleven-hour transit of the canal. He awoke only when his First Mate knocked on his door and reported that they were once again in the Mediterranean Sea and heading west. Ahead of them, they only had a week's worth of steaming through the Mediterranean and the Strait of Gibraltar, and then up the Atlantic coast past Spain, Portugal, and France, before plying the English Channel to Rotterdam.

He fell back asleep and awakened with the promising first light of a new day. The *Cygnet Dawn* remained on a steady course of three-four-zero, trudging along parallel to the Egyptian coast. When Brunelli checked his ship's position before going down to dinner, they had just crossed over to Libyan waters.

After dinner, it was Matteo's custom to enjoy his cappuccino and his pipe sitting out on the bridge wing. It was in that moment of tranquility that his reverie was rudely interrupted by a shout through the open doorway of the bridge from his second-in-command.

"Captain, I am seeing new radar contacts, and they are heading directly toward us," the First Mate reported as he looked up from the radar screen, eyes wide. "It appears they have come out of Derna. They are in a hurry, doing better than twenty-five knots."

Brunelli grabbed his binoculars from a console and stepped back out onto the open bridge wing. Whoever was approaching them should easily be visible. The Libyan coast was only about fifteen nautical miles to the south. Probably just fishing boats heading out, but why were they moving so fast? There had been reports of fighting in and around Derna, so maybe they were simply escaping the latest bit of chaos in the historically chaotic city. Whatever, Libyans fighting Libyans should have no bearing on him or his big vessel and its valuable cargo.

Brunelli quickly brought the oncoming ships into focus. They appeared to be a couple of frigates—small destroyers, maybe, but definitely warships —and from the size of the bow waves they were kicking up, they were indeed coming fast and aimed arrow-straight at the *Cygnet Dawn*.

This should not be happening. Not here. In the Persian Gulf or near

Yemen or off the coast of Somalia, yes, distressing but not surprising. But intruding on a blissful, Technicolor twilight in the Mediterranean?

The bridge-to-bridge radio speaker abruptly crackled, the urgency of the tinny voice summoning the Captain back inside.

"Motor vessel *Cygnet Dawn*, this is Second Regency Navy ship *Al Gharbella*," the speaker blared. "You have illegally entered Libyan waters without permission. You will heave to immediately and prepare to be boarded."

Brunelli grabbed the bridge-to-bridge microphone and answered, "*Al Gharbella*, this is the motor vessel *Cygnet Dawn*. We are a Panamanian flagged deep draft tanker transiting through to Rotterdam. Our navigation shows us well clear of Libyan waters. We claim the right of innocent passage under the UN Convention on the Law of the Seas."

The response came immediately. "*Cygnet Dawn*, you will heave to and prepare to be boarded or we will open fire without further warning." The speaker's voice had taken a decidedly harder tone. "The Second Regency recognizes no laws but those of Allah. You are under arrest and your ship will be confiscated for your illegal acts."

Brunelli watched as the two frigates came up astern of the *Cygnet Dawn*, one on the port side, the other on the starboard. He observed with alarm as the forward gun turrets on both warships trained around until he was staring directly down the gun barrels.

Then he spotted something else. Something equally concerning. A pair of helicopters flying out from the direction of the beach, on a course toward the three ships. They certainly would not be the good guys coming out to assist the oil tanker in escaping from this dicey situation.

Turning to the First Mate, Brunelli ordered, "Get on the GMDSS and see if you can raise any American Navy ships in the area. Inform them that we are being attacked and boarded by what we can only assume to be Libyan terrorists. If you can't raise any Americans, get the Egyptian Navy or the Israeli Navy. Hell, if all else fails, call the Italian Navy."

GMDSS—the Global Maritime Distress and Safety System—is a maritime communications system mandated for all large ocean-going ships for the purpose of emergency communications between ships and with shore stations. It is designed to rapidly pass safety-of-life information and to inform vessels of navigation hazards or distress situations.

Brunelli reached over and rang up "All Stop" on the engine order tele-graph. Then, with no immediate alternative, he said into the bridge-to-bridge microphone, "*Al Gharbella*, under protest, we are answering 'All Stop.' Please be aware that the *Cygnet Dawn* is a large ship and fully loaded with cargo. It will take at least fifteen minutes for us to come dead in the water."

There was no response.

One of the helicopters hovered out over the big ship's main deck while the other held station a few yards to starboard. That one had a heavy machine gun menacingly trained on the ship's bridge. When the tanker was fully stopped, ropes suddenly dropped down from either side of the first hovering bird. Then a squad of heavily armed men fast-roped down onto the tanker. The two birds quickly changed positions and another half dozen men came down ropes onto the *Cygnet Dawn*'s deck.

All the armed men rushed up the exterior ladders to the bridge. As they crashed into the wheelhouse, the First Mate dropped the GMDSS micro-phone, leaving it dangling from its coiled cord. He raised his hands in surrender and shook his head as he mumbled, "Captain, I only got a response from a Viking cruise ship out of Crete and the Malta Harbor Control station."

Brunelli knew that meant no warships were hurrying to their rescue. But at least the world would know that they had been hijacked by whomever these men were. There really was nothing to do but comply with whatever they were told to do. And wait for someone to come to their rescue.

The armed Libyans, wearing a uniform that Brunelli did not recognize, bound the Captain and his First Mate before manhandling them down two levels and into the mess decks. They were soon joined there by the rest of the ship's twenty-eight-man crew. Then, Brunelli could feel the *Cygnet Dawn* as she started to slowly move again. That meant these Libyans had enough expertise to drive his ship somewhere. But down in the windowless room, there was no way for the Captain to tell what direction or to where.

To find hope for their chances of being rescued, Brunelli could only come up with a couple of thoughts. It would be difficult to hide his massive ship. And the AIS transponder—the automatic identification system present on most ocean-going vessels—continuously broadcasting the ship's position was still busy informing the world exactly where they were located.

He could only pray rescuers came before these very efficient pirates decided Brunelli and his crew were expendable cargo, not needed for whatever their evil plan might be.

4

Ali Hakim Sherif followed Bijan Salemi and hopped off the launch, over to the small platform just inches above the water surface. The vertical side of the *Cygnet Dawn* seemed to blot out the sky as it stretched high above them. Ali Hakim clung to the lifeline as he followed the Iranian on the long climb to the main deck.

Huang Zhou was there to meet the pair as they stepped onto the ship's expansive deck. "Welcome aboard, my friends."

Ali Hakim glanced around and responded, "Thank you. This is truly a very large ship. But tell me one thing. Now that we have it, what do we do with it?"

Huang Zhou smiled and chuckled. "We will do our best to turn it into cash. That will add the money required to help finance the victorious conclusion to your revolution."

"Of course," Ali Hakim retorted, then paused before asking the obvious question, "But how?"

Bijan Salemi answered, "We tell the owners, this Swan Maritime Holdings, that we are confiscating the ship as a penalty for violating the laws of Second Regency. We make the fine equal to the value of the ship and cargo. There are two million barrels of crude oil on board. At today's prices, that

alone would be worth over two hundred million dollars. Add in the cost of
the ship and a little something for the Captain and crew, I suggest that we
tell them the fine is half a billion dollars, US."

It was Ali Hakim's turn to chuckle and proudly puff out his chest. "Such
a deal would be in the finest tradition of my ancestors, the famed and much
feared Barbary pirates. As the new head of the government, I will issue a
proclamation that the Second Regency claims all waters south of thirty-
four degrees latitude and inside lines extended from our eastern and
western borders as our territorial sea. This very large vessel ignored the
sovereignty of our nation. Any ship that wants to transit will have to have
permission—which they failed to request—and will be required to pay the
appropriate toll. If they do not, we will simply arrest them as we have this
violator and hold them for ransom." He paused to correct himself and
chuckled. "Well, not 'ransom.' Their 'levy' for violation of our maritime
laws." He chuckled again and went on, "Oh, I mean to say that we will
impound the offending vessel and arrest its crew until the assessed fine has
been paid. We do not want to appear to be too much in the style of the
Barbary pirates. But we can be like Brotherly Leader and Guide of the
Revolution Gaddafi as we establish an even more ambitious 'Line of
Death.'"

"That is perfect, Ali Hakim," Salemi offered, and Huang Zhou nodded
his concurrence.

The Libyan turned to Zhou. "Is one of your helicopters available? I
really want to get over to Benghazi and watch them as they unload the
long-suffering people of the Second Regency's brand-new submarine."

Ψ

Commander Henrietta Foster sat back and intently watched the big-
screen display that hung in the overhead above the command console, a
frown on her face. The image playing out on the screen was of the large
orange-yellow cargo ship that had begun to slowly sink into the sea as it
ballasted down. Anyone not knowing better might think it was sinking
within sight of the coast of Libya. The ship's huge main deck had been

cleared of the ersatz structure meant to resemble an oil rig. The submarine that had mostly been hidden under it while riding as a passenger on the semi-submersible heavy-lift ship's deck was now plainly visible. The cargo ship's name, *Xin Guang Hua*, was just a few feet above the waterline. An hour before, the letters had been high above the sea up on the vessel's towering bow.

Foster zoomed the controller in until the submarine filled the screen. "Nav, we recording this?" she asked.

Lieutenant Commander Sharon Woolsey, *Gato's* Navigator and current Officer-of-the-Deck, nodded and answered in her clipped New England accent. "Yes, ma'am, recording a high-resolution MPEG file. It'll be ready to upload when we query the satellite tonight."

"Good, good," Foster mumbled distractedly as she continued to study the activity on the screen. "Now that they have all the crap cleared away, I can finally see for certain what they're carrying. It's not agricultural equipment or Chinese-made Hyundais." She pushed the button on the Xbox controller that rotated the photonics mast view. Half a dozen small patrol boats darted about, circling the *Xin Guang Hau*, intent on keeping any curious boaters well away from this particular unloading.

"Nav, move us in so we are four thousand yards off that ship's beam," Foster ordered. "I want good close-up images of that sub to send back to Navy Intel. They're gonna love this." She swung the photonics camera back so that it centered on the ship and its cargo. "That sub almost looks like a Chinese *Yuan*-class, but something ain't quite right."

Sharon Woolsey glanced down at the ECDIS navigation chart. "Skipper, we've only got about a hundred and thirty feet of water under the keel right here. If we move in like you want, we'll be lucky to have a hundred feet if these charts are accurate."

Eric Householder, the XO, chimed in, agreeing. "That wouldn't give us much room to maneuver if something goes hinky."

Foster nodded. She was one of those submarine skippers who welcomed challenges—when properly offered—from her officers. She was usually right to start with. But it only took one mistake to make for a very bad day. "Yeah, I know that. But I figure we slip in real slow and careful-like.

We get some close-up pictures and then we slink back to deep water like the sneaky, steely-eyed killers of the deep that we are."

Householder took a closer look at the screen, leaning in, squinting. "The Chinese have been exporting these *Yuan*-class boats for a bit, but they're usually dumbed-down versions." He pointed to the stern of the Chinese boat. "See that? That looks like a propulsor where the screw ought to be. That's the first time we've seen one of those that I know of. It's always been a standard seven-bladed screw. I'm betting she's damned near as quiet as we are, and that's real damn quiet." The XO turned to Foster. "And I concur, Skipper. So long as we don't dig a ditch in the bottom, we sure as hell need to go take a closer look at this momma."

Woolsey cautiously and slowly maneuvered the *Gato* in the direction of the Chinese heavy-lift ship. The route took a bit of a zigzag as she was careful to stay well away from the patrol boats that appeared to be flitting around randomly. She almost had the *Gato* where she wanted it when one of the patrol boats made an abrupt turn and sped up, heading directly toward where the sub's mast protruded just above the surface. It would not be long before the little patrol boat would fill the screen.

To confirm what they were seeing, Jed Durham called out from sonar, "High-speed screws, increasing SNR, zero bearing rate!"

Woolsey quickly lowered the photonics mast and ordered, "Pilot, make your depth one hundred feet."

The fathometer watch called out, "Nine-zero feet under the keel."

The *Gato* slid down into the depths. Depths that were not so deep at all.

"Eight-zero feet under the keel."

Durham called out, tension thick in his voice, "Still zero bearing rate! Sucker's going to go right over the top of us."

"Six-zero feet under the keel."

Most people onboard the submarine could now clearly hear the high-pitched whine of the patrol boat's screws through the hull.

"Four-zero feet under the keel."

The pilot announced, "On ordered depth one-zero-zero feet."

Foster looked over at Jed Durham. "Can you tell what that patrol boat's doing now that he missed giving us one hell of a headache?"

Durham replied, "No change, now opening at high speed. Wide aperture array shows him at five hundred yards and opening."

"Bastard's probably got a hot date waiting in Benghazi harbor. Wasn't coming after us after all. Okay, let's get our pictures and get out of this fishpond," Foster said. "Nav, get us back up to periscope depth."

When the *Gato* was back up near the surface and could once again see the heavy-lift ship, water was lapping over the *Xin Guang Hua*'s main deck. The Chinese submarine was completely uncovered, plainly visible. As Foster and her control room watch standers looked on, they could see the submarine float free as her ride sank even deeper, out from beneath its cargo. The sun was also sinking, but it fell beyond the western horizon as a harbor tug took the now-floating-free submarine in tow and headed toward the Port of Benghazi to the east.

The *Gato* slowly headed back toward deep water, out beyond the twelve-mile limit. There, she would return to periscope depth once more and send her haul of very interesting information and compelling video back to Naval Intelligence.

"I'd give a dollar to see the looks on the faces of the intel weenies when they see this," Henrietta Foster said to no one in particular. "Libya taking delivery of a Chinese submarine."

"We need to get up a betting pool on what the boss tells us to do next," Eric Householder responded. "My money's on us spending lots of time loitering around the harbor of Benghazi, waiting to see what that new arrival does."

"And I say let's discuss your wager in the wardroom," Foster shot back. "It's grilled pork chops and applesauce tonight."

Ψ

The President of the United States, Sandra Dosetti, sat back and enjoyed the buttery softness of the calf-skin leather easy chair. The steward topped off her glass of chardonnay and then disappeared into the galley. Dosetti glanced out the window. The Rocky Mountains, thousands of feet below, steadily moved past like a lovely, snow-capped diorama. Honolulu was still over seven hours away, even with the preferential routing that Air

Force One always received. It was time for dinner, then an hour or so making nice with the press contingent that was riding in the back. Her PR team should have her remarks for tomorrow's Asian-Pacific Markets Conference ready for her review and edit by then.

But first, Vice President Sebastien Aldo was requesting a short-notice conference call.

The Air Force Master Sergeant in charge of communications on Air Force One knocked at the door and stuck his head into the presidential suite.

"Madam President, your call is set to begin in one minute. I need to set up the system."

Dosetti nodded and waved to the Master Sergeant to go ahead.

He took a remote-control wand from a side table and pressed a button. A panel on the after bulkhead slid up and out of the way, revealing a large flat-panel display. He handed the remote to the President. "Ma'am, I know this is your first opportunity to use this system. Just hit the large center button when you're ready to start. The Vice President is already waiting online for you. When you're done, just hit the same button again to disconnect. Call me if you need anything."

He backed out of the suite and closed the door, leaving her alone. Sandra Dosetti pushed the button. Sebastien Aldo appeared almost instantly. She noticed the concern on his face.

"Madame President, sorry to disturb your evening," the Vice President began. "But we need to discuss this pirate situation in the Mediterranean. I have the Secretary of State and Secretary of Defense here with me."

The camera panned around to verify that John Dingham and Alstair Bunch, the newly confirmed Secretaries of Defense and State, respectively, were a part of this meeting.

Dosetti smiled and nodded. "Al, John, good evening." She took a sip of wine before asking, "Now, what's the latest on the situation?"

"The Libyans are acting up again, but the new guy over there seems intent on taking over the world in his first month on the job," Sebastien answered, shaking his head. "So far, they've been shooting at each other about the same as they've done for most of recorded history. But then this. They just released their first communication and list of demands since they hijacked the oil tanker *Cygnet Dawn* in international waters. They're claiming, of course, that the ship was in their waters illegally. It's called the 'right of innocent passage' for a reason. But for that crime, they are demanding payment of a fine of half a billion dollars before they will release the ship and crew."

"That's BS!" John Dingham roared. A gruff, retired US Navy Admiral, Dingham had a reputation as a no-nonsense, shoot-from-the-hip style of leader. "That damn ship was a good twenty miles off the coast when they went out there and attacked and seized her. That's international waters in anyone's book. What we need to do is go on in there and kick this Ali Hakim Sherif's butt. Teach him a lesson right off the bat before he solidifies his position with his people, let alone the rest of the world."

Alstair Bunch, a Yale-educated lawyer and an associate of President Dosetti from her days on Wall Street, raised his hand, palm out.

"Easy, John. Let's not start another Barbary War just yet. The Wilayat Tarabulus Althaania—or the Second Regency of Tripoli, the English translation is a lot easier—are absolutely holding the ship and crew hostage. They have announced that all waters extending north from their borders to thirty-four degrees latitude belongs to them, and that comes from no less a decree than the edicts of Allah and by right of conquest by Suleiman the Magnificent." He chuckled and added, "Sort of interesting that they are claiming this big patch of water based on a war that happened six hundred years ago."

Dosetti broke in. "This ship is Panamanian flagged, I think I saw. Do we even have a dog in the fight?"

The Vice President answered, "The *Cygnet Dawn* is owned by Swan Maritime Holdings out of Bayonne, New Jersey. It was sailing under lease to Royal Dutch Shell. So, we have jurisdiction because of the ownership being US and under NATO because of the lessee. The crew is an assortment of Greek, Cypriot, and Malaysian. The Captain is Italian. No US citizens."

"Where is the *Cygnet Dawn* right now?" Dosetti asked.

"She's at anchor in the outer harbor at Tobruk," the VP answered. "Seems someone was thoughtful enough to leave the AIS transponder on, so it was easy to locate her." An aerial image of a large ship surrounded by smaller harbor craft appeared on the screen. "Here is a photo that one of our recon birds took this afternoon."

The President quietly pondered the situation for a few seconds, then she asked, "What are your recommendations?"

John Dingham answered without hesitation. "As I said, we send a strike team in to take back the ship. I can have a SEAL team or DELTA Force briefed, trained, and in there raising hell in a week. By then, I can also have two aircraft carriers in the Med to provide air cover for the operation. If we don't act now, and forcefully, they're just going to do it again. They obviously consider the Mediterranean Sea to be one big-ass ATM machine!"

"But what about the crew?" Bunch protested. "We go in kicking down doors, someone is surely going to get hurt. Why don't we try a diplomatic, negotiated approach first? We may be able to settle this dust-up without it being a bad action-movie scenario."

The Vice President said, "Well, there's another wrinkle here."

Dosetti raised an eyebrow. She recognized the tone in Sebastien's voice. There truly was some nasty kink in the situation.

"As it turns out, Swan Maritime Holdings is a wholly owned subsidiary of Rosenblatt Capital. You remember Magnus Rosenblatt, Madam President?"

Dosetti nodded slowly and pursed her lips. The other two cabinet members on the screen looked at each other, puzzled. "Yeah, the Wall Street banker. I've known Magnus for a long time. He has a finger in every-thing that involves massive amounts of money or Wall Street itself. So, he's in shipping now, too?"

Sebastien nodded. "Well, he called a few minutes ago. He talked to me since you weren't available. Oddly enough, it seems that he is not in that big of a hurry to get his ship back right away. It's fully insured. The insurance company will pay the fine."

Dosetti chuckled dryly. "I'm not sure what his angle is, but you can bet that Magnus has figured out how to use this situation to make a buck. Prob-ably betting on crude futures and the price going up while pirates and terrorists are over there seizing tankers like they're shopping at Costco."

"That's about what I figured," Sebastien replied. "He also felt the need to mention that he was working with the national party organization to set up a fund-raising gala in New York City for your re-election."

"That's rich. I haven't even been elected for the first time yet, and he's already planning my re-election. Trying to butter us up with promises of campaign support," Dosetti answered. She had ascended to the Presidency when the previous Chief Executive and Vice President became caught up in a potential scandal and abruptly resigned for "health reasons." "Okay, here's what I want you to do. John, go ahead and get your ships deployed, an assault plan devised, and a SEAL team ready to go. I'm not authorizing you to act yet. Just get it teed up."

Looking toward Alstair Bunch, she went on. "Al, go through diplomatic channels and let our European allies know that we view this action seriously and are reviewing our options, both diplomatically and militarily. While you're at it, let the Arab world know that this Second Regency of Tripoli, or whatever the hell they are calling themselves, is headed down the same road that Gaddafi went down, and it will end the same way. We must be careful not to appear weak or hesitant, but we don't want to spook the rest of the world, either. Or give the other party anything to slam us with."

She looked at each man's face on the screen, trying to see signs that everyone understood her position. Satisfied, she told them, "Now, if you gentlemen will excuse me, it's dinnertime in my time zone."

With that, the President disconnected the call.

Ψ

Ali Hakim Sherif stood and scanned the map hanging from the tent wall, not at all sure he understood what he was seeing. He could not decipher many of the symbols that cluttered the map, nor was there a legend anywhere that might better inform him of what they meant. That was a job for his generals anyway. His mission was to lead them to glory and that was exactly what he was doing.

He did not need the map to know that his troops were rapidly converging on the tiny desert village of Ash Shwayrif. The roadway just outside the tent rumbled with the near constant clatter of tanks and APCs hurrying past. Sand kicked up by the vehicles' passage seeped through the sealed tent seams. It coated everything and everyone inside with a powdery layer of fine red dust.

He did notice that the map symbols were concentrated on the only three roads that converged on the lonely outpost where Igider Ibn Gildo, the current Berber tribal leader—who was also the self-styled President of the Government of National Unity—had chosen to make a stand against Sherif's approaching forces. That showdown was now taking place. Sherif's command tent was only forty kilometers south of Ash Shwayrif, erected next to the road up from Brak, the next closest town, another two hundred kilometers to the south. But his armies were converging from Qaryat and Abu Nujaym, prepared to put a decisive and positive conclusion to this part of the takeover. Ibn Gildo's only escape was out into the trackless and waterless desert. Should they decide to retreat that way, his army would be easy to track down and destroy.

The Bedouin leader Bahri Dawoud Kahir ad-Din Misurata stood off to the side, intently watching a small laptop screen. What would his ancestors have thought of such a device and the view it allowed them? Smiling, he waved for Ali Hakim to come over and see what he was seeing.

"Ali, I truly believe these Iranian UAVs are magic," the elderly Bedouin excitedly proclaimed. "We have the same view as Allah on all that is happening at a place an hour's camel ride from where we stand."

The screen showed an aerial view of several T-55 main battle tanks careening down a rutted roadway. The lead tank, while still charging forward, trained its turret on something to the side and ahead of them. Then it suddenly belched flame and smoke. The camera quickly panned to the horizon, where what appeared to be an armored personnel carrier abruptly exploded and began to burn. No one escaped the doomed vehicle.

Then the camera operator shifted to another UAV. This view zoomed in to show a building in the village. A set of crosshairs, centered on the building, was super-imposed on the screen. The view brought the building rapidly closer. It grew until it filled the entire screen and then the monitor went blank. The operator looked up and smiled, then made an exaggerated slashing movement with his hand across his throat.

The building, and whatever or whoever it contained, was no more.

Bijin Salemi tugged on Ali Hakim's robe and pointed to another screen, the one he had been watching. This UAV showed vehicles kicking up thick clouds of dust as they departed from the Qaryat-Ash Shwayrif Road and came to a stop there. Ali Hakim could not tell from the image what vehicles might be churning up so much dust.

Salemi smiled as he explained. "The Twenty-Third Heavy Artillery Battalion has reached their objective, twenty kilometers from Ash Shwayrif. They are deploying their launch tubes now." He directed the computer operator to shift pictures. The new view was very similar, more billowing dust clouds behind vehicles that appeared to be leaving a main road, then pulling to a stop. Only this time, it was the Abu Nujaym-Ash Shwayrif Road. "That is the Fifty-Second Heavy Artillery Battalion deploying." With a click of the mouse, a third view came into focus. It was identified as the Seventeenth Heavy Artillery Battalion deploying off the Brak-Ash Shwayrif Road.

The numbers on a nearby digital clock ticked over to show it was now fifteen hundred hours. The UAV cameras showed the 152mm heavy artillery come to life in unison. Ninety cannons over three battalions sent their high-explosive death zooming into the tiny desert town. Again and again the guns roared until most of the little village had been reduced to rubble and ugly debris. There was no hint of answering fire or any other response from inside the village.

The buzzing of Ali Hakim's cell phone interrupted the show of destruction. The leader of Wilayat Tarabulus Althaania considered not answering it as he continued to watch the glorious fulfillment of his long-gestating finale—one that would finally make him his nation's undisputed leader—as it played out on the screens.

But it could be important. He pulled the offending instrument from his pocket. The voice on the other end of the call was familiar.

"Ali Hakim Sherif, this is Igider Ibn Gildo, President of the Government of National Unity. I surrender all my forces and appeal to you for mercy for my men."

There was a smile across Ali Hakim's hawklike visage. He had just heard the words he had so long craved to hear. Now, he could speak his own words, the ones he had looked forward to saying.

"There is no mercy for the *khayin*. The holy Quran demands death for treason."

He clicked the phone off, pointedly ending the call. Then he gave the orders to have his tanks begin their fast advance toward the village and for the artillery barrage to continue until the last available shell had been fired.

Ali Hakim said, "See that my orders are carried out to the last man."

Bijan Salemi nodded and smiled in agreement. It was, indeed, a great day for the Second Regency.

5

Admiral Jon Ward was breathing hard and sweating like—what was it Papa Tom used to say?—sweating like a seaman deuce at captain's mast. He had somehow not noticed when the hill stretching up and out of Alexandria had gotten so long and steep. It seemed like only a few weeks ago that he and good friend and Navy SEAL Captain Bill Beaman would go out and run pretty much all day, maintaining a consistent six-minute-per-mile pace even as they carried on a deep philosophical discussion. Somewhere along the way, though, these morning five-mile runs had morphed into an hour-long slog. Still, he refused to concede that age might be catching up with him.

Anyway, it was a beautiful spring morning in Northern Virginia. The sun was still low on the eastern horizon, over across the Potomac. The mockingbirds were chirping away like an inspired choir and every bush seemed to be an azalea ablaze with red, pink, orange, or pure white blooms, doing their best to impress during their too-short annual springtime show. He reflected that at least at this old-dude pace, he had plenty of time to take in nature's beauty as he plodded through the middle of it.

The crosswalk light at the corner of Beauregard and Seminary Road blinked red. That gave Ward an excuse to stop and lean against the pole, sucking in the cool morning air. Only a couple more miles home and, best of all, it would be a gentle downhill the whole way.

Just as the light changed and he stepped off the curb, Ward's cell phone chirped annoyingly. He hated having the device on him as he ran, but it was a necessity. As the Navy's top spy, he could not avoid the tether. It was a fast-moving world out there. He pulled the offending phone from his pocket, expecting to see the caller ID of Jimmy Wilson, his flag aide.

No. It was his son, Jim, instead. And he and his current state of affairs was another reason Jon Ward had the cell phone with him. The light and the rest of the run could wait. This call he would take.

"Mornin', Granddad."

The Admiral could hear the special lilt in his son's voice, but it took a second for the greeting to sink in.

"What...you mean...?"

"Yeah, Dad, you got yourself a grandson," Jim Ward proudly announced. "Born at 0337 this morning. Eight pounds, six ounces and twenty inches tall. The college recruiters are already calling, ready to draft him. I told them he is playing for Navy. Mother and son are doing fine. Li Min is resting but little Tom, in true SEAL fashion, is demanding breakfast."

"Tom?" was the only response that Jon Ward could muster.

"Yeah, we named him after Papa Tom. I can't wait to tell him."

Jon Ward's father—and Jim's grandfather, though he never knew him— was killed on a mysterious submarine mission when Jon was a boy. It was Tom Donnegan who acted as a surrogate father and mentor for Jon. Then, when Admiral Donnegan retired back to his beloved Hawaiian Islands, it was Jon Ward who relieved him as the Director of Naval Intelligence. Not replaced, Jon always maintained. Nobody could replace Tom Donnegan. Relieved, with hopes he could do half the job the Admiral had done to keep the world a safer place.

"Where are you now?" the elder Ward asked.

"We're at Bethesda Hospital. You need to get your run finished and get your butt up here to meet your grandson. Mom's probably already sitting in the car with the engine running, waiting for you."

"On our way, son," Jon Ward answered. "On our way!" The light changed to Walk, but Ward found an entirely new gear for the rest of the jog home. And all thoughts of the various points of strife and conflagration around the globe disappeared from his mind.

He set the fastest pace he had attempted since the time several years ago when he and Beaman raced up around Tantalus and Round Top Mountains above Honolulu, Hawaii. That was for the prize of a bottle of Glenlivet Single Malt Scotch.

Beaman beat him that day, but Ward knew he had already won the big prize on this bright, glorious spring day in DC.

Ψ

A cold spring rain blew in off the North Sea, painting Brussels a dreary gray. Even the bountiful flowers that normally brightened the ancient city appeared washed out and weary. Captured in an industrial park between two busy, wet freeways, the North Atlantic Treaty Organization's headquarters compound lacked even the floral decorations to ease the dreariness. The headquarter building's modern industrial architecture, all glass and gray steel that was intended by its designers to symbolize interlaced fingers, did nothing to brighten an otherwise drab day.

United States Secretary of Defense John Dingham took his seat at the large annular table in the expansive Meeting Room in the NATO headquarters. Most of the other representatives of the thirty-two NATO nations were already in their designated seats, quietly waiting for this latest round of the North Atlantic Council to begin. The huge walnut table around which they gathered had been built to impress but, at the same time, to accommodate the representatives of all the members without indication that any one of them had precedence over the others. The seats arranged behind the table, those reserved for myriad assistants and strap-hangers, aides, and advisors for the primary representatives, were filled.

The Secretary General called the special meeting of the NAC to order. This was the principal decision-making body for NATO and was made up of a Permanent Representative—called an ambassador or PermRep—an appointed official from each member nation. In special cases, the member state's Minister of State or Defense could attend. Secretary Dingham had flown in from Washington especially for this meeting and would be sitting in as the official US representative.

The crowd ominously quieted down when he first entered the room, but there was still a murmuring undertone among the group. Dingham sensed the rancor and discontent that permeated the gathering. This came as something of a surprise. His experience with NATO meetings back when he still wore his old Admiral's uniform had been mostly collegial. It always felt to him very much like an old-fashioned European men's club.

The Libyan situation was a key topic on today's agenda, the very first item for discussion, but that was not the primary reason the new Secretary of Defense had come winging across the Atlantic. With heavy commitments around the globe taxing available US assets to the limits, President Sandra Dosetti had decided that she was not willing to assume a leading role in this particular "regional" crisis. That was something that the NATO countries facing the Mediterranean Sea should have to take on. It was Dingham's job to deliver the message that the other members were going to need to pick up the slack. It would not be a communication they would welcome and most of them had already heard the rumors.

The presiding officer had just introduced Secretary Dingham and gave a brief description of his topic when the Italian PermRep, Arturo Vincenza, who was particularly irate and more than willing to express his disdain, signaled for the opportunity to speak. "Perhaps, if the United States feels that sea lanes across the Mediterranean are not of sufficient importance to require a vigorous defense, then we should also question their commitment to the Standing NATO Maritime Group Two, which we have created and funded for that very purpose."

Dingham raised his hand, indicating to the Secretary General that he desired to respond. Now was the time to head off irrational speculation. The Italian PermRep sat there, arms crossed, lower lip jutted out defiantly.

"Mr. Secretary General, members, please allow me to address Signore Vincenza's concerns honestly and directly. I believe they represent the apprehensions of others gathered here today as well. As President Dosetti has stated, both in her previous position as Secretary of State and now, as President, the United States stands firmly with our NATO allies. But, as has been expounded upon in earlier sessions of this gathering, US assets, and particularly those required for maritime contingency operations, are severely constrained at this time. Our utilization of those assets, both within NATO and with our other commitments worldwide, must be employed on a national priority basis. Given those limitations, it is our determination that the current Libyan situation, and especially in regard to their questionable claims for territorial waters, would and could best be handled by the SNMG-2. The US simply does not have the surface ships available over any extended period to contest this new 'Line of Death' declared by Libya's recently self-proclaimed head of state."

Dingham paused to take a drink of water and allow his words to sink in. The room was remarkably quiet. NATO members were accustomed to the United States saying things like, "We won't, we can't...but we will, regardless of the cost to us in military might or dollars." This stance was a markedly different one.

Dingham did not want his next words to be considered just the latest in the US's typical about-face. "That said," he continued, "we do have a submarine currently on mission in the area of the Mediterranean Sea. With the heightened tensions in the Eastern Mediterranean and with this Libyan situation, we intend to enhance submarine operations in that theater. To meet the support, logistics, and repair requirements for more extensive submarine operations, we had already planned to re-establish the old Submarine Squadron 22. But to do that, we require access to a base where we can conduct periodic submarine support activities."

He looked around the room. The French PermRep was watching a female aide nearby as she adjusted her short skirt. The Greek representative looked at the ceiling, refusing to meet Dingham's gaze. The Italian, Vincenza, had taken a sudden deep interest in something on a sheet of paper on the table before him.

Dingham had his answer. The Mediterranean NATO nations were not going to be of any assistance.

Ψ

The sun was heralding a new day as it cast first light on the dull brown hills behind the Libyan port of Benghazi. Steve Hanly, the on-watch OOD on the submarine USS *Gato*, continued to slowly pan the photonics mast cameras in a constant circle. The view from zero-four-zero to one-nine-zero was unremitting sand, now illuminated by the rising sun. The remainder of the circle was the dark blue Mediterranean. Hanly felt that he had been watching the same boring color palette for most of his life rather than just the past week. Nothing was happening, not since the Chinese diesel submarine had been towed behind the breakwater in Benghazi's outer harbor, out of view of the US submarine as she swam laps off the coast. Just steering course zero-three-five north until the fly-blown coastal village of Daryanah was abeam to starboard, reverse course until the equally fly-blown village of At Taribjah was abeam to port, then rinse and repeat.

Gato CO Henrietta Foster, carrying her signature oversized coffee mug, walked into the control room and watched for a long moment her crew members at work. Efficient. Professional. Bored out of their ever-loving minds. She strode over to the command console and watched the video display for a few seconds.

Hanly commented, "Pretty boring TV show. I give it one star. It's been like this all watch. Not even a fishing boat coming out. Not a single sunbather on the beach. Man, I wish that Chinese sub would come out and play and give us something to see."

"Careful what you wish for, Eng," Foster said with a chuckle. "Intel is saying that sub is being commissioned into the Second Regency of Tripoli navy as the *Sayf Alnabii*. That translates as the *Prophet's Sword*. Latest photo imagery shows her tied up, but with a whole lot of activity going on pier-side. And just to keep things interesting, it looks like at least two more of those heavy-lift ships are heading this way compliments of our Chinese friends. Gives a whole new meaning to 'Chinese delivery.'"

Hanly shook his head. "And I suppose that Sub Group Eight wants us to stay here making racetracks in the ocean until all the players are on the board."

It was Foster's turn to shake her head. "Nope, Eng. We just got orders to make best speed for Souda Bay on Crete. They want us to onload a Direct Support Element Team and all their special gear and gizmos. I'm guessing that once we have the DSE spooks on board, you're going to be seeing a lot more sand. But this time you'll be a bit more entertained. We'll be able to listen in on what Ali Hakim Sherif's little navy is up to, what with Christmas coming early this year. Anyway, come around to course north. When you get in deep water again, drop down to four hundred feet and ahead full. Nav will be up to lay in the track to Souda Bay as soon as she finishes breakfast. It's blueberry waffles with some blueberry syrup the cooks whipped up. Yummy."

Ψ

Bill Langley could not help holding his breath most of the time as the drill derrick slowly swung vertical, the winch groaning painfully as it pulled the massive structure to a fully upright position. It would take the better part of a week to complete construction on the exploratory drill rig. Then there would be a month or more of actual drilling. According to his careful calculations—admittedly more of an educated guess since this was an extreme situation—they needed to auger down to a depth of better than four thousand meters. This rig was designed to drill down to six thousand meters, so he could fudge his numbers a little. Still, that would require a tremendous stack of pipe and a lot of drilling mud, not to mention drill bits and the plethora of other equipment. He would need to get it all hauled all the way out here deep in the Western Egyptian desert. Every piece would have to be driven across more than 250 kilometers of sand and rock from Abu Minqar, the nearest semblance of civilization, and the roads out here had hardly been constructed for this kind of traffic. Where there were roads at all.

If the expense and risks of drilling a wildcat well in the trackless wastes were not worrying enough for Bill Langley, there was a more concerning problem that lay to the west. The Libyan border was only ten kilometers away in that direction. And the nearest Libyan military base—he still called the country Libya though word was they now insisted they be called the Second Regency of Tripoli—was Posto Trucchi. It was only 290 kilometers away, across the Great Calanshio Sand Sea, which consisted of more rocky plateaus than sand. The reports out of Libya concerning the erratic, power-crazed new leader Ali Hakim Sherif did nothing to ease Langley's concerns. If this Sherif character even got a sniff that there was an oil strike so close to his nation, and especially a discovery of this suspected historic magnitude, his Bedouins would be across that imaginary border in a heartbeat, ready to redraw the borderlines.

Langley needed to find out where the security detail that the Egyptians had promised him was, and when they would arrive at the drill site. He looked at his watch, as if that might answer his concerns. No, he should call back to the tiny army outpost at Abu Minqar yet again to check for an ETA. He began punching the numbers into his satellite phone.

The jangling ring tone had just begun when he heard the clattering of a helicopter approaching from the east. Then he could see it. A big, desert-tan, twin-rotor Chinook with the red, white, and black Egyptian flag on its tail. And the chopper was blowing up an impressive sandstorm as it stopped midair, checked for obstructions, and finally touched down at the makeshift landing pad a couple of hundred meters from the drill pad. As the rear door opened, a dozen soldiers dressed in desert camouflage uniforms clambered down, lugging behind them an array of crates and boxes of gear.

The leader of the squad marched importantly over to where Langley stood. He threw up a British-style open-handed salute and, in a drill field voice, announced, "*Sydy, Mulazim awwal* Lieutenant Hanbal Elmahdy. Second platoon, Bravo Company, 116th Mechanized Brigade, reporting for security duty. Where should my men set up our base of operations?"

Langley greeted the young Lieutenant with a much less formal salute and pointed him toward a flat spot a hundred meters from the drill pad. They may have been days late, but they were efficient. In fifteen minutes, the Egyptian soldiers had lugged their gear to their campsite and begun setting up tents and a portable latrine. Meanwhile, the Chinook, without ever cutting its engines, lifted off and hastily disappeared over the horizon to the east.

Langley shook his head. He finally had security on site. That is, so long as the Libyans—or whatever they called themselves these days—did not show up with more than a couple of camel drivers armed with BB guns. His own crew of oil field roustabouts probably made a better security team than Lieutenant Elmahdy and his small platoon.

Well, if things should go to hell in a handbasket, at least they had radios and maybe enough weapons and target practice with them to hold out for a while.

It would only have to be long enough for some more of the Egyptian Army to show up with a real fighting force. He could only hope they would do so in one hell of a hurry.

The news about this amazing find would leak out sooner than later.

6

Henrietta Foster was holed up in her stateroom on board the nuclear submarine *Gato*, nursing a large mug of coffee while she performed one of her least favorite tasks. She was reluctantly reviewing the file of Lieutenant Fitness Reports that the XO, Eric Householder, had forwarded to her. In Foster's mind, the only thing more painful than reviewing officer FITREPs was writing them. Fortunately, writing them was the XO's problem, but the review process was already giving her a monumental headache. And just so she would not start to feel complacent, the Chief's evaluations were stacked up right behind the file of Lieutenant FITREPS.

The phone hanging above her minuscule desk buzzed. For once, she was grateful for the interruption. Foster grabbed the handset and cheerfully responded, "Captain."

"Captain, Officer-of-the-Deck." It was Lieutenant Sharon Woolsey. "We have a flooded umbilical cable alarm on number one photonics mast. Recommend that we place number one photonics mast out of commission. Request to commence troubleshooting number one photonics mast."

Foster took a swig of coffee before she answered. She did not taste it at all. Any kind of relatively small problem could quickly become a major one while transiting a few hundred feet below the surface of the sea.

The *Gato* had two photonics masts, so there was a built-in redundancy, but the two were not identical. Number two was also called the low-profile mast because its sensor head was less than a third the diameter of the number one, making it much more difficult to be spotted when the sub was using it at periscope depth. But that reduced diameter came at a cost. The smaller head did not have room for all the antennas and sensors in the larger number one mast. The loss of the number one photonics mast meant that the *Gato* would be significantly constrained during the intelligence gathering mission to which they were about to be assigned. And that was about to become even more complicated.

"Place number one photonics mast out-of-commission and commence troubleshooting," Foster answered. "And, Nav, let's get a message off to Group Eight to have tech reps ready in Souda Bay to fix this when we get there. Clear baffles for coming to periscope depth. I'll be out there in a minute."

When Foster stepped out into the control room, she saw that the *Gato* was at 150 feet depth, heading west at ten knots.

Sharon Woolsey stood at the command console, studying the sonar picture. She looked up at her Captain and reported, "Skipper, we hold no sonar contacts. Our last BT showed a strong layer at ninety feet, though, so there could be some contacts being masked by the layer. Request permission to come to periscope depth."

Foster looked at the sonar display and the BT trace. Seawater at a different temperature could act to bend sound waves. A layer was a depth band where the temperature changed greatly, bending the sound waves away and effectively blinding sonar.

Before she could say anything, the 4MC emergency announcing system blared, "Fire! Fire! Fire in the laundry!"

The first hints of grayish smoke were already wafting into the control room. Daryl Collins, the pilot, grabbed the 1MC microphone and announced, "Fire, Fire in the laundry! Rig ship for fire!" The incessant "Bong! Bong! Bong!" of the general alarm set the crew racing to begin fighting the fire. "Rig ship for fire! Don EABs throughout the ship!"

Foster's eyes were already beginning to feel uncomfortable from the smoke as she grabbed an emergency air breathing mask, plugged the hose into a nearby manifold and slipped the mask on. She took in a couple of deep breaths of the clean air and then looked around to confirm everyone in the control room had donned their own EABs. She needed them to be breathing and alert until they were beyond this emergency.

Fire and smoke on a submarine are especially dangerous. There is no place to go to get away or get unbreathable air out of all the compartments until they could get to the surface. And even if they did safely get up there, it would take a while to do so. Bad things could happen to good men and women in that short amount of time.

"Control, scene," the 4MC blasted. "This is the XO. I'm in charge at the scene. The fire is out. Fire was in the dryer. There's heavy smoke in the lower level. Recommend emergency ventilate."

Good news, bad news. No more fire, but if any of the crew had not been able to get to a mask, he or she could be in bad shape by now from all that thick smoke. Foster looked over at Woolsey and ordered, "Officer-of-the-Deck, proceed to periscope depth. Emergency ventilate the operations compartment with the blower."

Sharon Woolsey glanced quickly at the sonar display. Nothing showed there. Then she commanded, "Pilot, make your depth six-two feet. Co-pilot, prepare to emergency ventilate the ops compartment with the blower. Number two photonics mast coming up."

Collins dialed in six-two feet as the newly ordered depth and watched as he allowed the automatic ship control to smoothly guide the mammoth submarine up toward the daylight and welcome fresh air. Meanwhile, the co-pilot toggled a few switches that aligned the submarine's ventilation fans and dampers for emergency ventilating the operations compartment. Then he raised the snorkel mast so that they could suck in a bunch of that clean Mediterranean Sea air as soon as they were at periscope depth.

The *Gato* headed upward at a sharp angle.

"One-two-zero feet, coming to six-two feet," Collins called out. Then, a moment later, "One hundred feet, coming to six-two feet."

"Ship is ready to emergency ventilate with the exception of testing the head valve," the co-pilot announced.

Woolsey was spinning the photonics camera around, searching for any underwater shapes they may have missed as the submarine headed upward. All she saw were various shades of blue.

"Ninety feet, coming to six-two feet." Collins was updating their depth every ten feet. "Eighty feet, coming to six-two feet."

"New sonar contact on the LAB array!" Jed Durham, the sonar supervisor, yelled with undisguised urgency. "Bearing three-zero-zero!"

The large aperture bow array was the *Gato*'s primary passive sonar. The horseshoe-shaped array of sensitive hydrophones that were wrapped around the submarine's bow was designed to search out ahead of the boat for other vessels, above or below the surface.

"Just popped up when we broke through the layer," Durham yelled. "He's damn close!"

"Seven zero feet, coming to six-two feet."

"Emergency deep! Left full rudder!" Foster ordered. They needed to get back down to the relative safety of the deep and do so quickly. Otherwise, this new sonar contact would likely be trying to occupy the same space that *Gato* was on the verge of occupying. That would be a far worse situation than laundry fire smoke. But turning away might just give them a little extra clearance and enough time to avoid a collision.

The "Emergency Deep" order automatically started several actions. Daryl Collins rang up "All-Ahead Full" on the engine order telegraph and went to "Full-Dive" on both the bow and stern planes even as he was dialing in a depth order of 150 feet. The throttleman, back in the maneuvering room, opened the throttles to answer the full bell as rapidly as he could. The co-pilot flooded water into the depth control tank and was supposed to lower all masts and antennas. With so much going on, he was slow on that order.

"Lower the photonics mast! Lower the snorkel mast!" Foster shouted when she saw what was happening. Woolsey was already lowering the photonics mast, but the snorkel mast still indicated "Up."

THUNK! SCCCRRREEECCCHHH!

Something had hit the submarine hard. Whatever it was shoved the big sub roughly and heavily over to port. Anyone not seated or braced was thrown to *Gato*'s deck. That included her CO. The loud grinding, tearing noise from somewhere outside continued for a seemingly long time.

Foster slowly picked herself up off the deck where she had fallen. *Gato* seemed to be okay. At least there were no reports of flooding or other mayhem. The lights were still on. The screw was still turning. And the nuclear reactor was making heat.

Something continued to bang repeatedly against the hull. Or maybe it was the boat's sail that was taking a pounding. The noise was definitely coming from somewhere above the spot where she now stood, braced against a table and checking herself for blood or bruises. There was no way to tell what the source of all that racket was until they could get to the surface and do an inspection.

"Pilot, make your depth nine-zero feet," Foster ordered. "We'll clear baffles above the layer and try not to hit anything else on the way to the surface to see what the damages are." Turning to Durham, she asked, "Is the LAB array okay?"

Jed Durham ran through some quick diagnostics and answered, "Yes, ma'am. Array is working like a champ. So is the wide aperture array. Ready to clear baffles."

As the Gato swung around in a wide circle, Durham and his team carefully searched their screens for any ships that might be close aboard.

"Skipper, completed baffle clear. One sonar contact. Sierra Two-Seven-Six. Bearing three-two-seven, range three thousand yards. Sierra Two-Seven-Six appears to be dead-in-the-water."

Turning to Sharon Woolsey, Foster ordered, "Officer-of-the-Deck, proceed to periscope depth and then surface the ship. Once we're on the surface, let's see if we can ventilate through the bridge hatch to clear this smoke."

It took another ten minutes to get the Gato up on the surface and then the bridge hatch opened. When Foster climbed up and looked out, she could see the dented and torn after part of the sail. The snorkel mast was mangled and bent at a sixty-degree angle. This was going to take some significant effort to repair, more than the limited personnel at Souda Bay could possibly provide.

Looking out to the northwest, Foster could see a large container ship about three miles away. Indeed, the vessel was "DIW." Dead in the water. Foster grabbed the 7MC microphone and called down to the control room.

"XO, Captain. Contact that ship to the northwest on channel sixteen. See if they need any assistance. Tell them that we are damaged but able to proceed without assistance." She felt an ache in the pit of her stomach. Thankfully, everyone seemed to be okay. But she knew this little fender-bender would generate much paperwork and bureaucratic hoopla, for sure. Plenty of ribbing, too—most of it good-natured, some not—from her contemporaries about her female driving abilities. And grumbling from some who still did not approve of a woman—and especially a Black woman—commanding a submarine. What had her dad always told her? "It is what it is. Do the right thing. Not necessarily the easiest thing. Always." Foster continued, "And prep an OPREP THREE NAVY BLUE message. We'll have to let the higher-ups know that we put a dent in daddy's Buick."

Ψ

Gato's OPREP THREE message rang alarm bells all over the Pentagon. Within COMSUBLANT and COMSUBGROUP EIGHT as well. With the submarine safely up on the surface and no reports of casualties, the immediate concern was to get *Gato* safely in-port somewhere so that repairs could be made as quickly and quietly as possible. Not everybody on the planet needed to know the US Navy was down a boat. But until a complete and thorough inspection was conducted, she would be relegated to steaming on the surface.

Some within those groups also knew *Gato* had suddenly become very important to the Navy and NATO as well as many other entities who had no idea what was going on in that corner of the Med.

Still others were more concerned about the public relations and political issues that might ensue from having a US Navy nuclear submarine plow into an innocent, unsuspecting cargo vessel in international waters a long, long way from American shores.

Then the Greeks decided that it was not appropriate to have a damaged nuclear submarine in a Greek port. Possible radiation leaks, they whispered. So, they nixed any plans to conduct emergency repairs in Souda Bay. As soon as the news broke about the Greek position on the situation, the Italian government jumped in and let it be known that the *Gato* would not be welcome in Italy in its current hazardous condition. It appeared the sub would have to make a long and uncomfortable surface transit all the way across the Atlantic, back to Norfolk.

Then the phone jangled in Secretary of Defense John Dingham's office. It was the Royal Navy's First Sea Lord, Sir James Allgood. He had gotten wind of *Gato*'s plight and was aware of her strategic importance at this particular time. He was calling to offer use of the Royal Navy facilities at Gibraltar.

Dingham smiled for the first time since he had returned from the testy NATO meeting in Brussels. Gibraltar was just about perfect. The Royal Navy maintained a good-sized modern base there and the old Royal Navy Dockyard, now a civilian-run facility, had a pair of drydocks that could easily hold the *Gato*. Plus, they already had most of the complex, heavy equipment that would be necessary to hastily repair her.

And as icing on the cake, Sir James offered up Gibraltar as the new home for Submarine Squadron 22.

"Sir James, next time I'm in the UK, I owe you a nice Oyster Stout," Dingham happily told him.

"Many thanks, my friend," Allgood replied. "But She Who Must Be Obeyed has pulled rank and has me off all nosh and ales of late until I drop some weight. Good luck with your boat. We're all counting on your keeping a lid on whatever is boiling up down there."

"We will. With your help, we will, Sir James."

Ψ

Sometimes, when he stood in front of his bathroom mirror shaving, or when he rode his exercise bike while watching the telecast of an Ohio State or Cleveland Browns football game, he could feel the gentle motion of the deck beneath his feet. It felt almost like the sensation he had once experienced when a submarine was at periscope depth, the waves on the ocean's surface above rocking the vessel ever so slightly. Sometimes, not so slightly.

But the movement nowadays was not caused by the swells of the sea. He was—at least in theory—ensconced in a massive structure anchored to solid ground. What he was feeling was usually nothing more than another minor earth tremor, a common occurrence in Yokosuka, Japan. The hilltop flag quarters that the US Navy provided him as on-base housing was supposed to be constructed to ride out the effects of such seismic activity, under the principle of flexing rather than breaking. In essence, a ship floating on a movable sea of earth and rock. But here in the middle of Planet Earth's "Ring of Fire," it was impossible to minimize all the motion when the ground trembled.

Admiral Joe Glass did not really mind. Not only did he have a spectacular view of the world's largest overseas naval installation out his window—Fleet Activity Yokosuka—but the movement of the deck beneath his feet brought back so many memories. Ones that reminded him of how much he truly missed being at sea aboard submarines with such dedicated shipmates, plying the depths of the seas, riding those amazing, sophisticated vessels on behalf of the good citizens of the USA.

That had been his job for most of twenty years, first as a junior officer and department head, then XO, and ultimately as CO, all aboard various classes of subs. In the process, he had experienced his share of both good times and harrowing situations, from beneath the polar ice north of the Arctic Circle to the steamy seas of the Far East to tense times in the vicinity of at least five of the world's seven continents. He regretted missing Australia and Antarctica and completing the sweep.

Of course, there were experiences he would never be able to tell friends or relatives about. Not even his wife. The tragedy of losing her and his baby son to a drunk driver had never really left him although he never spoke of it. It had been almost thirty years, but he could still picture the smiles and tears as he left for Holy Loch and his very first patrol as a brand-new Ensign. He never imagined that a glimpse of them out the plane window would be the last time he would see his wife and boy.

Nowadays, though, he rarely crossed the brow and stepped from the pier onto the deck of a submarine, even though he was Commander Submarine Group Seven. He still used any excuse, however meager, to go out and ride a boat and spend some time with the lucky bastard who had command, to drink real submarine coffee and visit with the crew. But even though his pay grade was much higher—he now held the rank of Rear Admiral (lower half) —he found fewer and fewer opportunities to enjoy the sights, sounds, and smells of submarines. That included the boats that he technically oversaw.

He spent far more time in his office or a briefing room somewhere on the sprawling base, reviewing boring reports, meandering memos, maintenance issues, and seemingly never-ending personnel problems.

On this Sunday, he had just finished a twenty-mile "ride" on the bike while watching on TV through a complicated satellite hookup as Ohio State kicked a field goal to beat Penn State in the final seconds. That was when he unexpectedly had his mostly mundane lifestyle abruptly redirected by a person who often popped up in those reminiscences. And someone who still had occasion to alter Glass's schedule rather dramatically.

A particularly energetic tremor during the workout had taken Glass back to his time as exec on the old *Sturgeon*-class boat *Spadefish*, to the time when he served as executive officer under then Commander Jon Ward, running drug-smuggling interdiction patrols between South America and the West Coast of the USA. Between the Buckeyes' win and those vivid remembrances, he almost missed the chime and the readout on the bike's screen informing him that he had hit the twenty-mile mark. He considered remaining aboard for another ten miles but decided he would get cleaned up, stop by the on-base McDonald's for the closest thing to American food he had found so far, and go over to the headquarters building to get a head start on Monday's paperwork stack.

As he hopped off the bike and started for the shower, he felt another substantial earth tremor even as his phone sounded a distinctive custom ringtone. The first few notes of the chorus of the Beatles song, "Yellow Submarine."

That told Glass the caller was his old CO, Ward, now an Admiral with four stars who held the lofty position of Chief of Naval Intelligence. Ward was thirteen time zones behind him. It was Saturday night back there, but Glass knew Ward was almost certainly in his Pentagon office.

Typical.

Glass grabbed a towel, dried the sweat from his hands, and picked up the phone.

Instead of, "Hello!" Glass started with, "Admiral, I assume you saw that big win and you're calling to congratulate your favorite Buckeye alum!"

There was a pause and a chuckle. "Wish I was, Joe. But I don't even know who they were playing." A subtle shift in voice tone confirmed the subject had already been changed. "Look, how quick could you get your sea bag packed and be on the way back here?"

"Two shakes of a lamb's tail, as my momma would have said."

Another pause, but no laugh this time. "Good. I need you to come see me. I've been talking with the CNO. We've got a job for you."

"Sure. What's up, boss?"

This time, there was no hesitation. "Joe, the Mediterranean is about to start boiling like an unwatched soup pot. We need somebody we can trust to go over there to direct a boat or two and try to find out what the hell is going on. And then help me figure out what we can do about it."

"You know I'll do my best, Admiral."

"Indeed, I do. Oh, and by the way, you're being sent in as the new Sub Group Eight."

Ψ

Ali Hakim Sherif strode through the historic stone gatehouse, unconsciously ducking his head as he walked beneath the portcullis's iron spikes. Inside the courtyard, the ancient ochre-painted stone walls were mostly hidden by vast swaths of red, black, and green bunting.

The Red Castle was a celebrated structure on Tripoli's waterfront, adjacent to Martyr's Square, and a thousand-year-old symbol of Libya's long and bloody history. On this day, the courtyard, its grounds and museum, normally a quiet respite from the bustling Souk al-Mushir, was crowded with men dressed in everything from military uniforms to business suits. More than a few were wearing flowing Bedouin *thawbs* and *serwals*. Some had been there for hours already, milling about, making nervous conversation. But regardless of their attire, these men were the country's leadership. The generals, bureaucrats, and tribal leaders. The men who held the nation's reins of power, and who had attained their positions in ways that ranged from savvy political moves to murderously brutal action. They were the men smart enough, unscrupulous enough, or violent enough to seize what they wanted. And what they most wanted was power and all that came with it.

Armed guards in glittering dress uniforms—but bearing loaded AK-74s —stood at every entrance while snipers on alert were arrayed along the rooftops. Men with serious faces, wearing mirror sunglasses and with their suitcoats showing suspicious, ominous bulges, stood around the perimeter warily keeping an eye on the crowd.

Respectful silence fell across the courtyard from the moment Ali Hakim entered. The crowd separated, making a clear path for their new leader to follow toward a stage at the far end of the courtyard. Most of them touched their right hands to their foreheads and bowed as Ali Hakim passed.

The stage had been erected so that the crowd would be facing the *qibla*, the direction of Mecca, 1,800 miles away. This placed the stage diagonally across the far corner of the open space. A green flag with three white crescent moons arranged on it, the ancient flag of the Regency of Tripoli, stood on one corner of the stage while the red imperial standard of the Ottoman sultan rested on the other. An immense golden crescent moon and the golden eagle, national emblem of Libya, formed the backdrop behind a single podium in the middle of the platform.

Ali Hakim leaped up the stairs and onto the stage, raising both arms in triumph as he stepped boldly to the podium. The crowd roared its approval, then, as one, fell silent as it was obvious their new leader was about to speak.

"My brothers! My tribesmen!" Ali Hakim shouted the words. They echoed off the walls around them. Then, looking toward a small contingent of foreigners, including Li Chung Sheng, the Chinese President's special emissary to Libya, he added, "And, of course, our friends from afar!" He waited for the renewed cheers to die down before continuing. "As you all are now aware, our journey back to our rightful position in the world order has reached an important milestone. We have defeated the traitors in our midst whose only goal was to steal the riches of our people and bring power to themselves, not to our nation. Now, as of this historic day, all of what the remainder of the world knows as Libya has become the cornerstone of the Second Regency of Tripoli." Ali Hakim had to wait longer this time for the hosannas of the crowd to subside. "Now, with the grace of

Allah, we are once again united under one government, the Wilayat Tarab-ulus Althaania. And, just as it was with the First Regency of Tripoli…" He turned and pointed toward the green flag on his left. A stray bit of breeze off the sea appeared to lift the banner in a flutter of acknowledgment. "…when my ancestor, Suleiman, ruled with an iron fist on behalf of our tribes, we will once again become one powerful empire, ruling from the Nile to the Atlas Mountains."

Ali Hakim basked in the deafening acclaim from those assembled there. As he did, he looked around the courtyard, enjoying the deluge of approval. Then, when the roar of the crowd abated, he pointed to the red walls of the highly symbolic fortress. "My ancestors rode out of Arabia and bravely wrested these very walls from the Romans. Suleiman the Magnificent then brought our tribes together as what history still considers to be the world's greatest empire. A hundred years later, Suleiman Safir, my father fifteen times removed, became the first *pasha* of Libya and was anointed right here in this very courtyard where we stand united today. The great Suleiman's heritage established our sacred right to rule these lands. Now, finally, it is time for us to take back what rightfully belongs to us. Allah has guided us this far. Though the task ahead will not be easy, he will continue to bless and smile on our righteous jihad as we reclaim and restore what is rightfully ours."

Ali Hakim paused as the crowd again roared its approval. It appeared that they may not stop, but, with a broad smile on his face, he raised his hand for silence. They obeyed his command.

"As we continue our holy quest, I am proud and humble to announce that I am the one who has been selected to lead you forward to victory, and that I will do so under my new title, Pasha Suleiman Jadid!" As the crowd cheered mightily, he pumped both arms in the air, then shouted into the microphone, "On to victory! On to victory!"

The assemblage picked up the chant. "On to victory! On to victory!" Then gradually changed to, "On to victory with Suleiman Jadid! On to victory!"

Ali Hakim Sherif—now Suleiman Jadid—continued to pump his arms and smile as he walked off the stage to what appeared to now be an unending ovation. Li Chung Sheng had stepped away from his small group and met Hakim at the base of the stairs leading down from the stage.

"Excellent speech," the Chinese envoy enthused, bowing, shaking the newly declared *pasha*'s hand. Then he looked Ali Hakim in the eye. "This crowd will follow you anywhere. But I must ask. You say you were 'selected.' Who selected you as Suleiman Jadid?"

Ali Hakim looked right back at Li Chung, stuck out his jaw, and answered, "I did. I am the new Suleiman."

7

Captain Brian Edwards zipped up his foul-weather jacket as tightly as he could get it. Spring weather came late to northern New England and the Portsmouth Naval Shipyard, located at the southernmost extension of Maine. Or in New Hampshire, if one happened to consult the fine gentlemen in that state's legislature. The border dispute was over two hundred years old and not likely to be resolved anytime soon. The base was experiencing a late-season snow squall. The cold night wind, howling in off the Piscataqua River, sent a shiver down his spine.

Edwards remembered the soft, warm Pacific breezes that blessed Pearl Harbor, Oahu, Hawaii. He had not really acclimated to Maine winters since driving the *George Mason* to these cold, northern climes for an extended overhaul after a dicey mission off South America. He had turned his submarine—his baby—over to his relief several months before. Then, in its infinite wisdom, the US Navy decided Captain Edwards was the ideal candidate to help guide submarine crews through the shipyard process there at PNSY. Tolerance for blustery weather was not a factor. He was stuck laboring as the Submarine Squadron Two Deputy for Engineering. Never mind his request to return to Hawaii and a squadron out there under the swaying palm trees. That missive may or may not still rest in an inbox on some Admiral's desk somewhere.

It had been a long night. Edwards had just completed an evening monitor watch, observing maintenance being conducted on a submarine's reactor plant. With the sun eight hours from making another appearance, he walked along the drydock wingwall and skirted the gigantic baby-blue crane erected there. It had been creatively named "Big Blue." He was on his way to his office to write up his notes, then he planned on breakfast at Galley Provisions, Kittery's only twenty-four-hour eatery. A breakfast supplying lots of calories and carbs, for medicinal purposes, of course, but one that would almost certainly disturb his sleep. His observations would be the subject of tomorrow morning's meeting between the squadron commodore, the PNSY commander, and the boat's CO, so they needed to be sent out tonight, before he went home to that waterfront rental up in York Beach.

A blast of sleet stung his face as Edwards headed down Perry Avenue and through the gates out of the "Closed Industrial Area." It was still several chilly blocks over to the Squadron Two building on Goodrich Avenue.

He was walking by the *Squalus* Memorial when his cell phone decided to add to his misery. He grabbed it and punched the button without even looking to see who might be calling at such an hour.

"Edwards," he snapped.

"Now, is that any way to talk to your old skipper?" Joe Glass laughingly protested.

"Captain...err, I mean...Admiral," Edward stammered. "Ignore this old grouchy sailor. It's good to hear your voice. What can I do for you, sir?"

"Brian, I got a hankering for *paella* and I understand the best in the world is served in Gibraltar. Care to join me for dinner there next week?"

Edwards stared at the phone for a second. Was his old skipper off his rocker? Glass would be calling from Yokosuka, Japan, where it was not quite noon tomorrow, so it was not likely *sake* causing Glass to talk such gibberish. And besides, Glass had never been much of a drinker. Or much of a kidder either.

Edwards laughed at his former XO's puzzled silence. Then he let him off the hook.

"Brian, they just gave me Sub Group Eight and they are standing up

SUBRON 22 again. It's going to be headquartered in Gibraltar. I need a Commodore there and I told SUBLANT that I wanted that to be you."

Another icy gust tore down the street between the old redbrick buildings, which acted to funnel the frigid blast directly toward Brian Edwards.

"Tell me, what's the temperature in Gibraltar right now?" Edwards asked.

Glass chuckled. He had spent time in Portsmouth as well. "Sixty-two right now with a high today expected to hit a sunny seventy degrees."

"I'm your man," Edwards shot back. "See you for *paella* next week."

Ψ

The *Gato* gently rolled in the Mediterranean swell as Henrietta Foster sat alone in her stateroom and reviewed the sonar tapes around their recent collision for what seemed like the ten-thousandth time. With the boat stuck on the surface and making best time for Gibraltar, she had plenty of time to consider "what might have been," Foster was mostly trying to figure out what she and her crew could have done differently that might have prevented the accident. That, and beginning to consider how she would answer the myriad questions at the inevitable board of inquiry.

Maybe they could have detected that big vessel—the Chinese flagged Overseas Container Line Ship *Hong Kong*—sooner. The decision to come to periscope depth was hers, of course, but it was based on all available indicators telling her that they were all alone in the ocean. And they did need to get to the surface quickly to ventilate. The fire and the smoke had added urgency to the situation.

Despite reviewing the sonar tapes that specifically concentrated on the sector where the *Hong Kong* suddenly appeared and turning up the gain to the max, there just was nothing there before they broke through the thermal layer at ninety feet. The temperature difference had been quite pronounced, more than enough to bend even the loudest noises back up and away from the submarine's sonar.

Reconstruction showed her that the *Hong Kong* had been pointed directly at them, too. That meant that the ship had presented a pronounced bow null. The bulk of the ship had masked its own noise. The tapes showed that the sonar team detected and reported the *Hong Kong* within two seconds of it suddenly popping up on the screen.

Now, looking at it from all angles, Foster simply could not see how her sonar team could have performed any better.

Maybe they—or she—could have reacted faster when the ship was detected. But again, the recordings showed in real time that only ten seconds elapsed from the initial report until the *Gato* was heading back down to the safety of the deep. The only outlier was getting the snorkel mast back down. The co-pilot was busy flooding the depth control tanks to help hurry them out of harm's way. That caused him to be a couple of seconds slow on that.

That was all history now. The future was, in Foster's opinion, much clearer. In a few minutes, they would be entering the inner harbor of the British Overseas Territory of Gibraltar. In all likelihood, she assumed, her replacement would be waiting on the pier, and she would be leaving her boat for the last time, off to appear before a board of inquiry. The Navy did not look kindly at ship commanders who got themselves involved in poten-tially catastrophic mishaps. When things happen that are not supposed to happen, it is usually somebody's fault. And that somebody is ultimately the CO.

Henrietta Foster shook her head and smiled ruefully. She had come a long way in this man's Navy, fought her way up every step of the way by being the best she could be, proving that she was stronger, smarter, and worked harder than anyone else. Now she was almost certainly going to lose her command, leaving in disgrace. At least her dad was no longer around to see such a thing.

There was a gentle knock on her door. "Enter," she mumbled.

Her exec, Eric Householder, stuck his head in. "Skipper, we just received permission to enter port. We are to moor, starboard side to, at berth forty-nine on the South Mole. The message says that the pilot and two tugs will meet us two miles southwest of Europa Point Light. Vessel Traffic Control will be on radio channel twelve. Recommend we station the maneuvering watch."

Foster nodded and slowly rose. Maybe getting to work would take her mind off what was about to happen to her and her Navy career. "Thanks, XO. Station the maneuvering watch for entering port."

Householder hesitated, then stepped inside and closed the door behind him. "Skipper, a personal word?"

Foster eased back into her chair and nodded.

"Skipper, there is nothing you or anyone else could have or should have done differently back there," Householder told her, looking Foster directly in the eye. "We were fighting a fire and we needed to ventilate to get the smoke out. Between that, the thermal layer, and the container ship being so close, there just wasn't time to avoid the collision. Skipper, sometimes shit just happens. And there ain't nothing you can do about it."

Foster stood and offered her hand to Householder. "Thanks, XO. And if I don't get a chance to say it later when the feces you are talking about inevitably hits the rotating air-circulating device, let me just say it's been great serving with you."

Householder took the offered hand, shook it, but also shook his head in disagreement. "Skipper, with all due respect, that's no way to look at this. You're not going anywhere except back to sea when we get *Gato* fixed. Now slather on some sunblock and grab your shades. The sun topside is vicious."

Foster half smiled. "Thanks, Eric. Already hit the sunscreen. I don't want to get a sunburn. And thanks for the discussion." She grabbed her ballcap. "Now, let's see if we can remember how to get the old girl into port without denting anything else."

She turned and headed up the ladder to the bridge while Householder stepped into the nearby control room. Foster knew that the XO was only trying to buck up her spirits, give her a positive outlook, but there was a difference between maintaining a positive outlook and facing reality. As with any challenge—including this latest one—she knew she should steel herself for those realities. They would be coming her way fast and furious in just a few hours.

Other than working around a half dozen freighters swinging at anchor in the approaches to the inner harbor, maneuvering into Gibraltar was uneventful. The port pilot guided them through the slot in the breakwater, past the South Mole Lighthouse, and down along the South Mole until they were abreast pier forty-nine. He deftly guided them between a British destroyer tied up at pier fifty and a frigate snugged up to pier forty-eight. There was just enough room to slip the submarine between the two gray Royal Navy warships. The tugs pushed the *Gato* firmly up against the camels while the line handlers made the submarine fast to the pier.

With the boat safely tied up and the Officer-of-the-Deck supervising bringing on the brow and shore power cables, Henritta Foster had a few seconds to check her surroundings. The iconic Rock of Gibraltar dominated the skyline like an image from a picture postcard. There was also a surprising amount of activity all around her and her submarine.

Then she spotted a couple of men standing beside an official car only a few feet from where the brow would soon rest. She recognized them at once, but these were a couple of guys she never expected to see on this side of the world.

Admiral Joe Glass and Captain Brian Edwards were both waving at her now that they had seen her on the bridge.

That confirmed her intuition. Edwards would be her temporary replacement. Joe Glass was here to officially deliver the bad news.

As the portable pier crane swung the brow over and lowered it, connecting the submarine to the shore, the pair sauntered over in the direction of the *Gato*. The brow had just kissed the deck when Glass hollered across the water, "Captain, welcome to Gibraltar. Permission to come aboard."

Foster cupped her hands around her mouth so that her voice might carry over all the noise from the tugs and the crane. "Permission granted. Coffee in my stateroom."

As Foster made the long descent back down into the boat, she heard the 1MC announce "Sub Group Eight arriving," followed by six bells. Then came, "SUBRON 22 arriving," followed by four bells.

She was puzzled. What was that all about? Last time she looked, Joe Glass was a one-star and Sub Group Seven, not a two-star. And Submarine Squadron 22 had been defunct for years, ever since the Navy left La Maddalena, Italy, back in the early 2000s.

The three officers showed up at Foster's stateroom at the same time. Glass held out his hand, smiled, and told her, "Commander Foster, you and your crew did a damn fine job getting *Gato* back here. Now I need for you to get her fixed ASAP and back in the fight."

"But..." She was confused. So confused she forgot to make the call to the galley for a pot of coffee.

It must have been the dumb look on her face, but Glass went on to hurriedly explain as they closed the door and found seats. "Here's the deal, Henrietta. Things have changed quickly and for good reason. I'm now Group Eight. We just stood Squadron 22 back up and Brian is the new commodore. *Gato's* going into the *Prince of Wales* drydock first thing tomorrow morning for a thorough inspection and to get that sail fixed. As I said, I need you back in the fight as quick as we can get you there."

"Then I'm not being relieved?" Foster asked, a little dumbfounded. "Pending an inquiry?"

Joe Glass shook his head and grinned. "I'm going to fire my best skipper? When we got Chinese submarines being delivered to a nutcase dictator in NATO's home lake? Whatever gave you that idea?"

"I just assumed, you know, bumping our heads on a cargo ship..."

A solemn look fell over Glass's face. "I do have one serious question for you, Commander."

"Yes?"

"Why the hell haven't you got us some submarine coffee in here yet?"

Ψ

Li Chung Sheng coughed loudly as he walked up to Ali Hakim Sherif's *bayt al-shar*, his Bedouin tent. This was a lesson the Chinese emissary had learned early in his time in this region. In keeping with Bedouin custom, such a subtle announcement of his presence gave the Libyan strongman ample notice that someone was approaching so he could be prepared. Li Chung then waited until he heard Ali Hakim tell him to enter. He slipped his shoes off and stepped inside the black wool tent.

Even though Ali Hakim had set up his current government headquarters in Ar-Rajmah, a picturesque small village in the hills above Benghazi, he insisted on living in a *bayt al-shar* as if they were still out in the desert somewhere, like any simple Bedouin nomad might. Such a show played well with his people when the images appeared on the front pages of news-papers and on the government television stations of Suleiman Jadid living in a desert *bayt al-shar*.

Ali Hakim rose to greet his guest and waved him toward a pile of cush-ions. "Make yourself comfortable. I'll have some tea made shortly. This is not exactly your Beijing teahouse, I'm afraid," he apologized, waving his hand to indicate the tent. "But it is serving its purpose quite well."

Li Chung smiled as he lowered himself onto the cushions. "I must admit that I have grown rather fond of your Bedouin tea. The sage and cardamom add an unexpected hint of spice to the flavor. And I understand the cardamom has medicinal value, supporting the immune system." The Chinese diplomat handed Ali Hakim a file. "While we are waiting for the tea to steep, perhaps you might want to see these photographs."

The first picture, obviously a satellite photo, showed a submarine, the *Gato*, tied up at the mole in Gibraltar. A second image was a surprisingly clear blow-up of the damage to the sub's sail.

"As you know, the American submarine collided with Orient Overseas Container Line Ship *Hong Kong* last week a hundred kilometers southwest of Crete. It is now in Gibraltar for repairs, thanks to the British Royal Navy. According to our intelligence sources, this USS *Gato* was the only American submarine in the Mediterranean at the time. Considering the usual bureaucracy and with the two navies having to coordinate to requisition even a single bolt or screw during the repair work, we will not need to worry about them for a while."

"Allah is good," Ali Hakim said with a rare smile. "It would almost appear that your ship was guided to that spot by the Almighty so He might smite the infidel. And I have already learned that the *Hong Kong* just tied up in Tripoli with only minimal damage. The supplies it is delivering will be quite useful, especially those long-range air defense missiles. They should provide a very nasty surprise for any NATO warplanes that might be stupid enough to challenge us and our new government."

It was Li Chung's turn to smile slyly. "Whether the *Hong Kong* arrived at that fateful spot near Crete by divine guidance, by design, or by pure luck will remain a mystery. But the OOCL has already filed claims in Admiralty Court for damages to the *Hong Kong* caused by the dangerously reckless operations of the American submarine. It will be quite ironic when the Americans end up paying for your missiles." Li Chung took a first sip of the hot tea, smacked his lips, and then enjoyed another taste before continuing. "And since we are speaking of submarines, the commander of our training crew has informed me that your men are performing very well in their training. They are now ready to take the *Sayf Alnabii* to sea. With our men supervising, of course."

"Good! But not surprising. We have a long heritage of sailors plying the waters of the Mediterranean, including the Barbary pirates. I knew our men would quickly master this maritime task as well."

"Well, these vessels are much more complicated than those lateen-rigged three-masted xebecs of yesteryear," Li Chung responded. "But you should be duly proud of the men we have trained on these modern warships."

"Yes, and with the American submarine no longer there, I am anxious to make good use of our own new underwater toy," Ali Hakim said. "We must put some teeth in the 'Line of Death.' Otherwise, it will be as meaningless and disrespected as the one Gaddafi attempted to establish almost half a century ago. The Americans only laughed at his futile posturing. No one will laugh at Suleiman Jadid and the Second Regency."

Li Chung looked up at the Libyan strongman with a serious face. "My friend, let us not rush this. We will soon get the *Sayf Alnabii* out to sea and make certain your men are completely familiarized with its operations, regardless of what they may encounter. With a well-trained, well-prepared crew, and with the American vessel now out of service for quite a while, ours will be the most capable submarine in the Mediterranean. And remember, there will be more underwater firepower to come, and very soon. I can report to you that our other two submarines are arriving early next week. With three submarines, you will control the entire Libyan Sea basin. And do so with little to fear from the NATO nations in the Mediterranean." The Chinese diplomat took a final sip of tea before replacing the cup on the silver tray, then he went on. "The final bit of information I have for you comes from our sources inside NATO headquarters. The new American President, that woman Dosetti, is refusing to provide American Navy ships to the organization to challenge you and your extended claims of territorial waters. The Italians and the Greeks, maybe the French, will be left to fend for themselves for the foreseeable future. Without doubt, the time will soon come for your new Barbary pirates to venture forth."

Ali Hakim sat up proudly. "I could not agree more. And thanks to our Iranian and Russian friends, we now have information about all shipments heading past our doorstep that may prove profitable for us and very embarrassing for the Western infidels."

Then his voice changed tone, becoming more serious. "I have a message for you to pass to your President, directly to Tan Yong. I request that you do not make any written reference to this message and to pass it with the highest possible security to the President only." He paused until the Chinese emissary nodded, confirming he would agree to Ali Hakim's provision. "Good, then. Tomorrow Suleiman Jadid will announce that we are nationalizing all foreign-owned assets in the Second Regency and expelling all foreign workers. That will give us complete control of our own oil and gas production and assure that the proceeds from such trade will remain with the people of our nation, not be siphoned off by oil companies of other nations. And it will severely impact the economies of Italy, France, Germany, and Spain. If Greece had any industry, it would cripple them as well."

Li Chung smiled at Ali Hakim's attempt at a joke, took the last swallow of tea from his cup, then replied, "That is all very good. And this move certainly advances my country's agenda as well as yours. But I must ask, what is the reason for all this secrecy?"

Ali Hakim raised his hand. "On it benefiting both nations, I agree. But the second part is more important. And it is the part where secrecy is vital, as you will see. I am now gathering forces on the eastern border, down on the Calanshio Sand Sea, where they will remain hidden by the vast desolation of the area. When I give the word, they will sweep across the Egyptian border and seize what the maps show as the 'Western Desert.' Trust me when I say that the history of the border between Egypt and the Second Regency is too complex and convoluted to quickly explain. In the end, it boils down to the fact that the Al-Ṣaḥrā'al-Gharbiyyah, or what the Egyptians so arrogantly call their Western Desert, is rightfully ours as passed down from Suleiman the Magnificent. And we intend to take what is ours."

Ali Hakim paused to take a breath and to look intently at the Chinese diplomat.

"Yes, go on."

"What I really need is for some outside crisis to keep the Americans busy. Something far away from our desert sand. Maybe more than one crisis. I need them so busy that they will not think to come to the aid of their Egyptian friends. I am requesting that the People's Republic stir up some American angst."

"But tell me, sir," Li Chung asked, a confused expression on his face. "Why are you so interested in committing this fighting force to capture scorpions, camel spiders, and tons of hot, dry sand when there is so much to defend in populated and more valuable areas of your nation?"

Ali Hakim took a moment to finish the last of his own cup of tea. "That I am not yet prepared to share. Not even with you, our most trusted ally. But be assured, this action will also be of great benefit to both our countries. In reality, it will be of almost indescribable benefit to us all."

8

"Madam President, we recommend that we bring pressure to bear on the Egyptians to prevent delivery of those two Chinese submarines." The State Department briefer glanced over at Alstair Bunch, the Secretary of State, for support. So far, the diplomat's face remained unreadable. "One of the Chinese heavy-lift ships is in the Red Sea and is scheduled to transit the Suez Canal tomorrow. The other one is in the Andaman Sea, expected to reach the canal in ten days or so. Our ambassador is standing by to deliver a démarche to the Egyptian foreign minister. With your permission, we would like to proceed." The briefer had finished with his prepared remarks but remained there, standing uncomfortably behind the podium.

President Sandra Dosetti sat back and steepled her fingers beneath her chin as if contemplating all the manifold permutations of the question now before the group. She had learned early on in her political career that a careful, thoughtful pause during a meeting could reveal a great deal of useful information. The lull in the give-and-take often had to be filled by the person doing the presentation. Frequently, they volunteered data or an opinion that was more than the questioner originally intended to pass along.

Secretary Bunch jumped in to fill the awkward silence. "We feel that this is a symbolically important move. Peacefully, but firmly, establishing our position in this situation." Both the French and the Italian Foreign Ministers had called Bunch to express their concern and support for a diplomatic solution. And then Magnus Rosenblatt, the Wall Street mogul, had called to discuss the situation developing in the Mediterranean. A lot of global heavy hitters were now playing in this game.

Secretary Bunch and Vice President Sebastien Aldo looked across the broad expanse of the cabinet meeting room table at the President, awaiting her decision.

Dosetti was still quiet, but she noted that her Secretary of State was clearly anxious for this démarche approach to go forward. It was not surprising it made sense considering the idea came out of his department, but was Secretary Bunch revealing something bigger behind his anxiety? Was there pressure from somewhere steering his decisions? She decided that she would need to keep her eyes open in that direction.

The President nodded toward John Dingham, the Secretary of Defense. Dingham cleared his throat and reported, "Madam President, we've been tracking these two ships since they left Guangzhou about two weeks apart. From photo intelligence when each of them transited the Malacca Straits, it appears that they are rigged to look like they are carrying drill derricks. That was the same thing the Chinese pulled with the *Xin Guang Hua* a couple of weeks ago, and only now do we know it had the submarine aboard, hidden under all that piping and canvas. However, there is nothing illegal about delivering an oil drill derrick. Or a submarine for that matter. And we cannot prove they are carrying anything else." Dingham paused for a moment, glancing down at his notes. Then he added, "AIS data shows that these two are both headed to Benghazi once they go through the Suez Canal. We do not care if that nutty bastard Sherif gets another couple of oil derricks. But I sure don't like him getting more submarines for that bullshit navy of his."

Dosetti looked over at Bunch. "Al, refresh my memory. I don't recall any legal or treaty limitations on what cargoes are allowed to transit the Suez. Is that correct?"

Bunch nodded reluctantly. "Yes, ma'am. We are basing our démarche on our treaty arrangements with the Egyptian government rather than any specific rules regarding the canal. Admittedly, it's a loose interpretation of the treaty terms, but the Egyptians may comply since it would absolutely be in their best interest to not have the previously mentioned nutcase next door in possession of high-end submarines."

Vice President Aldo chimed in. "And the Egyptians still may not comply with our suggestions. There are not many countries left on the planet who will risk getting on the wrong side of Tan Yong and the CCP. For that possibility, I recommend we have a backup plan."

Dosetti nodded. "Just what I was thinking. John, arrange for a couple of destroyers, those *Arleigh Burke*s that you sailors are so proud of, to escort those two ships to Benghazi. But they are to do so at a safe distance and not appear in any way to be harassing them. And get hold of Admiral Ward over at Naval Intelligence. I may have a sensitive job for him that would require some SEALs." She looked over at the Secretary of State and added, "Alstair, send your ambassador with the démarche, but don't hold your breath on it doing any good."

Dosetti pushed her chair back and stood. "Now, if you gentlemen will excuse me, I have a meeting with some group called the Society for American Education. They want to talk about removing from history books most everything that happened before 1870." Looking over at the Secretary of State, she added, "Alstair, we should be done in time for our meeting with the Japanese ambassador at two. If you would stop by fifteen minutes early, I would like to go over our discussion topics beforehand."

With that the President walked out of the room and turned down the hallway in the direction of the Oval Office.

Ψ

Commander Henrietta Foster climbed up the vertical ladder and out of the hatch of USS *Gato* to be greeted by a warm, fragrant Mediterranean-evening breeze. It was hard to tell it was nighttime, though. The Gibdock shipyard was awash with brilliant blue-white floodlights that completely washed out the night sky, canceling out the stars overhead. The submarine's narrow topside was congested with workers and all sorts of equipment. It was all she could do to skirt past all the shipyard workers busily working on the *Gato*'s damaged sail.

Foster stopped on the brow that connected her submarine to the drydock's wing wall. Looking back, she marveled at all that had been accomplished in just over a week. NAVSEA back home had loaded several planes with all the shipyard workers on the East Coast that they could corral and sent them to Gibraltar. Enough for three shifts a day, seven days a week, so this was no vacation for anybody. And the result was constant hammering, banging, grinding, and welding. All that noise made living on the boat impossible for *Gato*'s crewmembers. Fortunately, the Royal Navy made a barracks available for the crew and a block of rooms at the BOQ for the wardroom. However, those accommodations were a twenty-minute walk from the drydock, so Foster had declined a room and slept in her stateroom as best she could while wearing a pair of noise-cancelling headphones.

She was pleased to see that the after part of the sail no longer looked like so much mangled, twisted, junkyard-bound steel. It once again resembled a submarine sail. The new snorkel mast and the two after universal modular mast assemblies were lying on the wing wall waiting to be hoisted aboard, installed, and aligned. The UMMs allowed the damaged masts and lifting gear to be taken away and replaced as brand-new boxed units that slipped into place as a completed assembly. That meant most of the tedious work of making up hard-to-reach connections and ticklish alignments was all but eliminated, greatly simplifying and speeding the process. At this rate, the sail work would be all buttoned up and freshly repainted in another week.

It could not be soon enough for Foster. She readily admitted she never felt comfortable with solid ground beneath her feet. She needed to get *Gato* out of the shipyard and back to sea. That was where they both belonged.

The skipper stepped off the brow and onto the drydock wing wall. A big crane lumbered by, its bell clanging loudly to warn anyone nearby that the behemoth was underway and to stay clear. She waited for the crane, a large metal box dangling from its lifting hook, to pass before she quickly walked across the access road before some other prehistoric-like beast came along.

Brian Edwards waited for her there, a grin on his face, leaning against an older Land Rover Wolf that was painted the dull green color of the British Royal Army.

"This might be the most hazardous duty you've seen yet, Commander," he said in greeting. Busy overseeing the repair work on her boat, Henrietta had hardly seen Edwards or Joe Glass in her week in Gibraltar.

"Nice wheels you're sportin' there, Commodore," Foster responded as she saluted. "So, where we going? You were mighty mysterious when you asked me if I could spare a few hours."

"The ride's courtesy of His Majesty. Hop in and we'll give her a spin."

Foster instinctively reached for the right-side door of the vehicle just as Edwards grabbed for the same handle. "Henrietta, if you wouldn't mind, I'd better drive," he joshed. "After all, I know where we're going and you don't."

"I keep forgetting that the Brits drive on the wrong side of the damn road," Foster said with a laugh and headed around for the other door. "At least you didn't make any comments about women drivers."

Edwards spun the Land Rover around and gunned it, shooting out of the shipyard and onto Rosia Road. Edwards made a quick series of turns as he snaked through a labyrinth of narrow streets that edged up the lower slopes of the world-famous Rock of Gibraltar. Foster had long since lost her sense of direction, totally confused by the streets that angled off in all directions. Then they were suddenly out of town and on a relatively straight road that climbed sharply upward. Engineers Road abruptly ended in a tee, requiring them to turn onto Queens Road and continue the climb. That had them angling across the rock in the other direction. The roads formed long switchbacks as they ascended the steep slope.

Foster might have been hopelessly lost but she was still mesmerized by the fabulous view. The Mediterranean Sea stretched out forever in three directions under a half-moon. It seemed that a thousand ships were visible out in the Strait, their running lights Christmasy dots of red, green, and white. Morocco and the Atlas Mountains—the northern coast of the continent of Africa—were just visible as a broad, brown smudge against the starry night sky. That distant shore was banded with car headlights twinkling along the roads that ran along the southern horizon.

Edwards skidded the Land Rover to a halt in front of a metal gate with a large sign that declared the property on the other side of the fence belonged to the Royal Army and that no admittance was permitted. Any violation would be met with deadly force.

An armed guard wearing the double chevrons of a corporal waved them to a stop and purposefully stepped up to Edwards's window. Foster noticed that another guard, this one a lance corporal, was staying back while covering them with his SA80 automatic rifle. This pair looked serious about their jobs. And she assumed there were other eyes, electronic and human, on her and her chauffeur.

Edwards presented his ID card along with Foster's. The corporal took his time as he thoroughly inspected the cards and then checked the names against a list on his clipboard. Only then did he salute and offer a friendly enough welcome to HMCC, His Majesty's Command Center Gibraltar. He signaled to the lance corporal, who then swung the heavy metal gate out of the way and waved them through.

Foster looked over at Edwards and asked, "Boss, what the Sam Hill was that all about?"

"Henrietta, we are now on a facility that does not exist," Edwards answered as he swung past an old, run-down cement building that likely saw its best days around the time World War II was winding down. Just past the building, a tunnel opened unexpectedly, leading directly into the hillside. Edwards drove into the darkened entrance and continued for a hundred feet or more before emerging into a large, open room that most resembled a parking deck. He swung the Land Rover into a parking spot he appeared to own between a couple of very similar Land Rovers.

Jumping out, he said, "Come on. The tour is about to begin."

Foster climbed out and followed Edwards as he made his way for a heavy steel door. Going through the unmarked passage, the pair found themselves in a small, narrow room with another steel door at the far end. The only other features she noticed in the windowless space were a small video camera in one corner and a keypad next to the door. Someone not as accustomed to closed-in tight spaces as a submariner like Foster might have felt claustrophobic.

From nowhere, a metallic voice squawked in a heavy British accent, "Please enter your personal clearance number, Commodore."

After Edwards punched in a series of numbers on the keypad, the door obediently swung open. Foster blinked in amazement at what she saw on the other side. They were stepping from a dank, dark, run-down World

War II facility of undeterminable use into a command center right out of *Star Wars*. The huge, brightly lit room was filled with large-screen monitors flashing colorful pictures, graphics, and data that a group of fifteen or twenty analysts appeared to be busy digesting while simultaneously pecking away on keyboards or swiping and punching touchscreen displays.

Foster slowly looked all around, trying to make sense of what she was seeing. She was accustomed to such a control room on her boat but nothing as massive as this. "Okay, what is this place, Brian?" she queried. "And what are they all doing?"

"Just like the guy at the gate said, this is HMCC Gibraltar," Edwards answered. "Or at least the intel center part of it. The actual command center is in the next couple of rooms. Interesting, isn't it?"

"You can say that again," Foster answered. "But what...?"

"They get intel feeds from all over the Med and Europe, plus from a great deal of Africa. Satellite coverage gets fed directly into here along with any intercepted intel," Edwards explained. "Even all the Brit Link 16 data from their ships and planes gets routed to here. They're getting a very complete look at just about everything happening within...let's call it...a twenty-five-hundred-mile radius of here. All correlated in this room before it's fed into the next room and then back to Government Communications Headquarters outside of London."

"So, this is a listening post for GCHQ?"

Edwards shook his head. "Not really. You won't find any antenna farm anywhere close to here. In fact, anything digital coming in or going out is on undersea fiberoptic cables connected to dozens of stations around the region. This place looks like a black hole for any emitted electronic signals. Nothing in and nothing out. Like I said, it doesn't exist."

Edwards guided Foster into the next room. This one was even larger than the first and equally brightly lit. The walls were decorated with still more large flat-panel displays, but the space was divided into smaller work centers clustered around a large central briefing area.

Henrietta Foster was surprised to see a familiar face amid all the activity. Joe Glass sat at a desk just off the briefing area. He turned from his own keyboard and monitor to wave the two visitors over.

"Hey, Henrietta. How about this place, huh? This is the heart of the

HMCC and, for the last few weeks, the SUBRON 22 Ops Center. Welcome aboard, Commander!" Glass stood, smiled and shook her hand. "Our Royal Navy brothers are subletting us a couple of desks in here, along with access to their GCHQ tap as well as their comms systems. When we get you back in the water and in the fight again, we'll be directing you from here." He patted the desk. "It's a whole lot better connected than my Ops Center back in Naples is. In fact, it's so good that I'm going to use it for your ops. I asked Brian to bring you up here and away from your beloved *Gato* because I wanted you to see first-hand what we had set up to support you."

Foster nodded. "Impressive. Really impressive."

Edwards sat down at one of the desks and waved Foster to a seat. Glass keyed up an image of what appeared to be a heavy-lift ship on a flat panel suspended above them. "We are tracking two more Chinese-flagged heavy-lift ships heading for the Suez Canal. Looks like they are transporting a couple more Chinese subs just like the *Sayf Alnabii* you spotted last month trying to sneak into Libya...or whatever they're calling themselves now. We're going to try to get you out of drydock in time to hightail it over to Benghazi with a team of SEALs. You should be showing up around the same time as the Chinese and their cargo. We know you will be observing and sending all the data you can back here, and we'll route to Naval Intelligence and Admiral Ward at the Pentagon. We're not sure just what all you may have to do down there, Hen. The details are still coming together, but I want your team ready to go."

"Boss, you got it," Foster answered enthusiastically. "Just get me out of this cave and back to the boat safe so we can get her out of here and make ourselves useful."

Glass smiled and replied, "Sounds good, but first we have another assignment for you. They tell me you've been on your boat day and night, helping, observing. Well, Brian and I are of the opinion you could use a little downtime. We found a place downtown that serves a killer *paella*. Let's get ourselves a late dinner before we take you back to *Gato*."

Henrietta grinned. "Guess I have no options. As my daddy always said, 'Orders is orders!'"

Ψ

The Chinese-flagged, semi-submersible, heavy-lift ship *Hua Rui Long*, laden with what appeared to be a massive piping structure that completely filled the ship's main deck, cleared the Port Said breakwater and headed out into the far southeastern corner of the Mediterranean Sea. The orange-and-white behemoth soon plowed unconcernedly through the long, slow rollers, their rhythmic rise and fall splashing ineffectually against the ship's sides.

At a length of over eight hundred feet and a beam of two hundred feet, the *Hua Rui Long* could lift and transport just about anything it needed to. Theoretically, even an American *Gerald Ford*-class aircraft carrier could rest comfortably on the cargo ship's main deck, although two hundred feet of the carrier would extend out over the water. But today's manifest listed the *Hua Rui Long*'s burden as being one unit of a natural gas processing plant that was manufactured in China's Zhoushan Fabrication Yard. It was to be delivered to the newly nation-alized Wilayat Tarabulus Althaania National Oil and Gas Company, which had formerly been owned by a corporation principally controlled by British Petroleum. No more. Now it rightfully belonged to "the people of the Second Regency of Tripoli," according to the press office representing the newly installed government of Ali Hakim Sherif.

Buried deep under all the silver piping and gray steel girders, the *Hua Rui Long*'s real cargo had been skillfully concealed. It was the brand-new modified-*Yuan*-class submarine *Dire Alnabii*—the *"Prophet's Shield"*—and it would not see the light of day again until the natural gas processing plant paraphernalia had been disassembled and floated off the ship's deck. Even the expert Egyptian inspectors, who had toured the *Hua Rui Long* in Port Taofik before it transited the Suez Canal, had not detected the hidden submarine.

Once he had cleared the Port Said breakwater, if the master of the *Hua Rui Long* had searched out on his starboard beam, he might have spied the American *Arleigh Burke*-class destroyer *Harold A. Stanton*. The sleek, gray ship, the newest of the Flight III *Burkes*, was making lazy circles, loitering just at the horizon. The destroyer's advanced AN/SPQ-9 surface-search radar was tracking every surface ship within twenty miles of the *Stanton*, but they were paying particular attention to the Chinese leviathan just emerging from the northern reaches of the Suez Canal.

But the master of the Chinese freighter had no reason to care about other traffic in the vicinity so long as it kept out of his way. As far as he was concerned, he had just cleared the last potential obstacle to delivering his cargo to its destination.

"Bridge, Combat, Surface Track One-Seven-Six equates to our contact of interest. Correlates with AIS to the *Hua Rui Long*," Lieutenant Commander Scott Richter, the Tactical Action Officer on the *Stanton*, reported. "One-Seven-Six is bearing two-zero-six, range two-zero miles, tracking on course three-five-zero, speed twelve."

"We hold the target visually," Captain Jerry Baudsley, the *Stanton*'s skipper, replied. "And I can confirm that it is one big, ugly momma." Baudsley was another Captain who enjoyed sitting in his raised seat on the open bridge wing, enjoying the cool evening breeze. He put the 7x50 binoculars back to his eyes and scanned the Chinese ship one more time. The massive array of pipes and girders on her deck ran the entire length of the ship, looking more like some mad scientist's laboratory experiment than a ship at sea. Baudsley stepped over to the destroyer's "Big Eye" binoculars. With the stanchion-mounted 20 x 120 binoculars, the view made it appear that he was right up alongside the colossal vessel. He carefully scanned the orange ship, matching it against the photo supplied by Naval Intelligence.

"TAO, contact Bravo Alpha," Baudsley said into the microphone. "Inform him that we have the *Hua Rui Long* in sight, Track One-Seven-Six on our Link 16 feed. Commencing the mission." Sticking his head through the bridge door, he ordered, "Officer-of-the-Deck, take station on Track One-Seven-Six one-two-zero relative at a range of thirty thousand yards."

Baudsley sat back and watched as the OOD maneuvered the destroyer so that they were on the Chinese ship's after starboard quarter and just on the horizon, about fifteen miles away. From back here, they could watch everything the heavy-lift ship did and where she went, all while staying far enough away to not raise undue attention. It was surely going to be a boring mission, watching some Chinese merch haul crap down the Med to that loon over in Libya, but that would be their job for however long it took.

Jerry Baudsley sat back and sipped from his cup of coffee. He remembered listening to his father telling tales of sailing around the Mediterranean for the US Navy back in the eighties, keeping a wary eye on the activities of a similar Libyan loon. Everything old was new again.

"Captain, Track One-Seven-Six has changed course," the OOD reported. "Now on course three-three-zero, speed still twelve."

"Very well," Baudsley acknowledged. "Maintain station." The CO stood and stepped into the bridge house. He considered the radar picture, confirming that none of the thirty or so other ships in the area were likely to run over the *Stanton* for the next few minutes. Then he turned to the OOD and told him, "I'll be in my sea cabin. Your tasking for the rest of your watch is to maintain station on this guy. Don't be too obvious, but if he tries to contact you, tell him that you are an American warship on a military mission. Nothing more. Oh, and above all else, don't lose him. Got it?"

With that, Baudsley headed for his sea cabin. He figured at this speed and with their suspected destination, they had at least three days ahead of them tracking this guy and his sketchy cargo. For now, Baudsley decided, he might just take a break, email his dad, and see if he wanted to swap some sea stories.

Ψ

Jim Ward kicked back in his desk chair, raised his hands high over his head, and stretched his aching back. On the short list of things he despised, the veteran SEAL commander rated office work near the top. He would much prefer being out in the field somewhere, completing an important mission with his team, to being stuck here in this dingy office in Coronado, California, working through a slag heap of incessant paperwork. And it seemed any time he got near the bottom of a stack, it got replenished with even more wearisome paperwork. None of this was a reason why he attended the US Naval Academy. Or why he chose the SEALs as a way to serve his country. Not as a submariner, like his dad and grandfather. He felt confined inside one of those sewer pipes. Ward much preferred the wide-open spaces, even while trekking daunting distances in horrid weather and with bad guys shooting at him.

Ward stopped to remind himself of the good side of what he was doing.

Sitting there behind his desk, when he looked out the window, he could see the breakers of the Pacific Ocean lapping up on the Silver Strand where it connected Coronado Island with Imperial Beach. People traveled long distances and paid good money to enjoy such a view, but it was his for the taking anytime he looked up. But even better, when he left work for the day —after keeping office hours much like the civilian world—he drove home to his beautiful wife, Li Min Zhou, and their newborn son, Tom. They would be waiting for him in the little rental bungalow up in the hills above Chula Vista.

When he allowed himself to think about it, he realized just how good life was, even if it was leavened with stifling admin.

The desk phone buzzed, shaking him from his reverie. "WARCOM N-2, Commander Ward. This is not a secure line."

"Commander, this is Admiral Sturm's office. The Admiral would like to speak with you right now. Can you come up?"

Uh-oh. The Admiral usually went through the courtesy to schedule meetings with members of his staff. This summons sounded urgent. Ward's first thought was, *What have I done this time?*

"On my way."

Rear Admiral Jason Sturm was Commander, Naval Special Warfare Command, or COM WARCOM in Navy parlance. As a two-star Rear Admiral, he was Ward's boss several times removed. His corner office was three floors above Ward's temporary cubicle with an even better view of the Silver Strand. Before stepping out his office door, Ward checked his uniform in the mirror, then hopped up the stairs two at a time. He was pleased the trip did not cause him to breathe any harder. He had lost some of the sharp edge of fitness recovering from his wounds garnered during his recent South American adventure. The docs said that paper shuffling would be a good rest, but it was not especially good exercise. He was just getting back to full stride with his workout regime. He knew that he would need that SEAL level of fitness soon enough.

Once he was standing in Admiral Sturm's outer office, he checked his watch. Two minutes. Pretty damn good. And certainly met his boss's "right now" directive. The aide, who seemed surprised to see him so quickly, ushered Ward directly into the Admiral's office, then departed, shutting the door behind him. Sturm waved Ward to a seat.

"Jim, good to see you," the tanned and very fit senior officer said, friendly enough. "How are the wife and that new baby of yours doing? I never talk with your dad without him asking if I've met the tyke yet. You should bring him by sometime, let us make baby talk to him, maybe recruit him to the Navy."

Ward eased back in the chair just a bit. So, the unexpected call and summons were not for a butt chewing for some infraction that had finally caught up with him. Ward smiled and answered, "They're doing great, Admiral. Young Tom has the lungs and appetite of a SEAL already. He's always hungry and sure lets you know."

The Admiral nodded, then the expression on his face confirmed he had shifted gears and the conversation had turned serious. "I know it's a special time for you, and I hate to pull you away from your family," he said. "And I really hate to take you away from completing the lessons learned on that mission you and your guys just did. But someone way above us in the food chain has a job that needs to be done. They have specifically requested that you be the guy on the pointy end of the spear. I need for you to scrounge up that team of miscreants that you like to hang out with and get your young asses on a plane to Gibraltar. The Air Force is laying on a C-17. It has an ETA of Friday, noon, in Gibraltar, so you have three days from right now to gather your team and gear, get a preliminary briefing, and be on the tarmac."

"Admiral, can you give me any hint of what the mission is?" Ward questioned.

Sturm held up a thick file. "It's all in here." He handed it over to Ward. "The brief will tell you a little more. But, as usual, you'll have to do your own investigating once you're there. And by 'there,' I mean there," the Admiral said, pointing to the file envelope.

He escorted Ward to the door. The interview was over.

"Please extend my apologies to your wife and son for pulling you away," Admiral Sturm said as he shook Jim Ward's hand at the door. "But duty calls."

"I accepted that fact a long time ago, Admiral."

"Oh, and Jim, one more thing."

"Yes, sir?"

"Be careful over there."

Back at his desk, Ward opened the sealed envelope and removed the files. After quickly scanning through them, he began making a series of phone calls. Some were local, gathering up his team. One was back to the Pentagon.

"Son, great to hear your voice," Admiral Jon Ward announced upon answering his phone.

"Yours too, old man!"

"Please tell me you're calling to say you and Li Min are bringing that grandson of ours for an official visit? Mom's been threatening to abandon me and head your way if I don't take some leave time soon."

"Well, visiting you guys will have to wait a bit, I'm afraid. I just met with Admiral Sturm," Jim replied. "Looks like I am heading out on a job."

"Yeah," the elder Ward answered, "I got roped in, too. And I knew you wouldn't be taking a vacation anytime soon. Seems like the current occupant of the Oval Office has specifically requested the service of the Ward family warriors. Or at least the male ones. That is, the male ones over six months old."

"Dad, can you check with Mom and see if she can come out and help Li Min while I'm gone?"

Jon Ward chuckled. "Son, you must be kidding. A chance to hold her grandson? I don't think I could keep her away."

"Dad, what can you tell me about this mission? Gibraltar seems like an odd place for a SEAL team to be."

There was a long silence on the other end of the phone, then Jon Ward spoke. "Jim, they got a venomous snake over there in the Egyptian and Libyan desert that they call the sand viper. They blend in well with the sand and can deliver a deadly bite. One unusual thing about them, though. Unlike most vipers that only sit and wait to ambush their prey, these guys also go out and hunt aggressively if they think they need to. We got ourselves a sand viper on the south coast of the Med right now, and we may have to go in there and chop the head off the damn thing."

9

Wu Ming Jie stood back and watched quietly. The diesel engine burbled, emitting smoke and the smell of burned fuel into the night air. He felt the pleasantly familiar vibration in the deck beneath his feet. Gazing down at the brightly lit pier from his vantage point atop the submarine sail, he watched the line handlers on the pier as they patiently stood by to cast them off. All was ready to get underway.

The Libyan crew was progressing well in their training. Of course, they would never be able to operate the *Sayf Alnabii* like a well-trained People's Liberation Army Navy submarine crew could, but Wu Ming, who was overseeing their training, was impressed with how far they had come in only a few short weeks. His PLAN trainers were gradually becoming less teachers and more advisors. It would be many more months, maybe years, before the Libyans would become proficient enough to operate and fight these complex ships by themselves, but they had learned enough now to take the vessel out to sea and operate her in the role of a combat submarine.

"Captain," Wu said, addressing Lahal Nihad Rifat al Subay, the Libyan commanding officer of the *Sayf Alnabii*. "Let us cast off lines and head out. We rendezvous with the *Al Gharbella* at midnight at thirty-two-point-five-one degrees north and nineteen-point-three-eight degrees east. Let us observe with a critical eye how your crew and the *Sayf Alnabii* perform on your first operational mission."

"Captain Wu," Lahal Nihad responded, "just what will our first mission be? My crew is anxious to prove themselves worthy in taking the battle to the infidels."

Wu chuckled and held up his hand. "Let us do this in easy stages. As you are learning, a submarine is a very complex warship. Employing one effectively against a target requires much practice beforehand. Considering most potential targets can and are willing to shoot back, it is better to get this practice in controlled, easy steps against a much more benign opponent. Tonight, we will work with your frigate, the *Al Gharbella*, to find a tanker that is on course to enter our territorial waters early tomorrow morning. For this exercise, we will merely observe and, perhaps, make some practice periscope approaches. The tanker will never know we are there, employing him for our training purposes."

Lahal Nahid nodded. He understood the logic but was frustrated at what he saw as slow progress. Ming Jie's plan made sense, but Nahid also chafed under the ever-present Chinese sense of superiority. After all, Nahid's ancestors had plied these Mediterranean waters for centuries. Their galleys had been the scourge of all the civilized world long before the Chinese ventured out on the deep sea.

Lahal Nahid reluctantly returned his thoughts to getting his submarine underway and out to sea. After casting off lines and pulling away from the pier, it was an easy jaunt past the mole and breakwater at the harbor mouth and out to the deep blue waters of the Mediterranean Sea. The night breeze felt invigorating when they increased their speed to fifteen knots.

The *Al Gharbella* was waiting at the rendezvous location as expected. The frigate reported that they were tracking a ship on radar, one that was illegally traveling through their newly defined territorial waters. And this report was not part of any simulation conjured up for a drill. The AIS data showed the ship to be the Italian-flagged tanker *Dello Di Ulsan* and that she was bound for Genoa, Italy, with a load of fuel. The tanker's track had it passing one hundred kilometers north of the current position of the Libyan frigate and submarine.

The plan was simple. The two warships would steam north at

maximum speed and intercept the tanker right at dawn. This actual challenge of an intruding vessel would present a perfect test for the submarine and its crew-in-training.

The pair of ships headed north as the *Dello Di Ulsan* steamed westward, her Italian crew apparently unaware of the approaching Libyan navy ships. An hour before the scheduled intercept, the *Sayf Alnabii* slipped beneath the waves to make the rest of the journey hidden from view. The submarine increased its speed to twenty knots to race out ahead and arrive at their destination first. That way, it could be waiting at periscope depth, stealthily observing as the actual intercept and confrontation was made by the *Al Gharbella*.

The sun was just sliding above the horizon off to the east when the submarine's periscope popped above the surface. The sea was clear. Not a ship was in sight. And that was just as Lahal Nahid expected. The unarmed Italian tanker should be coming over the horizon in a few minutes just as the *Al Gharbella* would be aggressively charging in from the south.

"Captain, I have two sonar contacts to the east," the sonar operator suddenly announced. "One sounds like something big and heavy. Almost certainly the tanker. The other return is very faint, but sounds much smaller, maybe a deepwater fisher or something like that. Both bear one-zero-six."

Lahal Nihad spun the scope around and stared down the bearing to the new contacts. He could just make out the high masts on the tanker coming over the horizon. The other ship was still invisible. A fishing boat caught in the middle of the Libyan warship's confrontation with the Italian tanker would complicate things considerably. But it also offered an interesting training opportunity for the submarine's green crew. The more vessels up there to track, the better.

He spun the scope around to look to the south. As expected, he could now see their partner, the *Al Gharbella*, as she came racing over the horizon.

The radio receiver in the conn blasted, "Tanker *Dello Di Ulsan*, this is the Second Regency frigate *Al Gharbella*. You are in Second Regency territorial waters illegally. You are ordered to stop engines and prepare to be boarded."

There was no answer from the Italian tanker. The big ship proceeded on its journey as if nothing untoward was happening.

The Captain of the *Al Gharbella* waited for five minutes before repeating his demand. "Tanker *Dello Di Ulsan*, you are ordered to stop engines and prepare to be boarded. If you do not comply, we will be forced to open fire."

Lahal Nihad continued to watch the Italian tanker through his periscope. It did not respond in any way. But it was much closer to him now, no more than ten thousand meters away. Suddenly another ship came into view, the one that his sonarman had assumed to be a deepwater fisher. But the vessel he was watching was clearly a warship. It had been hidden by the tanker's bulk but was now racing out in front of the tanker, the water reaching high up on its bow as it pushed ahead.

Then, a truly troubling development. Lahal Nihad looked on as the vessel's main gun tracked around to aim at the *Al Gharbella*. The ESM intercept receiver on the submarine chirped as it detected the ship's fire control radar had also been activated. Probably tracking the *Al Gharbella* for the warship's gun.

This stare-down was dangerously ratcheting up!

Then, a new voice on the radio circuit. "*Al Gharbella*, this is the Italian warship *Commandante Borsini*. We are providing escort to our tanker ship that is operating in international waters. You will cease and desist in this attempted act of piracy. We are authorized to take you under fire if you persist."

The two ships were roughly the same size, but they were very different. Although relatively lightly armed, the *Commandante Borsini* was a modern Italian patrol ship with the latest weapons and sensor systems. The *Al Gharbella* was much more heavily armed with two turrets for twin 76mm guns and an impressive-looking P-15 Termit anti-ship missile launcher, but it was a Cold War–era hand-me-down frigate given to the Libyan Navy by the Soviets back in the 1980s. Nothing had been done to improve or modernize it in the ensuing years, and many systems, including the fire control radar and the anti-ship missile system, were not operational.

There was no response from the Libyan vessel. At least, not on the radio.

As Lahal Nihad watched through his periscope, there was sudden smoke and flame erupting from both barrels of the Libyan frigate's forward 76mm gun mount. Seconds later, there were huge splashes in the sea near the Italian patrol vessel.

The *Commandante Borsini* heeled over as it radically maneuvered to avoid any follow-up volley. Even as she ducked, the vessel's modern OTO Melara 76mm autocannon answered. The first shot crashed into the *Al Gharbella*'s forward gun mount and exploded spectacularly. The Italians' OTO Melara gun was capable of firing all eighty rounds in its magazine in under a minute, and they seemed intent on proving it. The shots rained down on the Libyan frigate without mercy, quickly reducing its topsides to a mass of flaming wreckage. Somehow, the warship remained afloat.

Lahal Nihad was aghast. He had never seen such destruction happen so quickly. Or so unexpectedly. He had to come to the assistance of his comrades. Allah demanded it.

"Prepare to fire torpedo tube one at the Italian warship," he ordered, eye still locked to the scope.

Wu Ming Jie started to object. This crew had never fired a torpedo before. Not even an exercise one. They had only shot virtual ones in the trainer.

"Captain, do you really believe…?"

Lahal cut him short. "Order your advisors to assist us. Our comrades are dying up there."

Wu nodded. "Captain, I recommend that you shoot two torpedoes, just to make sure. It will be difficult for a torpedo to separate the Italian warship from the big tanker."

Lahal immediately ordered, "Make tube two ready, as well."

"Captain, tube one is ready," the Weapons Officer reported. "Tube two will be ready in thirty seconds."

"Shoot tube one at the patrol ship," Lahal Nihad ordered.

High-pressure water flushed the YU-9 torpedo out of the submarine. Its battery-driven electric motor immediately accelerated the weapon up to better than sixty knots as its nose swung around to point at the Italian ships. As soon as it energized, the torpedo's electronically scanned sonar array detected a massively inviting target. Its guidance system steered it directly at the acquired target.

"Captain, tube two is ready," the Weapons Officer reported.

"Shoot tube two at the patrol ship," Lahal Nihad ordered. The second YU-9 was shoved out of the *Sayf Alnabii* and joined its sister weapon in racing toward its target.

Wu Ming Jie studied the control panel for the two torpedoes. Hair-thin fiberoptic wires connected them both back to the submarine. They sent data on just what the fish were seeing.

"This is what I feared," the Chinese submariner said. "The tanker is a much larger target so both weapons are aiming for it. Captain, steer the first weapon ninety degrees to port. That way it will no longer see the tanker. Then we will be able to guide it back onto the patrol ship."

When the torpedo obediently turned to port, it lost its sonar lock on the tanker and headed off to the west, searching for a new target.

"What about the second torpedo?" Lahal asked.

Wu shook his head and answered, "It will be complicated enough to just steer the one torpedo in for a hit. Do not bother with the second one. Allow it to hit the tanker."

Then Lahal Nihad watched as a flaming arrow emerged from a box launcher on the *Commandante Borsini*. A small rocket motor shoved a Harpoon anti-ship missile high into the air. The rocket motor burned out and dropped away while the Harpoon's tiny turbojet motor took over, driving the missile forward at just below the speed of sound. It dropped down to skim the wave tops for a few seconds before crashing hard into the flaming mass of *Al Gharbella*. The 221-kilogram warhead exploded, gutting the hapless frigate.

Lahal Nihad beat his fist against the periscope in helpless rage. His counterattack had come too late to save the *Al Gharbella*. There surely was no one left alive on the burning hulk.

But he would have his vengeance. The Barbary pirates would never have let such violence go without a brutal response.

Wu looked up from the graphical display of the torpedo attack that he had been watching. "Captain Lahal, the first torpedo has generated out to where it will no longer see the tanker. Steer it seventy degrees to starboard now and it should detect the escort ship."

Indeed, the torpedo had just steadied up on its newly ordered course when a light blinked on the control console. The Weapons Officer called out, "First fired torpedo has acquired on the patrol ship. Increasing speed." Then, almost immediately, he called out, "Second fired torpedo has acquired on the tanker. Also increasing speed."

They watched the graphical display as the two weapons raced toward their targets. The first torpedo zoomed right on past the *Commandante Borsini* without hitting anything or exploding.

Lahal Nihad looked questioningly at Wu. The Chinese submariner smiled and said, "Wait."

Right on cue, the Weapons Officer yelled, "First torpedo in reattack." The display showed the deadly fish had turned around and was now running directly at the *Commandante Borsini*.

Wu explained, "The target was small enough that the torpedo thought it might be a decoy. It went on past and did not see a new target. So, it circled back to attack the only potential target it had detected."

He had just finished his explanation when the *Sayf Alnabii* was rocked by a terrific explosion. Lahal Nahid looked toward where the *Commandante Borsini* had been, but he saw nothing but a massive boiling gray cloud with bits and pieces of wreckage sifting down from the sky.

The YU-9's warhead utilized a sodium hydride/seawater chemical reaction to generate a very large amount of high-temperature hydrogen gas. The temperature instantly reached over 2,000°C. The hydrogen then violently reacted with oxygen, causing a tremendous explosion.

The Italian patrol boat was gone.

Then a second massive explosion shoved the sub sideways. Lahal Nihad swung the periscope around to look at the *Dello Di Ulsan*. The huge tanker was improbably broken in half. Both parts were burning furiously. It was only a matter of time before it, too, disappeared beneath the waves.

Wu Ming Jie looked over and said, "Captain, I suggest we leave this area as quickly and quietly as we can. Soon this place will be the center of an intensive ASW search conducted by several nations. This is not somewhere we want to be."

Lahal Nihad nodded, avoiding a satisfied smile. He must not show any joy in the wake of the deaths of so many of his fellow defenders. But he and his submarine with its inexperienced but brave crew had found revenge already.

Then he ordered, "Make your depth one hundred meters, come to course zero-nine-zero, ahead full."

Ψ

The European Times newsfeed story about the violent sinkings in the Libyan Sea arrived on board the *Harold A. Stanton* even before the report showed up on the Special Intel message traffic update. *The Times* was reporting that the Libyan strongman Ali Hakim Sherif was screaming about the infidel Italians sending a battle fleet to ruthlessly attack one of his patrol ships. A ship that had been peacefully and innocently protecting Second Regency sovereign waters. The Italian Navy headquarters in La Spezia issued a statement that one of their patrol ships, the *Commandante Borsini*, had been escorting the Italian-flagged tanker *Dello Di Ulsan* on its voyage from Alexandria, Egypt, to Genoa, Italy, and were in international waters when both vessels were attacked without provocation by a Libyan warship. Reports were preliminary, but it appeared that both Italian ships as well as the attacking Libyan frigate had been sunk. A search for survivors had been initiated.

The Special Intel traffic did not have much additional information, just speculation that Sherif was flexing his muscles more than most intel organizations had anticipated. All US ships were advised to proceed with caution if they were steaming anywhere in the vicinity of the waters being claimed by the former nation of Libya.

Captain Jerry Baudsley sat in his chair on the port bridge wing of his destroyer, reading the disturbing messages as they poured into his tablet. It was obvious the intel weenies at Sixth Fleet were going bananas trying to figure this one out. And the N-3 Ops and Plans people were clogging the airwaves with conflicting orders and guidance. About all that Baudsley could figure out for certain was that the Libyans and the Italians had themselves some kind of dustup a hundred miles north of the Libyan coast.

Three ships and the bodies of their crews were all on the bottom of the Mediterranean.

But that made it far more than a dustup.

Baudsley checked the reported position of the incident against his current location. Based on the speed and course the Chinese garbage scow he was shadowing was traveling, they would be sailing just south of the point where this all happened sometime tomorrow morning. Of more concern, they would cross this Libyan wild man's "Line of Death" sometime in the next twelve hours. If he was in the mood to fling ordnance freely, it was best to be prepared for anything.

Baudsley looked at the attack realistically and some of it did not add up. The ancient Libyan frigate should have been no match for the modern Italian patrol ship. Even if they shot it out with each other like an old-fashioned western gunfight, it did not explain the tanker being sunk. No, there had to be another player in the mix. And Baudsley had a pretty good idea who that might have been.

It took a couple of hours, but his query about the current location of the new submarine gifted to Libya by China finally came back. The damn thing was missing from satellite images.

Baudsley had his answer. Grabbing the phone, he called his Tactical Action Officer in Combat. "Mr. Richter, stream the Multi-Function Towed Array. Make sure sonar is briefed up and alerted about that new Libyan submarine. And, Scott, contact Sixth Fleet and tell them I want a submarine out in front of us, sanitizing the area."

"Skipper, Sixth Fleet has already informed us that the only boat in the Med is in drydock undergoing repairs. The *Gato* won't be out of Gibraltar until the end of the week. Then, it's a three-day transit to get here. We won't get any help there."

That was not good news. Baudsley thought for a second, then he said, "In that case, tell Sixth Fleet that I need P-8 coverage out of Sigonella. If those Airedales are going to draw per diem for their Mediterranean vacation, then they damn well are going to earn it."

Scott Richter chuckled. The US Navy's land-based patrol aircraft fliers were well known and widely razzed for their propensity for living well while deployed to such hardship billets as Sicily in the springtime. Only candy-ass Air Force pilots had it rougher.

"You got it, Skipper," Scott Richter answered. "The MFTA is being deployed. And I have sonar lined up to go active on your command. If you're worried about a submarine threat, recommend we wheel out one of the MH-60s and have it on a ready fifteen."

Baudsley smiled. That was one of the things he liked about Richter. He always thought at least two steps ahead. Having one of their two anti-submarine warfare helicopters on the flight deck, already fueled and armed, ready to go in fifteen minutes would allow them to quickly pounce on anything that they might detect on the towed array. Anything like a Chinese submarine operating at the behest of a newly empowered Middle East madman.

"Good thinking, Scott. And make sure that it has a pair of Mark 54s dangling underneath. If we find a Libyan submarine, I want to be able to send them our very best."

Now that the TAO was getting the *Stanton*'s sensors and weapons ready to find and respond to the threat of a possible submarine, Baudsley needed to make sure his ship was ready for just about anything else. The Eastern Mediterranean did not seem nearly as peaceful as it had only a couple of hours before. In fact, it suddenly appeared to have become downright hostile. His ship needed to be ready for war.

Turning to the Officer-of-the-Deck, he ordered, "Mr. Johnson, sound General Quarters. When Battle Stations are manned, relax to Condition III cruising watch. And then set Material Condition YOKE throughout the ship."

Condition III Battle Stations was the normal wartime cruising condition for a warship. One third of the crew would be at their battle stations at all times. This allowed the ship to quickly respond to a surprise attack or rapidly transition to full Battle Stations if the ship went into battle. Material Condition YOKE caused most of the watertight doors and hatches to be shut unless people needed to pass through for some very good reason. This was more stringent than Condition XRAY, the normal peacetime sailing condition in which everything is left open, but not as stringent as Condition ZEBRA, where watertight integrity was maximized with all doors and hatches shut and most dogged shut.

Condition III and Material Condition YOKE made sure that the crew and the ship could maintain a high state of readiness for a long time. The *Harold A. Stanton* would be as prepared as they could be for anything that Ali Hakim Sherif might throw at them.

Anything above or below the surface of the Mediterranean Sea.

10

Bahri Dawoud Kahir ad-Din Misurata had returned to the place where he felt he truly belonged. He was deep in his beloved desert, far from the dangerous intrigue and the tribal fighting of the more settled and "civilized" world. No, this place of barren rock and blowing sand was his home.

His old Land Rover would never substitute for a reliable, sure-footed camel, but it was admittedly faster so long as there was enough fuel. The battered vehicle breasted a low ridge line. Bahri Dawoud signaled his driver to stop. He held his hand up to shield his eyes from the hot glare of the midday sun and squinted through the windshield. Dust clouds rising into the bone-dry air easily marked the advance across the wasteland that his men were making in three distinct columns.

The oasis of Al Jawf, with its surrounding green fields of center-pivot irrigation agriculture, was a day's journey behind them. Libya's mostly imaginary border with Egypt was just over the next rise. And their objective was ten kilometers beyond that point, out on the Calanshio Sand Sea.

The time had come to move his men into their attack dispersal. Bahri Dawoud grabbed the radio microphone and ordered, "Fazel Badir, swing your column around to the north. Nassif, swing your column around to the south. Move your men to within one kilometer of the camp but make very sure you are not detected. Attack hour will be 0100, precisely as planned. Any questions?"

Fazel Badir al-Din and Nassif Mohyeddin were both members of Bahri Dawoud's Misurata tribe and among his most trusted lieutenants. They were both veterans of many tribal battles, fighting alongside Bahri Dawoud. Even though this was to be a relatively small raid, requiring only a hundred fighters in twenty vehicles, it was important that their actions be coordinated, quick, and lethal. Fazel Badir and Nassif would ensure that would be the outcome and do so with minimum unnecessary communications.

Bahri Dawoud sat and watched as Fazel Badir al-Din's cluster of desert vehicles swung out in a broad arc to the north. Nassif Mohyeddin's vehicles pointed southward in a similar broad arc. Bahri Dawoud scanned the cloudless sky for the presence of any unexpected aircraft. There were none. He doubted any birds that flew higher than he could see—satellites in space—even bothered to scan this expanse of arid nothingness.

He took a long swig of water and waited for a few minutes before he sent his own column forward, directly toward their objective.

It was midafternoon when Bahri Dawoud signaled the next stop. According to his GPS, the objective was now a mere five kilometers ahead. It was time to send a scout patrol out on foot to find out for certain what awaited them. In the meantime, the rest of the force would hunker down in a predetermined *wadi* to rest, hydrate, and conduct a final check on their equipment.

The Chinese had provided the latest satellite images of the camp showing the towering drill rigs, the hastily erected equipment sheds, several trailers pulled in for offices and supervisor quarters, and the cluster of tents for housing the drill crew. Analysis of the images confirmed there were maybe thirty roustabouts working on site. They also revealed a small security force, certainly no more than a squad of soldiers. But that data was conjecture, totally based on some satellite taking pictures from several hundred kilometers out in space. It would take the scouts sneaking in close enough to observe the camp to confirm what they believed to be the case. They would count heads and determine what security was really in effect.

The sun had set and the moon had risen by the time the scouts reported back. The satellite numbers were accurate. The roustabouts and guards were not the least bit alerted. In fact, the scouts had observed them playing a pick-up soccer game against each other on a flat stretch of powdery sand.

It was time to head out. They should arrive in their attack positions a little before midnight. Then, after a few minutes for a breather and final checks, it would be time to fill the quiet desert night with flying bullets.

Ψ

Bill Langley was having a terrible time falling asleep. There was far too much to worry about, what with the investors breathing down his neck, expecting immediate and massive returns on their considerable outlay. He always wondered how they could have acquired so much wealth and yet still be so ignorant about how things worked in the real world. And though the petroleum engineer loved the treasure-hunt aspect of his job, running an exploratory drilling crew at the far end of a very long logistics train had its own set of challenges. Then, on top of all that, his find of a lifetime—his Holy Grail—had brought him to a spot on the map that was only a couple of miles of hot sand away from the border with a country controlled by a ruthless, greedy, and seemingly deranged dictator. A man who would certainly do whatever necessary to add Langley's new treasure field to his own portfolio.

All this was certainly enough to keep any sane man awake far into the night.

Langley looked at the glow-in-the-dark hands on his watch. It was just past midnight, but there was no reason to try to go back to sleep. Bitter experience had long since convinced him of the futility of forcing slumber. Better to go ahead and surrender to insomnia, get up, and get something useful done.

He kicked back the blanket, rolled over, and got up. Slipping on a shirt and shorts, he carefully dumped out his boots before slipping them on. Deathstalker scorpions and sand vipers both loved to hide in boots. Both critters could be deadly.

The engineer decided to see if he could scrounge a late-night snack and a cup of coffee from the mess tent before settling back in his own quarters to wage an attack on the mountain of paperwork. Stepping outside, he looked up and admired a crystal-clear night sky decorated with millions of pulsing stars. They were perfectly visible even though a full moon lit up the desert almost like daytime. He could even see detail along the rocky ridge that was almost three miles to the west of their drill field.

Something moved. Something over there near a pile of drill waste at the far edge of the camp. Langley blinked and looked again in that direction. Although rare and typically skittish, there were a few wild animals that had the audacity to roam this part of the Egyptian desert in search of food. The tiny Fennec fox and the little Dorcas gazelle both wandered across these sands at night. Maybe he had caught a glimpse of one of those tough guys.

Langley continued focusing on the bit of sand where he had seen the movement. There it was again, hardly enough to be noticed. But then he could tell it was not a fox or a gazelle. It was clearly a man. A man trying to slither across the sand on his belly like one of those Saharan sand vipers, moving from the waste pile to a point behind a stack of piping.

"Intruder! Intruder!" Langley called out as he stepped back inside his tent to grab his Glock. Luckily, he tripped on something and went down hard just as automatic weapons fire erupted from three sides, shredding the tents and the men sleeping inside them. With gun in hand, Langley crawled back to the doorway, spotted an attacker racing across open ground in his direction, and instinctively pulled the trigger. A quick three-shot grouping dropped the attacker into an awkward heap.

Hanbal Elmahdy's security detail—or at least the ones who survived the opening fusillade—spilled from their tents, crouching, trying to get their weapons ready. They ran directly into a hailstorm of hot bullets.

The massacre took only seconds. The young Egyptian Army Lieutenant fell with the first burst.

A few of the guards, those who had been on duty, continued to return fire but mostly only shooting blindly at unseen targets. Meanwhile, several of Langley's workers were doing their best to defend the drill rig with the sidearms they carried. But the incoming barrage only ramped up in intensity. Bill Langley could easily see that continuing the fight would be futile. They would all be needlessly killed.

He called out in Arabic, "*Tawagaf ean 'iitlaq alnaar! Nastaslima!* Stop shooting! We surrender!"

A voice answered in English. "Throw down your weapons and come out with your hands up."

Langley, the remainder of his crew, and the three Egyptian soldiers who had survived the attack were roughly bound and thrown to the ground to form a crude circle, surrounded by heavily armed men wearing tattered uniforms of the Libyan Army. One of the Libyans stepped forward and asked, "Who is in command here?"

"I am," Langley responded. "But I am only the engineer in charge of—"

"Stop! I am General Bahri Dawoud Kahir ad-Din Misurata of the Army of the Second Regency. You are our prisoners. You will be formally charged with illegally entering and occupying our country and attempting to steal our natural resources. Such action constitutes an act of war, and your violations will be treated as such."

"Bullshit," Langley spat. "You know as well as we do that the Libyan border is better than ten kilometers to the west. You attacked us in Egypt, and that, General, is an act of war. I demand that you release us."

Bahri Dawoud smiled. Even in the moonlight Langley could see an evil glint in the man's eyes. "You sound American. That, of course, will do a trespasser like you no good out here. This land has legitimately belonged to our people for centuries and Suleiman Jadid has reclaimed this land for Allah and the Second Regency of Tripoli. You are his prisoners. And it is our law that prisoners perform labor in payment for the expense of their incarceration. Those who refuse or who do not perform their assigned chores will be severely punished."

"I demand that I be allowed to communicate with the US embassy in —" the engineer started, but Bahri Dawoud stepped closer and clipped Langley hard on the temple with the butt of his pistol.

"You are under the jurisdiction of the world's newest nation," the General angrily spoke, "but the rebirth of one of its oldest and most powerful. We will determine with whom you speak and when. Obviously, it will be most convenient and best for each of you that you and your men continue your work here, doing just as you have been, and do so earnestly and effectively. However, from this point forward, you will be working not for wicked colonialists who would rape our land and pillage our home but on behalf of Allah and his most humble servant, Suleiman Jadid."

11

The gargantuan C-17 Globemaster III had the ability to haul a lot of stuff a long way, but not particularly quickly or in great comfort. Twelve hours sitting in the plane's cargo bay jump seats gave Commander Jim Ward adequate time to review the mission plans with members of his team. Or at least go over what he knew of the plans at this point. He and Chief Billy Joe Hurt pored over the files and charts that lay spread out over the top of a shipping container.

SEAL Chief Hurt hailed from north Alabama and his accent grew even more pronounced when things got tense. He rubbed his chin and drawled, "Skipper, you reckon the brass have done gone and figgered this whole thing out?"

"What you gettin' at, Chief?" Ward answered, unconsciously mimicking Hurt's accent.

"Well, the timeline they givin' us don't jibe, to start with," Hurt answered. Tracing out the track across the Mediterranean with his forefinger, he went on. "I guess this here is about fifteen hundred miles, give or take. It's gonna take the *Gato* the better part of three days to haul our asses to where they want us to be. Then assume we take a day scouting the place out." He scratched his head and frowned. "Boss, if *Gato*'s settin' thar ready to cast off lines as soon as we show up, it'll be a week before we can do anything to help the cause."

"I don't disagree, Chief."

Hurt reached over to the keyboard and punched up an image on his laptop. He showed the screen to Ward. "This is the latest satellite image of that Chinese heavy hauler, the *Hua Rui Long*. The picture is only three hours old. Looks to me like that ship is at anchor a mile or so off Benghazi." He zoomed in on the image until they could clearly see people working on the ship's deck. "It also appears that they're taking apart all that crap that's been hidin' the Chinese sub they're delivering."

Ward intently studied the image. "I think I see what you're saying, Chief. The Chinese managed to unload the last one in four days. If that's the case with this one, the Libyans will have their brand spanking new submarine safely inside the seawall at Benghazi well before we can even get close to take pictures, let alone do anything to delay the delivery."

"Yep, I reckon we best be planning on sneaking inside the harbor somehow to do our business...whatever that business might be," Hurt replied.

"You're right, Chief," Ward grumped. "And that complicates things more than a little. A longer swim, lugging more gear. And plenty more opportunity for the SOBs to see us. It sure would be nice if we had a Swimmer Delivery Vehicle. Or one of those new Dry Combat Submersibles. *Gato* ain't capable of haulin' either of those machines."

Hurt looked over at the rest of the team, who had been eavesdropping as they opened several of the palletized crates and checked out the dive gear that had been loaded on the C-17 back on North Island. The Chief asked, "Jones, LaCroix, you two checked out the DPDs yet? Looks like we might be needing them."

Chuck Jones and Gene LaCroix looked up from the pile of gear they had been inspecting.

"Get right on it, Chief," LaCroix answered as he nudged Jones toward the next crate in the row. Stenciled on the side of the gray-green crate in old-style block letters were the words "Diver Propulsion Device, Mod II, one of." Two other identical boxes were strapped down on the same pallet.

"Make double sure that the prop turns free and the batteries are accepting a charge. And make certain the recon-nav system is uploading and downloading," Hurt directed.

"Gee, Chief," Jones answered sarcastically. "I don't think me and Croy ever done this before. Could you please draw us a picture of where the ON/OFF selector switch is?"

Hurt shot back, "I'll show you the ON/OFF selector switch on my boot kicking your backside, wise guy." But he was laughing as he said it.

Hurt turned back to Ward, "Those DPVs will just have to be the answer to our problem. Not as quick or as comfortable as a DCS, but they'll get us there and back."

Ward nodded. "We got what we got. Are Martinelli and Dumkowski done checking out the ordnance?"

Chief Hurt had assigned Tony Martinelli and Joe Dumkowski to inspect the crates of weapons and explosives they would need.

"Yeah, looks like we have enough stuff to start a minor war, including several Russian-made limpet mines. And Hall has the comms gear all up and running. The only thing left to do will be for us to confirm we can synch with *Gato* once we're aboard. You remember that time, I bet."

"I remember that time," Ward said, nodding. Every SEAL had a "that time" memory of the comms gear not synching. It was usually a crypto foul-up of one sort or the other. Then the confusion when no one could talk to anyone else.

Just then, the Air Force loadmaster walked over to where Ward and Hurt stood. "Excuse me, Commander, but we're beginning our descent. Can your guys button this stuff up for landing? Winds blowing across the Rock can make for a bumpy approach here. And the pilot asked if you would like to go up to the flight deck and grab the jump seat for the landing. It's a pretty good view."

Ward turned to Hurt and said, "Chief, have the guys stow everything. We can finish the checks once we're on the ground. I'm going up front and finishing this ride in first class."

Ward climbed the ladder up to the flight deck and stepped through the door into the cockpit. The co-pilot waved him to a seat behind the pilot and pointed toward a radio headset. Ward plopped down and donned the apparatus. The first thing he heard was, "Air Force Zero-Zero-Eight, Gibraltar

ATC, you are cleared to approach runway two-seven. Winds ten knots, gusting to twenty-five from the southwest. Bird threat normal. Be advised possible windshear off the Rock has been reported."

Ward looked out the cockpit windscreen where he saw a short, narrow runway that crossed a tiny neck of land with water on both sides. The near end of the runway started right at the edge of the Mediterranean Sea and the far end jutted a thousand yards out into Gibraltar Bay. It was hard to imagine they could land something the size of a C-17 on that strip. And to make matters worse, the runway appeared to have been shoe-horned into a very narrow space. To the north, a major city crept right down to the runway's edge. To the south, the massive bulk of the Rock of Gibraltar rose almost vertically only a few yards away.

The copilot smiled at the SEAL's apparent unease. "Commander, be glad we're landing to the west today, from out over the Med. If we were landing to the east, we would be doing a continuous turn around the Rock to avoid Spanish airspace. We wouldn't be able to steady up until we were on final approach. It can reach sphincter-level ten when we come in that way."

"You guys have done this before, then?" the SEAL asked.

"Naw, first time for everything, you know," the co-pilot responded, but with a big grin.

A voice crackled in the headset. "Air Force Zero-Zero-Eight, Gibraltar ATC, traffic control confirmed in place. You are cleared to land on two-seven."

The co-pilot explained, "The only road between Gibraltar and the border into Spain goes right across the middle of the runway. That's the Kingdom of Spain just north of the airport. We can't land until they stop traffic on that road and put the gates up. Sorta like a railroad crossing except to allow planes to land. Interesting place. Now make sure your harness is tight. The landing will be bumpy."

The Rock loomed out of the windscreen beside Ward as the pilot slammed the C-17 onto the deck. He applied reverse thrusters to bring the bird to a stop just as Ward was sure they were going to skid out into the water. The pilot smoothly swung the bird around and taxied over to the RAF hangers, bringing the C-17 to a stop, and then proceeded to shut down.

Ward looked out to see a small crowd standing at the edge of the apron. A welcoming party? He immediately recognized Joe Glass and Brian Edwards—Ward and his SEAL teams had been along with those guys on some bang-up missions over the years—but he was not sure who the other people were. Several trucks were already moving toward the C-17's rear cargo hatch as well. The passenger door swung open, and the ladder dropped down a few feet behind where Ward sat. He unstrapped and hurried down the ladder to greet Glass and Edwards.

Joe Glass grabbed Jim Ward's extended hand and then tugged him closer, enveloping him in a warm bear hug so tightly that it caused Ward to groan. Glass stepped back and said, "Sorry, I forgot you had been winged on that last gig. But damn it's good to see you, kid."

Jim Ward laughed. "It's good to see you, too, Joe...uh, I mean Admiral. Oh, I'm good. Just twinges when there's rain in the weather forecast."

The wound was a souvenir of a recent mission involving some especially bad guys in South America.

"Good to hear," Glass answered. "Grab your bag and jump in the car. My guys will help your team unload and get everything down to the pier. I want to haul your happy ass up to HMCC and get you briefed up."

"HMCC?" Ward questioned as he got a similar handshake from Brian Edwards, but without the hug.

"His Majesty's Command Center Gibraltar," Glass answered. "It's the best classified command center that I've ever used. And for that we can thank the Brits. Otherwise, we'd probably be running this show out of a Motel 6 somewhere. You hungry?"

"Now you're talking," Ward said with a laugh. "Only thing I've had to eat in the last twelve hours were cardboard sandwiches from those Air Force boxed lunches and that lukewarm dishwater they call coffee. Everybody tells me I have to do the *paella* and local *vino tinto* here."

"I got the same advice and it's spot on," Edwards interjected. "Not as good as submarine food, but you'll like it."

Joe Glass threw an arm around Ward's shoulder and led him off to the waiting Land Rover. Laughingly, he said, "That we can do. And catch up on all the latest news including an update on that new little guy of yours. Then the brief."

Ψ

The KH-11 Block 6-3 electro-optical reconnaissance satellite USA-376 made a routine sun-synchronous orbital pass six-hundred miles above western Asia. From this altitude, the satellite's nano-technology mirror allowed a system resolution of a tenth of an arcsecond. What that really meant was that the satellite continuously photographed a swath of Planet Earth that was over a thousand miles wide with a resolution such that analysts could read the sports page of a newspaper if someone on the ground or shipboard left it open.

Satellite USA-376 uploaded its digital images to a stealth communication satellite hovering in an inclined geosynchronous orbit twenty-three thousand miles above a spot in the central Pacific. The data feed bounced at the speed of light between comms satellites until it was ultimately downloaded to the National Reconnaissance Office's National Geospatial Intelligence Center, located inside the heavily guarded gates of Fort Belvoir, Virginia. Deep inside the massive, modern pile of concrete and steel, teams of specially trained analysts armed with the most cutting-edge artificial intelligence technology scrutinized every inch of the imagery. The analysts had barely started studying the data from Northern Manchuria when alarm bells started ringing. Something was up and it was big.

By the time the analysts got to the East China Sea and the Taiwan Strait, panic was setting in. Everywhere they looked, they saw the Chinese People's Republic's military mobilizing on a massive, unprecedented scale. The AI "assistants" were reporting what sounded like the stuff of best-selling military-thriller fiction. It determined that what they were seeing presaged the People's Republic going to a war footing. But why and over what? These were not questions for these analysts to answer. Nor was it something that the AI programs were even programmed to consider.

The Joint Chiefs of Staff, along with John Dingham, the SecDef, rushed to meet in an emergency session in the National Military Command Center deep below the Pentagon. But they did so in a way that such a hastily convened meeting would not draw the attention of the media.

USA-376's images were shown in excruciating and vivid detail on the large screen monitors that covered the Command Center's blast-proof concrete walls.

The military brass admitted to each other that they had been caught flatfooted. This disturbing information was a bolt from the blue. The data begged two questions: What were the Chinese planning and how should the US react? The arguments covered the full gamut from, "This is only a Chinese readiness exercise—admittedly much larger than anything they had done in the past, and thus was not a cause for concern," to, "The Chinese have decided to start a major war, we need to go to DEFCON ONE and get everything in position to defend Taiwan right damn now, so why aren't the STRATCOM bombers in the air yet?"

John Dingham motioned the Chairman of the Joint Chiefs to the side and quietly conferred with him before he called President Dosetti in the White House Situation Room on the high security line.

"Madam President, we are not sure what Tan Yong's intentions are here. No one has ever seen the PLA mobilize on this scale before. We are seeing that every warship the PLAN has is getting underway. It's also looking like the PLAF are moving everything that flies to airfields in the Jiangxi, Fujian and Guangdong Provinces. Those are the ones right across the straits from Taiwan. Interestingly, Intel is reporting that they have not ratcheted up any of their nuclear forces yet. Their land-based launchers are maintaining normal alert, and we are tracking the only SSBN they have at sea. It's currently in the South China Sea about four hundred miles east of Hainan Island."

"All right," Sandra Dosetti responded. "What is your recommendation? What will be our response?"

"We go to DEFCON THREE. Immediately deploy all our carrier battle-groups to the Pacific with the idea of keeping them out beyond the range of those DF-26 anti-ship ballistic missiles. That has the side benefit of not being as confrontational as steaming right up to the Taiwan Strait but delivers the message that we are here and ready and keeping a close eye on whatever it is they are doing."

"Are we actually ready to do those things?" Dosetti asked.

Dingham hesitated for a second before he answered. "Well, with two carriers in shipyards, three in deep maintenance restricted availabilities, and two more just starting their pre-deployment work ups, we'll be lucky to get four battlegroups there within a month. Two more could show up a couple of months later. We can have four submarines in the area in a week and ten in a month. Not much good for a show of force, but real helpful if ordnance starts flying."

Dosetti thought for a few seconds and then asked, "John, what does this mean for our preparedness everywhere else?"

"Madam President, I'll be honest with you," Dingham answered. "This will stretch us to damn near the breaking point. We'll be back-of-the-cupboard bare everywhere else in the world."

Dosetti sighed deeply, her frustration obvious on the audio link. "Well, I guess we have to do what we have to do. Get ready for anything until we know something. Go ahead with DEFCON THREE and get the ships into position as fast as you can. Secretary Bunch is talking to the Chinese ambassador, but we aren't getting anywhere on the diplomatic scene."

"Yes, and our usual intel is baffled on intentions. We can see what they're doing but we're blind on why," Dingham said.

"You know, it's almost like they want us to generate some kind of a big response," Dosetti mused. "Like they're wanting us to duck instead of dodge."

"Yes, ma'am, it does."

"Maybe it's time to check with that Admiral that heads Naval Intelligence. Ward, right? He usually has a pretty good pipeline into Beijing and a way of applying what he sees to what is happening." The men could hear President Dosetti tapping on a desk with fingertips or a pencil. "And let's pray he's got some idea what Tan is up to this time."

Ψ

Ali Hakim Sherif's cell phone buzzed. He punched the "talk" button and gruffly responded, "*Mrhban*, hello." He had been busy reading the glowing stories about his new administration and policies in his country's two major newspapers, both strictly government controlled.

The voice on the other end of the line had an Oxford accent but did not sound English at all. Maybe oriental. "*Pasha* Suleiman, this is Nian Huhu

De. I am the Special Ambassador Plenipotentiary for the People's Republic of China. President Tan Yong requested that I speak with you personally and proudly inform you that the People's Republic has delivered the diversionary crisis situation that you requested. The Americans have already responded in the expected ways and they will be very busy for some time far from the Mediterranean Sea. President Tan urges you to please profitably use the time this affords."

Ali Hakim smiled. Finally, it was time for the next phase. He summoned Bahri Dawoud Kahir ad-Din Misurata.

It was time to set the rest of the plan in motion.

12

Zawiyat Production Platform Six was a bridged-type offshore oil platform. It stood in nine hundred feet of water in the Mediterranean Sea ten miles offshore from the village of Sidi Barrani, Egypt. Its job was to service a dozen petroleum wells located deep below the sea surface. One-hundred-twenty men lived and worked three shifts a day on Production Platform Six to keep the black gold flowing from deep in the earth and back toward the shore. The wells were all connected to the platform with a series of infield pipes. The ten-inch-diameter pipe was currently moving over six thousand barrels of crude oil per day. Once ashore, the oil and gas were mixed and sent to a processing facility just outside the tiny desert town.

Platform Six was only one of ten similar platforms in the sprawling offshore field. And they were all busily tapping into the vast Zawiyat Offshore Oil Concession. All combined, the platforms were sending over a hundred thousand barrels of crude oil and two hundred million cubic feet of gas to the Sidi Barrani processing facility every day. There, the natural gas was separated out from the crude oil and the resulting products— liquid and gas—were piped to the port of Ad Dakhilah. That pipeline ran across more than four hundred kilometers of hot desert sands. Finally, it would all be loaded aboard tanker ships and floated away to feed the thirsty cars, homes, and factories of northern Europe.

The desert countryside south of Sidi Barrani was also the location of the dozens of producing oil fields that made up the Barrani Oil Concession. All these wells were also connected to the Sidi Barrani processing facility. Indeed, the facility had been constructed ten years before specifically to service the Barrani Concession when those massive fields had first been tapped. Within the past year, the busy processing plant had been enlarged to handle the newly discovered offshore fields. All those sources and the active processing complex formed a major part of Egypt's contribution to the world's petroleum production, placing the country within the top thirty of all oil producing nations.

From the Egyptian viewpoint, the big worry was that this crucial operation lay only fifty kilometers from the Libyan border. Even before Gaddafi, there had been rumblings that Egypt's next-door neighbor might use some ancient tribal claim to this once useless territory as an excuse to grab the oil-rich area. That fear had grown considerably once the Sidi Barrani processing facility and all those fields were producing. To counter that threat, the Egyptian armed forces had constructed several army barracks and air bases out there in the desert. But while these were being built, the realities of the considerable expense to man and maintain these remote bases became apparent. With the single exception of the Habata Air Base—which conveniently did double duty as the civilian airport for Sidi Barrani —the other airfields were left with only their runways completed. The blowing sands quickly hid those. The desert barracks did continue to be manned with a few squads of soldiers, but they were there more to act as local police than to provide any serious military protection.

The tribal leader Bahri Dawoud Kahir ad-Din Misurata sat in his tent just on the Libyan side of the border, reviewing the attack plan yet again. There were two key elements, and though they were far more advanced than the ones his ancestors had employed in their day, he was sure these would lead to success. The first task was to take out the Habata Air Base immediately, before the Egyptians could react and stage any airstrikes out of there. The second was to seize control of the oil fields before any action could be taken to defend or destroy them. After all, the oil was the goal of this attack. Everything else they would be seizing in the process was just so much worthless sand.

Huang Zhou ducked into the tent. The Chinese pilot carried his flight helmet tucked under his arm. His flight suit was clean and neatly pressed. Somehow, the officer could maintain the appearance that he was always ready for an inspection regardless of the dirt and heat.

Huang looked at his watch. "General, we are ready. I will personally lead the flight of ten Z-10 attack helicopters. We will depart at moonset, twenty-two hundred. It will be completely dark, and we will be flying low, just above the sand. The Egyptians will never see us approaching. It is only sixty kilometers to Habata, so we should hit them at twenty-two-fifteen. Xiao Chen is leading the Z-20 transports. They will be five minutes behind us and will put a hundred of your warriors on the ground."

Bahri Dawoud nodded, not allowing the ire to show on his face. Sometimes the Chinese treated him like an ignorant camel driver. Of course he knew the details of the geography of the upcoming mission. He pointed to the map. "I've already deployed a brigade-sized unit under Massif Mohyeddin, as we have discussed. They crossed the border a couple of hours ago. Their ETA at the airfield is just before sunrise. Your team will only be required to hold the airfield until they arrive to relieve you. Then you will be gone before the Egyptians and the rest of the world begin questioning who assisted us in such a highly successful operation."

"That should not be a problem," Huang said, almost jauntily. He spun and strutted out of the tent toward the makeshift flight line.

Minutes later, Bahri Dawoud involuntarily ducked as the Chinese attack helicopters roared overhead. It felt like they were only inches above the fabric, as if Huang had deliberately buzzed his tent to shake him up.

The flight across the sand for the Chinese choppers was uneventful. Bahri Dawoud's attack brigade lit up the Z-10's Blue Sky navigation system's FLIR as the attack birds roared past, just thirty meters overhead. Nothing else alerted on either the FLIR or the terrain-following radar. Even the YH-96 electronic warfare suite remained silent. No one was out looking for such an assault. No one had been alerted to the menace headed toward the oil facility.

One kilometer from the Habata perimeter, Huang popped up to fifty meters and lit off his own synthetic aperture radar. The picture that it painted on the screen was combined with the FLIR images so that Huang could see in his holographic heads-up display the airfield and all equipment parked there. It was as if it were a bright day outside his cockpit instead of a moonless night. Huang immediately spotted two MIG-29s sitting in hardstands at the south end of the runway. At a stroke of Huang's finger, two CM-50IGA air-to-surface missiles dropped away from his helicopter and rocketed toward the hardstands. The two MIGs disappeared in terrific explosions, lighting up the night, leaving nothing but burning, smoking wreckage.

Huang did not see any other fighter aircraft there, but a couple of C-130s were parked on the apron next to the small terminal. His PX-10A 23mm chain gun made short work of the two fat birds, also leaving them ablaze. The rest of his helicopters went searching for anything that moved, sending rockets and missiles into hangars and other buildings. Trucks, cars, and anyone dumb enough to run outside received the attention of their chain guns.

By the time Xiao Chen's transport helos arrived, Habata Air Base was mostly charred and smoking ruins.

Ψ

The second prong of Bahri Dawoud's attack was aimed directly down Egyptian Route 40M, the Coastal Highway. Another full brigade of over two thousand troops riding in T-72 main battle tanks and Puma armored fighting vehicles made up the main striking power in this group. The attack would be backed by several ancient MIGs that were left in the Second Regency's Air Force, the few Russian planes that were still flyable. Not that their fitness for combat mattered. Bahri Dawoud did not expect any resistance. The only "armed forces" ahead who might try to impede their charge were the local traffic cops in El Salloum, the only real town on the route.

It was little more than an eighty-kilometer scenic drive along little-used paved highways directly from the border to Sidi Barrani. Bahri had given Fazel Badir al-Din command of this assault. So far, it had been nothing more than a nice starlit drive along the road where the desert met the sea. After his brigade blasted through the border checkpoint at El Salloum—"blasted" being a few well-placed rounds to hurry along the fleeing guards

—his troops had the four-lane highway entirely to themselves for the rest of the trip. Even the beach road through the tiny village of El Salloum was deserted except for the one traffic cop who obligingly stopped the few cars on the road at that hour to allow Fazel Badir's column to pass through without slowing down. Of course, the policeman's cooperation might have had something to do with Salloum being primarily a Bedouin community and the traffic cop a proud member of a subtribe of Fazel's Misurata people.

Dawn found Fazel Badir firmly in charge of the Sidi Barrani processing facility. The workers arrived for their work shift to find that they had new bosses. It was late afternoon before Ali Hakim's Second Regency government could send the right engineers to the facility to take charge and start the process for turning the Western Egyptian oil wealth into a very generous money source for the Second Regency.

The Egyptian Air Force, after some quick planning and even quicker briefings, launched their first strike mission just after noon. Ten Dassault Rafale fighters of 34 Squadron lifted off from Gebel el Basur. At about the same time, twenty F-16C Fighting Falcons of 75 Squadron roared away from Jiyanklis New Air Base. The Dassaults zoomed down the coast with the intention to hit Fazel Badir's brigade, who were resting from the previous night's fun in the meager shade of the date palms outside Sidi Barrani. The Falcons were targeted against the invasion forces that had formed a perimeter surrounding the Habata Air Base.

The two fighter squadrons were barely airborne when they were first detected by sophisticated Chinese-made and, at least for the time being, Chinese manned HQ-22 air defense systems that had been quietly set up on the Libyan/Second Regency border in recent weeks. Those systems automatically identified and began tracking the inbound aircraft. The attacking warplanes were still a hundred miles from their targets when the first salvo of supersonic HQ-22 missiles blasted off and raced in their direction at Mach 6. A second and third salvo quickly followed. The missiles' semi-active radar homing locked on their quarry and guided the HQ-22s with deadly accuracy. The pilots didn't have a chance. Their radars didn't see the incoming missiles, and at Mach 6, they were only visible for a split second before impact.

Within minutes, the desert was littered with flaming debris from more than two dozen hits. One of the F-16s survived only by jettisoning his weapons load and diving for the deck. The badly frightened pilot rocketed across the desert in full afterburner, flying at Mach 1.2 a mere hundred feet above the deck, raising dust plumes and punching out flares all the way home.

Dispatches had already gone out to the world's media and through diplomatic channels during the day to confirm that the Second Regency of Tripoli had reclaimed sovereign territory that had been brutally stolen from its people many years before. And that the government had nationalized all petroleum facilities contained within the newly liberated area, making those natural resources once again the property of the people of the Second Regency, as Allah intended.

All such missives concluded with the declaration that the Second Regency was prepared to defend this rightfully reclaimed territory, not only in international venues and forums, but on the battlefield.

Ψ

President Sandra Dosetti sat back in her chair and took a deep breath. The Oval Office was quiet for once. It was a perfect time to catch up on reading some of the voluminous files that crossed her desk. The only feasible way to do this chore was to set aside a couple of hours every evening. Her secretary and office factotum, Natalie Byrant, kept the two hours inviolable. No one entered that door unless the country faced some imminent and existential danger.

So, she was surprised when there was a quiet knock. The Director of the CIA, Cyril Brown, walked in and, without seeking or receiving permission, took a seat across the Resolute Desk from the President. Dosetti knew Brown as the quintessential Washington insider. He knew everyone and where all the bodies were buried. And he employed that knowledge in what she considered his ruthless climb to the top.

Brown calmly crossed his legs, carefully adjusting the knife-sharp crease in his trousers before he spoke. "Madam President, I regret to inform you that President Smitherman has passed away." His voice was flat and calm. There was not a hint of sorrow or compassion. No surprise either.

The man Sandra Dosetti had succeeded to the highest office in the land was no friend of the Director. "It seems he was fishing on Lake Palestine in East Texas when he suffered an apparent massive heart attack. The body is being transported to his ranch right now, and once there, the media will be advised. There will be a state funeral, of course, but we will try to keep our involvement—yours and mine—out of the limelight."

Dosetti nodded. Something about how this news was being delivered did not feel right. And she really did not like the comment about involvement in Smitherman's unexpected passing. She unobtrusively reached under her desk and hit the button that energized the office recording system. At the same time, she asked, "Why am I hearing this from the CIA? Isn't this something for his Secret Service detail or the FBI? Last time I looked, your charter was for everything outside our borders. Even though you don't like it one bit, Texas is still inside the USA."

A thin smile creased the Director's face as he pulled something that looked like a rather fat fountain pen from his jacket pocket. A little yellow light atop the object was brightly flashing. "Madam President, it would be best if we did not record this conversation and thus kept it off the record."

She shut off the recording system. The light on the device in the Director's hand stopped blinking. "Am I correct in assuming that the CIA had something to do with President Smitherman's death?"

Brown shook his head dismissively. "Some questions are best left unasked. Much like the questions about how it was that you so suddenly ascended to this office."

Yes, Dosetti had become President when both the sitting President—Harold Smitherman—and his Vice President resigned their offices, not at the same time but still within a suspiciously short timeframe, ostensibly for health reasons. When Smitherman appointed her as VP after the sitting VP resigned, she became the next in the line of succession. While the whole thing raised howls among the press corps, abundant conspiracy theories throughout social media and the all-news TV channels, and speculation about what was going on even among those who rarely followed politics, no one ever learned the true reasons—or the complicated mechanisms employed by Dosetti—for the unprecedented change in America's top office. If the true story were ever unveiled, both she and her Vice President would surely be impeached. Even if they had staged their "coup" for all the right reasons, to remove the corrupt President and his veep.

She nodded, understanding the implications and the very thinly veiled threat from the head of the Central Intelligence Agency. Brown was a deadly viper she would have to handle very carefully until the problem could be resolved. But in the meantime, he could still be very useful to her.

"What about Osterman?" she asked. The last she had heard, the former Vice President was working to obtain some cushy job with one of the Ivy League schools. She had no idea which one, nor did she care.

Brown chuckled. "Well, it would certainly appear to be a little suspicious if the Vice President met an untimely end at about the same time as the President, even if both have well-documented health issues. Especially since there are still rumblings about the timing of their both leaving office in the first place. Osterman is in the Vermont woods, suffering from a painful case of shingles. He really should have gotten that new Shingrix vaccine, but it is well known that he is stubborn about such things." The Director shook his head, still chuckling. "Not that it would have done any good against the particular strain he has contracted. It's really strange. That variety of the illness only occurs in the remote jungles of central Africa. And, as with the more common strain, it can lie in wait in the human body for decades before becoming so painfully active. One has to wonder how and when he might have caught the virus."

Dosetti mumbled, "Yes, one has to wonder." She had very little doubt that Brown was behind Osterman's painful malady.

Cyril Brown shook his head as if awakening from a reverie. "Well, it's really an academic question. Former Vice President Osterman will most likely suffer a massive stroke in a month or so."

Dosetti's phone buzzed before she could ponder the Director's prediction. It was Natalie. "Excuse me, Madam President. President Tan Yong is on the red phone. He says that it is urgent that you speak."

The red phone was a secure hot line that connected directly between the White House and Tan Yong's office in the Forbidden City. It had been used extensively during President Smitherman's time in office, though not necessarily for official state business. Not so much since.

"Excuse me, Director," Dosetti said as she reached for the red phone.

"We are going to have to make an appointment so that we can continue this discussion. I need to speak with the Chinese President right now."

Brown stood, nodded, and quickly exited the office. He had come to deliver a message to Sandra Dosetti and he had done just that. He had no doubt there would be further discussion about the ramifications of the timing of the fatal health issues of the former Chief Executive and his number two. And about what the Director was angling to accomplish in light of such developments.

"Mr. President," Dosetti said into the phone, her voice devoid of any emotion. "What can I do for you?"

"Madam President," the Chinese strongman began, "I think that it would be beneficial for us to discuss the current situation between our two nations and come to an understanding, only the two of us, leader to leader. First, as we have told you many times before, having your aircraft carriers and submarines loitering off the coast of our province of Taiwan is not conducive to a peaceful resolution of our differences. The chance of an accident becoming the lighted fuse for a much greater and more destructive detonation is real, President Dosetti."

"President Tan, as you well know, the US Navy is there at the request of the duly elected government of the free nation of Taiwan, the Republic of China," Dosetti replied, her voice flat, emotionless. "They will stay there until your PLAN forces stand down from their current state of high alert. And I will once again ask that you and your military make certain there is no...as you put it...'accident.' If you really want a peaceful resolution, if you truly want to avoid the accident of which you speak, then standing down would be the logical beginning."

She paused before continuing as an indication she was now changing the subject. The Chinese President waited patiently for her to go on. Both knew the complaint about Taiwan was not the primary purpose of this call anyway. Dosetti promptly got to what she now knew to be the real reason. "And meanwhile, you can also stop sending weapons and advisors to help Ali Hakim Sherif and Libya. I think he's calling himself Suleiman Jadid these days."

"We are only coming to the aid of a downtrodden people, and even then, only at their request," Tan Yong answered. His tone sounded as if he was reading the carefully honed words of a scripted reply. "The people of the Second Regency of Tripoli are trying to throw off the yoke of Western hegemony. They have rightfully requested the assistance of the People's Republic of China in their quest. And in so responding to that request, we have already suffered losses of equipment and men."

Dosetti allowed her anger to show as she shot back, "Whatever Sherif asked for, he invaded Egypt and attacked and sank an innocent tanker and its escort in international waters without provocation. It is nothing more than a naked grab for the oil riches there as part of some dream empire Sherif intends to create. Egypt, which has already lost aircraft and men as well, has requested our assistance. There is a very real possibility that even more of your advisors will be caught up in the fighting and may suffer the consequences. And that more of the expensive equipment you and your people are supplying that madman will be destroyed. Only you can prevent that from happening. Now, if you will excuse me, I have a state dinner to attend."

She placed the phone back in its cradle without giving the Chinese leader an opportunity to respond. If he bothered to check her published schedule—and she doubted he would—he would see she had no such state dinner.

President Sandra Dosetti took another deep breath and said, out loud, "Check, President Tan. Your move."

Then she resumed working her way through the massive stack of files.

Ψ

The sun was dipping below the hills behind Algeciras, the Spanish city directly across the Bay of Gibraltar from the area's famous rock, when the two commercial tractor tugs finally showed up, ready to pull the *Gato* away from Pier Forty-Nine on the harbor's South Mole. US Navy Commander Henrietta Foster was standing with the Officer-of-the-Deck and the civilian harbor pilot in the tiny "playpen" structure at the top of the submarine's sail. The playpen's temporary pipe stanchions allowed them to safely stand high above the sub's deck so they could have an unobstructed view of everything happening down on the pier as they cast off. This evening,

SEAL Commander Jim Ward joined them there. For the past hour, they had gripped the stanchions and waited impatiently while the Gibraltar Port Authority used their tugs to complete another task, apparently one with higher priority, pushing a massive trans-Atlantic cruise liner up against the Western Arm pier. With the cruise ship safely tied up and the tourists heading off to board buses for their shore excursions or to enjoy the Gibraltar City night life and spend lots of money, the two tugs finally made their way down to pull the *Gato* away from what had been her temporary home at His Majesty's Naval Base Gibraltar.

It did not alleviate Henrietta Foster's frustration that Sir James Allgood, the Royal Navy's First Sea Lord, was still standing down there on the pier with Joe Glass and Brian Edwards, making small talk, but, despite his power, doing nothing to hasten *Gato*'s departure. Allgood had flown down from London for the express purpose of observing this underway. Henrietta could do nothing but watch from her perch up on the sail as the British Admiral's presence only contributed to the delay.

It was twilight when the two tractor tugs were at last made fast to the *Gato* and all was finally ready to get underway. Foster happily ordered all lines cast off. When the last line dropped into the water, the quartermaster, standing behind Foster, blew his whistle and unfurled the stars and stripes on the mast. The night breeze off the Med caught the flag so that it snapped crisply, as if offering its own sharp salute. According to the laws of the sea, the newly repaired submarine was officially underway.

As the two tugs strained to pull the sub away from the pier, Joe Glass cupped his hands and yelled up at Foster, "Smooth sailing and good hunting!"

Foster and Ward both gave a thumbs-up and saluted. At "ahead one-third," the submarine slowly proceeded toward the north end of the mole where they would have access to the deeper waters of the bay. Steaming cautiously through the narrow slot between the South Mole and the Detached Mole, the submarine was finally clear of the inner harbor and technically back at sea again. Foster could feel the faint Mediterranean swell gently pitching her boat. It seemed as if the big vessel beneath her feet, like a dolphin released from captivity, was elated to once again frolic and be free in its natural environment. It felt good.

Turning to Lieutenant Jim Sanson, the current OOD, Foster ordered, "Officer-of-the-Deck, come to course south. When the pilot is on board his tug, cast them off and come to 'ahead standard.' Have the bridge rigged for 'dive.' I want to submerge as soon as Europa Point Light is abeam to port."

Foster shook hands with and thanked the harbor pilot, then watched as he made the long climb down the sub's bridge trunk, only to emerge a minute later on the main deck. Then he hopped over into the tugboat that waited to take him ashore. She turned to Jim Ward. "Commander, we best get below. It's about to get real wet up here."

The *Gato* slipped beneath the waves and headed east, but not before performing one last task, copying the latest intel on the high-data-rate antenna. The extremely high frequency satellite communications system connected *Gato* to the rest of the world at gigabit speed.

Back down in the quiet of the depths, Jim Ward and Henrietta Foster sat in her stateroom and read through voluminous intelligence reports. Each report would likely have considerable impact on their future tasks. The satellite imaging printouts were the most immediate. They confirmed that the heavy-lift ship *Hua Rui Long* had completed offloading the newest Chinese/Libyan/Second Regency submarine and that the boat was now docked safely behind the mole in Benghazi harbor. The images also revealed the third heavy-lift ship, the Cosco Heavy Transport *Guang Hua Kou*, as it entered the Suez Canal with what looked like another deepwater drill rig onboard. Everyone involved knew differently. The US Navy destroyer *Harold Stanton* was racing back to Port Said to greet *Guang Hua Kou* when the ship emerged from the canal.

"Captain, did you see this?" Ward asked, pointing to one of the reports. "The Libyans—or Second Regency-ers, or whatever the hell they're calling themselves this week—launched a serious attack just across the border into Egypt. And it looks like they weren't messing around. Two columns at brigade strength or better and some kick-ass firepower."

"You can call me Hen. Everybody else does," Foster responded, nodding. "Yeah, that jumped out to me, too. Ali Hakim is going after the oil, not the sand or so-called sovereign territory. And his Chinese pals are sure helping him out. They pretty much wiped out an Egyptian air strike that responded, and they weren't using slingshots shooting camel turds, either. Makes our mission even more dicey, you know."

Ward shook his head. "No doubt...Hen. And please call me Jim since it looks like I'm your guest here at the *Gato* VRBO. It's pretty clear that things have ramped up while you were in the body shop back there, but the *Stanton* and us are the only US shooters left in the whole damn Med. Everybody else is suddenly going balls to the wall to get to the Pacific where there's a bunch of smoke but, at least so far, not much fire. You gotta wonder if there's a connection between all that posturing over there and what's for sure going on here." He winked at Foster. "A little bird told me some folks in high places are beginning to think so."

"It has occurred to me how screwy it is that they're making a show of gettin' all busy off China while they're delivering all kinds of high-tech weapons to Libya on this side of the globe, like FedEx at Christmastime," Foster agreed.

"But one thing you can bet on," the SEAL said. "We're about to be busy. First off, my gut tells me we'll be targeted against that third Chinese sub. I'm going to get my guys busy planning for that mission. And you have a bunch of Tomahawks in your vertical launch tubes. I figure you'll be suddenly and aggressively off-loading a few of those when the time comes."

"Yep," Foster answered with a grin. "But I only have twelve Tomahawks. The VPM tubes each have a Conventional Prompt Strike bird in them. Gives us a Mach 7 dose of whomp-ass. You might also add the twenty ADCAP torpedoes and the two Harpoons down in the room. I sure as hell would like to suddenly and aggressively off-load some of those bad boys in the direction of those PLAN subs, too." She glanced at some notes on a legal pad on her small desk. "Here's what we do know for certain. We got four days in transit for us to have it all figured out. And the same four days to be ready for whatever calamity we're cruising toward at 'ahead standard.'" Then she looked up. "Speaking of Harpoons, it's time to tube load one of those. Where we're going, with all the small patrol boats nosing around, they can be a lot more valuable than a Mark 48. And, if we need one, we'll need it quick."

"Most likely," the SEAL agreed.

She grabbed the microphone and ordered, "Officer-of-the-Deck, back-haul the weapon in tube three. Load a Harpoon into tube three."

13

Joe Glass stood with Brian Edwards and Sir James Allgood on the pier and watched as the *Gato* departed HMNB Gibraltar, heading out toward open water. After the submarine disappeared around the turn, the trio walked back toward the battered Land Rover, the vehicle they had been allotted for inconspicuous transportation. Glass turned to the First Sea Lord and said, "Sir James, I hope you can go up to the HMCC and review the situation with us. This whole Libyan thing is changing quick. I have a feeling that the mission we gave *Gato* this evening won't be the mission she actually does."

Allgood raised his hand. "I'd be happy to, Joe, but this is an American show. There is no reason for you to feel compelled to keep us in the loop. You certainly don't need our agreement on any of this."

"True," Glass agreed. "But you have provided us with invaluable and timely assistance. And the intel resources coming through the HMCC will almost certainly prove to be crucial. I don't want you to be blindsided by any blowback that might result from your assistance so far. Besides, Admiral Ward, our Director of Naval Intelligence...I think you know him well...has suggested we spend some time with you discussing the various aspects of this mess."

"Then I shall accept your kind invitation," the Brit promptly replied.

Edwards jumped into the driver's seat and started the engine. Allgood climbed into the passenger seat, fastened his seatbelt, then reached up to get a good grip on the handhold. "Reliable sources have warned me of your driving, Captain," he joked. "Same source is telling me that the price of *paella* is spiking downtown. Rumor is that some crazed Yanks are eating the restaurants out of their stock of saffron."

Edwards slipped the Land Rover into "Drive" and, with a mock scowl, said, "Vicious propaganda, all of it. My driving is fine and Admiral Glass is single-handedly responsible for the run on *paella*." He laughed, gunned the engine, and sprayed gravel as he shot down the mole.

It took twenty minutes to negotiate the town's traffic while they wound their way up to the HMCC's hidden entrance. Once inside the command center and seated around the conference table, Sir James held up a finger, indicating the other two men should watch the trick he was about to perform. With a flourish, he touched a hidden door on an inconspicuous side cabinet behind him. It popped open and a shelf lifted up. On the shelf were three crystal glasses, a small water pitcher, and a bottle filled with golden-brown liquid. He picked up the bottle and inspected its label and top for a moment.

"One advantage we Brits have over you Yanks is that we never suffered through Josephus Daniels," he said as he offered the bottle to Edwards and Glass for inspection. All three knew Daniels as Woodrow Wilson's Secretary of the Navy and the man who banned all booze on US Navy ships. "Lagavulin Sixteen, you see, is a very smooth, peaty whiskey. Or in your colonial version of our language, 'a damn fine Scotch.'" He poured a dram in each glass, then offered the other two men the water pitcher. Both Glass and Edwards demurred. Splashing a little water into his own glass, Allgood lifted it up and offered a toast. "To the king," and took a sip.

"To Josephus Daniels," Edwards said. "May he forever remain thirsty." The two Americans dutifully joined in the toast, then quickly acknowledged how good the whiskey was.

Settling comfortably around the table, the three men got busy reviewing the latest intel messages as they sipped their libations. With the aid of the command center staff, they projected various satellite photos, maps, and graphics on the large flat-panel screens that surrounded the conference table.

"Our friends from the Middle Kingdom seem to be taking an inordinate interest in Ali Hakim Sherif's rise to power, and in assisting him in establishing himself as god of the southern Med coast," Allgood commented. "One thing is for certain. The men who make up most of his fighting forces would be incapable of manning these weapons we are looking at, let alone maintaining them." He zoomed in on an image of an HQ-22 air-defense missile launcher system parked somewhere out in the desert. "My analysts at NID tell me that this is the very latest HQ-22 variant, something the Chinese are calling the HQ-22C. It is only now being deployed to the PLA back home. Why has Tan Yong given it to Ali Hakim when his own army is only just now receiving it?"

Joe Glass responded, "Same question we have on those submarines. The boats that Ali Hakim is unloading have propulsors. That's technology we haven't seen yet on the PLAN vessels."

Brian Edwards flipped up an image of an encampment on one of the panels. "We also have evidence that Tan Yong and the Chinese are not our only problem. They have some other scary friends and benefactors." He zoomed in on the image until individual people were identifiable. "You see the guy to the right of Sherif? The one with the really cute black turban? Intel has him pegged as a guy named Bijan Salemi. He has a really impressive resume. He's a major operative in the Iranian Revolutionary Guard Quds Force and ranks way up there on the terrorist hit list. He's been reliably linked to at least three dirty operations against Israel in the last couple of years and is an expert on unconventional warfare. If he's cozied up with Sherif, as this image appears to show, you can bet Iran is playing a big role in the Second Regency. Or at least they really want to."

Joe Glass studied the screen for a bit and then offered, "The two things that all these players have in common is oil and wanting to somehow put the screws to NATO and to us. China needs and wants all the oil it can get. Both Iran and Sherif, of course, know how valuable it would be if they pump all the oil they can and sold it to the Chinese."

Allgood took another sip of his Lagavulin before asking the obvious question. "So, what do we do about this unholy triumvirate? The Egyptians have already proven rather tragically that flying airstrikes against this bunch of simple nomads is not a good plan."

"It would have to be land-based air, if we did try more airstrikes," Glass pointed out. "All our carriers are racing off for the Western Pacific in response to Tan's shenanigans over there. Where are your flattops?"

"*Prince of Wales* just finished a port visit in Sydney and is heading north to join your carriers somewhere west of Guam," Allgood answered. "That transit will take a bit. *Queen Elizabeth* is in drydock for a scheduled maintenance period. So, we are in the same condition as you blokes."

"Well, that leaves us with two Tomahawk shooters, *Gato* and the *Harold Stanton*, and we could quickly put up about eighty birds of various kinds," Glass responded. "Plus, one SEAL team. I'm not even privy to what our other teams are up to or where they are, but I know they ain't here where we need 'em." Glass swirled the remaining few drops of the whiskey in his glass, then quickly downed it. "I suggest we quit worrying about what we don't have or can't get on station here anytime soon and put what assets we do have to work. Sir James, do you have any Tomahawk shooters available?"

"We have a Type 45 destroyer and a couple of Type 23 frigates that we can get underway and in range in three or four days," the First Sea Lord answered. "Those orders will have to come from the Prime Minister down through the Minister of Defense. You know they'll have to weigh the political effect any potential shooting might have, but, as you Yanks like to say, I'll get the ball rolling. And I'll put a call in with my old friend John Dingham just to make sure we are coordinated. Your SecDef and I go way back. And I know he appreciates a good whiskey as much as I do so that makes him a worthy partner in any endeavor."

Joe Glass put his hands down flat on the table and rose. "And as you Brits like to say, 'Jolly good show, chap.'"

But there was no humor in his words or the expression on his face.

Ψ

President Sandra Dosetti had made it her policy to never answer the phone herself. Even her personal cell phone number was routed through her executive assistant for screening purposes. Natalie would then vet the call before informing Dosetti. Or tell the caller to go away, nicely or otherwise, depending on who it was. The process kept nasty surprises for the

President to the absolute minimum, and even sometimes snagged the computer-generated randomized robo-call.

For that reason, Dosetti was startled when the device suddenly rang without Natalie's intervention. And with a blank caller ID on the screen. She let it chirp a couple of times before curiosity overcame caution and she punched the answer button.

"Yes?"

"Madame President, thank you so very much for taking my call."

Dosetti immediately recognized the voice. The thick Slavic accent overlaid with a hint of Brooklynese. A memory, sometimes pleasant, sometimes not, from her days on Wall Street.

"Good afternoon, Magnus," she answered. "I know better than to ask how you managed to get your call directly through to me."

Magnus Rosenblatt chuckled as he answered. "That would be prudent. Let's just say that I have my ways and leave it at that."

"But you know you could go through the usual channels," she chided him. "And I will be happy to return your call."

"I understand, Madam President. Sometimes those channels move very slowly. Today I have some matters of considerable urgency. And I have no time for 'slowly,' understand?"

Rosenblatt Capital was one of the largest privately owned investment banks in the world. Very little happened in the financial industry anywhere on the planet without Rosenblatt Capital—and by extension Magnus Rosenblatt—being involved in some manner and degree. Rosenblatt was a force to be reckoned with, powerful enough that he could not be ignored. Not even by the President of the United States. And if the guy wanted something, he usually got it. But at least this time he was asking for it first.

"Sandra, it's been quite some time since we last spoke," Magnus said, pointedly segueing to the first matter he wanted to discuss. "Since before your rather abrupt ascendency into the Oval Office. If I didn't know better, I would say that you have been avoiding me."

It was Dosetti's turn to chuckle dryly. "I think that you can appreciate that I've been a little busy lately. What with wrestling with the economy, trying to reach some kind of working relationship with the other side of the aisle in Congress, and generally keeping the world safe for democracy, I haven't had much time for social calls. Now, what can I do for you?"

"I understand, Sandra. But I'm sure that the Vice President relayed to you my offer to host a campaign kick-off fundraiser for you here in New York. It's never too early to start filling the coffers for your first turn before the voters, you know," Rosenblatt answered. "I understand the initial polling is rather lackluster."

Dosetti closed her eyes for a moment and took a deep breath. So, this was simply an effort on Rosenblatt's part to obtain some political leverage with the relatively new Chief Executive. That was to be expected, of course. Dosetti had no illusions. If someone from the other party were sitting in her chair, Magnus Rosenblatt would still be on the phone with him or her, making the same offer. He did not play political favorites. He played for power. The power money almost always bought him.

"Your kind offer is much appreciated, Magnus," Dosetti replied noncommittedly. "And we have already placed it under consideration for when we kick off the campaign. If we decide to run, of course."

She suspected there was another reason for this call, though. Rosenblatt knew the offer to Vice President Aldo would have been all it took. She was about to try to politely end the call when the financier said, "I understand. The offer stands. But that is not the only reason for my call. I am becoming very concerned with the situation in North Africa."

"And what situation are you alluding to, Magnus?" she asked. She needed to know his involvement there and how much he actually knew about this crisis.

"I'm sure you remember the *Cygnet Dawn*, the petroleum tanker that Ali Hakeem Sherif's pirates grabbed off the Libyan coast. This very day, I have authorized the payment from my personal account of the ransom that the bastard demanded for the release of the vessel's crew. They are supposed to be flying from Tobruk to Tangier tonight, as I am sure your intelligence sources and news media will soon be able to confirm for you. The tanker itself is no more than an insurance write-off. It will be cheaper in the long run to allow the ship itself to rust away in Libya than to pay the fine they are demanding."

"Thanks for the heads-up on the ransom," Dosetti acknowledged. "That gives us a chance to prepare a statement and pretend we know what's going on."

"Sherif now appears to be greatly expanding his domain," Rosenblatt went on. "He openly brags of his intentions to rebuild the Ottoman Empire. I am guessing you have been briefed on the details of his drive to forcefully and brutally take the Sidi Barrani oil fields. Rosenblatt Capital is heavily invested in Egyptian oil and especially in the Zawiyat Offshore Oil Concession and the Barrani Oil Concession. We stand to lose hundreds of billions if that sand crawler and his nomads are not pushed back across the border."

In truth, Dosetti knew very little of the details about the events Rosenblatt was describing. There had been only a quick blurb in her daily brief. Still, she replied, "Of course, Magnus, but this kind of regional flare-up is something you need to discuss with the Egyptian government, not with us. We find ourselves very heavily involved with a little crisis developing in the Western Pacific right now."

"As do we," Rosenblatt answered. "You can imagine our investment in not only oil but, for example, all the elements necessary for electric-car batteries in the Pacific Rim and South China Sea region. But be assured we are in discussion with Egypt about the situation there. However, it will take some time for them to pivot to the west and mount an offense after concentrating so long on Gaza and Yemen and other issues elsewhere in that region."

The President realized there was more Rosenblatt had to tell her. She assumed he would need no prompting, but she did some anyway. "So, what do you want the US to do about this?"

"Madam President, the takeover of the coastal facilities is not actually our primary concern when it comes to Sherif," Rosenblatt responded. "You will learn of this in the news or likely even in your intelligence briefings. One of my companies is financing a wildcatter named Langley who has made a startling discovery down in an area of Egypt called the Great Calanshio Sand Sea. It is a good four hundred miles south of the Mediterranean coast but only a short distance from Sherif and the Libyan border. The most godforsaken place you can imagine. Anyway, Langley was prospecting down there. Data now confirms that he has found the largest oil field anyone has discovered in recent history. We are talking billions of barrels of oil and trillions of cubic feet of natural gas. Enough that its coming to market will have to be managed carefully to avoid crashing the petroeconomy entirely. And managing carefully is not something this new leader of what he is calling the Second Regency of Tripoli knows anything about."

"I'm sensing that you are leading up to the primary reason for this call, Magnus," Dosetti pointedly responded. "Something more than a fundraiser chat."

"Of course I am," Rosenblatt shot back. "Langley was conducting the activation of test wells and overseeing initial development. But now, we have lost all contact with him and his crew. Last word from him was two nights before Sherif's fighters hit and seized Sidi Barrani. Please keep in mind, Madam President, that Langley and much of his crew are American citizens. The Egyptians have already told us they do not have the capabilities to scour such isolated territory when their neighbor is already making themselves at home at currently working facilities that are actively pumping black gold to the world as you and I speak."

"And...?" The President suspected what was coming next.

"I need your help as Commander in Chief to learn what happened out there in the desert and to bring Langley and his men back safe," Rosenblatt answered.

"And make sure all that oil gets pumped, processed, and paid for to a subsidiary of Rosenblatt Capital and not to some tin-pot dictator looking to fund his dream of a twenty-first-century empire," Dosetti told him.

"Should those American citizens be successfully rescued, we might also expect ownership of the discovery to remain with the people of Egypt and the investors who funded the risky exploration in the first place," the financier responded. "And that much of the world's petroleum needs would be met by entrepreneurship and free enterprise and not so much by enemies of the USA."

Dosetti thought for a moment before responding, "Magnus, I could not have spun it any more beautifully myself."

14

Ali Hakim Sherif stood next to his car and watched as the orange-and-yellow tractor tug nudged his latest gift, another brand-new Chinese submarine, up against the pier. Soon, the *Dire Alnabii* would double the power of his fleet. The new Libyan strongman could already envision this black beast stalking the seas, preying on those ships who dared defy the newly reawakened Ottoman Empire and the will of Allah. Even better, soon the third modified *Yuan*-class submarine—already named the *Khinjar Alnabii*, the *Prophet's Dagger*—would join its two sisters in helping assure the Second Regency of Tripoli's return to respected dominance across the entire region. With three such modern, powerful submarines, Sherif was sure that he would and could rule the Mediterranean. Even the Americans would be fearful of challenging such mighty warships.

"Give us two months to train your crewmen and the *Dire Alnabii* will be ready to join the *Sayf Alnabii*." Wu Ming Jie, the Chinese PLAN representative, stood beside the Arab dictator, pleased by the proud look on the man's face. "The trainers for the *Dire Alnabii* are every bit as good as my team on the *Sayf Alnabii* and you already have proof of how well they can do their job."

A cruel smile flitted across Ali Hakim's face. "Yes, they taught the Italian Navy that they must respect our rightful borders. But, Wu, I am very anxious to get all three submarines out to sea. We need them to be ready to fight, and fight effectively, before the American Navy comes. And we know they will come once they understand the potential effect of what we are doing on their petroleum supply and prices."

Someone leaned out of the car window and said, "*Pasha* Suleiman, we need to leave now if we are going to be in Sidi Barrani before nightfall." It was Li Chung Sheng, the Chinese diplomat. "We must allow Wu Ming to do his job training your sailors so they may accomplish your plan. Huang Zhou has your helicopter ready to fly."

For Li Chung Sheng, the incursion along the Egyptian border was a perfect time to prove to his nation's new partners in the region the effectiveness of the modern Chinese weapons that had been delivered to the Second Regency. Since that incursion had been such an easy success, it was time to flaunt those weapons and the damage they had inflicted on the Egyptians, to provide Ali Hakim Sherif proof of the value of being a friend of the Middle Kingdom. This little jaunt over to Sidi Barrani was designed to be much more than a sightseeing tour.

It was a quick twenty-minute drive out to Benina Airport, where Zhou had positioned the helicopter. Inhemed al Megharief Road was pretty much a straight shot from downtown Benghazi to the airport, a modern four lane highway, and the police escort made certain that traffic did not hinder the presidential motorcade. Arriving at the airfield security gate, Ali Hakim's little entourage did not even slow down, blasting right on through as the security guards vigorously waved them on.

The motorcade drove straight out onto the apron before screeching to a halt alongside the Z-20 helicopter. Zhou had outfitted it as the official state helicopter, including having Sherif's newly designed presidential shield painted boldly on each side. He had positioned it at the airfield, always fueled and ready to go. With Sherif and Li Chung comfortably seated aboard, the presidential Z-20 lifted off into a cloudless sky. Behind them, two Z-10 attack helicopters, both fully armed, lifted off to provide a protective escort.

Before heading east, Zhou made a loop so that they could fly over the harbor. It was an opportunity for his passengers to get a bird's-eye view of the two submarines that sat there, nestled up against the pier. Then Zhou swung the helicopter east, out over the Jebel Akhdar, the only forested area in the whole Second Regency. As the town of Tobruk flitted past the windscreen to the left, the landscape abruptly changed from forest and agriculture to desert wasteland.

Zhou swung the aircraft around to the south and flew along the old borderline for a few kilometers before they overflew what looked like a large truck park. Pointing, he said, "That's one of your new HQ-22 longrange air defense batteries. That one and another one just like it farther south are defending the Second Regency from Egyptian air attacks. And air attacks from anyone else who might decide to attempt to stop you." Sherif felt the need to scoff at Zhou's mention of any possible challenge, but before he could say anything, Zhou interjected, "Ali Hakim, remember that the Egyptians have the most powerful air force in the Middle East. Beyond these helicopters, you have practically no assets to put into the air. Those missile batteries are fully capable of protecting your oil fields for now. Until our partnership assists you in being even better equipped against attacks."

They flew in silence for a few minutes. Not actually in silence. There was no conversation. But there is no such thing as silence while traveling in a military helicopter.

Finally, Huang Zhou pointed out toward some scattered heaps of blackened wreckage that littered the desert sands to their left. "We are approaching Habata Air Base, now. Those are the remains of some of the Egyptian Army that tried to defend it. Our troops who so bravely claimed the base have renamed it as the Suleiman Jadid Forward Attack Base."

Zhou glanced over to confirm that this bit of news had, indeed, caused Ali Hakim to smile.

The airfield appeared in the distance and then rushed closer. But even from that far out, they could tell it was busy. Men and vehicles rushed about and there were both military helicopters and heavy-lift transport aircraft parked on the apron.

"We are using the base for staging and for airlift," Zhou explained as he pointed to a pair of large jets being unloaded and cargo taken into a concrete bunker. "Those are an Ilyushin IL-76 and a Tupolev TU-154. They were carrying reloads for the HQ-22 batteries, flying them in from Djibouti and up through Sudan to avoid prying eyes."

"Very good," Sherif said, clearly impressed. "Very good."

Zhou banked the Z-20 around and made a broad orbit of the airbase. "See the prop planes unloading by the terminal? Those are a pair of Iranian C-130s. Two loads of UAVs. Very useful weapons and they are now in your inventory. But for now, we must refuel."

It took ten minutes for the Z-20 and the two escorts to top off their tanks, time for the passengers to get out and stretch their legs.

Soon they were airborne again, still aimed south, passing over more trackless desert. The sun was low on the western horizon when the unmistakable silhouette of a single oil rig appeared, sprouting like a determined tree out of the sand and rock. Zhou completed a circle around the small, lonely facility before settling down on the makeshift landing pad.

Li Chung Sheng looked out as the side door slid open to allow a hot blast of desert wind and sand inside.

"So, this is the Great Calanshio oil field?" the diplomat asked. "The source of all we need to complete our ambitious plan? I must say, it is not very impressive."

Ali Hakim Sherif smiled and answered, "Not yet, sir, but beneath these sands is enough oil and gas to fund our entire revolution for the next hundred years. And to be certain the energy needs of our best friends will be met for even longer. All we need to do is get the product out of the ground and pumped up to the coast."

Li Chung replied, "And for that I am sure you know you will need help from the Middle Kingdom."

"The reason for this little jaunt is not only for you to show me what our partnership has already accomplished," Ali Hakim said. "I am quite aware of our success thus far. But it is also for me to show you the reality of what is needed and the promise of the rewards. Now, let us go enjoy refreshments and have a chat with a few people who can explain just how important this bit of desert is to the future of the Second Regency and the history of the world going forward. This bit of arid land will soon become yet another birthplace of a new civilization. But even with the resources of your government, the treasure beneath our feet, the blessings of Allah, and the will of my long-oppressed people, we will likely still have only one opportunity to accomplish our goals. We must leave nothing to chance. And we cannot flinch from doing what must be done."

By the end of his speech, Ali Hakim Sherif was shouting, sweat pouring from his hairline. As they stepped down into the sand, none of the others had any doubt the man meant exactly what he was saying.

Ψ

Henrietta Foster stood and intently studied the big flat-panel display. She toggled the Xbox controller so that the camera zoomed in on the Chinese heavy-lift ship, the Cosco Heavy Transport *Guang Hua Kou*. The massive vessel had just dropped its anchors a mile offshore from the port of Benghazi, ready to begin offloading its cargo. A flock of small craft—including a couple of patrolling gun boats—milled about near the giant Chinese ship. That effectively prevented Foster from driving the *Gato* in for a close-up look, no matter how stealthy they might be in doing so. However, the photonics mast's advanced optics easily compensated for that impediment. Even from a couple of miles away, she had a view much like what she would have enjoyed had they been right there, up close and personal.

"They'll be starting to flood down soon," Eric Householder, standing beside Foster, predicted. "It took the last guys a couple of days to offload all that drill rig crap before they could even get to the sub."

Jim Ward stepped up and studied the screen closely. Finally, the SEAL team commander said, "If we're going to make that black tub a mission kill, looks like we have a two-day...really a two-night...window. Whole lot easier to do this job when they're floating around out here than to have to swim into the harbor. What you think, Chief?"

Billy Joe Hurt nodded in agreement. "I'm with you, boss. Gotta figger we need four swimmers and two diver propulsion devices. It's gonna have to be tomorrow night, though. We don't have enough time to get the plannin' done, get briefed, and make the swim tonight."

"So how long you figure this mission will take?" Foster asked.

Ward scratched his head before he answered. The skipper needed to know, and the answer should be as close to accurate as he could make it. "If we do a lock-out a couple of miles out, two hours for the lock-out and swim, an hour under that big boy for the mission, and then two hours to swim back and lock-in, all told, it should be about five hours. I'm figuring in probably an hour of contingency time, too."

"So, we set 'go time' for twenty-one hundred tomorrow night? That's twenty minutes after sunset," Householder calculated. "Then we rendezvous again at about oh two hundred."

Ward nodded. "That'll work." Turning to Hurt, he told him, "Chief, get the guys together to break out the gear and get busy checking it out. Let's you and me put our heads together and start planning this out."

The SEAL team spent the entire night checking and double-checking their gear and then going deep into the SEAL mission-planning process. By the time the sun was rising over the horizon on the sea surface above them, they had completed the plan, worked out the contingencies, and redteamed the whole thing to try to discover any hidden gotchas. Finally, it was time to get some sleep.

Jim Ward was deep into a pleasant dream starring his wife and new son when Jason Hall shook him awake. "Boss! Time to wake up. Almost go time."

Ward reluctantly sat up, swung his feet to the deck, and quickly jumped into his uniform. After splashing some water on his face and making a quick stop in the wardroom for a cup of coffee, he trotted down to the torpedo room to meet up with his team.

They were already in their wetsuits, their Mk-25 rebreathers draped over their shoulders, clearly set to go to work. Chuck Jones, Gene LaCroix, and Tony Martinelli under command of Chief Hurt would be the first team on this mission, the ones who would swim all the way to the target and do the assigned job. Jim Dumkowski and Jason Hall were suited up as the backup team. They would stand by just in case help was needed. Jim Ward would be staying back, overseeing everything from the submarine. He was not happy about missing the action, but the rest of the team had finally convinced him that he was not needed on this swim. Instead, he was far more valuable for command and coordination. Ward knew they were right and relented.

Together, they all traipsed up to the lockout trunk where their gear was already staged and waiting. Master Chief Cortez, *Gato*'s COB, met them there along with two of his crewmembers, his phone talker and trunk control operator.

"All set to go, COB?" Ward asked, impulsively checking his wristwatch.

"Just about, sir," Cortez answered. "The pilot is bringing the ship to a hover now. Your guys can go ahead and enter the trunk, though. As soon as we're at zero speed, we can commence with the lock-out."

Swimmer lock-out from a submerged submarine is an inherently dangerous evolution. Although *Virginia*-class submarines like the *Gato* were specially designed for such swimmer operations, those hazards still existed and were very real. To do a lock-out safely, the submarine had to maintain a rock-solid depth control—normally at eighty feet—with a tolerance of plus or minus only one foot. A submarine changing depth while swimmers were locking out could result in enough of a rapid variation in pressure that the divers experienced a painful and potentially deadly embolism. The other absolute requirement was zero speed. A swimmer emerging from the hatch could easily be swept away and sent tumbling into the propulsor even if the submarine was only making a couple of knots. For these reasons, the whole lock-in/lock-out process was a carefully controlled and well-practiced evolution.

Jones, LaCroix, Martinelli, and Hurt crowded into the confined lock-out trunk and shut the hatch.

"Ready to flood the trunk, y'all." Chief Hurt's normally deep voice sounded tinny over the loudspeaker.

"Flood and equalize the trunk," Master Chief Cortez responded.

Hurt opened the flood valve and positioned himself so that his head was up behind the flood skirt. That would allow him to keep his head out of the water so that he could use the speaker, even when the trunk was "fully" flooded. The other three SEALs donned their rebreathers, sat in the bottom of the trunk, and started sucking oxygen. When the trunk was fully flooded, Hurt equalized the pressure around them with the outside sea pressure.

"Trunk is flooded and equalized," the voice blasted over the speaker.

The COB checked with the OOD in the control room to confirm that all the safety criteria were met. Then he ordered, "Swimmers, open the upper hatch and exit. Hurry back for breakfast."

The four SEALs emerged from the submarine and out into the night-darkened sea. Hurt grabbed the controls for the first DPD sled waiting there for them and oriented the navigation system. He felt a bump as Martinelli took hold of the passenger handles on the diver propulsion device. Next, he glanced back to confirm that Jones and LaCroix were ready to go. They were. He flipped the switch to turn on the DPD's power and headed east on a bearing that would take them directly to the *Guang Hua Kou*.

The water was pleasantly warm and the night was calm. To conserve both oxygen and battery power, the team cruised just below the surface. With the rebreathers, they did not even have to worry about leaving a bubble trail. At an efficient cruising speed of a knot and a half, the journey to the big Chinese cargo ship took almost two hours. Right on schedule, the jet-black wall of the vessel appeared ahead of them.

Before getting close enough to be seen from the ship's deck, the SEALs dove down and moved closer, reaching the point where they would be hidden under the ship's flat bottom. The two sleds rendezvoused there. Martinelli remained with the sleds. Hurt, Jones, and LaCroix grabbed their Russian limpet charges and swam upward. The explosives they were using were named for a sea snail they resembled, had a timed fuse, and could be attached to targets with their strong magnet. It took almost half an hour of swimming through, around, and under the confusing array of drill rig apparatus that had already been off-loaded before they finally found the submarine floating just above the keel blocks on the *Guang Hua Kou*'s main deck. The sub was staged for off-loading once the sun came up. They had arrived just in time to wreak havoc.

The SEALs found it a little disorienting to have a large ship's deck below them as they went about their business attacking the submarine above them. The steel below meant that they only had a narrow window to escape if they needed to.

Hurt swam aft and stuck his limpet charge as far as he could reach inside the propulsor shroud after setting the timer for two hours. LaCroix attached his mine under the sonar dome on the sub's bow. Jones placed his about midships on the keel.

The three SEALs rendezvoused and wormed their way back out of the labyrinth before dropping down to meet Martinelli. Then the four pointed their sleds back toward the *Gato* and the promised breakfast.

They had just cleared the mass of ships scurrying about on the surface above them when Hurt saw a red light on his control panel.

The sled's control system was hearing a high-frequency active swimmer-detection sonar, pinging at a much higher frequency than was audible for a human. Someone on the *Guang Hua Kou* had abruptly lit off their security system. There was no way to tell whether that meant the SEAL team had been detected or if someone had just turned it on for some other reason. But it did not matter then. The SEALs opened the throttles on their sleds wide and began a pattern of random dives and rises, doing their best to mimic porpoises at play. They knew the sonar could only reach out a thousand yards or so. They still had a couple of hundred yards to go before they would be out of range and safe from detection.

And they would continue doing their best porpoise impression the whole way.

Ψ

The security officer on the *Guang Hua Kou* just happened to look down and notice the diver security system had not been activated the previous evening when the day's work by maintenance divers had ended for the day. He cursed, promised himself someone would be reprimanded, and immediately turned it on. As it came to life, he noticed something. It could have been a fleeting glimpse of a possible contact, but he could not be sure. Just to be safe—and deciding it would be a good unannounced drill—he issued a call for a security swim.

To everyone's surprise, the divers quickly found and detached two limpet mines that Jones and LaCroix had planted, the one on the submarine's keel and the one under its sonar dome.

The *Guang Hua Kou* and the security boats went on full alert, furiously searching for the divers who had planted the two mines. However, the Second Regency had lost the only surface ship with an ASW sonar in the fight several weeks before with the Italian Navy. All the security boats could do was race around and churn up the calm waters.

The four SEALs were just locking back in onboard the *Gato* when the remaining limpet mine, the one that Chief Hurt had planted inside the Chinese sub's propulsor, detonated. The blast blew the propulsor completely off the submarine while jamming the shaft back into the vessel. The flooding around the damaged shaft was far greater than the submarine could handle.

If one of the Chinese training crew had not had the foresight to slam shut the door into the engine room, sealing off that compartment, Ali Hakim Sherif's newest prize, the *Khinjar Alnabii*, would have quickly sunk back down on the *Guang Hua Kou*'s main deck and rolled over on its side.

Even so, it would be many weeks before either ship could possibly be returned to service.

15

The roar rudely jolted Bill Langley awake. It was the sound of ten thousand jet engines revving up somewhere just outside the trailer where he was sleeping. The oil engineer rolled out of his bunk and stared out the window. A million stars twinkled in the desert night above and to the east. To the west, though, there was an ominous solid wall of blackness. Langley had spent years in the Western Egyptian desert. He immediately knew what he was seeing and hearing.

A full-blown major *haboob*, a desert sandstorm, was bearing down on them. If the Sahara Desert was the undisputed daddy of sandstorms, the Calanshio Sand Sea was the birth mother. Hurricane-strength winds were not uncommon at all in such broad cyclones. The wind-blown grit could sandblast the paint off any unprotected surface, blind anyone dumb enough to be outside with his face and eyes unprotected and fill his lungs full of powdery life-smothering sand.

If their Libyan captors had only allowed Langley access to his computer, satellite imagery would have given them plenty of warning, with time to get prepared, lash everything down, and duck. But this rude wakeup call had come much too late. Libyan Lieutenant Hamaqa Fakhoury, who had been left in charge of the well site and the hostages, would not allow any connections to the outside world. Certainly not to the internet. So now they were all waking up to a very nasty surprise, a major *haboob* bearing down on them at the speed of a locomotive and for which they had taken no preparatory precautions.

Langley shouted a warning to the others being held captive in the trailer, hoping his voice would be carried above the noise from the rising wind. He grabbed a pair of goggles from a drawer and wrapped a wet towel around his face to cover his mouth and nose before he rushed outside to try to get to the others. It was far too late to lower the drill derrick, but maybe there was time to shore it up enough to withstand the howling wind before the full force of the storm overcame them. Or secure loose objects that would soon become deadly projectiles.

Lieutenant Fakhoury met him as soon as he stepped outside. The annoyingly officious Bedouin military officer had been nothing but a pain in Langley's backside since he and his men took charge of the drill site. Even so, it had been easy to deal with his incessant demands to continue the exploratory drilling when he had no concept of the engineering involved. So far, Langley had taken advantage of the man's ignorance by simply drilling horizontally, mumbling to his head roustabout to explore "a thousand feet too soon and in the general direction of East Bejesus." The engineer figured there was almost zero chance of hitting anything but sand snakes and desert rat nests by boring that way. He was certainly not about to bring in a major oil find to enrich the regime that had so brutally taken him and his crew as prisoners. He knew, of course, that if they ever figured out what he was doing, he would pay dearly for sabotaging such a potentially lucrative project.

The worst for Langley, though, was how the officer and his squad were treating his crew. As far as Fakhoury was concerned, they were all infidels, and they were to be treated as slaves. The work was brutally hard, and the Libyans were unrelenting. Food was rationed out at only a survival level. Verbal and physical abuse were common if they even suspected the oil field workers were slacking off.

"Langley, what do we do now?" Fakhoury asked plaintively, his face revealing near panic. Langley was about to answer when the leading edge of the black wall of blowing sand swept across the drill site. Visibility immediately plunged to zero. Wind-blown debris became dangerous missiles. A piece of two-by-four lumber zipped past Langley, impaling itself into the wall of the trailer mere inches from his head.

He grabbed the hapless officer by the scruff of his neck and threw him through the door before diving inside himself and jamming the door shut behind him. The trailer had been tied down when it was brought in, just to secure it against the usual gusty winds out here, but now it shook and trembled, rocked back and forth, threatened to topple over and go flipping away as if kicked by the foot of some giant. Despite his many years working in the desert, Langley had never experienced a sandstorm this intense. But he knew that the bigger *haboobs* were also the most persistent and long-lived. This storm could last for days. There was no telling what emergency assistance they would need when things finally calmed down. And certainly no way to know if this trailer and the four others like it where the rest of the crew and the Libyan soldiers huddled—their only shelter—could possibly survive this beastly dry maelstrom.

Hamaqa Fakhoury—a city boy who had no experience in weather like this despite his long familial lineage of desert dwellers—curled up in a ball on the floor. Langley thought he might be sobbing. He shook the Bedouin leader.

"Lieutenant! Lieutenant!" he pleaded. "You got to get your act together and right damn now. Call back to your headquarters. Nothing they can do now but we're gonna need help when this thing blows over. If it hasn't carried what's left of us halfway to the Red Sea by then."

Just then his head roustabout burst into the trailer, tumbled to the floor, then required the help of Langley and several of their men to get the door closed again.

"Bill, we got ourselves some problems. The comms antennas just got carried away," he said and then swallowed hard. "And the blowout preventer just actuated. We hit oil!"

Langley did not know what to say. All he could come up with was, "Damn!"

Ψ

Ali Hakim Sherif—now known as Suleiman Jadid—stood at the

entrance of his *bayt al-shar*. A cool sea breeze wafted up from the Mediterranean carrying the faint smell of the sea overlaid with the sweet scent of almonds blooming on the plains below. He could see the anti-aircraft batteries and tanks surrounding the mountainous ridge top, high up in the Akhdar Mountains.

"Ali Hakim, if you must live in a tent, this is certainly the ideal place to put it," Li Chung Sheng ventured as he joined the Bedouin leader.

Ali Hakim smiled. "The tent provides a unifying image for my people. They see a leader who is truly one of them." He waved his hands expansively. "But it doesn't hurt to experience this image in comfort, surrounded by the natural beauty of this region."

The recently self-crowned leader moved over and plopped down on a pile of cushions. "Now, let me pour some tea to enjoy while we discuss some business." He reached for the *abriq alshaay* and filled two cups. He offered one to Li Chung before sipping from the other. Looking over the cup's rim, he offered, "The affair with the *Guang Hua Kou* heavy-lift ship and our new submarine, the *Khinjar Alnabii*, was most disturbing. My people are demanding revenge for the slight to our honor."

The Chinese diplomat sipped from his own cup before he answered. "Yes, most unfortunate. However, we were able to lift the submarine out of the water when we re-floated the *Guang Hua Kou*. My government has decided that the best course of action is to return both the lift ship and the damaged submarine to the Middle Kingdom for repairs. I am afraid that it will be a year or more before we can return your submarine to you."

Ali Hakim seemed to not have heard the dismal estimate. "We are sure the Americans are behind this attack?" Ali Hakim phrased the query as a question but stated it more as a fact.

Li Chung nodded. "We found Russian-made limpet mines that they used to throw us off. One of their submarines, the one that was in Gibraltar for repair, is missing and not accounted for. The evidence points to the Americans."

Ali Hakim took a sip of tea. "I agree. As I said, my people demand revenge. So do I. I have decided that since we lost a warship, the Americans must lose two. I am sending the *Sayf Alnabii* out with orders to sink the destroyer the Americans have lurking off the coast of Egypt. And then, at the successful execution of that mission, they are to search out and destroy the American submarine. We can and must demonstrate our ability and willingness to defend our empire."

Ψ

Rear Admiral Joe Glass carefully cleaned his reading glasses before taking a sip of coffee. Then he punched up the next message on his JWICS account. The Joint Worldwide Intelligence Communications System was the military's intranet for top secret and SCI—sensitive compartmented information—communications. A lot of email traffic on the system was unclassified administrative drivel—what users called "JWICS spam"—but Glass knew at once that this email warranted being sent via JWICS. The message had been passed through Glass's immediate bosses, Commander US Sixth Fleet and Commander Naval Forces Europe, and they added directions for him to take appropriate action. However, the message originated much higher up the food chain. The Secretary of Defense and the Joint Chiefs of Staff, with the President's approval, had a crucial mission for Joe Glass. It was dangerous, complicated, and required covert execution.

"Hey, Brian," Glass called across the command center. Captain Brian Edwards was studying his own monitor. "You need to see this. We got ourselves a job to do, and we need to get a move on. I'm forwarding it to you on JWICS."

Edwards read the message, read it again, and then whistled softly. "Damn! This is gonna be a ton of fun." He looked up at the digital clock hanging above the flat-panel monitors that covered the far wall. "And it's going to take some work to get all the pieces into place. Suggest we set up a conference call with all the likely players. *Gato* is busy clearing the area from that little SEAL action off Benghazi. She's not scheduled to communicate for another six hours while they hightail it out of there."

"Sounds about right," Glass answered, his face blank as he did calculations in his head. "Why don't you get your Ops Officer to start writing the OP ORDs and working out the water space management. I'm going to see if we can get Sixth Fleet to set up the coordination with the Egyptians. I figure they'll be more than willing to help."

It was well past midnight inside the Rock of Gibraltar when Brian Edwards was finally successful in getting some early plans in place and setting up the conference call with all the players.

"We have everyone?" Joe Glass asked as he started the meeting. "Chime in."

"*Gato* here, Admiral." Henrietta Foster's voice came over the speaker, as clear as if she were sitting there in the command center, sipping from her own monstrous coffee mug. "I have Commander Ward from the SEAL team here with me."

"*Stanton* up on the call," Jerry Baudsley chimed in from his quarters on the US Navy destroyer.

"Gentlemen, and lady," Glass said, officially opening the meeting. "I'll start by explaining the situation. Understand that this mission comes from the very top, White House tasking. Apparently, our friend Ali Hakim Sherif, who we hear is now calling himself Suleiman Jadid, sent a raid into western Egypt, well south of all the fighting that is making the news of late. Anyway, this raid took a bunch of American citizens as hostages. They were a part of some kind of oil exploratory outfit that was working under an Egyptian contract. Intel shows that they are being held prisoner at their camp. It's located down there in a region they call the Calanshio Sand Sea."

"Sand sea, huh? That sounds like a real garden spot," Jim Ward interjected. "Something with a name like that ain't likely to be a Club Med vacation."

Glass chuckled. "Jim, if it was a tropical vacation spot, we wouldn't be sending in you and your little band of pirates to kick ass and take names, now would we?"

"Admiral, you have a point," Ward answered ruefully. "Guess you got all those picture postcards I've been sending after all."

"Anyway, someone very high up in the administration wants these people back and you guys drew the short straw. But don't you get the big head. You're about all we got in the neighborhood right now. Busy time for everybody, I guess. Your job is to go in and get them. Their camp is something over four hundred miles from the beach, so the logistics are going to be a little complicated. Commodore Edwards is going to tell you how we think this is going to lay down."

"Good morning, everybody," Edwards started out. "The distances are long, for certain, but that's not the only problem. It looks like the Libyans have set up a pretty effective air defense system already. You don't buy this stuff at the military surplus store. Their Chinese buddies have supplied them with several HQ-22 air defense systems, and it looks like the Calanshio Sand Sea site is under their umbrella. Don't ask why they took hostages and set up sophisticated air cover to protect a trillion acres of sand, but they did. And there's probably a reason. But back to that distance thing. Since surprise is key to this operation, aerial insertion is not a good option."

"We talkin' Avis Camel Rental?" Jim Ward asked. "That's a long hike even for supermen like me and my frogs."

"Not quite," Edwards responded. "We're arranging a rendezvous and PERSTRANS for you and your team from the *Gato* to the *Stanton* tomorrow night. Hen, Jerry, the coordinates for the rendezvous are being forwarded to you as we speak, and the math should work if you both hustle."

"Check," was the confirmation from Henrietta Foster.

"Got it," Baudsley said.

"Jerry, as soon as the SEALs are aboard your vessel, we need for you to hightail it east. The moment the Abu Suweir Air Base in Alexandria is within range of your bird, get it in the air and ferry the team over there."

"Roger that."

"Jim, leave all your gear on the *Gato*," Edwards continued. "We're staging everything for you out of Abu Suweir. We'll even have a change of underwear waiting for you. We also hope to have a bit more detail on what you'll be running into down there. The Egyptians will be loaded and ready and will fly you down to a little outpost called Abu Minqar. It's two hundred and fifty klicks from there to your objective, and since we're in a hell of a hurry and air temp is well above a hundred, you'll be going cross country on a couple of ALSVs. Those dune buggies will be just what you need for this jaunt. And a hell of a lot of fun to operate, I might add. We're working on staging a pair of MV-22 Ospreys for your exfil. That gives enough space to bring out the anticipated number of hostages plus you guys. Any questions?"

"Who do we call when the shit hits the fan and we need support?" Jim Ward asked. "Both of which will happen for damn sure."

"If you need ordnance on targets, *Gato* and *Stanton* will both be standing by ready to light the fuse on their Tomahawk inventories," Edwards answered. "And we will have a Reaper flying out of Djibouti. Those drones carry heavy ordnance nowadays and could be helpful if the guys with the joysticks can keep it clear of the HQ-22s. But we have no Air Force assets in range. And we don't know yet if the Egyptians are up for another tussle with the Chinese dart-throwers. They got hurt pretty bad last time."

"If you really want to put the hurt on somebody in a hurry, I have four tubes loaded with Conventional Prompt Strike Missiles," Foster offered up. "At something better than Mach 7, the CPS is a real quick way to give bad guys a throbbing headache. Just send us the coordinates and we'll deliver, hot and fresh."

"Now, that sounds promising," Ward replied. "With what little we know, that's my biggest concern right now. They got to figure somebody's gonna try to get those hostages back. But, hey, I'm sure more factors will come up as we plan this in more detail."

Glass waited for a few seconds, then he said, "If there are no more questions, that will conclude this call. Each of you, get with your team and look at your part in this operation. Any big rocks in our way, let us know quickly so we can look like we know what we're doing. First step is tomorrow night."

Ψ

Room 180 in the Old Executive Office Building, across the street from the White House, had once been President Richard Nixon's hideaway office. It was a place he felt he could go to when he needed to be alone to think. The spot had the added benefit of being well away from the prying eyes of the press, who kept close tabs on the comings and goings of the Oval Office. President Sandra Dosetti saw some usefulness in Nixon's idea and appropriated the ornate Victorian room for the same purpose as he did.

Vice President Sebastien Aldo sat in his usual place at the right side of the gold brocade settee. Dosetti had chosen the matching wing chair across the coffee table from him. She carefully placed her cup on the table and, in her usual direct way, started the discussion.

"Seb, we need to strategize what we're going to do about Cyril Brown."

Aldo leaned forward and quietly responded, "I never trusted that SOB. You ever watch his face when he talks? I swear he never blinks his eyes. Almost reptilian. And I hate reptiles."

Dosetti chuckled. "They say the eyes are the windows to a person's soul. His case, you are looking into a cold, dark, void. The man so much as admitted to me...no, 'gloated' would be a better word...that he had Smitherman murdered and was planning the same for Osterman. Then he threatened us with exposure if we didn't play his game, whatever it is."

Sebastien snorted. "Remember the immortal words of that slimy New York Senator a few years ago? 'Don't mess with the CIA. They can screw you six ways to Sunday.' You know we need to be real careful here, Madam President."

"True," Dosetti answered. "But why does that snake choose to raise his head right now, when we have so much else on our plate? We finally got a budget passed, even if we did have to play dirty pool with the opposition. Then the Chinese are doing even more than the usual sword rattling over Taiwan. And, to top it off, that crazy land pirate in Libya thinks he can recreate the Ottoman Empire the old-fashioned way, marching in, killing people, and staking his claim, and he has the help of our friends in Beijing to try to pull it off."

"Has Brown given you any idea of what he wants?" the VP asked.

"Not yet, but you can bet it won't be cheap," Dosetti answered. "He'll probably want both our souls and our firstborn but he'll happily settle for some extremely valuable political capital. To him, power is worth far more than money. He'll leverage this over us for some significant position. He'll wait for just the right time to reveal his demands; right for him, that is. The question is what do we do in the meantime? Until we find out what his game is, I don't like this 'waiting for the other shoe to submit to gravity' stuff."

"There isn't much we can do except wait and watch," Sebastien answered. "We play along until we don't. Hell, he might even be useful at some point. Do you think he'd ever reveal what he knows about the untimely health issues of the previous POTUS and veep? His hands are dirty there. Can we deal with him?" He took a sip of his now cold coffee and made a wry face. "We gotta assume he's not playing alone, and we have no idea who is really involved. Or who our friends are over in the intel field. Or even if we have any. Last thing we need is to—"

Dosetti raised her hand for Sebastien to stop rambling. "We do have one friend in the intel world that we can trust. Remember that Admiral who turned us on to Smitherman's dealings with the Chinese? Admiral Ward. He's not a part of the more nefarious underbelly of the spy world but he might be useful. I'll call him to the White House for a meeting. But this all may take some time. What do we do if Brown decides that Osterman should suddenly have his stroke?"

"Issue a news release and send flowers," Sebastien answered. "As to Osterman meeting an untimely end because of the CIA Director's terrible timing? *C'est la guerre.*"

President Dosetti whispered, "Yes, *c'est la guerre.*"

16

Captain Jerry Baudsley stood on the port bridge wing of his US Navy destroyer, scanning the quiet, empty Mediterranean Sea. The *Harold A. Stanton* seemingly had the whole swimming pool all to herself. From horizon to horizon, nothing else interrupted the calm waters.

He put down his 7x50 binoculars and yelled through the open bridge door, "Officer of the Deck, call down to CIC and see if they have contact. We're at the right rendezvous position. That damn submarine has to be somewhere close by."

"Captain, CIC reports no sonar contacts," Steve Johnson replied.

"Typical submarine maneuver," Baudsley growled. "They're going to sneak in and pop up fifteen hundred yards off our beam. Probably launch a flare first, just for giggles. Call down to CIC and tell the TAO that they'd better find that SOB first or they're going to draw duty days in every liberty port for the rest of this run."

Johnson grabbed the phone and was speaking with the Tactical Action Officer in the combat information center when the starboard lookout hollered, "Green flare! Two thousand yards off the starboard beam."

Jerry Baudsley angerly threw his ball cap down onto the deck and stomped it. "Damn! What did I tell you!"

Just then the bridge speaker blared, "Bridge, sonar. Passive contact on the MFTA and the SQS-53C. Best bearing three-five-four. Range estimate two-seven hundred yards."

"Bridge, CIC. New radar contact on the SPQ-9. Bearing three-five-two, range two-nine hundred yards. Possible submarine periscope."

Steve Johnson sheepishly reported, "Captain, TAO reports they have contact on a confirmed sub. And it's one of ours."

Baudsley replied caustically, "Well, tell them that is real helpful. If he had been shooting ordnance instead of a flare, we could track him together from our life raft."

The starboard lookout yelled, "Surfacing submarine off the starboard beam." He pointed out to where the *Gato*'s sail was just breaking the surface, a black hulk abruptly knifing through the sea in a spray of white foam where only a few seconds before there had been nothing but placid blue water. The submarine rose higher and higher out of the water as it steered a course parallel to the destroyer.

Suddenly the bridge secure radio speaker squawked, "Alpha Lima Six, this is Quebec Three Charlie, how copy? Over."

Baudsley grabbed the red handset and answered, "Quebec Three Charlie, this is Alpha Lima Six actual. Copy you five by. Nice entrance, Hen. Over."

"Jerry, I thought we'd get in a little covert attack practice while we were at it." Henrietta Foster's voice was distorted a bit by the encryption system, but the chuckle came through plainly. "So how did we do?"

"Impressive, but we detected your flare launch," Baudsley answered grudgingly. "Suggest slowing to four knots and conducting this transfer. I'm launching my RHIB now."

"Roger. Slowing to four knots. Sending personnel topside."

Baudsley glanced over at the *Gato*, still steaming on a course parallel to the *Stanton* and at about a thousand yards off the beam. Someone waved from the bridge of the submarine. Baudsley waved back. Then he could see a hatch swing upward on the submarine's main deck and people emerging from inside the huge black tube.

"Ready for PERSTRAN," the radio crackled. "Seven PAXs and luggage to move."

The *Stanton*'s seven-meter RHIB—rigid-hull inflatable boat—pulled alongside the submarine. Several parcels were passed over to it and then seven men hopped on board the little boat. Even as the RHIB pulled away, the men topside on the sub were already dropping down the hatch and swinging it shut behind them.

The radio crackled again. "Transfer complete. Departing on mission."

Baudsley replied, "Roger. Good hunting."

By the time the RHIB was back alongside the *Stanton*, the *Gato* had once more disappeared beneath the waves.

"Officer-of-the-Deck, I'm going down to the helo deck to greet our guests. Set flight quarters and come into the wind," Baudsley directed as he headed off the bridge.

He was on his way down the passageway when the bosun's whistle tweeted and the 1MC announced, "Now, flight quarters, flight quarters. All hands, man your flight quarters. All personnel stand clear of the flight deck."

The recent arrivals would not be spending much time on the *Stanton*. The big Sikorsky MH-60R out on the destroyer's flight deck was already spooling up, preparing to depart, when Baudsley entered the hangar deck. Seven men dressed in desert camo stood apart from the destroyer crewmembers who were bustling to get the bird ready to fly. Baudsley hurried over to where they stood.

"Commander Ward?" He had to shout to be heard above the helicopter's screaming turbine engine.

One of the men stepped away from the group and answered, "Yes, sir."

"Commander, wish we had time to extend some surface Navy hospitality but we're already in range to Abu Suweir Air Base in Alexandria. We'll have you airborne and on your way as soon as we can get you aboard and your gear stowed. The Egyptians are standing by to get you down to Abu Minqar. They're reporting a major sandstorm, something they call a *haboob*, covering the Calanshio Sand Sea. Satellite imagery confirms. No way of knowing how long it will last."

Ward nodded. "May hold us up. May be useful for cover. I guess we'll see when we get there. Thanks for the lift." The SEAL commander grabbed his rucksack. "Captain, we do appreciate your ever so brief hospitality."

Ward saluted, spun and trotted out onto the flight deck and into the ready bird. With even more noise, the MH-60R lifted off and flew away to the south, toward the Egyptian coast.

Ψ

Although the clock showed a little past noon, the precious little sunlight that managed to filter through to the oil field trailer had a decided dull gray-red hue. Bill Langley tried to look out the window to see if he could discern any let-up in the storm, but the glass had been sandblasted to the point of being barely translucent. The wind had been howling unabated for almost four days now. Langley had suffered through his share of such storms in his many years in the desert but never experienced a *haboob* that lasted anywhere near this long. He had not even heard of one like the vicious cyclone howling without pause on the other side of the shelter's thin metal walls. There was no way to know how much more of this they would have to endure. Or how long the simple structure could withstand the force of the wind and sand.

It had also been four days and nights they remained trapped in this trailer with Lieutenant Hamaqa Fakhoury. The overbearing Libyan officer had recovered from his initial panic as the storm first swooped down upon them and resumed his tyrannical approach.

The first couple of days, the young Bedouin officer had tried to keep the crew at work, drilling for oil. The men, threatened at gunpoint to continue, tried as best they could. Inevitably, Mother Nature won out. Fingers and toes were crushed and bodies were badly bruised as they tried to move drill pipe and set equipment. Grit solidly clogged air filters. Pumps seized when sand infiltrated the lubrication. Crucial apparatus was buried beneath wind-driven dunes. Finally, they lost electrical power when the last diesel generator failed. Someone had calculated that the typical Saharan sandstorms moved more than five hundred million tons of dust per year. This one was not typical, and it seemed to Langley and his crew that a great proportion of that annual total had now been dumped directly on top of them in less than a week.

After the second day, the sand was piled so high that Langley was no longer able to open the trailer door to take a peek outside. They were truly trapped. But at least all that weight would keep them from getting blown away. There was nothing to do but wait for the storm to abate and then figure out how to get out of what amounted to a thin metal coffin.

Langley sat down with a couple of his foremen who had ended up in this particular shelter and spoke with the others via radio to take stock of their situation. Between this and each of the other surviving trailers, there was plenty of food. Even accounting for the appetites of their captors. The water tanks, thankfully, had recently been topped off and were nearly full. They had been taking it easy with their walkie-talkies and most still had about half of a full battery charge. He calculated that they would be fine for a few more days.

Surely, by then, the *haboob* would blow itself out. And maybe somebody would be coming to rescue them, both from the effects of this monstrous storm and from the radical bastards who had kidnapped them at gunpoint.

Surely.

Ψ

After transferring Jim Ward and his SEAL team to the *Stanton*, Commander Henrietta Foster pointed the bow of the *Gato* west. There was a job to be done back there. Someone needed to get in close and personal with Benghazi to keep tabs on those Libyan/Chinese submarines. Those vessels were not stealthily hauled halfway around the world as tourist attractions or for fishing. *Gato* would be the one to watch and try to determine what they were really up to.

The Second Regency honchos were probably still miffed about what had happened to their newest undersea toy. They had also probably figured out that the not-so-subtle message had been delivered by a submarine and underwater demolition team. Foster anticipated that the Libyans would not hesitate to throw ordnance at anything that even appeared to be a submarine swimming around in their newly declared territorial waters. But she also knew that the Libyan Navy was still very limited in warships, crew, and training so they would not be able to do much. Those two remaining Chinese *Yuan* submarines were the only credible naval threats that the Libyans could launch. As long as she was reasonably careful, she calculated that the *Gato* would be safe while still watching for either of the two remaining submarines to come out and play.

The COB, Jesus Cortez, and the XO, Eric Householder, joined Foster in her stateroom. "XO, COB," Foster began, "we should be back on station off Benghazi on the evening watch tomorrow. I want *Gato* to be ready when we get there. COB, get the Chiefs to do a complete damage control equipment inventory and checkout. I want everything tuned, primed, and working. XO, have sonar do a complete sound-silencing checkout. I want this boat so quiet that fish bump into her. Tell Weps to fully wring out both the torpedo and missile fire control systems. When I want to put the hurt on someone, I want to know the systems work."

"You think we're going to see action, then?" Cortez asked.

"Let's just say I ain't taking any chances," Foster answered.

"What about the SEALs' little trip?" Householder chimed in. "I thought we were supposed to stand by to launch Tomahawks if they called for help."

"True," Foster responded. "But those guys won't be heading in until tomorrow night at the earliest. If we launch somewhere off Benghazi, we will be sending our birds across Libya and that puts them behind those new Chinese HQ-22 missile batteries. They'll have a whole lot better chance to make it in the back door than if they were tootling along right out there in front of those launchers." Foster looked hard at the two submariners. "XO, COB, I want to man battle stations tomorrow at noon, before we round the headland and make our way down into the Gulf of Sidra. I expect we will stay at battle stations until we've sanitized our op area. That could take a while. So, make sure everyone, including you two, gets a good night's rest tonight. It could be a while before any of us get to hug our teddy bears again."

Ψ

The sand-brown Egyptian Air Force CH-47 flew low across a stretch of desert terrain that exactly matched the bird's paint job. When Commander Jim Ward looked out the port at the other two Chinook helicopters flying in formation with the one on which he rode, he noted just how good the camouflage was. From above, the helicopters simply disappeared against the landscape. That, however, was about the only good part of this flight. The howling T-55-715 twin turbines were giving him a roaring headache while they threatened to vibrate the old warbird right out of the sky.

"Commander Ward, Abu Minqar is reporting that they are socked in." The pilot's heavily accented English was just understandable on the intra-plane communications system headset. "We are directed to set you down near the town of Farafar. It is seventy kilometers northeast of Abu Minqar. My apologies for not being able to get you closer."

Ward glanced back at the Advanced Light Strike Vehicle strapped down in the Chinook's cargo bay. With its fuel bladders topped off, the four-wheel-drive dune buggy had a thousand-mile range. An extra seventy kilometers might add an hour to the mission. No big deal.

The major problem was the wall of dust that stretched from the ground up to several thousand feet, totally blotting out the western horizon. It was no complication for them yet but they faced more than two hundred miles of cross-country driving in pretty much zero visibility through a trackless wilderness of sand and rock. To top it off, that wilderness was claimed by the Second Regency, and those guys had already shown they were willing to shoot trespassers on sight. Then, once the SEAL team reached their sand-blasted destination, all they had to do was rescue a bunch of hostages from an unknown number of bad guys and then figure out how to get everybody back to civilization.

The SEAL motto was never truer. "The only easy day was yesterday."

Ward had long since decided there were too many complications—known and unknown—involved with this mission for him to be comfort-able. But being uncomfortable was not supposed to be a deterrent to a Navy SEAL.

The three big helicopters settled down in their own cloud of dust kicked up by their massive twin rotors, foreshadowing the conditions they would soon experience compliments of Mother Nature. They were a kilometer south of town and a hundred meters from the Al Farafa-Al Wahat highway, the only reliable auto route through this part of the country. The two-lane paved track wound its way down to Abu Minqar and then eventually to the nation of

Somalia six hundred kilometers to the south. But Ward and his team had no interest in the not-so-scenic drive to the Somali border. It was the Libyan boundary that drew their attention, and it was three hundred kilometers to the west. Or just a little less now that the Second Regency was redrawing the maps.

The SEALs made quick work of offloading the three ALSVs from the Chinooks, stowing their weapons and stores on the sleek-looking sand rail vehicles, firing up the 160-horsepower Porsche diesel engines, zeroing the GPS navigation systems, and then racing off across the sand toward the distant hazy, tan horizon. Although the vehicles could easily hit eighty miles an hour on the highway, the SEALs quickly figured out that twenty was about as fast as they could go across the rough, open ground. Even at that speed, it was a bone-jarring, teeth-rattling, ass-bruising ride.

Three hours in, Ward called a halt. It was an opportunity for a head break and for everyone to stretch his legs, walk around for a bit, and grab some chow. It was also a good time to check over the ALSVs and move some fuel from the bladders to top off the vehicles' tanks.

Jim Ward was sitting against the tire of his "dune buggy," sheltering from the wind and snacking on a First Strike Ration pack while booting up his Toughbook laptop when Billy Joe Hurt found him.

"Hey, Skipper," the SEAL Chief said as he squatted down beside Ward. "Dibs on the peanut butter bar."

Ward tossed him the dessert ration. "Here you go, Chief." He grinned as he added, "But don't you dare ask for my Zapplesauce."

Ward moved the laptop so that Hurt could see the screen.

"No new intel," Ward said, "and nothing new on our mission. Satellite imagery is still showing nothing but blowing sand."

"This ain't normal," Hurt stated. "From what I've heard, these *haboobs*, even the really big ones, rarely last more than a day or two. We're looking at almost a week now this thing's been blowing."

"Yeah," Ward agreed as he shook his head. "We got to get ourselves a new travel agent for sure. All this dust makes the drive a lot of fun. Near as I can calculate, we have another seven hours to go at this pace. That'll get us to this drill rig about midnight tonight."

"Any word on extraction yet?" Hurt asked. He pointed at the three passenger ALSVs and added, "Ain't no way we're bringing a bunch of oil field roughnecks out on these rattle traps."

"Still planning on AFSOC coming through with a CV-22," Ward answered, "but that's not confirmed yet."

"Those blue-suiters better get a move on," Hurt harumphed. "We're already halfway into this op and we still need a way out. I sure ain't planning on some Lawerence of Arabia stuff and riding out on a camel."

Ward was still chuckling at the mental image when Tony Martinelli walked up. "Hey, boss, we got a problem. The fuel bladders are contaminated. We got enough good fuel for maybe another 250 klicks."

"You sure about that, T?" Hurt asked.

"Yep, Chief," Martinelli shot back. "Had Jones test it too, just to double-check. Looks like someone doctored the fuel the Egyptians gave us."

"Makes you wonder what else they may have doctored, and how they knew about our missions in the first place," Ward said. He checked the map. "But damn glad you guys caught it. That gives us a fifty-kilometer buffer to get to the well site. We either scavenge for fuel there or we get a camel for the Chief if the Air Force doesn't come through. Let's get those bladders off-loaded. No sense hauling them around anymore if the gas is hinky. I'll send a message back to the Admiral telling him of our little problem and see if they have assets to try to figure out if this is just random mischief or somebody knows what we're up to and wants to leave us stranded out here. Then we need to get a move on. Midnight arrival will only give us a couple of hours to scout around before we hit them at first light."

"What you reckon the odds really are that they know we're attempting an extraction?" Hurt asked.

"Doesn't matter," Ward answered. "We got to assume they'll be all ready to give us a nice, warm welcome to the world's biggest sand trap."

Ψ

Lahal Nihad Rifat al Subay sat in his stateroom reading and rereading the orders that had just been delivered by courier to his submarine, the *Sayf Alnabii*. They were quite clear. He and his crew were to get underway immediately. They would then systematically search all of the waters claimed as part of the Second Regency looking for an intruding submarine. And should they find such, they were to destroy it. But first they were to sink the American destroyer patrolling east of Sidi Barrani. The missive was signed by Suleiman Jadid himself.

Lahal Nihad smiled as he folded the orders. His country's new leader, the strongman anointed by Allah specifically to restore his homeland to its rightful destiny, was personally sending him on a mission to defend the *albalad alam*, the homeland. It was, at the same time, a great honor and a hero's path to immortality. All he needed to do was to complete this mission successfully. With this remarkable and stealthy new vessel, with the destructive power it held, and with a dedicated crew well on its way to becoming proficient in its operation, he was confident he could do just that.

Wu Ming Jie, the leading Chinese advisor on board the *Sayf Alnabii*, stepped into Lahal Nihad's tiny stateroom without knocking. "I see that our mission orders have arrived," he said as he plopped down on the only other seat in the room. Without invitation. "Ambassador Li Chung advised me that they were on the way."

He reached for the folded orders. "May I?" It was not a request.

Lahal reluctantly passed the paper to the Chinese submariner, then steeled himself for the usual negativity. The old man would probably go into a very long and involved discussion of all the reasons why Lahal Nihad and his crew were not ready or capable of completing this or any other mission. Lahal Nihad was aware that Wu Ming had a very low regard for the seamanship and learning abilities of the *Sayf Alnabii*'s crew.

Wu Ming glanced at the sheet of paper and nodded. "Yes, this is just as I expected. Intelligence has confirmed that the sabotage of the *Khinjar Alnabii* was an attack by swimmers attaching and detonating limpet mines against the submarine. Our divers found several of the devices before they detonated. But, unfortunately, not all of them. The mines that were discovered were marked as Russian-made. Someone was cleverly trying to point a finger of blame at our Russian friends. We suspect that a submarine delivered the divers, either an American SEAL team or a British SAS team, so they could carry out this sneak attack."

Lahal nodded and announced, "Exactly. This is the scenario that I have already suggested to my superiors. And it will be our duty to go to sea and avenge this dastardly sneak attack on our country. We will blast this submarine from the sea."

Wu Ming shook his head, a slight smile on his lips. In the same tone he might have used to chide a small child, the Chinese advisor said, "Lahal Nahid, my impetuous friend, I am afraid that you are about to find that hunting an American or British submarine is very different from shooting a hapless, unsuspecting, and mostly defenseless Italian frigate. This time, your target can and will shoot back. Maybe even shoot you before you are aware he has detected your presence."

The Chinese officer slowly rose, stretched, and stepped toward the door. He turned and said, "Captain, I suggest that we get this submarine out to sea first thing in the morning. We will not find the enemy and the glory you seek while you remain tied to the pier. Instead, your vessel could well be next to be sabotaged while you sit here scheming, threatening glorious vengeance."

17

It was just past midnight local time when Jim Ward brought his little dune buggy convoy to a halt. GPS said that the drill site seized by the Libyans should be straight ahead and over the next ridge. He climbed out from beneath the steering wheel and stretched mightily, relieved the long, bumpy ride was over. Now, the fun part. It was time to send out his scouts to see for sure what awaited them just over the stone escarpment. It was worrisome that they knew so little about what they were about to wade into, how many hostage takers there might be, what type of defensive weapons they may have brought in, any escape vehicles or aircraft that could be standing by. Normally, they would have planned the mission based on detailed satellite images of their objective, but the sandstorm had made that impossible. The only pictures they had were pre-assault. All they showed were tough men, sweating as they labored away in the new oil field.

Meanwhile, Ward needed to call home to see if there was an update on the status of their ride out of this place, their "exfiltration." Thankfully, the *haboob* that had been blowing sand in their faces for their entire journey had died down considerably. Ward still could not see the stars overhead, but the swirling dust had settled just enough that he could discern the ridgeline a couple of hundred yards in front of them. His men should have a good view into their objective if they found a proper overlook. But there was no way to know if there were bad guy lookouts posted on that high ground. If they had been spotted already. If they were seconds away from being ambushed.

"Dumkowski, you and Jones circle around to the north," Chief Billy Joe Hurt directed. "Hike up to the high spot on that ridge to the north. Find someplace where you can look down on the camp. As you know, the likely spots are marked on your map if this little dust-up didn't blow 'em away. Let me know what you see." Hurt looked at his watch. "Sunrise is at 0300Z. I want to start the fireworks and give 'em a wake-up call at 0215Z. So, you got four hours to get in position and make yourselves comfy. And remember, make sure you don't shoot into the trailers. That's got to be where they're holding the hostages. Any questions?"

The SEAL team members had heard it all before. Multiple times. Joe Dumkowski nodded. "You got it, Chief." He grabbed his Mk 17 SCAR-H assault rifle and night vision goggles. "One thing. You didn't say if you wanted Jonsey to take his sniper rifle."

"Lord a-mighty, Dumkowski, do I have to tell you when to take a dump, too?" Hurt growled. "Of course I want you two to lug that cannon up there. If we're lucky, you can shoot a bunch of bad guys while you're sittin' up there on your asses. And that fine example of military hardware sure as hell ain't gonna be much use if you leave it down here in the back seat, now is it?"

Chuck Jones pulled the M107 Barrett .50 caliber sniper rifle from the cargo area of his ALSV. With a night vision scope, bipod, and a box of ammo, the weapon weighed almost fifty pounds. Carrying it up the ridge would be a chore. Dumkowski grabbed the spotter scope and several extra boxes of .50 caliber ammo and the pair started the trudge up the hill, wading through loose, wind-blown sand.

Hurt turned to Tony Martinelli and Gene LaCroix. "Okay, I want you two frogs to skirt around the camp the other way. Same thing I told Dumkowski and Jones, find someplace where you can look down on the site and see what and who you can see. Let everybody know what you observe. Remember what I said about not shooting into the trailers. Fireworks start at 0215Z unless what you guys see tells us we shouldn't. Now get movin'. That sand's gonna make for slow going."

Jim Ward sat down next to his ALSV, leaned back against a big rear tire, and opened his laptop. In a few keystrokes, he had synched with the comms satellite. It took mere seconds before he was texting with Joe Glass back in the HMCC, buried beneath the Rock of Gibraltar. Ward shook his head as he watched Glass's words scroll out on the screen. No surprise that his boss and team were on the job, assisting Ward and his team even in the middle of the night. But the technology was still impressive. Here he was, in a desolate wilderness over two hundred miles from the nearest civilization, but he was texting in real time with his boss who was in a cave more than two thousand miles away.

"In position, one mile from drill site. Opposition unalerted," Ward typed. "COMEX rescue planned for 0215Z. What is status of exfil?"

A few seconds after Ward hit Send, a window popped up. "Acknowledge arrival. AFSOC holding exfil by CV-22 until HQ-22 threat neutralized. Working problem. Request you hold in place until exfil resolved."

Ward stared at the screen for a few seconds. He understood perfectly what Joe Glass was telling him. The Air Force would not be coming to get them and risk their nice little Osprey aircraft until the Chinese missiles had been taken out.

Ward ran the list of alternatives in his head. It was a short one. There was no way he could carry everyone back to safety using his dune buggies. One consideration was the possibility of finding enough trucks or other work vehicles down at the camp to evacuate everyone. That just might work. He had a quick mental image of them using the ALSVs to lead a parade of vehicles across the desert, like a scene from a *Mad Max* movie. But they would hardly be out of danger using that method either. The trek would take several days, and the Libyans would certainly want to prevent them from getting away and sharing their tales of woe with the world. And the Second Regency obviously had Chinese warplanes and lots of loyal tribal warriors in the region to see that did not happen.

In the meantime, what Ward knew for sure was that he had the element of surprise on his side. If they executed the rescue as planned, if their estimate of the expected resistance was accurate, and if they could quickly escape the oil field with all hostages, prisoners, and his team, the mission had a very good chance of succeeding. If they sat around on their butts and waited for however long it took for this missile threat to be eliminated before they even launched the hostage rescue, failure was a much higher probability.

Ward started typing. "Proceeding with rescue as planned. Discuss exfil after rescue successfully completed. Ward out." Then he sat back against the tire and waited for Glass to give him a "no go." There was none. Just an acknowledgment, a wish for good luck, and an "out." That was another reason it was so good to work with Admiral Glass. He instinctively knew what Ward and his SEALs were up against.

Ward folded up the laptop and stowed it in the ALSV. Billy Joe Hurt had been reading over Ward's shoulder. He murmured, "Okay, then. Now what?"

"Well, Chief, like I told the boss, we take out the bad guys, control the situation, and then we see what we do next. Remember, indecision is the key to flexibility," he answered with a dry chuckle. "And if it was easy, they would've sent somebody else. Let's get these buggies up near the ridge. I want to slip them in as close to the drill site as we can before anyone notices we're out here."

Ward, Hurt, and Jason Hall inched the ALSVs quietly up to just below the ridge top. Ward and Hurt then slithered up to where they could look down on the encampment below. It was a very quiet predawn scene. Ward had to search the camp for several minutes before he finally spotted some sentries. And all three were soundly asleep at their posts.

Hurt chuckled and shook his head. "Now, that's something. We may have to wake up the guards just to take them prisoner."

"Don't get overconfident on me, Chief," Ward counseled. "I'm more worried about the shooters. We have no clue how many they have or how well they're armed or just how vigorously they'll be willing to fight to keep their hostages, but we know they got them. I'm guessing a dozen but could be a bunch more. And we have to assume they're well armed and just as well trained."

Ward's intra-squad radio crackled. "Skipper, Dumkowski. We're in place. Not seeing any activity."

"Skipper, Martinelli, ditto. In place, no activity. We're ready whenever you are."

"You guys seeing the same three guards we're seeing?"

"Roger. Three sleeping beauties."

"Affirmative. Looks like they got Chinese Type 95 Bullpup assault rifles, but none of the three has his weapon close or at the ready."

Ward asked, "Jonesy, you got your Barrett ready and all your calculations done?"

"You betcha, sir. For shots on all three."

"Okay, so they apparently have no clue we're dropping in for breakfast," Ward responded. He checked his watch and noted the time. "Cover us. We're heading in."

Ward jumped behind the wheel on the ALSV while Jason Hall slipped into the gunner's position. He charged a round into the .50 caliber M2A1 heavy machine gun and gave Ward a thumbs-up. They slowly eased over the ridgeline and headed down toward the cluster of buildings. Chief Hurt jumped into the second ALSV and pulled right in line behind Ward, following him over the top.

Then both SEALs pushed hard on their accelerator pedals and charged down the slope toward the camp, no longer concerned about noise. It would probably serve as an asset, maybe causing the bad guys to panic.

Joe Dumkowski, watching through his spotter scope, saw one of the guards jump to life, startled, and try to locate his assault rifle. Chuck Jones's M107 roared once. The guard's head exploded. At a little over 1500 yards, the man never had the chance to shoulder his rifle and get off a shot in the direction of the ALSVs. Jones swung over to the second guard, who had jumped to his feet, mouth and eyes wide. He was reaching for his weapon when Jones sent another .50 caliber round downrange.

The sentry was blown backward, hard. Two guards down.

Gene LaCroix, who had slithered along in the sand to within five hundred yards of the main part of the compound, took out the third guard with his SCAR-H assault rifle. Again, it took only one bullet.

The whole compound suddenly came awake. Lights flashed on. Trailer doors, recently shoveled free of blocking sand, slammed open. Men poured out, barely awake, struggling to get their shoes on while working their weapons. Tony Martinelli and Joe Dumkowski added to the fire from

LaCroix and Jones. The emerging soldiers dived for cover, but they left behind several inert lumps that now littered the ground.

Chief Hurt pulled up fifty yards short of the compound. He moved smoothly and in one motion from the driver's seat to the gunner's. His .50 caliber M2A1, aimed at the cowering Libyans, only added to the din and confusion. Several of the guards tried to hide by diving behind a large pile of drill casing. The M8 armor-piercing rounds had no trouble powering through the material and finding vulnerable human flesh on the other side.

Ward boldly drove right on into the center of the camp as Hall swung his machine gun around, blasting anything that moved but making sure not to fire anywhere near any of the portable buildings.

The fight was over in a few moments. A white flag was fluttering weakly out a trailer window.

"Come out slow!" Ward ordered. "Show me your hands!" He used English, but in a tone that left little doubt what he was saying.

A man in a dusty, dirty uniform, walked out slowly, still holding high the white flag—a bath towel—with his hands above his head.

"Do not shoot. We surrender," the officer pleaded, also obligingly using English.

Ward jumped out of the ALSV, looked at Hall, and said, "Cover me." Then he walked deliberately toward where the Libyan stood, knees shaking. The SEAL commander's rifle was constantly trained on the officer.

"Tell your men to drop their arms and muster out here," Ward directed, loud enough to be heard throughout the compound. "All of them. They stay peaceful, and you live." He circled the man slowly, then shouted, "Hostages! Stay where you are! We're here to rescue you!"

It took a few minutes before fifteen Libyan fighters were clustered in the open area in front of the tool shed. Jason Hall was busy checking for concealed weapons and binding their hands with zip ties while Billie Ray Hurt covered him with his heavy machine gun.

In the meantime, Jim Ward found Bill Langley and his roughnecks hunkered down inside one of the trailers. With Langley's help, all were quickly accounted for, and available vehicles inventoried.

Tony Martinelli came marching in from the south with a pair of Libyans walking despondently in front of him. "Hey, boss, look what I found," he announced. "Looks like they were out for a morning stroll, but in one helluva hurry."

So far as they knew, no one had made it to a radio to report what was happening out here. Still, the kidnappers likely had regular check-ins scheduled to be sure all was going according to their nefarious plan. And, of course, estimates on when oil would be pumped from the ground for the benefit of the new regime. It was only a matter of time before someone outside deduced what had happened.

Ward pulled his Toughbook out, set it on the fender of one of the dune buggies, booted it up, and texted Joe Glass. "Operation successful. Thirty hostages rescued. Fifteen prisoners. No friendly casualties. Available transport at site for twenty personnel max. Need exfil. Repeat, need exfil."

Ψ

Joe Glass leaned back and ran his fingers through his thinning hair, a sure sign to those who knew him that the submariner was doing some deep thinking. It was Jim Ward's text pleading for an exfil that was rattling around inside his head. Everyone involved with the hostage rescue mission knew that getting people out of that sand pile was going to be the tough part. And sure enough, the SEALs' precarious position demanded a quick and effective solution. Glass simply did not have one to offer. The fliers over at Air Force Special Operations Command were understandably unwilling to endanger their special operations CV-22 Ospreys and their crews to fly directly into the faces of the Chinese HQ-22 long-range missile batteries. Joe Glass certainly understood their stance. Although the CV-22s were a lot faster and offered longer range than helicopters would and were equipped with the latest avionics and missile defense systems, they would still be sitting ducks for those high performance Chinese anti-aircraft missiles.

Glass had to find a way around this conundrum. It was only a matter of time before the Libyans realized something was up. And that was why his head was pounding.

"Why don't we just go ahead and lob some Tomahawks in there?" Brian Edwards offered. A former submarine skipper himself, he had certainly drilled such a scenario many times, and even done it for real a couple of times. "We shoot from the *Stanton*. Half an hour later, those birds have turned those missile sites into ashes and dust."

"*Stanton* needs a precise address to deliver a package. Problem is we don't know exactly where the sites are, just that they're close enough to have already caused some grief for the Egyptians," Glass answered. "Remember, those hummers are road mobile. Where they're located ten minutes ago ain't necessarily where they are now, and especially since they know we'll have an aim point once they light off their radar or shoot something. By the time we get targeting data, send it to the *Stanton*, and get the birds on target, they will have moved. We end up using a million-dollar missile to rearrange some sand and gravel. And the launchers, radar, and command unit are all separate, too. Hitting any one of them will not take out the whole system."

"Yeah, I do recall it was easier when we were told to drop a wallop at a specific set of coordinates, we dial them in, and light the fuse," Edwards agreed. "You got an alternative, boss?"

Glass scratched his chin. "I'm thinking, Brian," he mused. "I'm thinking."

The Admiral leaned back, hands behind his head, and silently stared off into space for a few minutes. Long enough that Edwards needed to check that he had not dozed off. Finally, Glass jerked alert and announced, "I think I've got a plan."

Glass pulled up a map of the Great Calanshio Sand Sea, eastern Libya, and western Egypt. He used the mouse and keyboard to draw a circle around the drill site where the SEALs, hostages, and prisoners were stranded.

"Intel says that the HQ-22 has a one-hundred-mile range," Glass explained. "Just to be on the safe side, I've drawn a two-hundred-mile radius around Ward's camp."

"That's a whole lot of empty sand," Edwards whistled.

"Not necessarily. I think we can whittle it down a lot," Glass responded. "There is no reason for us to believe that Ali Hakim Sherif's minions have anything to the south. No reason for them to since they're not causing any mischief down there. So, we can discount that whole half-circle, right?"

"Still leaves a hell of a lot of territory."

"Yeah, but if they have any of them located back in Libya, the sites would be out of range for doing their job of defending the Second Regency troops from air attack. That cuts out another quarter of my pretty little pie. That doesn't leave much more territory to be worried about. Essentially, we're left with a quarter circle to the north and east."

"Okay," Edwards agreed. "But that's still way too fuzzy to start lobbing arrows and hope they hit something. Now what?"

"This is the fun part," Glass said with a broad smile. "Ward and his pirates aren't doing anything right now but babysitting. We send them out on recon. The Air Force has an EA-37B Compass Call EW aircraft stationed down at Djibouti. We get that bird in the air, way behind the lines in Egypt but close enough to pick up the HQ-22's radar. They could vector Ward right up to the radar site. He finds the command trailer, which will be somewhere close, and gets the precise coordinates they need for *Gato*'s lawn darts. Henrietta Foster will be sitting out there, ready to launch her Conventional Prompt Strike missiles. Ward sends her the targeting coordinates for the command trailer, and she smashes the thing, putting them out of business. At Mach 7, the Chinese would have about one minute to see the missiles on radar. Not enough time to do anything but make their peace with Allah. Then we send Tomahawks in from *Stanton* to make scrap iron out of the rest of the system."

"That sounds like a plan, boss," Edwards said as he excitedly jumped up. "What do you want me to do?"

"You get Ward moving and coordinate with Henrietta," Glass directed. Then he chuckled. "I guess I better call back to the Joint Chiefs to make sure we have complete and whole-hearted Air Force support on this."

18

Jim Ward closed the Toughbook, his face screwed up in deep-thought mode. He cocked his head, looked up at Chief Billy Joe Hurt, and said, "Chief, we got work to do. Get the boys gathered up and find Bill Langley and invite him to the party. We need to discuss some stuff."

The little group gathered around where Jim Ward sat on the front tire of his ALSV. Myriad stars winked at them overhead in what was otherwise nearly complete darkness. Chuck Jones was munching on some chow while Tony Martinelli was using his knuckles to rub sleep from his eyes.

"So, what's up, boss?" Joe Dumkowski was the first to ask the question that was on everybody's mind. "Lemme guess. Air Force called ahead to see what we want for our in-flight beverage? Make mine a Jack and Coke."

Hurt swatted at Dumkowski, who deftly dodged. "Dummy, you think you can be serious for once in a row."

"Naw, ain't never happened yet," Jason Hall interjected before Dumkowski could defend himself.

Ward held up a hand. "Guys, we got a little job to do before the blue-suiters show up. Seems they're worried that those Chinese HQ-22s might scratch the pretty paint job on their shiny new Ospreys. We're being sent out to find the missile launchers and send back coordinates to the *Gato* so they can hammer them. We're supposed to search out an arc two hundred miles north and east of this garden spot here."

Gene LaCroix whistled. "Skipper, that's a big chunk of sand. Must be better'n ten thousand square miles."

Ward nodded. "Actually, it's a little better than thirty thousand, but the Air Force is going to help us out. They'll have a bird in the air sniffing out the radars from those missile launch sites. They'll triangulate the bearings and send us the fixes. We just need to mosey on over to wherever that location is and get eyes on the command center, which they figure won't be far away at all. Easy little jaunt in the sandbox."

"Okay, but what do we do with everybody here at the drill site in the meantime?" Hurt asked. "We got prisoners, remember."

Ward answered, "That's why I asked Mr. Langley to join us here to discuss." Turning to the petroleum engineer, he went on. "This trip there and back shouldn't take more than a couple of days. Do you think you and your boys can lie low here and keep the Libyans under guard? No reason to expect that their headquarters are going to get curious for a bit and send anyone out. They know the storm damaged the comms out here. We'll leave you a team radio so you can call us back if you need to, though."

Bill Langley nodded his understanding, then countered with, "Commander, I got a slightly different suggestion. Ain't nobody that knows this desert better'n I do. I've been out here knocking around looking for oil for nigh onto thirty years and I think I know every rock and dirt pile. And, by the way, a couple of my guys are almost as grizzled as I am. I'm suggesting that we team up and one of us rides in each of those dune buggies with you. Ain't more than half a dozen places out in that sand where they could drive and park the kind of heavy equipment they'd need for missile launchers. We got some motivated folks here who will be happy to keep an eye on the prisoners."

Ward smiled. That was exactly the ace in the hole that he needed, and especially if the EW aircraft sniffing did not pan out. "Well, time's a-wastin'. Dawn's here in an hour. I want us out of here by first light. Top off the fuel tanks and get these dune buggies ready to roll."

Dawn was just a hint on the eastern horizon when the three ALSVs rolled away from the drill field. Langley sat in the passenger seat of Jim

Ward's vehicle as they headed almost due north. Their destination was eighty miles to a *wadi* that Langley thought was the most probable spot. Billy Joe Hurt and Tony Martinelli drove the other two ALSVs as they fanned out across the desert, each headed toward other potential missile sites.

"You see a McDonald's, Chief, get me an Egg McMuffin!" Dumkowski called over to Hurt.

Hurt shot him a middle-finger salute and pulled away, steering out of sight behind a hillock.

Ψ

It was a knock at the door that brought Commander Henrietta Foster fully awake. She was barely sleeping anyway, keyed up from keeping track of all the moving parts on this mission.

"Skipper, sorry to wake you," Eric Householder said as he stuck his head through the door, eyes averted. "Got two things you need to look at, though."

Foster glanced over at the clock above her desk. It was a little after 0300Z. It was still about an hour until sunrise and nearly two more hours until she would need to relieve Householder as the CDO, the command duty officer. But she knew she might just as well get up now. No way was she going to get back to even the shallow sleep she had been doing.

"What you got, XO?" she asked as she swung her legs out of the bunk and grabbed her robe.

"New message traffic from Group Eight," Householder answered. "Admiral Glass wants us ready to launch our prompt strike birds on short notice. From what I'm piecing together from the traffic, our SEALs are going to send us eyeball targeting data for some missile sites. The Admiral wants them taken out ASAP. And taken out for damn sure. No misses allowed."

Foster punched up the message on her screen and quickly read through it. "That's the gist of it all right. Get the Weps. I want to make sure he goes through all the procedures for putting third party targeting into fire control for those CPS birds and that the birds are ready to fly."

"Will do."

She looked back at Householder. "You said there were two things."

"We're getting indications that one of those *Yuan*s is getting ready to go to sea. Lots of message traffic intercepts and now somebody's tuning their MRK-50UE radar. Nine thousand megahertz, phase-shift-keyed. No mistaking it for anything else they might be doing. Best guess is this boy will come out to play early this morning."

"When it rains, it pours," Foster said with a chuckle. "We complain about how boring these I-and-W missions are, and then they pile everything on at once. Let's plan on doing both 'indications' and 'warning' for as long as we can. Get the boat in position to slip in behind the *Yuan* when it comes out. If it comes out. But I agree with you. All the signs are there. I'm going to grab a shower and some breakfast. I'll be up to relieve you in an hour or so."

When Foster stepped into the control room, she found it a hive of activity. Jim Sanson, the Weps, and two of his fire-control technicians sat in front of one console for the AN/BYG-1 fire control system, grooming the CPS missile launch system and reviewing the procedures for inputting targeting. The men had drilled the procedure plenty of times, but none had ever lit off one of these missiles at an actual target.

Steve Hanly had the section tracking party busy watching the *Yuan* submarine as it was, as expected, just now leaving port. He had the video camera on the photonics mast zoomed in on the outbound submarine as it cleared the breakwater at the mouth of Benghazi harbor and steamed their way.

Foster found the XO huddled over the ECDIS table, watching as the tactical situation developed. Housholder looked up at her. "Gettin' a little busy all of a sudden. Watching our little friend coming out of his playpen. We have designated him Master One since we have visual, EW, and sonar contact on him. If he plays per normal, he will pull the plug and go under at the fifty-fathom curve. That's about two miles out on this course. At his current eight-knot speed, that'll be about fifteen minutes from now. Recommend we go to battle stations before he dives."

Foster looked at all the information laid out. She nodded and said, "Sounds about right. Cookie made some really good sticky buns. They are right out of the oven and still warm. I'll give you ten minutes to run down and grab a couple before I man battle stations."

She did not have to tell him twice. As Householder disappeared out the front door, Foster turned to Steve Hanly and ordered, "Officer of the Deck, have radio deploy the BRA-24 floating wire." The floating wire antenna would allow them to receive radio messages even after they dropped below periscope depth. But the sub would be restricted in dive angle and rudder angle to keep the wire out of the propulsor, and it was receive only. There was a minimal chance that someone on the surface would see it floating by.

They watched on the big flat-panel display as the Libyan submarine arrowed farther out into the blue Mediterranean waters. Hanly maneuvered the *Gato* so that they were six thousand yards south of the *Yuan*. With the high-powered cameras in the photonics mast, they could easily watch as the men on the Libyan submarine prepared to dive.

When Eric Householder walked back into the control room, munching on a sticky bun, the Libyans were still scurrying around.

"Sure taking their time," Hanly mumbled.

Householder laughed. "They're just being courteous, Eng. Allowing me time to finish my breakfast."

"Let's get this show on the road," Foster ordered. "Man battle stations, torpedo."

The order was really superfluous. Everyone was aware of the situation. The word had been passed around the crew, so everyone had already drifted to their battle stations, ready to take over as soon as the order was passed. The COB, Master Chief Cortez, slid into the pilot's seat and promptly reported, "Ship is manned for battle stations."

Senior Chief Stumpf, the sonar coordinator, announced, "Hearing loud transients from Master One. Sounds like he's diving."

They watched as Master One slipped below the waves. Chief Stumpf reported, "Broadband contact on Master One, tracking on the large aperture bow array, bearing zero-zero-two. Also hold Master One on the wide aperture array. Range six-one-hundred yards."

Foster ordered, "Pilot, left ten degrees rudder, steady course two-nine-zero. Make your depth one-five-zero feet. Lower all masts and antennas."

With that, the *Gato* dropped down into the depths, keeping an eye—or to be more precise, an ear—on the other submarine, while still remaining ready to launch weapons, at the sub or at anonymous targets in a distant desert, if and when called upon to do so.

Ψ

An hour after sunrise, the *Sayf Alnabii* slipped her moorings. In a cloud of diesel smoke, she pulled away as her propulsor bit into the dingy harbor water. The boat easily maneuvered through the harbor and out past the breakwater. Thirty minutes later, when the water beneath them was deep enough, the submarine submerged. The vessel's commanding officer, Lahal Nihad Rifat al Subay, watched proudly as his crew handled the new Chinese-manufactured submarine with apparent skill. Clearly the training plan was working. In the last couple of months, the crew—most of whom had never been inside a submarine before their assignment here—had been molded into a well-trained and smoothly operating team.

Wu Ming Jie sidled over to where Lahal Nihad stood. He easily read the Libyan's mind. The expression on the man's face was a dead giveaway. "I caution you, Lahal. There is still much room for improvement and the need for still more instruction and practice," the Chinese advisor offered. "But I will grant that they are noticeably improving. Eagerness to learn is a valuable trait."

The Libyan submarine commander frowned. "Wu, my critical friend, with my crew and with this fine machine that your country has so generously gifted us, we are ready to rule the sea."

Wu Ming shook his head and smiled ruefully. "Lahal, with a few more months' training, your crew might be a match for the Spaniards. Or maybe even the French if you are lucky. But you must not delude yourself. Your crew would be no match for the Americans. If we should encounter one of their vessels, we would necessarily have to play dirty. Even then, we would need to be very lucky to prevail."

"You are too much of a pessimist," Lahal shot back, growing impatient. "We have one advantage the Americans do not. We have the blessing of Allah."

Wu Ming had long since grown tired of trying to convince this overly conceited Bedouin of his limitations. "This discussion serves no useful purpose. Let us begin the sonar search plan and steer toward our patrol area. If we are going to defend the Second Regency, we had better find what is out here that now threatens."

Lahal Nihad nodded. "Finally! Something I can agree with." He turned to the watch officer and ordered, "Go north for a hundred kilometers, then turn to the east. We are heading out to patrol off Sidi Barrani and protect our newly liberated lands. Make ten knots and stay alert for any vessels. Especially submarines. But our initial attention shall be on locating the American destroyer."

"*Naeam, qayid*," the watch officer sharply replied, acknowledging the orders. "The torpedo rooms report that they have loaded torpedoes in all six tubes. The *Sayf Alnabii* is ready for *maeraka*."

Lahal laughed and slapped the watch officer on the back. "May we soon find the battle you so lustily crave. But for now, attend to the sonar."

Lahal Nahid's sonar technicians—with their Chinese advisors carefully looking over their shoulders—manned the submarine's advanced H/SQG-04 passive sonar, searching the deep blue Mediterranean waters for any signs of a submarine.

The *Sayf Alnabii* slowly plodded to the north through waters claimed by the Second Regency. Only a few months ago, this area would have been teeming with shipping traffic carrying all manner of cargo along the ancient trading routes that crisscrossed this sea, but today the waters were eerily empty. The submarine's sensitive sonar did not detect any activity beyond the abundant sea life that inhabited the basin. Sea life that cared nothing for territorial claims or self-proclaimed borders.

Nor did the sonar detect any hint of the deadly black shape that lurked a mere six thousand yards astern.

19

EA-37B Compass Call aircraft tail number DM25813 lifted off from Camp Lemonnier, Djibouti, in full darkness. Sunrise was still two hours away as the heavily modified Gulfstream G550 smoothly climbed up to its cruising altitude. At fifty thousand feet, the world stretched out beneath them for over two hundred miles in every direction, but the sensitive antennas that bulged out along the aircraft's fuselage were already searching far beyond the horizon.

Tail number 813 had barely leveled off at 0.8 Mach when Major Bartholomew "Buck" Fuller, the pilot on this flight, engaged the autopilot and eased back in his seat. Fuller liked to think of himself as an old-school, seat-of-the-pants fighter jock, but he was flying one of the Air Force's newest electronic warfare birds. The heavily modified aircraft, originally designed as a luxury, long-range business jet, was a long way from being an F-15. Any fighting it did would be in cyberspace, using ones and zeroes instead of Gatling guns or air-to-air missiles.

Fuller keyed his intercom. "Hey, Legs, you gettin' anything on your TVs back there yet?"

Captain Samantha Wilson, the mission crew commander, sat in the windowless back compartment of the aircraft, surrounded by flickering computer screens, with her crew busily deciphering their content. Buck

Fuller was the only person in the Air Force with the total lack of political correctness to dare to call her or any other female officer "Legs." But he did and she allowed him to get away with it.

"Nothing interesting yet, Buck," she answered. "But we're still lighting off systems back here. We got two hours before we hit the racetrack. I don't expect to see those target radars until we get in the vicinity." She added, "Besides, I'm busy brewing a hazelnut latte back here. Don't bother me for the next half hour while I enjoy a cup or three."

"What, none for those of us up here driving the bus?" Fuller whined, winking at his co-pilot.

"How would it affect your macho fighter jock image if I let it be known that you begged for a hazelnut latte on a mission?" Wilson shot back with a laugh. "They'll drum you right out of the 'Good Ole Boys Club.'"

She did not wait for a response and instead checked in with Mission Control, located almost four thousand miles away in Mildenhall, UK. The aircraft had just crossed the imaginary line that was the border between southern Egypt and Sudan. From a distant seat, deep in a concrete command center, Mission Control would be directing 813 on this flight and receiving in real time all the data the aircraft sent.

"Buck, our racetrack will be from Kharga to Bawiti," Wilson reported to Buck Fuller. "I've loaded the coordinates into the flight computer. So, if you just keep your greasy palms off the stick and let the computer take over, we'll be just fine."

"Legs, I only got one stick up here and it ain't what I use to steer this plane with," Fuller answered. "We got a wheel for that."

Wilson just shook her head and did not bother to respond to his usual off-color commentary. Fuller might be a pig, but he was still the best pilot she had ever flown with. That had to count for something. She got up just long enough to fill her big mug with the aromatic, freshly brewed coffee.

They had just arrived above Kharga, a small oasis in the southern part of the Western Desert and barely visible almost ten miles directly below them, when her EW intercept operator called out, "Getting a hit! Positive ID on an HQ-22 search radar!"

Bingo!

"Got a bearing line?" Wilson quickly asked.

"Best bearing three-three-nine. Signal strength five," the operator answered. "Best guess range is two-fifty nautical miles."

Wilson immediately texted Mission Control with the contact information to be sure they noticed. She added a query. "You want us to light him up?"

The EA in EA-37B stood for "electronic attack." The powerful electronic emitters that the plane carried could jam, confuse, or outright fry targeted equipment. "Lighting them up" in this case would be an electronic attack.

The reply from Mission Control was quick and unmistakable. "Negative! Permission denied for electronic attack. We need a hard kill on this one. Obtain triangulation of emitter position." Someone needed to put ordnance on this target, destroying it completely, and not just damage some circuit boards and components. To do that, they needed more bearings to triangulate precisely where this radar was located. Then they could direct a hard-kill attack on it.

"Boss, picking up a second emitter, best bearing three-one-five," the EW intercept operator reported. "Best guess on range is three-fifty nautical miles."

"Okay, let's get good numbers on the closer one first and then—" There was a hard bump in what had so far been a normal, smooth flight. Coffee splashed out of her cup onto her console.

"Legs, we got a problem." It was Buck Fuller on the comms, interrupting her. His voice carried what sounded like a hint of concern. That, by itself, was disconcerting. "Uh, looks like we just lost number two engine, and the cockpit is lighting up like a Roman circus. Every alarm and buzzer we got is sounding. Look, I'm not sure how long number one is going to hold out either. It goes, we're a glider. And a damn sorry one, too."

Wilson felt the plane suddenly bank over hard and it was obvious they had started a steep descent. Her mug slid off and crashed onto the deck. Latte splashed everywhere. It suddenly got very quiet in the aircraft. Where was the lulling hum of the plane's two engines?

Fuller announced, "We had a dual engine flameout. Odds of that... well...I just declared an air emergency and immediate divert to El Kharga Airport. Everybody, grab an oxygen mask, strap in and hold on. This might be a little rough."

The Gulfstream screamed down from fifty thousand feet to twenty thousand in only a few seconds. Fuller leveled off there, slowing their hurtling descent four miles above the desert. They needed to be at or below twenty thousand feet to do an engine restart. The copilot grabbed a check-list and started reading it out loud.

"Crew oxygen on – Check"

"Power levers idle – Check"

"APU generator on – Check"

"Left/Right engine bleed, off – Check"

"Left/Right continuous ignition on – Check"

"Left/Right fuel control run – Check"

Then, "Buck, one of the damn things should start."

But nothing happened. With the alarms manually silenced, the cockpit was deathly quiet. Both engines refused to restart. Something was catastrophically wrong. Redundant systems had failed. They needed to be on the ground to find out why and fix it.

Truth was that gravity was taking care of the "getting them on the ground part." Fuller just needed to make sure the trip down was a safe one and that it ended on a nice, smooth runway, not nose first in the desert.

"Angels fifteen," the co-pilot called out. "Vector to El Kharga one-one-seven. Seventy miles out."

Buck Fuller muttered as he trimmed up the balky plane as best he could manage. Seventy miles would be the hairy edge for the EA-37B to be able to stay in the air with no power. With the slab-sided antenna units, it had the glide characteristics of a brick. Instinctively, he held the aircraft at a ten-degree nose up and nursed every inch of altitude that he could muster while trying not to bleed off too much speed. Still, the bird sank toward the sand and rocks below much faster than the glide path to El Kharga called for.

He searched the ground ahead, doing his best to will the airport to appear. The plane was passing through five thousand feet—still falling—when the co-pilot called out while pointing to a fuzzy splotch on the far horizon, "There it is, Buck! Ten miles out. We're cleared on runway one-eight. We gotta come around to course south."

"That turn will cost us some altitude, but we can't land crossways, I don't reckon." Fuller carefully eased the plane around to the required heading, wrestling with the unresponsive controls, but was able to line it up with the runway. He had to be careful not to oversteer, since there would be little chance of correcting. He also knew he was still well below the optimal glide path, much lower than he should be for a safe landing. But there was nothing to do about that other than nurse out every horizontal inch that he could and hope there was no building or tower or rare tree in his way.

Flying the aircraft dead stick, he just cleared the runway apron when he completely ran out of airspeed. And, simultaneously, lift. Again, more from instinct than anything else, he anticipated the threshold of the runway and slapped the aircraft down the last few feet. There would be no reverse of the engines to slow them down.

But they were going so slow by now that the broken aircraft coasted to a smooth stop halfway down the runway with only minimal braking necessary. The airport's only emergency vehicle—a rusty, old pickup truck—puttered out to meet them.

"Ladies and gentlemen, welcome to El Kharga International Airport. Please remain seated with your seatbelt fastened until we pull up to the terminal and the Fasten Seatbelt light is turned off," Fuller announced. "Thank you for flying Spook Airlines."

Ψ

Ali Hakim Sherif—but now the self-proclaimed Pasha Suleiman Jadid —paced angrily back and forth, from one side of his command tent to the other, muttering to himself. The aide currently on duty, there to immediately respond to and set in motion any order his new leader might issue, was hesitant to say or do anything to try to calm him down. He wisely chose to simply remain in his corner, standing at loose attention, awaiting a command. Any command.

The sabotage of the Second Regency of Tripoli's newest submarine, the *Khinjar Alnabii*, so generously supplied by their Chinese allies to help defend the nation's rightful waters and territory and his ascendancy to leadership, was what still had Suleiman Jadid in a rage. It affected his ambitious plans on several levels. It was, of course, a painful wound to his pride, to the sense of achievement of the Second Regency. But more importantly, it would be viewed by others as a sign of weakness. Especially those Sherif had shouldered aside in his ascent to his rightful place at the helm of the nation and the growing empire. Others who still waited to stab back if they saw even the slightest chink in his armor. So, the attack on the submarine was something that no powerful warrior leader—like Suleiman—could ever tolerate. There must be a savage response.

The hostile deed against his sub had been accomplished by the Americans for sure, though there was no hard evidence of that. He and his military advisors were sure that only the Americans could have pulled off such an attack. This demanded that Suleiman embarrass the Americans just as they had embarrassed him.

No matter how much he paced and fumed, there seemed to be only one thing he could do immediately in that regard. He stopped traversing the tent and turned to the aide.

"Contact the commander of the *Dire Alnabii* submarine," he ordered. "I want the submarine out to sea today. If they find a ship with an American flag—and I am confident they will, military, civilian, cruise ship, whatever—I want it sunk without warning! And relay this message to our Chinese friends."

By the end of the command, Suleiman had grown even more red-faced, raging. The aide swallowed hard and scurried off to do his master's bidding before he too became a target of Suleiman Jadid.

Ψ

Commander Jim Ward had his ALSV rocketing across the sand dunes as they ran northward, following Bill Langley's suggestions. Jason Hall sat back in the dune buggy gunner's seat and held on for dear life as they jumped over one crest and roared down the backside, then right back up the next one.

Langley sat in the passenger's seat, also holding on as best he could, and watched their progress on the GPS. "Commander, there's a nasty rock ridge coming up in half a klick. You need to steer to the northeast to avoid it."

Ward swung the wheel over, skidding in the loose sand, and then gunned the dune buggy in the new direction. The trio had been zigzagging across the Calanshio Sand Sea for more than two hours, always running in a generally northern direction but swinging wide to avoid rocks and ridges the ALSV would never be able to manage. As near as Ward could figure, they had covered a little over forty miles of the eighty they needed to make to get in the vicinity of the suspected *wadi*. And until they heard from the Air Force radar sniffer, this was the most likely place to start looking for the Chinese missile launchers. The trip had been bruising but so far uneventful.

"Hey, Skipper, can we pull over for a sec?" Jason Hall's voice came over the intra-squad radio. "I really, really gotta take a leak."

"Can't you just hang it over the side and water the grass?" Ward shot back. There was not a sprig of vegetation within sight.

"Way you're driving, you'd bounce me right out of this damn buggy if I ain't strapped in."

Bill Langley laughed. "Guess nothing changes. The kid in the back seat always needs to stop."

Ward took his foot off the throttle and eased down on the brakes, gliding to a stop. "We need to check comms anyway to see if there are any updates. Let's take fifteen. Stretch your legs and grab some chow. And you can weewee, Jase."

The SEAL commander hopped off the ALSV and grabbed his laptop. Hall was doing his business on the far side of the ALSV when Ward called out to him. "You get done, see if you can contact the Chief and Martinelli. See how they're doing with their tour guides. Meantime, I'll check in to HQ and see if the Admiral has any updates."

Ward grabbed a couple of First Strike Ration packs, tossing one to Langley before breaking the other open for himself. He munched on a pocket sandwich while he booted up the laptop. A half minute later, his face screwed up, he grunted and said, "Damn! Just our luck."

Langley, chewing a piece of jerky, asked, "What's the problem?"

"The Air Force bird is down. Some kind of mechanical problem has them grounded in some place called El Kharga," Ward answered with disgust.

"Yeah, I know where that is," the petroleum engineer said. "If you had a sick camel, they could probably get you going. A fancy Air Force aircraft? Not likely."

"They were able to get us bearing lines to two different sites before they went offline. But that's it. No posits. And you're right. Likely no more help from the blue-suiters."

Ward tapped out a couple of keystrokes. A map of western Egypt appeared on the screen. The bearing lines from the EA-37B bird were shown in red. One of them crossed very close to where Bill Langley already had them heading. The other one looked to be very near to where Billy Joe Hurt was bound for a look-see, based on Langley's knowledge of the terrain.

"Jase, you through to the Chief or Martinelli yet?"

"Got them both online, Skipper," Hall answered. "They're looking at Admiral Glass's message as we speak. They're asking what you want them to do."

Ward thought for a second, then said, "Tell Chief Hurt to head for that site to the northeast. That's pretty much where he was heading anyway. Tell Martinelli to hang back. He'll be our reserve if we need him anywhere else. And he can keep his eyes open for any sign of recent traffic in the area."

Ten minutes later, they were once again rocketing across the desert.

Ψ

US CIA Director Cyril Brown's Gulfstream G800 dropped down from its 51,000-foot cruising altitude in preparation for landing. The twelve-hour nonstop flight from Washington's Joint Base Andrews was finally over. Brown looked out the window as the sleek jet descended. The deep-blue waters of Turkey's Lake Van, formed by a volcano eruption in prehistoric times and one of the few lakes of such size with no outlet, no way for its cold, salty water to escape, stretched out before him. The lake gave way to the brown Anatolian highlands and the surrounding snow-capped mountains. Soon, he could see the city of Van, a municipality of more than a half million souls, directly ahead.

"Sir, we have been cleared straight in to land at Van Ferit Melen Airport," the pilot announced from the cockpit. The CIA pilot and co-pilot were the only other two people on this flight. "The other two aircraft we expected are already on the ground. We are being directed to park between them on the helo pad at the north end of the runway."

Brown nodded and smiled. "Good. This shouldn't take long. Please attend to refueling while we're meeting. I want to depart as soon as we're finished."

The Gulfstream was already swinging around to the southwest to line up with the airport's single runway. After touching down, they quickly taxied directly to the designated spot, coming to a halt between a Falcon 50 business jet that carried an Iranian Air Force paint scheme and a Chinese Y-20 jet transport.

The CIA pilot had barely shut down the twin Rolls Royce Pearl 700 engines when a lone figure appeared from the doorways of each of the other two aircraft and strolled casually toward the Gulfstream. Brown greeted them at the door, inviting them to step aboard the luxury jet.

"Director Brown, I must say that you fly with class," said Nian Huhu De, the Chinese ambassador, as he looked admiringly at the exotic wood and fine leather interior. The dignitary was dressed impeccably, nodding, smiling, the perfect diplomat. "Your American taxpayers are most generous."

Brown returned his smile. "It is good to see you again, your excellency. I trust that your flight was comfortable, even if not as plush as this."

The second man up the stairs was wearing the uniform of a colonel in the Iranian Revolutionary Guard. Bijan Salemi was the Director of the *Vezarat-e Ettela'at Jomuri-ye Iran*, the Ministry of Intelligence of the Islamic Republic of Iran, or "VAJA" for short. There was nothing diplomatic about Salemi's appearance or demeanor.

Brown turned and shook hands with him. "Colonel Salemi, it is good to see you again, as well." He waved toward the luxurious leather seats and told them, "Sit and make yourself comfortable. I am sorry, but with a view toward maximum security, I could not bring a flight attendant along, so we are quite without services. But please help yourselves to the libation of your choice."

The three were soon comfortably seated, each with his preferred beverage from the opulently stocked bar. Brown gazed over the rim of his glass of Talisker twenty-five-year-old single-malt Scotch and promptly started the business part of the meeting. "Gentlemen, while it is good to meet with you once again to discuss our mutual benefit, I must ask why you were so determined that a face-to-face meeting was necessary. Not only are world events involving our nations quite muddled right now, but our new President, that Dosetti witch—and please pardon me for being so open in my disdain for my new boss—but she is proving quite obstinate in coming around to our ways of doing business. Ways that have worked so well, not only for maintaining peace between our countries but for us all to ascend to the positions we seek. To maintain world peace, of course, while assuring open trade from which we certainly get our due. But understand that if she catches a whiff of this off-the-record meeting, she will be very suspicious and that would make her even more difficult to deal with."

Nian took another sip of his Blanton's Single Barrel Kentucky Bourbon as he formulated an answer. "Director Brown, President Tan informs me that he has spoken with President Dosetti several times and that he echoes your feelings that she is quite difficult to deal with. We respect that she would not be as pliable as President Smitherman was, especially in her early days in the White House. But we must convince her that seeking her own elected term will be difficult without our help. And it is true that in both the near term with our operations in the Second Regency and for our future mutual profit, we need to convince her to join in on our way of doing business. Convince her that if peace and prosperity for all—and by 'all' I include the three of us as well as Madam President—if they are to be her primary goals, she will need to listen to us and become an ally. It is the way the world works now."

Bijan Salemi picked up the conversation as Nian took another sip of his whiskey. "Director, please be aware that my men are prepared to load a thousand kilograms of gold bullion onto your aircraft when given the go-ahead. That is an amount valued at about eighty million dollars US. It is completely untraceable. That should prove useful in your endeavors to bend President Dosetti to our will. I suggest that you tell your pilot to allow the cargo to be taken aboard and make him aware of the added weight."

Brown smiled. "That should help pay for some activities where I don't want any paper trail." He looked at his watch. "Gentlemen, there is a KH-11 satellite pass over this area in forty minutes. I really don't want some eager young analyst in Fort Belvoir to see our three aircraft suspiciously huddled at this out-of-the-way Turkish airport. It will raise more questions than I care to answer."

Nian Huhu De put down his now empty glass and rose. He was just a bit unsteady on his feet from the whiskey. "Well, then, I would say that we should depart and allow you to manage this particular part of our plan. Director, I trust that you have the tools you need to complete your task. President Tan is anxiously waiting the report of your success. One that I believe you are receiving ample recompense to successfully bring to fruition, with much more to come." With that, he ducked his head and exited the aircraft.

Salemi paused for a long moment and looked hard into the eyes of the CIA Director. A chill wind blew in from across the nearby mile-high Lake Van.

"And I know you realize that failure to achieve cooperation from your Chief Executive could lead to consequences none of us wish to ponder," he quietly said.

Then the Iranian headed down the stairs and back toward his own aircraft, still carrying what remained of his beverage of choice, a can of cold Bud Light.

20

Faqir al Batsi was sitting in his stateroom on board the Second Regency submarine *Dire Alnabii*, reviewing the day's training schedule with Pinqiong de Xipan. Pinqiong was the Chinese submarine expert tasked with training Batsi's crew. He nodded occasionally as the Libyan officer read off details of the previous few days' work and the plan for this day's cruise, but he did not allow himself a smile. There was so much more the green submariners needed to learn. Batsi and his superiors—all the way up to the country's new leader—were so unreasonably impatient. So overly optimistic about what it took to properly operate a vessel as complex and dangerous as the *Dire Alnabii*.

The phone at Batsi's elbow jangled loudly, startling both men. He picked it up, listened for a few moments, and nodded. His only words were, "Yes, sir," repeated several times.

When he replaced the receiver, he turned to the Chinese submariner, unsuccessfully suppressing a smile. "We have urgent orders. That was Suleiman Jadid's aide. The Supreme Commander has ordered us to sea and to make war on the Americans! We are to sink any Americans we might find, but more specifically we are being sent to work with the *Sayf Alnabii* to attack an American warship that we believe to be over near Sidi Barrani." He looked squarely into Pinqiong de Xipan's eyes as he added, "And your men are to go to sea with us to assist us in our holy war."

Pinqiong de Xipan frowned. His assignment was to train, not shoot. In his evaluation, the Libyans were neophytes, far from ready to go to war in a submarine. His counterpart on the other working *Yuan* held the same opinion, he knew. Even if his small team of instructors did most of the work and made the bulk of the decisions, it would be difficult to be successful. In truth, it would be extremely dangerous.

But he was aware that these were now his orders. His commander back home had made it clear that Pinqiong and his men were to do whatever the Second Regency's leader asked of them. Whatever.

"Well, Captain," Pinqiong said as he turned to an empty page in his notebook and began writing out a list. "If we are going to get underway today, there is much we must do, and we will have to do it very quickly. First, I suggest you call and arrange to offload the exercise torpedoes we have and onload a full complement of war shots. We could not sink much more than a rowboat with the exercise weapons. And have your supply officer load up on fuel and supplies, enough for at least a month at sea. We have no idea how long it will take to find our prey, and then how long we will be required to hide from the inevitable attempt at retribution. Now, I will go and check with my technicians. The systems will need to be properly groomed if we are going to war."

The Chinese submarine expert abruptly rose and stalked out of Batsi's stateroom without saying anything more. There was much to do and no time for the normal courtesies.

However, once away from the ship's Captain, Pinqiong's first priority was to seek guidance and confirmation. He slipped topside and found a spot at the bow where he was alone before he dialed his cell phone. Li Chung Sheng answered on the second ring. The Chinese ambassador was expecting Pinqiong's call, ever since he had gotten word of Ali Hakim's ambitious intentions. He really had no choice but to go along with the suicidal plan if China was to keep the Second Regency as a strong ally. And Li had already confirmed with his own superiors that this would be his nation's stance on the matter.

Li Chung Sheng informed Pinqiong de Xipan that he and his team of submariners were to assist the crew of the *Dire Alnabii* in every aspect of their war patrol, that he had the full backing of the People's Liberation Army Navy and the PRC government in Beijing. That included attacking American ships. But it was imperative that they kept Chinese participation in this mission an absolute secret.

Pinqiong recognized that he and his team were being sacrificed, pawns in the Middle Kingdom's drive for world dominance. He had no choice; he disconnected and went directly to work.

By noon, the *Dire Alnabii* was teeming with activity. To save a great deal of time, the exercise weapons had been launched out of the torpedo tubes and were being fished out of the harbor. War shot torpedoes were being loaded through the weapons loading hatch forward. Food, spare parts, and other supplies were streaming down the ramp through the midships hatch. Meanwhile, the engineers were topping off the fuel and liquid oxygen tanks aft. Trucks lined up along the congested pier, vying for parking spots so they could offload their cargo. Their sweating, frustrated drivers leaned on their horns and yelled colorful expletives at each other. Belowdecks, the submarine was so crowded with people trying to load and stow stores, to shift torpedoes, or to just get their usual jobs done, that it was next to impossible to move about.

Almost as if by plan, as the sun dipped to the western horizon, the last truck pulled away from the pier, the last crate of oranges was lowered below, and diesel smoke wafted from the boat's exhaust. *Dire Alnabii* was ready to go to sea, as were most of the men aboard.

Pinqiong de Xipan stood on top of the sail alongside Faqir al Batsi as the *Dire Alnabii* cast off lines and moved away from the pier, out into the harbor. The two men did not share moods. The Libyan was proud, smiling, ready to strike a blow for his nation and Supreme Commander. Pinqiong was none of those things. He could only hope they would have as much luck as they did enthusiasm.

The black submarine quickly cleared the breakwater, cutting an arrow-straight wake as it headed out into the Mediterranean. Pinqiong turned and gazed behind them as the last hint of dry land fell below the horizon off their stern. The veteran submariner was almost overwhelmed by the uneasy feeling that this might well be the last time he gazed upon terra firma.

He shook his head and then climbed down the ladder into the depths of the submarine. Minutes later, *Dire Alnabii* eased smoothly down beneath the wavetops and struck a course due north.

Ψ

"It should be just over the next ridge." Bill Langley raised his hand to point to the steep, rocky spine that rose like a wall a few hundred feet in front of them. "But I'd also bet this fine dune buggy of yours will never be able to climb up there."

Jim Ward slid the ALSV to a halt and glanced up at the rock-strewn slope. "We could climb that," he grunted. "But we'd have to make a lot of noise and be at risk of rolling this rattle trap." He studied the GPS topo map to see if there was an obvious better route to the valley on the other side. "Going around will take too long. Looks like we best go all mountain goat and start climbing. Bill, you stay here with our wheels. Jase, saddle up. We got a hike."

Langley started to object, but Ward raised his hand. "Bill, this is not a discussion. I need a shooter, and far as I know, you're not trained as one." He slapped the steering wheel of the ALSV. "Besides, somebody needs to guard our ride home."

Ward grabbed his SCAR-H automatic rifle and checked that it had a full magazine. Then he strapped on his HK45CT tactical pistol and grabbed his pack. Reaching behind his seat, he pulled a spare SCAR-H from the rack and handed it to Langley.

"You know how to use this?" he asked the geologist.

Langley took the rifle and laughed. "Well, I figure you put the fat end against your shoulder, point the skinny end toward whatever you want to shoot, and you pull this here trigger thingy." He paused a moment and then continued. "Look, Commander, you don't trek around way out here without knowing how to defend yourself. That's a good way to end up buried in a shallow grave. I got a dozen M16s at the well site, and if we had had a chance to get to them when those bastards surprised us, you guys could have stayed home."

Ward nodded. "Good to know. Now, sit tight. We should be back in an hour or so, one way or the other. And let's hope your hunch about where those launch sites are turns out to be spot on."

Jason Hall had already shouldered his pack with the satellite radio and snatched his own SCAR-H. "Okay, Skipper, let's get hiking. I really, really wanna see what's over that ridge."

The two SEALs hurried across the open space, then scampered up the rock-strewn slope. It took better than forty minutes of hard, tough climbing before the sweat-soaked SEALs crested the ridge and looked down on the broad *wadi* that now stretched out in front of them.

"Jase, set up the comms behind that rock," Ward ordered, pointing to a sharp boulder jutting above the ridge top. He crawled forward to the edge of the opposite downslope. There he had a panoramic view of the valley below and could see for miles and miles in the clear, dry air. He grabbed his binoculars and started a slow, deliberate search of the area. It only took a few minutes for him to spot and map out all the elements of an obvious HQ-22 site. Whoever had set it up had not really been concerned about any kind of attack. Two radar units were parked high up on the ridge to the east where they could easily scan for incoming aircraft, but both were in plain sight. They looked to be large, flat-panel, electronically scanned arrays. Both were raised into operating positions. Judging by the diesel smoke pouring from the adjacent generator units, the radars were busy searching the skies.

Also, he saw four launcher trucks, huge and deadly eight-by-eight units, parked in a line across the middle part of the valley floor. It took Ward a few minutes to find the command-and-control trailer, but he finally located it in the shadows of a cliff face off to the north and east.

Ward took his laser targeting unit and zeroed in on the command-and-control trailer. The unit linked automatically to Jason Hall's satellite comms radio. In seconds, the precise target coordinates appeared on Joe Glass's screens back in the HMCC beneath the Rock of Gibraltar. From there, it was relayed to Henrietta Foster on the USS *Gato* and a quick digital data burst echoed back to Hall's radio to confirm for Ward that the data had been received and verified.

The SEAL commander next shifted the laser targeting unit to the radars on the bluff and then to the launchers in the middle of the *wadi*. Those coordinates were also sent and receipted for by all parties within seconds.

"Jase, scoot back down and get your sniper rifle," Ward said. "We got some time before the party starts and I want to be able to add our own little bit of zing to the fireworks."

Hall grinned and headed back down to the ALSV while Jim Ward settled in to keep an eye on the launch site below just in case something moved.

Ψ

STI Jed Durham sat watching the *Gato*'s LAB array broadband display in front of him. This job should be exciting, in trail of a hostile submarine, but Durham was bored to tears. The Libyan *Yuan*-class submarine, identified as Sierra Two-Six in his system, should be presenting him with a difficult challenge to track, but this one was turning out to be incredibly easy. It was painting a broad white track down the BQQ-10 display that a blind duck could follow. And, just to add to the malaise, Sierra Two-Six was painting an equally vivid track on the wide aperture array. They did not even need to maneuver to solve the TMA problem. The WAA was rocking along, delivering to them a constant feed of target range.

Sierra Two-Six was a slave to consistency. Course one-zero-five, speed a little better than six knots, proceeding straight as an arrow to wherever it was going. There was only one deviation, and it was regular as clockwork. Every twelve hours, precisely 0600 and 1800, Two-Six would slow to four knots and go to periscope depth where it would snorkel for an hour. Durham checked the clock. Two-Six should be slowing about...now.

Jed Durham glanced at his display. Sure enough, received frequency and bearing rate were going up, range was dropping.

"Possible contact zig," he reported in a monotone. "Contact has slowed. And it's the expected time for him to go shallow and gulp air." Durham took a swig of coffee and watched the display generate on his screen. The coffee was the only thing keeping him awake, and he doubted that it would work much longer. This was about the dullest movie he had ever sat through.

Jim Sanson, the OOD, looked at the tactical display on the BYG-1 fire control system as Sierra Two-Six performed its usual song and dance. The computer confirmed that Two-Six had slowed down to just under four knots. It also showed that the *Gato* was creeping up on Two-Six. Sanson's orders were to stay outside of five thousand yards, lessening the chance of their being detected by the Chinese/Libyan sub, and he was now getting close to that fence.

"Left ten degrees rudder," Sanson ordered. "Steady course zero-six-zero. Make three knots by log."

"Coming left to zero-six-zero, three knots by log." Master Chief Jesus Cortez, the COB, was standing watch as pilot. He dialed in the new course and speed. The ship control computer did his bidding and smoothly swung the *Gato* around to the northeast while slowing its forward speed to three knots.

Henrietta Foster, finishing her morning tour of the boat, walked into control just as the *Gato* steadied up. She quickly glanced at the navigation picture on the ECDIS table and then looked up as Sanson joined her.

"Anything happening, Weps?" she asked.

"Naw, Skipper," the OOD answered. "Been real quiet. So easy the Navy may want us to forfeit our sub pay. Two-Six is on his routine schedule. Zero-six-hundred comms check and snorkel period. I swung to zero-six-zero and three knots to avoid closing him. If he holds to pattern, in an hour he'll speed back up to six knots."

"Weps, we're getting targeting data!" Scott Nielson, the OOD Under Instruction, suddenly called out. He was sitting at the missile launch console when the data suddenly started appearing.

Foster stepped over and looked for a few seconds at what was being displayed. Then she ordered, "Weps, man battle stations, missile. Hover the ship at one-five-zero feet. Prepare the Conventional Prompt Strike missiles in tubes seven, eight, nine, and ten to launch."

There was no time to run somewhere far from Sierra Two-Six before they launched. They needed to get their birds in the air. The SEALs were depending on prompt delivery. They would have to take their chances that Sierra Two-Six would not react violently.

Turning to Jed Durham, Foster said, "Keep a real close eye on Two-Six. Sleepy time is over. For us right damn now, and in a few minutes for those guys."

It only took two minutes for the *Gato* to be fully ready and manned for Battle Stations, Missile. Steve Hanly relieved Jim Sanson as OOD so that Sanson could supervise the impending launch of the missiles.

XO Eric Householder was still chewing something when he rushed into the control room and stepped up beside Foster. "Skipper, why do we always do these things when I'm trying to finish up breakfast?"

Henrietta Foster chuckled. "XO, Doc tells me that you're getting a little chunky. This is part of the USS *Gato* weight control program." Turning serious, she went on. "I need for you to take care of Two-Six. Get a torpedo ready. He has no idea we're here but we're about to let him know in a spectacular way. If he so much as sneezes, shoot him."

Householder nodded. He ordered, "Make tube one ready in all respects. Flood and open the outer door on tube one."

Jim Sanson sat at the missile launch control console and looked over his shoulder. "All target inputs are entered. We meet all launch parameters for CPSW launch. Four-missile ripple launch."

"Very well," Henrietta Foster acknowledged. "Conduct a four-missile ripple launch of the missiles in tubes seven, eight, nine, and ten."

Sanson pushed the launch order buttons on the missile launch control console. Back in the payload module, aft of the operations compartment, the missile tube upper hatch for tube seven swung up and open. The massive steel hatch had barely moved out of the way when the gas generator, sitting under the CPS missile, ignited and filled the tube with pressurized gas. The gas shot the missile to the surface. As soon as the missile sensed that it was out of the water, its hypersonic rocket motor ignited, quickly shoving the bird up to above a hundred thousand feet and to a speed of Mach 7.

The first missile was still climbing when the second one, in tube eight, leapt up in the air and soared to chase its partner. The third quickly followed.

The missile in tube ten, the fourth one, seemed to be on its way as well. But once above the surface of the Mediterranean, the motor failed to ignite. Gravity yanked it back down into the water. As it sank, it bounced off the *Gato*'s hull, banging loudly, before it continued its inevitable plunge to the bottom of the Mediterranean. It would not explode. The device was programmed to do its damage at its assigned destination. But the lick on the submarine had been substantial.

"Active sonar from Sierra Two-Six!" Jed Durham yelled. The submarine they had been trailing was awake! "Plus fifty SPL. Probability of detection better than fifty percent!"

Householder called out, "Firing point procedures, Sierra Two-Six, tube one!"

Steve Hanly immediately answered, "Ship ready."

Householder looked at the system solution of the Libyan submarine and saw that it was tracking. He announced, "Solution ready."

Scott Nielson, sitting at the torpedo launch console, replied, "Weapon ready."

Householder glanced over at Foster, who was still watching the missile launch but paying close attention to their other potential problem. She nodded at her exec, so he ordered, "Match bearings and shoot."

Just as the Mark 48 ADCAP torpedo was flushed out of *Gato*'s tube one —and before Foster or Householder even had time to consider if they might be shooting too soon—Jed Durham yelled, "Torpedo in the water! From Sierra Two-Six! Best bearing one-three-zero!"

As it happened, they had not shot soon enough.

Foster turned and forcefully said, "It's time to get out of here! Secure from missile launch. Ahead flank! Make your depth one thousand feet. Come to course two-nine-zero."

"Incoming torpedo bears one-three-one!" Durham reported, his voice noticeably breaking from tension.

"Pilot, launch two evasion devices. Wait thirty seconds and launch two more," Foster ordered. "And keep launching until you run out of the damn things."

"Incoming torpedo bears one-three-one!"

The *Gato* angled down and sprang ahead. It was a race with death. The submarine had no chance of outrunning the incoming torpedo. But maybe, just maybe, it could get outside the incoming weapon's acquisition cone, get to a place where the torpedo could not find and kill them.

"Hearing loud transients from own ship!" Durham reported. What? Something on the *Gato* was raising holy, noisy hell. "Incoming torpedo bears one-two-nine. It's in active search."

The approaching torpedo was actively stalking *Gato*. And from the distance from which it had been launched, there was a good chance it would find its prey.

"Skipper, we got a problem," Jim Hansen said. "Missile tube ten's upper hatch indicates not shut. Probably got damaged when that dud missile fell back on it." So, that was where all the noise was coming from.

Foster nodded. "Not much we can do about that now. Have a team try to manually override it shut. We need to stop that racket."

"Incoming torpedo bears one-two-eight!"

"Launch the port side CRAW at the incoming torpedo!" Foster ordered. "Then launch the starboard one."

The CRAW, or Compact Rapid Attack Weapon, was a miniature, six-inch-diameter torpedo designed to go out to meet and destroy incoming torpedoes. Each of the *Gato*'s two external countermeasure launchers had a CRAW stowed and ready for use. And those were about the only hope they had left if they were not able to dodge the incoming weapon.

The two miniature torpedoes blasted from their launch tubes as their lithium-hydroxide-powered SCEPS engines came up to speed, pushing the CRAWs up to more than sixty knots. They both arrowed toward the incoming torpedo.

"Incoming torpedo bears one-two-seven! Upshift in frequency! It speeded up!" Durham's voice was now a high-pitched squeak.

The torpedo had obviously found what it was looking for and was now rushing in for the kill.

A blast rocked the boat mightily, knocking Foster and Householder off their feet. The air was instantly filled with dust, insulation, and other loose debris.

Henrietta Foster lay on the deck, stunned. But she was aware enough to listen for any reports of flooding or major damage. But when she heard only positive reports on the boat's comm system, she sat up and glanced over at Eric Householder, who was just climbing to his feet. The CRAWS had done their job.

"XO, that was too damn close."

Ψ

Captain Lahal Nihad Rifat al Subay had been gazing out of the periscope of the Second Regency submarine *Sayf Alnabii*. It was a glorious sun-filled morning, perfectly matching the mood of the ship's commanding officer. The pleasant lull in activity while they snorkeled and recharged the submarine's batteries was a good time for him to relax and enjoy being in command of this fine warship without undergoing the constant criticism from his Chinese training advisor. Indeed, it was Wu Ming Jie who annoyingly insisted that they keep the batteries topped off, even though with the air-independent propulsion system they could operate for over a month without ever needing to snorkel. But the advisor was not aware that by not conducting training or running drills during that blessed hour it allowed Lahal Nihad a nice break. He had never imagined that he would equate the roaring noise of the submarine's diesel engines as they charged his vessel's bank of batteries with peace and rest. But Wu Ming's training regime was so demanding that this had been his only chance to find some solace.

The CO idly swung the periscope in slow full circles, gazing at the confluence of sky and sea. There was nothing out there other than those various shades of blue. The only exception was the occasional seagull wheeling and diving for its breakfast.

Wu Ming stepped up onto the periscope stand and interrupted his reverie. "We have received all of our messages for this period. We do have one new order that will affect us. We are ordered to rendezvous with the *Dire Alnabii* tonight and then to coordinate our attack on the American warship."

Lahal Nihad frowned—it bothered him that the Chinese officer looked at the ship's messages before allowing its Captain to do so first—but he did not bother to take his eye away from the periscope. So, his commander did not believe he and his crew could complete the mission on their own. He kept walking in a slow circle, then finally responded, "Wu Ming, would you oversee the navigation to get us to the rendezvous point."

He did not hear the Chinese submariner's response. A sudden brilliant flash of light at the corner of his vision grabbed Lahal Nihad's attention. By the time he had swung the periscope the few degrees so that he was looking in that direction, there was nothing to see but a trail of gray smoke heading up into the sky. Then, as he watched, there was a second bright flash of flame and a smoky track pointing skyward. Someone beneath the surface—certainly a submarine—was launching missiles.

"Loud noises on bearing three-two-two," bellowed the loudspeaker, the voice emanating from sonar.

Lahal Nihad watched a third flash before he could gasp then announce, "A submarine! Launching missiles!"

Wu Ming shouldered the submarine CO aside and took his own look through the periscope. There were three gray, smoky columns heading up into the heavens. Just then, a dark-green cylindrical shape popped up out of the water, hung there for an improbable instant, and then fell back into the sea with a huge splash. Wu Ming recognized an American submarine launching missiles. And common sense told him some valuable facility somewhere in the Second Regency was about to be obliterated.

Here was a chance to destroy a dangerous enemy while he was most vulnerable.

"Sonar, go active on the bearing," Wu Ming ordered. "Fire control, make the torpedo in tube one ready to launch."

Lahal Nahid just stood aside, mouth open, watching. At first, he was aghast that the Chinese officer had taken control of his ship. But he had no idea what he should do about it. Then it dawned on him that his vessel was about to do precisely what his country's new leader had ordered him to do. And Lahal Nahid vowed to himself that he would make certain he got full credit for this imminent and wonderful victory.

The sonar operator, one of Wu Ming's trusted Chinese experts, reported, "Positive return, bearing three-two-two, range four thousand meters."

Wu Ming breathed deeply, confident of the success of the blow he was about to inflict, and ordered, "Launch tube one at the American submarine."

Standing behind him, Lahal Nahid was now literally hopping up and down with excitement.

Up forward, in the torpedo room, the YU-10 heavyweight torpedo in tube one was launched out into the sea. The Otto-fueled engine started and rapidly came up to speed, thrusting the torpedo toward its target at sixty knots. It had barely zoomed clear of the *Sayf Alnabii* when it went active and began searching for the American vessel.

"The target has maneuvered," the sonar operator shouted. "He has launched noisemakers and is attempting to run away."

The fire control operator, another of Wu Ming's Chinese experts, was watching a screen on the torpedo fire control panel. The YU-10 torpedo was connected to the *Sayf Alnabii* with a hair-thin fiberoptic wire. The operator was seeing exactly what the fish was seeing. And he liked what he saw.

"Detection! Our fish has detected the American submarine! Commencing final attack!"

The Libyan sub Captain was dancing, barely able to contain his excitement.

"Incoming torpedo!" the sonar operator suddenly shouted, first in Chinese, then in Arabic. "The American has fired at us! American Mark 48 torpedo! Inbound!"

Wu Ming instinctively knew that there was very little chance to avoid the American torpedo. But, still, he would try. There was no other option. "Ahead flank! Make your depth four hundred meters!"

The submarine immediately angled down and sped into the depths.

"American torpedo bears three-three-one!"

"Launch the noisemakers!" Wu Ming ordered.

Two cannisters were dropped into the *Sayf Alnabii*'s wake. The lithium hydroxide in the cannisters reacted with seawater and released a wall of bubbles to hopefully shield the escaping submarine from the approaching American torpedo. The *Sayf Alnabii* was speeding along at better than twenty-five knots when it leveled off at four hundred meters below the sea surface.

"American torpedo being masked by the noisemaker!"

Wu Ming breathed a sigh of relief. Lahal Nahid puffed out his chest proudly and smiled broadly. He had never doubted they would outsmart the American torpedo.

But then: "American torpedo bears three-three-one. It blasted through the noisemakers."

Wu Ming was searching his mind for what to do next. Anything. Any way to outsmart this weapon and live for more than another few seconds. His thoughts were interrupted by a loud, distant explosion.

"Our torpedo sank the American!" the fire control operator joyously announced.

"Suleiman Jadid will be so proud!" Lahal Nahid crowed. "And you, Wu Ming, you said our crew was not yet ready to—"

"American torpedo bearing three-three-one! Torpedo is speeding up!" The sonar operator's voice was thick with desperation. He dropped his head to the console, surrendering to what was now inevitable.

The Mark 48 ADCAP relentlessly bore in on the Libyan submarine. With its logic circuits satisfied that the solid body in front of it met all the criteria of a valid target, it sent a pulse that energized its own internal arming circuit. Next, sensing that the object it sought was now close aboard, the arming circuit immediately detonated six hundred and fifty pounds of PBXN high explosives. The torpedo was only a meter below the *Sayf Alnabii*'s operation compartment when it violently detonated.

Wu Ming only had a split second to glance at the grinning face of the still unaware Lahal Nihad before both their worlds were instantly terminated.

The mangled remains of what had been the Chinese submarine and the three dozen souls aboard it sank to the ocean floor a hundred fathoms below.

21

Jim Ward never saw or even heard the first missile. But he sure as hell spotted the blinding flash of light when it hit its target. The explosion and sonic boom from the missile's Mach 7 descent arrived at the same time. One second, he was looking at the HQ-22 command trailer sitting happily in the shade of a rocky escarpment. The next, he saw rocks tumbling down from above the trailer, virtually burying it while his ears were ringing from the combined thunderclap of the sonic boom and the impressive explosion on the far side of the *wadi*.

The SEAL team CO was still processing what had just happened to the command trailer when one of the portable radar setups met a similar blinding, deafening fate, disappearing in a flash and roar. Then, without warning, one of the truck launchers exploded.

Ward waited expectantly. There should be a fourth missile. The *Gato* was loaded with four Conventional Prompt Strike missiles. The plan had been to send them all. But so far, no fourth missile.

Even so, the previously formidable site was missing its vital command trailer, one of its two radar units, and one of its four launcher platforms. That left one functional radar and three launchers, including twelve lethal missiles. They could still present a serious risk if those weapons were able to be utilized. And if the fourth CPS missile from *Gato* continued to be a no-show. Ward did not know the answer to those two big "ifs," but he could not afford to take any chances.

"Get on the horn to HMCC," Ward said to Jason Hall. "Looks like we're gonna need a Tomahawk strike to finish things off."

While Hall was sending the message back to headquarters, Jim Ward watched a few troops emerge from hiding and begin working to try to dig out the command trailer, glancing skyward all the time for another bolt of high-tech lightning. Given the time required to set up the TLAM launch Hall was requesting, and then the missiles' half-hour flight time, it would be most of an hour before they could expect anything to rain down any more destruction. Meanwhile, Ward decided that he and Hall should do something more than sit, wait, and watch.

He grabbed Hall's M107 sniper rifle. Flipping the bipod down, Ward snugged the big gun up against his shoulder and carefully sighted on the diesel generator that supplied power for the lone remaining operational radar. The laser range finder said that it was fifteen hundred yards away. Taking a deep breath, then expelling half of it, he eased back on the trigger. The M107 roared and bucked. The .50 BMG armor-piercing round flew for a full second and a half before it slammed into and completely through the block on the diesel generator's engine. There was still plenty of smoke, just not from the exhaust stack. Ward was confident the thing was dead. And the bad guys would be blind from a radar perspective. Just to be sure, he quickly shifted his attention to the radar itself. A couple of the damaging rounds blasting through the control cabinet at the backside of the radar antenna left that unit a smoking wreck, unusable.

"Skipper, you takin' my toy and having all the fun?" Jason Hall asked, grinning. "HMCC receipted for our report. They tasked the *Stanton* for the TLAM strike." Hall checked his watch. "Time on target in three-seven minutes. Now can I have my pop gun back before you start claimin' it's yours?"

Ward laughed and shifted positions so that Hall could fall in behind the M107. "Jase, it's time to see what damage you can do to those launchers. I'm not sure how long we can stay here before those guys down there take exception to us shooting at them. I don't know how many there are or how well they're armed, but I'd rather not find out the hard way."

Ward picked up his SCAR-H and slipped a 40mm grenade into the underslung Mk13 grenade launcher. Checking his laser range finder, he found that the nearest Libyan missile launcher was a little over seven hundred yards away. The grenade launcher was advertised as being effective for up to six hundred meters. The whole meters-to-yards conversion was just too hard. He decided to shoot anyway. Taking aim, he lofted the first grenade up into the air. It fell with a "karumph" ten yards short and a little to the left, its blast doing nothing more than raining down rocks and dirt onto the launcher and truck. The second shot was a couple of yards long and had the same undesirable effect.

The third shot—and the last grenade Ward had—landed smack on the truck's cab, exploded, and left the vehicle burning and fatally damaged. At least it could not move the launcher anywhere else.

Small-arms fire began peppering the hillside around them. Someone down at the missile site had figured out where their tormentors were and was now returning fire.

The M107 bucked a couple more times at Jason Hall's command. "I'm out of ammo," he shouted. "But those other two launchers aren't going anywhere anytime soon."

He laid the M107 aside and grabbed his own SCAR-H. Both SEALs began returning small-arms fire downslope, but it was clear that they were heavily outnumbered by some truly pissed off people. It was only a matter of time before they figured out that there were only two shooters pelting them. If they had not realized that already.

"Jase, grab your gear," Ward ordered. "Time for us to make ourselves scarce."

The pair scurried back down the backside of the slope to where they had parked the ALSV. Bill Langley was waiting for them, sitting behind the M2 Browning heavy machine gun and wondering which side had been making all that noise.

Ward laughed. "Bill, you look like something out of that old World War II movie *Desert Rats*."

Langley threw his head back in a pose and answered in a forced English accent, "I rather fancied myself as Sir Richard Burton."

"Well, let's get your movie star butt out of here before somebody shoots it off," Ward suggested. "We really stirred up an anthill over there. You hear anything from Chief Hurt?"

"Yeah, he called in a few minutes ago," Langley replied. "Said he came up dry on his *wadi*. They're going to continue northeast for another two hours. If he still doesn't see what he's looking for, he's heading back."

"Okay," Ward answered. He cranked up the ALSV and checked the fuel gauge. All was well, assuming they did not have to take any long detours. "Let's move a couple of miles and get in a position where we can see the TLAM strike on what's left here. I want positive verification that those HQ-22s are permanently out of the picture before I climb aboard an Osprey to get out of here and become a juicy target. Gotta be careful. I'm a daddy now, you know."

He slipped the dune buggy into gear and shot off, skirting around the base of the ridge, searching the horizon for a safe vantage point to observe the expected mayhem.

Ward slowed to a stop when he spied a possible overlook. But then the trio heard the roar of a helicopter over the ALSV's idling engine, even before Jason Hall spied it. The bird was flying low and coming in their general direction across the desert. He pointed and yelled, "Hey, that's a Black Hawk! Glad to see 'em but what's it doing this far downrange?"

Ward shook his head. "Look again, Eagle Eye. That's not a Black Hawk. It's a Chinese Z-20. Jase, get that Browning ready to go and pray our camouflage paint job works. It ain't gonna be good if he sees us. He probably has a pair of 12.7mm mini-guns on door mounts, and those things can chop us up like stew meat."

Langley jumped out of the way as Hall took his place. The SEAL pulled back the charging handle for the heavy machine gun and swung around so he could begin tracking the rapidly approaching helicopter.

"I think he's found us," Langley yelled and pointed.

The Z-20 had suddenly spun around and was now headed straight at them. Almost immediately, a pair of rockets arrowed away from the helicopter, aimed directly toward them. Ward yanked the wheel hard over and floored the accelerator. The ALSV skidded around and charged forward, leaving twin rooster tails of sand.

The two missiles slammed hard into the ground, exploding exactly where the Americans would have been had they not reacted so quickly. Even so, they were spattered hard with rocks and sand and nearly deafened by the blasts.

Hall opened fire with the Browning M2. Brass shell casings hailed down as he squeezed off burst after burst of .50 caliber rounds. The helicopter's door-mounted 12.7mm mini-guns—the ones Ward had been so worried about—were launching withering fire, sending up eruptions of dirt all around the evading ALSV.

Ward kept the throttle to the floor, bouncing across the rocks and sand as fast as the ALSV would go, constantly sawing back and forth erratically on the vehicle's steering wheel. The Z-20 doggedly raced after them, trying to get into a better position to take them out. Hall kept the auto-stabilized Browning trained on the attacking helicopter. Most of the slugs were hitting the target but doing no apparent damage.

"Keep shooting, Jase!" Ward yelled.

"I am! You just keep duckin' and divin', Skipper!"

Langley remained quiet, hanging on to keep from being tossed from the speeding, swaying buggy.

Then one of Hall's bullets struck something vital. The helicopter abruptly skewed downward and to the left, as if slapped hard by a huge hand. The bird had been skimming the ground anyway, trying to get a better angle on the fleeing ALSV. That meant that there was no room for the pilot to maneuver or pull up and away, even if he still had control of the chopper.

The Z-20 flopped over onto its side. Its five-bladed main rotor struck earth, sending shards of metal whirling off in all directions. The helicopter tumbled to the ground, bounced hard, began coming apart, and as it did so, it skidded across the desert floor on its right side before coming to a hard stop and erupting into flames. A ball of fire, a wall of black, billowing smoke, and bits of flung wreckage rolled out from the crash site and across the sand.

Ward slowed the ALSV to a stop. The three men jumped out and crouched down behind the vehicle. They watched the wreckage burn for several minutes, punctuated by small explosions from inside the fiery hulk.

Satisfied nobody survived the violent crash, Ward, Hall, and Langley got back into their ride, took deep breaths, and raced forward again. It was about time for the next round of fireworks and Ward still wanted to see for himself that all the anti-air capability had been snuffed out.

They had just reached an overlook along the *wadi* ridgeline when four Tomahawk missiles showed up, flew overhead, then crashed spectacularly into the valley floor. Nothing was left of this former HQ-22 site and sophisticated equipment but smoldering ruins.

"Okay, boys, let's head home," Ward announced, slipping the buggy into gear and pushing hard on the accelerator pedal.

"Jesus, did what just happened really happen?" Bill Langley asked, still hanging on tightly, knuckles white, face pale.

"What?" Ward responded. "Blowing up stuff and getting our asses shot at?"

"Just another day down at the office," Jason Hall said. But there was no sign of a grin on his face.

Ψ

"Where's my pilot?" Ali Hakim Sherif angrily demanded. "He was supposed to be here with my helicopter at three o'clock. It is now four thirty." Ali Hakim stamped around the tent impatiently. "I must be in Sidi Barrani to see the new anti-ship missile installation this evening before sunset. Huang Zhou knows this, too. How dare he allow any delay? We must assure everyone, and especially our brave fighters, that the clocks in the empire run on time and at my command."

His aide was too cowed by the tirade from Ali Hakim Sherif—no, Pasha Suleiman Jadid—to do anything but try to hide in the far recesses of his boss's "symbolic" command tent, quaking with fear. Others who had not reacted as quickly as Suleiman required seemed to soon disappear from the planet's face.

Ali Hakim glared at the useless aide and grabbed the cell phone himself. He punched in the numbers.

Li Chung Sheng, the Chinese ambassador, answered on the second ring. "Good day, Suleiman Jadid. How may I be of service to you, Excellency?"

"Where is Huang Zhou?" Ali Hakim growled. "He was supposed to be here over an hour ago to fly me out to Sidi Barrani for an important event."

Li Chung's voice took a decidedly solemn note. "There has been a most unfortunate incident. I was just about to inform you. Huang Zhou was scheduled to fly a crew of technicians out to the Calanshio Air Defense site. His aircraft is late and is now presumed lost. We have also lost contact with the air defense site."

Ali Hakim nodded, as if Li Chung could see him, and answered, "That is most unfortunate. He was a very good pilot and dedicated to our cause." Then he abruptly shifted gears, ignoring the importance of what he had just been told. "I need a backup pilot. That anti-ship launcher that you have so generously provided us is supposed to be ready this evening. I want to be there to observe its first use. And have representatives of our media cover my presence."

Li Cheung responded, "Yes, and if we have lost the helicopter and the air defense system to hostile action, we must not allow there to be any hint that such a setback has occurred. Not to your own citizens. Not to the world. I have arranged to have Xiao Chen fly you. He will be there within the hour." There was the briefest pause, then, with no input from the Libyan leader, Li Cheung continued. "I think that I will accompany you to the site, Excellency. We have not deployed the YJ-12 system overseas before. This will be the system's introduction to combat. I am most anxious to watch and report back to Beijing."

"Of course. Of course."

The Chinese emissary changed topics. "Have you heard from the *Sayf Alnabii* today?"

"No, should I have?" Ali Hakim asked. Why would Li Cheung ask such a question? As the Supreme Ruler of the Second Regency, Suleiman Jadid would not expect to receive daily messages from a subordinate several layers down in the chain of command. Certainly not a mere submarine commanding officer. If there was something of importance to tell Suleiman, Bahri Dawoud would have done so.

"No, I was merely wondering." Li Cheung realized he had touched a nerve. He tried to play down the question. "It is just that Wu Ming Jie, our advisor aboard the submarine, was expected to report training status this morning. As of now, we have heard nothing. That is unusual for Wu Ming. And with the other recent activity..."

Ali Hakim waved off the concern with a brush of his hand, again as if the Chinese diplomat could see him. "Probably just a communications glitch. Those submarines are so terribly complicated. Unable to talk when they cruise beneath the waves. I am sure they will report in by morning. Meantime, please be sure that I can get to this event in Sidi Barrani so I can demonstrate that the nation's new leader is strong and in command."

Ψ

Admiral Jon Ward, the head of US Naval Intelligence, entered the Old Executive Office Building and was immediately led to Room 180. He was surprised when President Sandra Dosetti greeted him at the door. She was the one who had so urgently requested that he come meet with her, but he expected an aide to open the door and greet him. "Admiral, I really appreciate your coming over to this side of the Potomac on such short notice."

"Well, Madam President, you are my Commander in Chief so..."

Then he noticed Vice President Sebastien Aldo was waiting for them inside the large office. He stepped over, shook Ward's hand, and said, "It's good to see you, Admiral. We want to thank you once again for your help in uncovering the previous administration's corruption plot and, just as importantly, in keeping it under wraps while we took care of that mess. It could have been quite a blow to our national psyche if the public had gotten wind of what they were doing."

"Just an old sub sailor doing his best for the country," Ward replied, a smile on his face.

"And let me thank you for your service, sir," Sebastian said.

"Indeed. Thank you," Dosetti said as she ushered both men over to the settee and wingback chairs. She claimed one wingback while Sebastien took the other. Ward plopped down on the settee, wondering who else had done the same thing, having a sit-down on this settee and then proceeding to say and do things that changed the course of history.

"Admiral, we need to ask for your assistance and that of your overseas sources once again," Dosetti said, immediately getting to the point. "As you will soon understand, this is extremely sensitive and no one outside the three of us is to be privy to any part of this. To cut quickly to the chase, we have very good reason to believe that the Director of the CIA is working counter to the good of this country, possibly in conjunction with one or more foreign governments. Or, at the very least, in close cooperation with them."

Ward looked perplexed. He made no effort to keep the puzzled expression off his face. "Madam President, are you saying that Director Brown is a foreign agent, a spy for someone else?"

Dosetti answered, "We're not sure what Brown's game is. He could be a spy. He tells everybody he is his country's 'top spook.' Or he may just be corrupt as hell. No matter how we label it, he may well be committing treason for money and political gain. We don't know but we believe you may have the sources to find out. And we understand those sources are loyal to you and you alone."

Ward was temporarily speechless. It was as if an enemy torpedo was in the water, aiming for his submarine, so he could not remain so. "Tell me more," he urged.

Dosetti continued, "If you try to use any federal intelligence assets in this task, Brown will surely be tipped off. We've known for a while that he has built a strong network within not only the CIA but other intelligence agencies around the world. We need you to employ only your office and those foreign assets that have been so valuable in the past. And even then, only the ones you implicitly trust. This could get very ugly if anything leaks. And we need this accomplished very quickly. Within hours would be better than within days, since we believe much of the trouble we are seeing in various hotspots are related to what Brown and his cohorts are doing."

Ward nodded, still shocked by what he was hearing. He had just been handed the most difficult and dangerous task that he had ever faced, and he could tell no one. Not even his direct superior, the Chief of Naval Operations.

As he walked out of the Old Executive Office Building and toward where he had parked his car, he was still shaking his head. But mostly wondering where in hell to start. Still, he had a good idea. There was one person with whom he could share this bit of earthshaking information.

And that person was a member of his own family.

Ψ

Henrietta Foster stood at the sonar consoles in *Gato*'s control room. Senior Chief Jim Stumpf, the Sonar Leading Chief, stood beside her. Both looked over Jed Durham's shoulder. Foster glanced over at Dale Miller, the OOD.

"Officer-of-the-Deck, increase speed to four knots," she ordered.

As the submarine reached the ordered speed, Foster asked, "Hear anything?"

Durham shook his head. "Still quiet. No rattle."

"Good," Foster said. "Let's do six knots now."

"Still quiet."

"Eight knots."

A few moments later, Durham shook his head. "Now I hear the rattle. Same as before."

Stumpf flipped through the displays and listened intently to the headset. "Skipper, we're seeing this racket on all the hull mounted arrays. The TB-34 towed array is hearing it, too. If we go any faster than six knots, we might as well have a siren and blue flashing lights. Everybody in the ocean is going to know we are here playing cop."

"Thanks, Senior," Foster grunted. "Good analogy. I'll steal it when I write my memoirs someday. Gather up the Weps, the COB, and the XO. Let's meet in the wardroom and see if we can figure out what we need to do." Turning to Dale Miller, she added, "Meanwhile, limit your speed to under six knots."

Five minutes later, Foster walked into the wardroom, filled her oversized coffee cup from the coffeemaker, and sat at the head of the table before taking a sip. Eric Householder had already grabbed the chair to her right. Jim Sanson plopped down in the one to her left. Jim Stumpf and Jesus Cortez grabbed the next two seats.

Sanson started the conversation. "Skipper, whatever that damned bird hit when the engine failed and it fell, it damaged number ten missile tube hatch." He flipped through a couple of screens on his laptop. "We've tried everything in the troubleshooting chart. Cycled it by hand, manual override, even tried to cycle it while backing down. Nothing." His voice betrayed his frustration.

"We ask for outside help?" Eric Householder offered.

"Yep. But NAVSEA is as stumped as we are," Sanson answered. "Their big insight was that something has broken loose and that's what's rattling back there. They're good at stating the obvious."

"Well, I agree their analysis was certainly insightful. Now what do we do?" Householder's voice was heavy with sarcasm as he referred to the engineers back in Washington, sitting in their safe, quiet cubicles.

Foster answered, "Way I see it, we have two choices. We can either slink back to Gibraltar with our tail between our legs for repairs again, or we can stay out here as a really slow ASW platform and Tomahawk shooter. Either way, it's a decision for Admiral Glass, not us. XO, draft up a message. Tell the Admiral the situation and the alternatives. Tell him that I recommend we stay here for a bit, at least until we get the SEALs extracted."

Foster's JA phone buzzed. She grabbed the handset.

"Captain, Officer-of-the-Deck. On course one-one-two, speed five. We just picked up a new sonar contact on the TB-34, bearing two-three-six, ambiguous bearing three-four-eight. Classified submerged submarine."

"Thanks. Update me every time he farts or sneezes." The CO hung up the handset and looked at the faces of the men around the table. "You guys remember that submarine shooting at us a few hours ago? The one we sank?" They all nodded solemnly. "Thought you might. Well, that guy's sister may be in the vicinity. We've just seen her. Let's pray she doesn't see us."

22

Li Min Ward pushed back from the dinner table, smiling in appreciation at her mother- and father-in-law. She had just finished the largest meal she had enjoyed since giving birth to her son. Her and SEAL Commander Jim Ward's son. Admiral Jon Ward's grandson. Turning to her mother-in-law, Ellen Ward, she said, "Mom, that was delicious. I need to get your recipe for that sweet potato casserole."

"The secret is the selection of spices and genus of sweet potatoes," Ellen told her. "And I grow most of those out in the greenhouse and the raised beds in the backyard. You could probably get what you need at Harris Teeter, but..."

"That's what I get for having a botany professor for a mother-in-law, right?" Li said with a grin and started to rise. "Now let me help you with the dishes. I know from experience that the Ward men don't do dishes."

Ellen Ward laughed. "Yes, that was a hole in my training plan. I'm afraid 'like father, like son' in that department. But I'll clear the table. I think Jon wants to have a private word with you."

"See, I once again rescued you from a dismal fate," Jon Ward said with a nod, then stood and led Li Min into the living room. But Ward was not necessarily kidding about having rescued Li Min from dicey situations. The two had quite the history from well before she and his SEAL son met and fell in love. Once the two were in the living room, and after closing the door leading back into the dining room, the Admiral poured himself a healthy Scotch and offered a drink to Li Min.

She shook her head. "Pediatrician says that I should lay off while I'm nursing. Otherwise, little Tom may grow up to be a sailor." After a chuckle, she turned serious and asked, "Dad, you have something we need to discuss?"

Li Min Zhou Ward was much more than Jon Ward's daughter-in-law. Before the family ties, she had established an effective and far-reaching intelligence network, based in Taiwan but reaching to the highest levels of the People's Republic of China in Beijing. Her work had proven invaluable to Ward on many occasions, and vice versa. For that reason, and because the fewer ties that existed, the easier it was to maintain secrecy, she insisted on only communicating through Admiral Ward. She simply could not trust anyone else. Since marrying Jim and then having their son, she had pulled back only a bit from her life's work, still producing useful intelligence while working from a rental bungalow in Chula Vista, just south of San Diego. But one equipped with state-of-the-art covert communications systems and secure computer capabilities that far exceeded the average cable modem, router, and PS-5.

After Jon Ward had laid out the entire situation with Cyril Brown to her, he said, "Li Min, I need for you to tap into your intel resources and find everything you can on Director Brown. How dirty is he and with whom? Listen, I don't want to put you or little Tom in any kind of danger. I see no way you or I could be connected to these kinds of inquiries. But even so, I'm ordering a protective unit to watch your place and to tag along wherever you go. Most people would never know they were there, but I know you will, so I'm giving you a heads-up."

Li Min smiled and shook her head. "Dad, I already have my own protective unit. And no offense, but it's a whole lot more discreet and effective than one of your federal units." She reached into the ever-present diaper bag and pulled out a Glock 40 Gen4. "Besides, I'm pretty good with this."

He did not doubt her. Before she spent most of her spook time on a computer keyboard, she had done her share of down-and-dirty skirmishing. She put the automatic pistol back into its built-in holster inside the baby-boy-blue diaper bag.

"Gives a whole new aspect to the term Huggies," Ward deadpanned.

"Look, there have been rumors for years that Brown was dirty," Li explained. "And that he had tentacles in lots of places. He is one reason I've been so adamant about only talking with you. I'm sure he has a personal arrangement that goes all the way to Tan Yong. And to the Ayatollah in Iran. And a couple of others you could likely guess. Though I have nothing solid, he probably also has some kind of setup with Russia. At the highest level. I don't have anything definitive on that one but let me Google it, if you know what I mean. The others? Bank on it. But I'll get you all the proof you need."

Ward nodded. "Thanks, Li. I know I don't have to say it, but let's keep this our little secret, at least until Jim gets back. I don't want to worry him. Or Ellen."

"Speaking of Mom, I'll have my people keep watch over her as well. And this place, too," Li Min told him. It was not a request for permission. "And I suggest that you start carrying again. You have a weapon?"

Ward reached under his jacket and pulled out a Colt M1911. "And I visit the range often enough to keep my skills up."

Li Min smiled. "I might have expected you to carry an ancient cannon like that."

"Gotta maintain that grandpa stereotype, right?"

"Speaking of which, I think I hear your grandson screaming for dinner," she said. "Then I got some work to do."

Ψ

Faqir al Batsi was only mildly worried. The *Dire Alnabii* was performing well and—at least judging from everything he observed—his Libyan crew was learning quickly. They had not seen signs of any shipping, American or otherwise, so the voyage had been uneventful so far. Nothing more exciting than the constant drills that Pinqiong de Xipan insisted on running. The Chinese submarine expert seemed to fancy a dream where he could turn what he considered to be nothing more than illiterate goatherds into a keen-edged fighting machine in just a couple of days. The truth was many of the men were, in fact, illiterate goatherds. That was the crux of Faqir's worry. His men were anxious and willing to master most of the simple evolutions, things like diving and surfacing the submarine, but they still stumbled through the more complex tasks like shooting a torpedo. Or, he assumed, dodging a weapon launched by another submarine.

Faqir took a sip of tea and leaned back in his chair, lost in thought. Suleiman Jadid had personally ordered him to accomplish this vital mission. To fail was unthinkable. As the Holy Quran says, "You shall fight them, for God will punish them at your hands and grant you victory over them."

A knock at the door disturbed Faqir's musing. It was Pinqiong de Xipan, the man Faqir had just been thinking about. He stepped into Faqir's stateroom and took a seat.

"Faqir, my friend," the Chinese submariner began, "at this speed, we will be in the area of the American destroyer by tomorrow afternoon." He hesitated for a second while he gathered his thoughts. Then he continued, "It is my assessment that your crew is not yet ready for combat. Even with my best men assisting, I fear for the outcome if we should rush in and attack the Americans."

Faqir knew there was truth in what Pinqiong was saying, and its logical extension, but he was not willing to give up on his chance for fame and immortality quite so easily. The *Dire Alnabii* would continue the attack. The American warship would feel the sting from his weapons.

"Pinqiong, in two days we will attack and sink the infidel warship," Faqir said calmly. He was merely stating a fact, something already recorded in the book of fate. "My *al-makarboun* will fight to the death, if need be."

Pinqiong laughed dryly as he shook his head. "That is all well for your crew, but I have no reason to become a victim of your mad dash toward martyrdom. I am afraid there are not seventy virgins waiting to greet me on the other side."

Faqir stood and threw his arm around the shorter man's shoulder as he effectively turned him out into the passageway. "Come, let's walk around and see what our warriors have learned today."

Their first stop was the *Dire Alnabii*'s cramped sonar shack. Faqir looked at the many screens, but the dancing dots meant nothing to him.

Pinqiong stared at one screen intently. He pointed at a series of bright spots low on the screen. They were almost ready to drop off the display, out of view.

"What are those?" he asked.

"Some kind of rattling sound," came the answer from one of the Chinese advisors. "It was a series of quick transients and then it disappeared. I am guessing that it is some fisherman with a noisy crane hauling in his nets, probably at least fifty kilometers away. But we will continue to evaluate and see if it returns. It offers an excellent training opportunity, yes?"

"Yes. Yes, it does," Pinqiong replied, but with little enthusiasm.

Ψ

Admiral Jon Ward answered his cell phone on the second buzz. He was out for a run on the Alexandria, Virginia, area's Mount Vernon Trail and had just entered the shaded Dyke Marsh Preserve. Though often busy with other runners, this was always a good route when he needed to think about things. It was a smooth, easy path along the river and the views of the Potomac seemed to help clear his mind. Today, he was trying to figure out his next step after the disturbing meeting with President Dosetti and her urgent and surreptitious tasking.

He pulled up and stepped to the edge of the boardwalk that crossed the marsh before he checked the caller ID on his phone. Nothing. Oh well. He hit the answer button.

"Ward."

"Admiral, this is Magnus Rosenblatt. I don't believe that we have ever met, but Sandra Dosetti speaks highly of you."

Jon Ward stared at the phone for a second. Magnus Rosenblatt was perhaps the most powerful man on Wall Street. Of course Ward knew who he was. But why would he be calling him? And on his private line? And why was he dropping the name of the POTUS?

"Nice to hear the boss likes me," Ward said.

"Admiral, I will make this short. I have learned of your meeting with our President and the mission that she has assigned you. I'm afraid that Sandra and her inquiries have aroused some very powerful people, and those forces are hell-bent on thwarting your mission. Cyril Brown is alerted, and he will stop at nothing...nothing...to protect himself and his position. You will need to proceed with the utmost caution."

"Mr. Rosenblatt," Ward responded. "How exactly did you get this information?"

Rosenblatt chuckled dryly. "Let's just say that a man in my position must always be seeking valuable, accurate information and must have the resources to do so." He paused for only a second and then added, "And we are very discreet. Even with your resources, if you check, you will find that this call never happened."

Ward started to reply, but he realized he would now be talking to no one. Magnus Rosenblatt had hung up.

He watched a great egret flap its wings and take off from the murky water of the marsh, likely searching for prey. Then Ward did all he knew to do.

He jogged on.

Ψ

"Skipper, we have a leg," Jim Sanson reported. "Coming right to course zero-seven-zero."

Henrietta Foster studied the tactical display on the ECDIS table. The contact they had designated Sierra Nine-Seven, another submerged diesel submarine, was fifteen thousand yards away, steaming a straight course of one-one-zero and making a speed of about ten knots. She was not sure how much longer they could hold contact on the diesel boat. Due to the damage to the *Gato* and the noise it made when exceeding about six knots, she was steaming due east at that precise speed. That gave Sierra Nine-Seven a four-knot speed advantage and the vessel had already turned that into a seven-mile lead. Sonar contact was becoming tenuous. Another couple of miles and they would probably lose the sub altogether.

Senior Chief Jim Stumpf, *Gato's* senior sonarman, stepped away from the sonar consoles and stood beside Foster. "Skipper, way I figure it, we got maybe fifteen minutes before we lose this guy. What you thinkin' for the next move?"

"I'm thinking, Senior," Foster answered, "we could just let this guy march over the horizon and hope the *Stanton* picks him up. And that they will be able to track him." The tone of her voice was a good indicator that she did not prefer that course of action.

Jim Stumpf shook his head. "Skipper, I don't think that's a good idea. Never seen a skimmer yet that could track a quiet diesel boat for any length of time. Can't we just run out ahead of him? You know, like they did in World War II, the old end-around?"

"That racket is so loud that we'd have to go around north of Crete just to keep from being counter-detected," Foster replied, then she had a thought. "Maybe we can use all that noise to our advantage. How is our active working?"

"It all checked out before we left Gibraltar," Jim Stumpf answered, "but we ain't used it since."

"Well, get your team to check it all out," Foster directed. "And run the latest METOC data through the SFMPL active prediction program. Let's see what parameters it recommends and what we can expect."

The Navy Meteorology and Oceanography Command collected weather and oceanographic data from all the world's oceans. They then prepared and sent out to each ship oceanography data messages tailored for their particular ocean area. The METOC data was a vital input to the Submarine Force Mission Program Library application to predict active sonar performance in the complicated and complex undersea environments like the Eastern Mediterranean Basin.

"Aye, Skipper," Stumpf answered. "It'll take a few minutes." He stepped back over to the sonar consoles and got his team moving.

Henrietta Foster turned to Jim Sanson. "Mr. Sanson, proceed to periscope depth. We need to call the boss and tell him what we're doing."

It took almost ten minutes for Foster to convince Admiral Joe Glass that her plan would work and was the only possible sure way to keep tabs on the rampaging Libyan submarine. That was a necessity considering this boat's sister had so recently tried to sink the

Gato. By the time she had bent Glass to her way of thinking, and they had arranged coordination with the *Harold Stanton*, Senior Chief Stumpf's team of sonarmen had completed tuning the *Gato's* Large Aperture Bow Array to conduct an active tracking of Sierra Nine-Seven.

"Skipper, there is a real strong layer at one-four-zero feet. As long as Nine-Seven stays shallow, best search depth is one-two-zero feet. If he goes deep, best search depth is three hundred feet. So far, he's stayed shallow the entire time."

"Thanks, Senior," Foster said. "Line up to go active on Sierra Nine-Seven for active trail." She turned to Jim Sanson and ordered, "Officer-of-the-Deck, make your depth one-two-zero feet, come to course one-four-five. All ahead standard. I want you to get between eight and ten thousand yards off his port quarter and maintain that position. Conduct an active trail on Sierra Nine-Seven."

As expected, when *Gato* sped up beyond six knots, the rattle started. Then it increased in amplitude as the submarine went even faster. But that noise was no longer a concern to Commander Foster. Every thirty seconds, Senior Chief Stumpf's sonarmen were directing two hundred forty decibels of acoustic energy at the Libyan submarine.

"Positive active return on Sierra Nine-Seven, bearing one-three-one, range nine-two-hundred yards."

After the third ping, Jim Stumpf called out, "Sierra Nine-Seven is cavitating, speeding up. Sounds like he's decided to go deep."

Sharon Woolsey was watching the solution on the fire control panel. She announced, "Contact zig. Looks like he's making twenty knots."

Jim Sanson ordered, "Pilot, make your depth three hundred feet, ahead full."

The rattle quickly became deafening inside the hull of the *Gato* as they jumped up in speed. It sounded like someone was standing outside the submarine, beating on it with a sledgehammer. It was so loud that Foster had to shout to make herself heard.

"Snapshot, tube one, Sierra Nine-Seven!" Jim Sanson looked questioningly at his skipper. "Just getting the gun cocked," Foster explained with a grin. "Our friend could well take exception to our active sonar. We've already seen they tend to get aggressive when stalked. So, I want to be ready."

Sanson nodded. With the tube flooded down, outer door open, and the torpedo powered up, it would only take a second to launch the weapon. Those saved seconds could be the difference between life and death if the Libyan submarine launched an attack.

"Positive return, Sierra Nine-Seven," Senior Chief Stumpf called out. "Bearing one-three-one, range nine-seven-hundred yards." The diesel boat was still trying to run away, but so far, with *Gato* running fast now, his efforts were futile.

Sharon Woolsey yelled, "Solution tracks, he is making twenty-four knots, course one-two-two."

Foster watched it all develop on the ECDIS display. If the Libyan had a fully charged battery when he started to run, and if his powerplant was as capable as a standard Chinese *Yuan*-class submarine, he could be able to run at this speed for about two more hours. Then his battery would be completely exhausted. He would be forced to slow and come up to the surface to run his diesel engines to charge back up. Foster figured she only needed to keep goading him with the active sonar until then.

Unless, of course, he got totally pissed and turned around to shoot.

Ψ

"Captain, we are hearing those transient noises again," the sonar operator on the *Dire Alnabii* announced. "Bearing three-two-two. I still think it is a fishing boat with mechanical difficulties."

Pinqiong de Xipan snatched a sonar headset and clamped it to his ears. After listening for ten seconds, he calmly removed them, dropped them, then turned and slapped the sonar operator hard on his cheek.

"You idiot!" he shouted. "That is a submarine with some kind of very noisy problem."

Almost as if to emphasize Pinqiong's announcement, the sonar intercept receiver suddenly sounded an alarm. The Chinese submarine expert looked hard at the intercept receiver, reading the output screen. He yelled, "American *Virginia*-class active sonar! High signal strength!" Turning to

Faqir al Batsi, the Libyan Captain, he ordered, "Ahead flank! Go deep, one hundred meters!"

Wide-eyed, al Batsi passed along the order. The *Dire Alnabii* angled down and shot ahead. The skipper then joined Pinqiong de Xipan, alternately watching the sonar display of the pursuing submarine and the battery amp-hour meter as it clicked down alarmingly. The main motors voraciously consumed the energy stored in the batteries. The meter told them that they could only run at this speed for a little more than an hour. If they could not escape from the stalking American submarine before then, they could well be forced to fight.

Pinqiong tried every trick he knew to evade the pursuing Americans. Fishtailing the rudder to create eddies, porpoising through the layer, even launching an evasion device. Nothing seemed to work. No matter what they did, the intercept receiver told them that the chaser was relentless.

And still, the amp-hour meter ticked over.

"It is time to fight, while we still have enough battery to elude," Faqir said forcefully. "Make tube one ready. We will shoot that bastard."

Pinqiong held up his hand. "Faqir, be aware that if you shoot, we die. I have no reason to become a martyr to your cause."

"But you have no other choice!" al Batsi shot back. "We will fight together and, if necessary, die together. Besides, I am the commanding officer of this vessel. There is nothing you can do to stop me."

"Oh, there is one thing," Pinqiong countered. He reached above the ballast control panel and flipped a pair of levers. Immediately, the roar of high-pressure air became deafening, blasting water from the vessel's ballast tanks, replacing it with air, and sending the sub upward toward the surface. Another measuring device—the depth meter—provided the most telling bit of information. It started slowly clicking upward, picking up pace, then rapidly reeled off the remaining distance before they reached the surface.

The Libyan submarine leaped high out of the water before splashing downward spectacularly. It slipped back down to twenty meters and then bobbed right back up to the surface. Finally, it floated there like a rather large, breached whale.

"We can surface and surrender." Pinqiong aimed a pistol at a point between Faqir's eyes as he completed his statement. "That is another choice we have."

Ψ

"You don't see that every day."

Henrietta Foster stood beside Eric Householder, watching the large panel command display with great interest. What they were witnessing could just as easily have been some computer-generated scene from a submarine thriller movie. The display was aligned to the number two photonics mast. They zoomed in on the view of the surfaced submarine so that they had a close-up look at the vessel's bridge. A large white sheet was dangling from its periscope.

Householder responded, "So that's what a *Yuan* looks like up close and personal. You think they're playing honest, Skipper?"

"I'm not inclined to try to find out," Foster answered. "Could be a ploy just to get us on the surface and drawn in closer. Get on the horn with the *Stanton*. This is the job for a skimmer. At least according to the NTDS display, they're about sixty miles to the east. See if they can get their MH-60R airborne and over here. Much as I'd like to shoot those SOBs out of the water, once *Stanton*'s chopper is on top, we can turn all this over to them and call it a day."

23

Admiral Jon Ward was working late, as usual, at his office desk, putting together some of the first info Li Min had provided him about CIA Director Cyril Brown's nefarious activities. His phone buzzed. To preserve his chain of thought, he almost did not take the call. Then he took a look. He recognized the caller ID. It was his daughter-in-law.

"Dad, we need to talk." No hello. No other greeting. She sounded anxious. Totally out of character for her. "Right away, but not at the house. Can you meet me outside Murphy's Tavern in Pentagon City in twenty minutes?"

Ward grabbed his uniform blouse, slipped the M1911 into its low-profile holster, and grabbed his cover. Heavily armed for a drink with Li Min, he thought, but the tone of her voice told him it might be a good idea. As he dashed out of the office, he shouted to his aide, Jimmy Wilson, that he was heading out to meet his daughter-in-law for a drink. That he would be back in a couple of hours.

"Tell her Jimmy says 'hey,'" Wilson called after him.

"Will do."

The Metro from the Pentagon station to Pentagon City took five minutes. He arrived in the courtyard outside Murphy's only seconds before twenty minutes had passed since taking the summoning call. He immediately saw Li Min, inconspicuously sitting on a bench with the diaper bag at her side. Fortunately, there was no sign of little Tom anywhere. He waved and walked quickly across the courtyard in her direction.

When he was only a few steps from the bench and Li Min rose to greet him, he noticed some movement to his left. Four men emerging from the parking garage at the other end of the broad open area. They were half running toward them. Something about their demeanor caught Ward's attention at once. He did not recognize the first three, but Cyril Brown was the last in line. The Director of the CIA? What the hell was one of the world's most powerful intelligence agents doing out here with three thugs in a light drizzle on a dark night? And running his way? His intuition told him this was not a bunch of college buddies meeting for drinks at Murphy's.

Ward shouted a warning to Li Min and grabbed for the grips of his automatic pistol.

The three heavies were already pulling what looked to Ward to be MP5Ks from inside their own jackets. The little 9mm submachine guns were ideal for this kind of close-quarters work. Ward knew that he was dealing with professionals. And that they were intent on performing the deadly task they were trained to do.

Ward did not take time to make any value judgements. His M1911 roared and bucked just as Li Min took her first shot with her Glock. The leading two attackers dived for cover. Ward hit the ground, making himself as small a target as he could.

He had a quick glimpse of one of the heavies going down hard as the others opened fire in full automatic. He rolled over and squeezed off a second shot. One more shooter went down.

Ward was dimly aware of a few bystanders diving, running, in panic. He hesitated before firing again.

Then, just after he shot off three more rounds, he felt a hot knife slam into his chest, right side, just below the collarbone. His shooting arm went limp, useless. Fog quickly clouded his vision. He struggled to retain consciousness, fighting back the dizzying gray that threatened to envelop him. He needed to stay alert, to remain in the gunfight. Needed to protect his daughter-in-law.

But then, despite his determination, Admiral Jon Ward's world went black.

Ψ

Joe Glass read the intel report. Finally, something he could act on and maybe end this operation.

"Brian, you read this?" he said, pointing to the report. "Looks like Suleiman Jadid has finally lifted his ugly head somewhere besides in that show tent of his. The guy is on the move. I'd say he has something planned and it's about to go down. Brilliant guy that he is, he's also moving all his leadership to one location. Surely, he knows there are lots of people who would like to dispatch all of 'em to dictator hell in one fell swoop."

Brian Edwards looked up from the screen he was reading. The two had their corner of His Majesty's Command Center Gibraltar all to themselves. "Yeah, boss. I was just reading it. Looks like he's heading for some place called Sidi Barrani. Something is up there. You have any idea where the Egyptians are with their re-attack plan now that we've made the skies a hell of a lot more friendly?"

"Egyptian General Staff says they are still a couple of days away but they're short on ground attack aircraft. They're getting their armor all marshalled for a push west," Glass answered. "This is too big an opportunity to pass on. Can we get Ward's bunch of SEALs up there in time to join the soiree?"

"Latest report has them about three hours to the south," Edwards answered. "You want me to get them moving that direction?"

"Yes, please," Glass replied. "Let's put our heads together and figure out exactly what we want them to do when they get there. And how we plan to extract them and the folks back at the oil field." He changed pages on the screen to see the report from Henrietta Foster out on the *Gato*. "And while we're at it, we need to figure out what we want to do with *Gato* and that *Yuan* that surrendered to her. I see that *Stanton* has one of their MH-60Rs on top just now."

Brian Edwards flipped through a couple of other screens, looking for a specific bit of communication. "*Stanton* has just reported that they have radio comms with the sub. Some guy named Pinqiong de Xipan—even got his picture here—claims he is now in charge of the Second Regency submarine *Dire Alnabii*. Says he is Chinese and is a commander in the PLAN. Yep, our intel has confirmed that last part. Now, this dude is demanding that he, the crew, and their submarine be turned over to the Chinese Navy so they can take it home."

Joe Glass let out a dry chuckle. "That's a good one. What with all the mayhem he and their other sub just set loose out there in the Med? Have *Stanton* inform this Pinqiong de Xipan character that they are all under arrest for international piracy and for acts of terrorism. And tell *Stanton* to escort the *Dire Alnabii* to the Egyptian Naval Base at Alexandria. If they even act like they might balk, send them to the bottom and save us all a bunch of trouble and paperwork."

"They're going to love this on the skimmer," Edwards said with a laugh.

Glass thought for a moment. "Well, I guess I'd best make a call back to the 'five-sided puzzle palace' and let them know that they are about to have an international diplomacy conundrum."

Ψ

Jim Ward shook his head as he read the message on his Toughbook. He had just brought the team back together and was about to lead them south, back to the oil field, so they could be extracted with the drill team and their prisoners. Based on the new orders, that extraction had just become an Air Force problem. Admiral Joe Glass wanted him to head north and see what they could do to mess up Suleiman Jadid's little party.

In light of this change in plans, Ward did a quick inventory of his assets. The three dune buggies had just enough fuel for a run to the coast. There would not be much of a safety margin. The team was all healthy. So were the three civilians who were tagging along. Weapons and the supply of ammunition might or might not be adequate for what they could be getting themselves in the middle of. Regardless, Ward did not see where he had any choice in the matter.

As all SEALs knew, you do what you can with what you got, not what you wish you got. They were ready to roll.

Ward whirled his finger over his head and pointed north. Each member of his team frowned. That was the opposite direction from the one they expected. Not the way to their ride home. But they shrugged and settled in.

Ward hit the gas and accelerated out across the trackless desert, kicking up a plume of sand, rocks, and dust behind him. The other two ALSVs followed in hot pursuit, off to wherever it was they were going to do whatever it was that they had been called upon to do.

Ψ

Jon Ward had never felt so disoriented, so nauseous. Not even in the roughest of seas when he had been forced to keep his submarine close to the surface. As the fog slowly cleared, he still had no idea where he was or what time it was. Only that there was a bright white light dangling above him.

"Admiral Ward? Admiral Ward?" He could faintly hear someone calling him. "Admiral, time to wake up."

Ward's mouth felt as if it was full of cotton balls. He croaked, "Okay, okay, I'm awake. But only if I can get a cup of wardroom coffee."

A face, mostly covered by a surgical mask, hovered over him. "Admiral, welcome back. You've been out for a bit, but you're going to be okay. I'm Dr. Bashwani. My team removed three slugs from your chest. No permanent damage, but a couple of them came very close to things you do not want to be hit by flying projectiles."

"Where am I?" Ward asked, followed by an involuntary groan.

"You're in the surgical ICU at Bethesda. There are some people here who are waiting to see you. You up for company?"

"Long as they're not shooting at my happy ass," Ward said weakly, nodded, and then groaned again. The movement involved with even a small nod had, in retrospect, not been a good idea.

Dr. Bashwani looked over at the rack of monitors that were bleeping and blinking, tracking Ward's vital signs. Everything looked to be within safe limits. "Admiral, I'm going to step out for a couple of minutes so you can be alone with your family. Hit the nurse call button if you need anything. And remember, you are still getting some pretty strong pain meds." The doctor disappeared.

His wife, Ellen, and daughter-in-law, Li Min, floated into view. Ellen kissed him on the forehead and then scolded, "Damn it, Jon, I don't know how many times I've told that SEAL son of yours to remember to duck. I didn't think I needed to tell you, too."

Li Min came into view. "Just Mom and me in the room now so we can talk. Dad, we're proud of you! You got all three of the pro shooters with that antique cannon of yours. Brown came out of hiding with the intention of finishing you off. We don't think he was interested in me professionally, but they were almost certainly going to eliminate me as a witness. But that snake won't be bothering anyone anymore."

"You tell you-know-who what happened?" Ward asked. President Dosetti. She and her minions would have lots of obfuscation to accomplish in a very short time frame. There were too many details that the public—and many in government—should never learn concerning what this shootout was all about.

"Yes, I made an initial report on the way here. Through myriad twists and turns so no one knows my involvement. The President is planning to stop by later tonight, once all the press interest has been put to bed. She can fill you in on how they're spinning this whole thing. Typical DC crime. Mugging gone wrong. Perps down. Two government officials shot, one fatally. You need to be in on the details so you all can keep your stories straight. I hope you can lie with a straight face."

She glanced at Ellen, who confirmed, "World class at that particular skill." Then she stepped back and said, "I assume you two have a few other things to discuss. I'll go call the babysitter and check on our little boy."

Once Ellen was gone, Li Min leaned over and touched her father-in-law's hand. "Suffice it to say that my Beijing sources came through. Brown was about as dirty as you can imagine, to the tune of billions of dollars. Maybe even dirtier than we imagined. He was tied in with about every despot and dark side leader on the planet and selling them your country's deepest secrets in exchange for cold, hard cash, gold, silver and crypto. And even God could not help anybody who got in his way." She shook her head. "We'll probably never know where all the bodies are buried."

Ward looked up at her and grinned weakly. "Thank God we know where a couple more intended bodies won't be! At least not yet."

"I'm so sorry you got caught in the line of fire, Dad," Li said. "You're not supposed to be a target for your country anymore. I should have picked another spot. Been more careful and observant."

"Aw, not your fault, Li," Ward responded, his voice fading. It required effort to talk, to keep his eyes open. "But you need to figure how Brown and his gunmen knew we were meeting, and that you and I were onto him."

"Wheels are turning already, Dad. Now, why don't you let those meds work and get some rest? We might need you back on the job..."

But Admiral Jon Ward was already back to deep, deep sleep.

Ψ

Suleiman Jadid stood at the back of the room and watched impassively, though he had no idea whatsoever what he was observing. The room, a portable structure, was designed as the control center for the YJ-12B anti-ship cruise missile launchers that were arrayed high on the bluff looking down on the village of Sidi Barrani and then out to the Mediterranean Sea beyond. It was not designed, however, for the creature comforts of a dozen high-ranking Second Regency generals and a collection of Chinese officials who tried to crowd into the structure, each elbowing his way to the place of honor he felt he deserved.

Tonight's entertainment was supposed to be the spectacular destruction of an American warship. A vessel that had the temerity to sail blithely into Second Regency–controlled waters even after repeated warnings delivered by various means, including in multiple speeches before the United Nations General Assembly right in the nest of the infidel New York City. No one could claim they had not been warned about intruding into the sovereign historical waters of the Second Regency.

The Chinese Yaogan-45 high-resolution optical imaging and synthetic aperture radar satellite sat in a geosynchronous orbit 36,000 kilometers above the Mediterranean Basin sending nearly real-time images of the American destroyer on a link down to the command center. The warship was steaming along defiantly only a little more than one hundred kilometers away. Puzzlingly, the images revealed another ship, much smaller, in company with the American vessel but the image quality was not sharp enough to identify it.

That there were two ships sailing together was not the primary complication they were facing. Suleiman was more than willing to attack them both. The problem was technical. The launch computer was not talking to the missiles. So far, they had no way to tell the missiles where to go or what to attack. And no idea what was causing such a frustrating glitch.

Suleiman was beside himself. First the HQ-22 anti-aircraft launcher south of the Siwa Oasis had dropped offline and was not answering any messages. It was as if they had disappeared. Now the anti-ship cruise missiles were no longer operational. The Libyan dictator was losing faith in the high-technology weapons that his Chinese patrons had been supplying. Supplying at a steep markup, all to be paid in oil from the new fields his loyal Bedouin troops were busy liberating. Perhaps he should re-evaluate his partnership with the Chinese, who were unable to even swat away such a sand fly as Taiwan. Maybe look for another place to shop. If only Russia was not so deep in war with its former satellite nations.

Li Chung Sheng stood stolidly watching his technicians as they sweated, trying every technique and trick they knew to make the recalcitrant system respond to their queries. And gauging the frustration of Libya's new leader, who clearly knew little of such technology, but who might, at any moment, explode violently.

Nothing his technicians tried seemed to work. The sophisticated missiles still sat in their launcher boxes, ignoring every plea.

Finally, Suleiman Jadid threw up his hands in disgust.

"Li Chung, are you going to get your *sawarikh hamaqa* ever to work? How can we fight the Americans and the rest of the world if I am unable to launch any weapons to mount the simplest of defensive efforts?"

Li Chung looked over his shoulder and stared at Suleiman. "Ali Hakim, I beg to differ with you. These are not 'crap missiles,' as you so colorfully describe them. They are the most advanced anti-ship cruise missiles on the planet. We merely need to download an update to the software. It will require a couple of hours. I suggest that you take your staff and repair to your tent. I will send for you when we are ready."

"As I observe, your advanced anti-ship missiles are good for nothing more than providing shade from the sun for the scorpions!" Suleiman Jadid turned on his heels and marched out of the control center. His general staff followed him out and down the hill to where his *bayt al-shar* had been set up. The tea was already hot. Sweet *rangina* and *qatayef* were laid out on trays for them to nibble on as the men sat and discussed what they hoped would be the night's events.

It was well past midnight when Li Chung stuck his head into the tent and signaled Suleiman Jadid that all was ready. The men traipsed back up the hill and jammed themselves into the command center, more than ready for the show to begin.

24

"Boss, you seeing what I'm seeing?" Billy Joe Hurt whispered, using his throat mike.

Hurt and Chuck Jones had crawled across open ground until they were only two hundred meters from the command center near Sidi Barrani. Hurt watched as the little building filled to the point that the doors could no longer be shut. Light spilled out into the surrounding darkness as did many voices in heated conversation.

"That's Ali Hakim Sherif in the flesh," Hurt whispered when he recognized the tall Bedouin stepping out of the darkness and others being tossed out so he could enter the building. "Something big is up, for sure, if it gets him way out here and away from that tent of his."

Jim Ward had parked the ALSVs in the moon shadow of a date grove a couple of klicks to the west of the missile site. He and the rest of the team then scooted up to where they were hidden in a low swale a hundred meters behind Hurt and Jones. That afforded them a good view of the command center. They again left the petroleum engineer, Bill Langley, and his two roustabouts back at the ALSVs to wait for them.

Ward keyed his mike and whispered, "Roger, Chief. That's Suleiman Jadid for sure. Looks like most of his general staff, to boot. Don't recognize the Chinese gentlemen, but they must be real muckamucks to be way out here with the big guy."

"What's the play, boss?" Hurt asked.

Just then, a brilliant flash of light and a loud roar erupted from the missile launchers further up the ridge. A YJ-12B shot out of its launcher box, its rocket booster shoving it up high into the air before its ramjet engine ignited and sent it quickly on its evil way. Another missile lifted off, followed immediately by a third one, each bearing more than enough fire-power to do real damage to ships and people. A rousing cheer went up from those inside the little jam-packed building.

"Whatever the plan was, it just got changed," Ward said. "Let's get in there and bust them up before they can launch any more." He led Tony Martinelli, Joe Dumkowski, Jason Hall, and Gene LaCroix in a low run toward the command center. The SEALs fanned out as they covered the short distance. They were almost halfway across the dark, open ground before a sudden shot rang out. Someone was alerted, but the shot was wild, raising dust in the open area fifty feet in front of the SEALs.

"Chief, give us some cover fire," Ward grunted into his mike.

Chief Hurt and Chuck Jones immediately opened fire in quick, three-shot bursts. Someone in the darkness up ahead screamed in agony and then fell silent. People began spilling from the command center, running senselessly out into the open. Several of the military officers drew their automatic pistols and sprayed bullets randomly into the night, threatening only sand and rock outcroppings in the nearby hills. But then the wild shooters fell as quickly as the two SEALs, Hurt and Jones, could take aim and fire.

Somewhere off to the right, headlights stabbed into the night sky. Heavy engines were growling as vehicles raced up the incline toward the top of the ridge. Jim Ward figured those had to be reinforcements on the way to help the troops and rescue those trapped inside the command center. They sounded like big trucks, troop carriers.

Of course, there would be troops out here to protect their cockamamie leader.

Time was short. The SEALs did not have the firepower or manpower to get in the middle of any kind of major firefight. Their only chance had been —and remained—a quick hit-and-run assault.

Then Ward heard the heavy drumbeat of a .50 caliber heavy machine gun opening up. A line of tracers led from the ridgetop down to what were now obviously on-rushing armored trucks. Trucks loaded with troops carrying weapons.

Then two more fifties opened fire from somewhere on higher ground.

"Skipper, we figured you could use some help." It was Bill Langley's voice that came over Ward's earpiece.

Ward chuckled. Langley and his boys were continuing to be useful. But it would not be good to get caught in crossfire between a bunch of enthusiastic oil well workers and some nut job's fiercely loyal militia. "Bill, think you guys can get those buggies down here to our position? We're going to need some quick transportation here shortly."

Ward heard a double click in his earpiece—Langley had been paying attention to SEAL comms procedure—and then he made out the roar of the ALSVs as they raced down the slope toward him.

The SEALs charged across the last bit of open ground as Billy Joe Hurt and Chuck Jones sprayed cover fire into the command trailer. Ward dropped to the ground just at the edge of the lighted area. He called out in his best Arabic, "In the trailer, surrender or we will blow it up."

Someone came running out of the command center, indiscriminately spraying his AK on full automatic. The shooter got chopped down before he could cover ten feet.

"Last warning. Grenades are next!"

A plaintive cry came from inside. "Wait! We surrender!" Six men, all except one in Chinese military uniforms, marched out with their hands above their heads. The last man was also Chinese but wearing a business suit.

Ward ordered Martinelli and Dumkowski, "Cover me." He stood and strode across to where the Chinese men stood. Nobody else in the area seemed to be moving. Seconds later, Jason Hall and Gene LaCroix emerged from the darkness, into the light. It took only a few seconds to make sure the Chinese were disarmed and to zip-tie their hands behind their backs.

The civilian, in a demanding tone, said in English, "I am Li Chung

Sheng. I am the duly recognized Chinese ambassador to the Second Regency of Tripoli. I demand to be treated as a diplomat."

Hall shoved Li Chung off to the side while Ward said, "I don't think your diplomatic mandate covers supervising an armed attack on the assets of another sovereign nation. You're coming with us."

Just then Billy Joe Hurt walked up, pushing along in front of him a man in Bedouin robes. "Looky what I found trying to sneak off in the dark like a scalded possum."

Ward looked the man up and down and grinned. "Damned if it ain't ole Ali Hakim Sherif, hisself, in the flesh."

"Suleiman Jadid," the man spat. "I am Suleiman Jadid, the head of state of the Second Regency of Tripoli. I demand to be addressed as *Pasha* Suleiman Jadid and to be given the respect my position deserves."

Ward pointed at Ali Hakim and then to Li Chung. "Guys, please make sure these two are strapped down in the ALSVs. They're going to be our VIP guests, and we'll let somebody else determine what needs to be done with this scum. Put the others back in the trailer and secure the exit door from the outside. We'll let their commanders know where to come rescue 'em and let them pick up the...uh...trash we left. Let's make tracks toward the harbor. No way we can exfil back across that desert."

"Got it, Skipper."

Tony Martinelli yelled and pointed down toward where Ali Hakim's generals had parked their armored transports, "Boss, we got more company coming! Suggest we beat feet outta here, but fast!"

A stream of headlights was snaking up the hill from the east, rapidly approaching the SEALs' location. Judging by their speed and the way they were dancing up the rough approach road, they were probably more armored personnel carriers. A second, similar gaggle was roaring toward them from the west. The only escape was directly down the steep embankment toward the town.

Ward ordered, "Saddle up! Looks like time for some runnin' and gunnin'." He jumped in the lead ALSV with Bill Langley in the passenger seat and Jason Hall manning the M2 machine gun behind them. Ali Hakim Sherif was bound to the rear seat, beside Hall. Ward aimed the dune buggy down the steep slope and jumped on the accelerator.

They had just cleared the compound when the first mortar shell landed, almost precisely where they had just been parked.

Billy Joe Hurt yelled into his intra-squad radio, "Boss, looks like they are real pissed that we snatched their supreme leader."

"You could be right," Ward answered. "But it looks like they are more interested in revenge than in protecting him. You'd think they'd be more careful where they're shooting if they wanted to save the bastard's life."

The three all-terrain vehicles bounced and bumped down the slope, threatening to roll over and spill everyone out. But, between the ALSV's low center of gravity and the SEALs expertly sawing their steering wheels back and forth downslope, they remained upright with the seatbelts keeping everyone inside.

A stream of tracers tore through the night, ricocheting off the rocks ahead of the ALSVs. Hall traversed the weapons station and opened with his .50 caliber machine gun, blasting at the vehicles racing after them from the west. Maybe he could cut them off at the bottom of the slope. Two short bursts from the heavy machine gun caused the lead Spartan APC to erupt in a ball of bright, hot fire. Hall quickly shifted his sights so that his outgoing tracers were forming dots in the darkness, headed for the second one.

Chuck Jones sat in the gunner's seat in Billy Joe Hurt's dune buggy. Jones was busy working on the column coming at them from the east. Whatever the lead vehicle was, its shots were getting annoyingly close. Jones sent several well-aimed bursts into the vehicle before it suddenly veered off the road and rolled over.

Direct hit!

"Good shootin', Jonesy!" Hurt whooped.

Flames burst from the column leader as it tumbled down the slope. From the very quick glimpse he got, Jones thought it was a LENCO Bear Cat, but his eyes had been affected by all the flashes and he could not be sure.

Joe Dumkowski, gunner in the last ALSV, was cussing loudly and straining to clear a jam. "Sand! Damn sand," he grumbled, mostly to himself. Bouncing down the slope while trying to clear a jammed M2 was not going to work. Instead, Dumkowski grabbed his SCAR-H. The 7.62mm rounds were not nearly as effective as the .50 caliber ones would have been. But damn it, they were better than nothing.

For the moment, it appeared they had stymied the guys who had been chasing and shooting at them. The three ALSVs reached the bottom of the slope and roared off across open ground toward the town of Sidi Barrani, a couple of kilometers away.

Ward had no plan for what they would do when they reached the town. He would figure that out when he got there.

Ψ

The US Navy destroyer *Harold A. Stanton* was steaming about fifty miles north of Ras El-Kanayis, Egypt. It was a calm, quiet night. The sea was a sheet of black glass, reflecting the quarter moon and array of bright stars overhead. It looked almost like somebody's prized computer-constructed image on Pinterest. Except for the surrendered Libyan submarine *Dire Alnabii* steaming in close company a thousand yards astern, there was nothing else man-made in sight.

For Captain Jerry Baudsley, it was like so many other peaceful nights steaming across the Mediterranean. Steve Johnson, the OOD, was maintaining a course straight for Alexandria at fifteen knots, a speed that the surfaced submarine could easily maintain. That it so far had willingly maintained. Baudsley leaned back in his bridge chair and enjoyed the night air. The breeze was from the south and it brought a spicy desert tang to his nose. He would sit out here on the bridge wing and observe for the first hour of the midwatch, just to make sure no more surprises cropped up. Not that he expected any. Johnson was a seasoned veteran as OOD. Scott Richter, down in CIC, was the finest TAO in the Atlantic Fleet. And taking charge of the Libyan/Chinese submarine had gone surprisingly smoothly. The Chinese PLAN officer aboard made it clear that he was giving up the submarine and would do whatever Baudsley told him to do rather than go back down and get stalked and sunk by the American submarine. He had kept his word. Everyone had been told to remain aboard the *Yuan*. There was no risk of anyone trying to escape. It would be a very long swim to land.

"Skipper, you want some coffee?" The messenger was making his rounds. Baudsley held up his cup for a refill, took a sip, and sighed. This was what life at sea was supposed to be like. Cool, clear, fragrant night. Smooth seas. Fine crew that could be trusted completely. A cup of hot java. And an enemy that steamed right up to them, waving a white flag, surrendering without a shot being fired.

"Vampire! Vampire!" the CIC announcing system speaker suddenly blasted out. "Three hostile tracks inbound! Range five miles. Speed Mach 3! Bearing two-zero-zero. Sons of bitches are trying to shoot us in the ass!"

Baudsley dropped his cup to the deck as he vaulted from his chair and jumped into the bridge house. He grabbed a microphone and ordered, "Combat, Captain, weapons free on all hostile tracks. Engage! Repeat! Engage!"

The incoming missiles were already much too close for either the big SM-6 or the SM-2MR/ER anti-aircraft missiles that the *Stanton* carried in her vertical launch cells for just this purpose. That left one option. The SeaRAM launcher spun around in the direction of the detected weapons and promptly spit out its complete load of eleven RIM-116 Rolling Airframe Missiles.

In seconds, the storm of five-inch-diameter, nine-foot-long missiles were spearing out toward the inrushing cruise missiles. The two groups of deadly ordnance were racing toward each other at a closing speed of better than five times the speed of sound.

Meanwhile, a bigger missile launched up from the *Stanton*, reaching a hundred feet before it burst open and launched a NULKA active countermeasure, which hovered there to attempt to attract the attention of the incoming missiles. The Mark 36 Super Rapid Bloom Offboard Countermeasure (SuperRBOC) launcher sent up clouds of aluminum foil chaff to try to confuse the missile seeker. A pair of Mark 59 decoy launchers sent inflatable balloons over the side to try to do the same thing.

The *Stanton* was concealed in an envelope of deception. Baudsley and his crew could only hope it would be enough.

"Vampires classified Chinese YJ-12 anti-ship missiles!" Richter's voice was barely a squeak. Good to know. And three of them were more than enough to send the *Stanton* to the bottom of the Med, alongside centuries' worth of shipwrecks and the skeletons of thousands of sailors.

Then, as Baudsley watched, his lips moving in a silent prayer, a flash of brilliant yellow-white light rent the night, followed quickly by the thunderingly loud blast. The chainsaw rip of a Phalanx CIWS joined the battle cacophony. The close-in weapon shot a stream of 20mm cannon shells like darts tossed out at 4,500 rounds a minute. They, too, zoomed out to attempt to intercept the incoming missiles.

Another loud explosion and brilliant flash tore the night apart.

"One Vampire left!" Scott Richter announced hopefully. Two gone. One deadly SOB remained.

Somehow, the last Chinese YJ-12B had avoided all the counter-weaponry and countermeasures the destroyer had launched. Then, the missile's terminal homing radar abruptly sensed a target, dead ahead and close by. The weapon's very smart onboard computer did precisely what it was programmed to do. It ordered the missile to dive down, run straight toward the target, and destroy it. And that is what it did.

Direct hit!

The missile tore right through the thin steel shell that made up the outer skin of the sail of the *Dire Alnabii* submarine. Then the YJ-12B's two-hundred-kilogram warhead detonated in the middle of the masts and antennas that filled the submarine sail's crowded interior. The awful explosion tore the sail structure almost entirely off the submarine.

Pinqiong de Xipan and Faqir al Batsi had not been enjoying the mellow Mediterranean evening nearly as much as Captain Jerry Baudsley had. They had been standing on the cramped bridge of the submarine, still arguing about Pinqiong's abrupt and unauthorized surrender, when the blast in the sky above from the intercepted missile stopped them cold. When the second one exploded a few seconds later, they could only look at each other and wonder what was happening.

The third missile, so recently launched from Sidi Barrani, killed both men instantly.

Hot metal shrapnel blasted downward into the submarine, eviscerating everyone in the control room and the mess decks directly below the control room.

The *Dire Alnabii* sat low in the water, the waves lapping up over the burnt scar where the sail once stood and then poured over, dribbling down into the burnt-out interior and onto what remained of the Second Regency of Tripoli crewmembers below.

Ψ

Jerry Baudsley stared at the low-lying hulk for a moment, surprised it remained afloat after such a powerful direct missile strike. His own ship had suddenly gone silent, disbelieving. The explosions had ceased and there were no more rapidly approaching pips on the radar screens, but there was no way to know if more death might soon rain from the sky. This time, there was little for the destroyer to toss out in hopes of confusing the incoming weapons. Nor was there any other nearby vessel—now that the Chinese *Yuan* lay so low in the water—that might offer the missiles a likely diversionary target.

The CO shook his head and then ordered, "Mr. Richter, get a damage control party in the number two RHIB and get them over to that sub. See if there are any wounded we can help. And see what we can do to keep it afloat and take it under tow. We got people who will want to take a good look at that boat even if it is a little bit dented. And get Gunner busy reloading the SeaRAM and CIWS just in case. We're going to keep an eye on the sky, and we best be ready if they try again to pop us."

25

The rising sun was barely a glimmer on the eastern horizon as the three heavily armed SEAL-team-driven dune buggies roared through the dusty streets of the town of Sidi Barrani, headed for the waterfront. They did not slow a bit as they raced through the old *suq* and past the ancient mudbrick Tamoil Mosque.

The pursuing Libyans were somewhere back behind them. Jim Ward figured the only escape was to lose them, at least for a few minutes, in the warren of narrow streets and alleys that made up the medieval *albaldat alqadima*, the old town. The ALSVs could squeeze through the ancient passageways, barely wide enough for a donkey or camel to pass. The Libyan combat vehicles were far too large to navigate the old town. They would be forced to wait on the outskirts and send in foot troops. Ward needed to engineer their escape before the Libyans figured that out.

The *al'aziqa* provided a winding, confusing maze. Dusty streets and dark alleys headed off in all directions, twisting and turning every few feet. Ward did his best to generally head toward where he thought the water might be. Finding and probably stealing a boat was their one hope to escape and to take their prisoners with them.

Finally, Ward turned a corner and saw the dark Mediterranean directly across the street. They hurried toward a point at the head of a rickety old fishing pier that jutted out into a shallow lagoon. A light dangling from a pole out on the end of the pier illuminated a pair of fishermen, heads down, loading their small boat for a day's hard work out on the water.

Jim Ward and Bill Langley jumped out of the lead ALSV and jogged in their direction while the rest of the SEALs and two roughnecks began unloading. As they approached the fishermen, Bill Langley put his hands together, gave a slight bow, and said, "*As-salaam 'alykum.*"

One of the fishermen, considerably older than the other, answered in English, "And peace be upon you, too." He bobbed his head in a quick bow and then continued, "I am Asenth Gomaa and this is my son, Amr. How may we help you, our early morning visitors?"

Ward could tell the man was aware of his sweat-stained battle fatigues and the weapons being unloaded from the futuristic vehicles there at the end of the pier. The two men with their hands bound, too. What must he think of them, showing up like this? Langley answered, "We want to rent your boat for a few hours. We will pay you very well, in American dollars. Far more than what a day's worth of fish would make for you and your son."

Gomaa shook his head. "No, we are honest fishermen. We will fish for our livelihood."

Then both Ward and Langley realized that the fisherman had finally recognized one of the bound men the SEAL team was escorting down the length of the pier toward them. Gomaa gestured toward Ali Hakim Sherif.

"The Libyan invaders are no friends of ours. We have no interest in assisting him in any way," he said, then spat in the general direction of Sherif. "You may have my leaky old boat to do whatever you must if you free us from the treachery of this man and his minions." He waved toward his son, who looked on, wide-eyed. "Amr will guide you and run the boat while I remain here and hide your vehicles. That should slow any search the Libyans might mount for their so-called leader."

Ward clasped the old man's hand. "Be careful, my friend. His warriors are not far behind. They will not be gentle if they find you with our equipment or suspect you helped us escape."

Asenth Gomaa smiled wryly. "I have lived all my years in Sidi Barrani. If I hide something here, no Bedouin is going to find it. If the Libyans are so close, you need to leave quickly." He shooed Ward in the direction of the boat.

With the SEALs, Bill Langley and his men, plus the two prisoners, and their weapons and supplies, the old fishing boat was loaded down. The freeboard was so low in the water that it appeared anything greater than a gentle ripple could swamp the vessel. The SEALs tossed their heavy weapons and most of their gear over the side and watched as it sank out of sight in the deeper water. The jettisoned weight helped, but the boat still rode dangerously low should the wind and waves pick up.

The boat's ancient diesel engine spat and sputtered but finally coughed to life. While Ward and Hurt cast off the lines, Amr yanked the levers to put the boat into some forward gear. The boat putt-putted out of the harbor, emitting a thick cloud of blue smoke into the brightening sky.

Once they were clear of the harbor—and without challenges or even minimal interest from anyone—Jim Ward booted up his Toughbook and quickly found a chart of the local area. He pointed to a spot about twenty miles north and west of Sidi Barrani.

"This is where we need to go. How long will it take for us to get there?" he asked the young fisherman.

Amr Gomaa stared at the chart for a few seconds. He carefully measured the distance with his thumb and forefinger. "That is thirty kilometers from our present location. It will take about six hours to get there, assuming no unexpected headwind. But I do not believe we will encounter unfavorable winds today. One problem I do see, though. I am not sure that I will have enough fuel to return. My father had only planned to fish close to shore today." Pointing toward the boat's single mast, he went on, "But don't worry. We can always raise the sail. Much slower, but I doubt we ever run out of wind."

"Well, Amr," Ward answered with a broad smile. The boy could hardly be more than fourteen or fifteen years old. "I think you are going to get a chance to ride on an American submarine. Unless you want to sail home alone."

Amr grinned as Ward looked at his watch. "Six hours will get us there about noon local. Go in that direction but let's take it slow and easy. We won't be making the rendezvous until after sunset. Only when it is dark."

Turning to Hurt, Ward added, "Chief, make sure our guests are comfortable and quiet, as far down there in the bilge as you can shove them." He picked up the boat's single sail. "Let's get this spread to give us a little cover and shelter from the sun. Anybody happens to pass by or fly over, this is nothing but a fishing boat doing what fishing boats do."

The old, sun-faded, orange sail covered the open midsection of the boat. The SEALs huddled under it, grabbing much needed sleep, while Bill Langley stood with Amr in the tiny wheelhouse. An hour into their transit, the boy and the petroleum engineer had become fast friends. After two more hours, old bachelor Langley claimed he was ready to adopt the smart, resourceful kid.

Ψ

Henrietta Foster stood by the ECDIS table and watched as Sharon Woolsey checked the latest GPS position of the USS *Gato*. The Navigator looked up and announced, "Skipper, GPS plots us two miles northeast of the rendezvous position. Course two-two-one is a good course. ETA in thirty minutes, noon local time."

Foster nodded and looked over at the sonar display. For the moment they were only tracking two contacts. Sierra One-Two-One had been classified as a merchant vessel, bearing three-five-four, range in excess of fifty thousand yards, past CPA and opening.

The other contact they had just picked up. Sonar was calling it a fisherman, Sierra One-Two-Four, bearing two-one-nine, range seven thousand yards and closing. It appeared their soon-to-be passengers had arrived early.

"Let's go up and take a look," Foster said. "Officer-of-the-Deck, come to periscope depth."

Steve Hanly responded, "Periscope depth, aye, Skipper." Turning to the ship control party, he ordered, "Pilot, make your depth six-two feet. Number two scope coming up."

The *Gato* smoothly ascended until the low-profile photonics mast broke the surface. Watching on the large flat-panel command display, Foster and Hanly could see the deep-blue image turn gradually lighter until there was a splashy mix of sea, foam, sun, and sky. This rapidly changed to a view out onto an almost pan-flat sea. The tiny image of a fishing boat was just visible on the horizon. It was hard to tell for sure, but it looked like the boat was slowly making its way toward their position.

"Conn, ESM," the 21MC speaker blasted. "Receiving X-band radar. Detection threat! Equates to a Chinese KLJ-1 radar. Carried on Chinese Harbin Z-9 helicopters. Signal strength plus forty."

Hanly was lowering the periscope even before ESM had completed their report.

Foster ordered, "Let's drop back down to 150 feet. Nobody invited those jokers. And we sure as hell don't want that guy to maybe see us in this clear water."

Everyone aboard the *Gato* could feel the sub's decks tilt as they hurried back into deeper water.

Ψ

"We got company coming," Bill Langley called out. His report was unnecessary. The howl from the rapidly approaching helicopter's twin turboshaft engines would have been impossible to miss.

Ward yelled back from his hiding place under the sailcloth, "Make like you're fishing. Don't forget to smile and wave."

Amr kicked the boat into neutral. While it drifted, he and Langley struggled to dump some fishing nets over the side. Langley had long since donned a dirty, wrinkled tunic and turban that Asenth Gomaa had left belowdecks. The two of them smiled and waved enthusiastically as the pale gray bird barely cleared the boat's mast. It flew out a few hundred meters. Then, when Langley and the boy thought it might be moving on, it circled back. The bird came to a noisy hover a few yards from the fishing boat, threatening to swamp the low-riding vessel. The pilot looked out and pointed to the microphone he held in his hand. Then he held up his fingers in a one, then a six. He wanted someone on the boat to talk to him on the radio and do so on channel sixteen, the international maritime channel. Amr shrugged broadly and shook his head. The boat was too small and poor to have any modern conveniences, much less a two-way radio.

The pilot gave up trying to communicate. He made widening circles around the boat. Then he disappeared over the eastern horizon.

Jim Ward peeked out from under the sail. "Think we convinced him we are nothing more than poor fishermen?"

"Don't know," Langley responded, "but I suggest we keep pretending we're fishing. He might get real suspicious if he suddenly came back around and we didn't have nets out."

While Langley and Ward conversed, Amr stood in the wheelhouse scanning the horizon. He suddenly yelled and pointed toward the north. "Mr. Bill, what is that?"

Ward and Langley both looked in the direction Amr pointed. There appeared to be a gray telephone pole poking up out of the water less than a thousand yards away.

"Our ride has arrived," Ward announced. "But let's just see if the fish are biting until the sun goes down."

Ψ

It took the remainder of the night and well into the morning for the surviving crew from the *Dire Alnabii* and the work party that came over from the *Stanton* to stabilize the submarine enough so there was not as much of a chance of it sinking. They made progress, even with the significant language difficulty, since the Libyans had only a rudimentary understanding of English—mostly gleaned from American movies and TV shows —and the *Stanton* sailors were entirely ignorant of Arabic. They worked out rudimentary sign language. Some of the surviving Chinese trainers served as quasi-interpreters.

Together, the men managed to complete a crude cofferdam, plugging the holes in the pressure hull where the sail had so recently stood. That served to keep most of the water out. The submarine's pumps, aided by a portable pump from the *Stanton*'s damage control locker, were able to at least keep up with the flooding.

The *Dire Alnabii* would not be going anywhere under its own power. The damage was just too severe for that. Taking it under tow was the only alternative to letting it sink. It was after noon by the time the bosun mates on the *Stanton* had rigged out the towing hawser, towing bridle, winch, and assorted other equipment needed to take the *Dire Alnabii* under tow behind the American destroyer. Without a towing plan for the Chinese submarine, it was all guesswork. Calling back to the NAVSEA engineers did not help. They had never towed a damaged Chinese submarine before, either. With the damage topside and lack of both submarine towing equipment and knowledge, they had to jury rig the bridle to the *Dire Alnabii*'s mooring cleats as best they could manage. At long last the damaged submarine was as ready as it could be for the American destroyer to pull it back to a port.

Not really trusting all the jury-rigged and "best guess" arrangements, Jerry Baudsley decided to err on the side of caution and limited the tow speed to three knots. The two ships would enter the Egyptian Naval Base Alexandria, two days later, just as the sun was setting to the west, back toward Libya.

Ψ

"Boss, we got company coming. Fast, too."

Billy Joe Hurt's words jarred Jim Ward awake. The SEAL team leader was lying on the rough deck beneath the boat's sailcloth, but sleeping soundly, deep in a dream. He was home, sitting on his couch with Li Min by his side and little Tom happily bouncing on his knee. Li Min was just telling him to be less rough with the boy, that he was not one of his rough-and-tumble SEAL team members. At least not yet.

But the dream evaporated in an instant with Hurt's loud warning. Ward sat upright and peeked out over the gunwale. There, out on the southern horizon, a blip was just visible. A small ship. Quickly heading their way.

Hurt mumbled as he watched through his binoculars. "Don't recognize it, but it's certainly a warship."

Ward shielded his eyes from the afternoon sun and squinted to better see the fast-approaching vessel. "Yep, looks like a gunboat of some sort," he agreed. "I can see a gun mount forward. These waters, the chances he's friendly are slim. *Gato* still around somewhere close?"

Hurt pointed with a thumb, back over his shoulder to the north. "Last time I saw her periscope was up that way, maybe half an hour ago. Surely, she's still here and didn't go out for pizza."

The gunboat was fast approaching. A wave rose high on either side of its knife-sharp bow as it sliced through the water. She had, as the old submariners would say, a bone in her teeth.

Then the boat abruptly slowed. They could easily hear the change in the pitch of her engines. The forward gun mount slewed around ominously, until it was pointed directly at the little fishing boat.

"Jesus," Hurt said. "He's not just gonna start..."

The gun spat once. A geyser of water popped up only a few yards ahead of the boat, and then just as abruptly collapsed back into the sea.

"That son of a bitch is shooting at us!" Hurt growled.

The gun sent another projectile their way. This time the column of water was directly alongside the fishing boat. Close enough the water drenched everyone on the deck.

"He's found the range!" Ward shouted. "Everybody over the side before he turns this thing into matchsticks."

Bill Langley and his two roustabouts did not need a second invitation. They immediately dove into the crystal-clear water. Billy Joe Hurt and Tony Martinelli were only a split second slower. Chuck Jones roughly shoved Amr over the side, then followed the boy into the water. Gene LaCroix reached down into the bilge, yanked Li Chung Sheng up by his collar and, in one continuous motion, tossed the Chinese diplomat over the side. Joe Dumkowski did the same with Ali Hakim Sherif before the two SEALs left the boat behind them.

Jim Ward looked around to make sure everyone had gotten off the vessel. Suddenly, he felt a blast of heat on his face and had the sensation of being flung high into the air. Then, before he fell back into the sea, his world went dark.

Billy Joe Hurt had swum only a few yards away from the boat when he looked back to make sure everyone was overboard. He saw the boat take the hit, the explosion turning it into little more than flying kindling. What little remained of the wreckage burned furiously, sending a column of smoke high into the air.

He also saw a person being flung surprisingly high into the air, coming down only a few feet from where he floated. Hurt swam the few strokes over to where the man—obviously one of his SEAL brothers—now floated face down.

He flipped him over. Jim Ward. Hurt felt for a pulse. There was one but it was very weak and reedy. The CO could be badly hurt. He needed medical attention quickly.

There was no one around to help. And the people shooting at them were now coming closer, most likely so they could admire their handiwork and finish off any survivors.

With Ward down, Hurt was CO. But for the life of him, at that moment he knew nothing else they could do.

Nothing but tread water and hope that sub could come to their aid.

26

The *Gato* steamed about a mile north of Jim Ward's fishing boat, back at periscope depth in a so-far empty sea. It was still two hours until nightfall. These waters were far too dangerous to surface the big submarine and pick up the SEAL team in broad daylight. All the bad guys had satellites parked above the Med and would immediately know something was up. Besides, there appeared to be little ship traffic in the area right now, so the safe, conservative method was the best one. That meant there was little for them to do but watch and wait for darkness at this watery bus stop.

"New sonar contact, designate Sierra One-Four-Seven," Jed Durham abruptly called out, destroying the quiet hum of the control room. "High-speed screws, bearing one-seven-nine. Sounds like a fast patrol craft of some kind. And she's headed for the fishing boat."

Henrietta Foster slewed the photonics camera around and stared down that bearing. With the camera at maximum magnification, she could see the warship on the command monitor. And then make out the flag the vessel flew. The bright red background, crescent moon, and star of the flag of the Ottoman Empire. The one recently adopted by the former nation of Libya.

"That chopper must've called in somebody to investigate," Foster deduced.

Whatever this vessel was, it certainly was making directly for the fishing boat. That could not be a good thing. Then she saw flames and smoke erupt from the little warship's forward gun.

"The bastard is shooting at the SEALs!" Foster shouted. "Snapshot with the Harpoon in tube three, Sierra One-Four-Seven. Bearings-only launch."

The Harpoon anti-ship cruise missile was the ideal weapon for this particular situation. The fast patrol craft was too small and had too shallow a draft for the Mark 48 ADCAP torpedo to be effective. And the missile would attack at 0.7 Mach. That would quickly stop the gunboat's attack. Foster could only hope they could get it out and on its way in time to save the guys on the fishing boat.

Jim Sanson's fingers danced across the fire control panel as he brought the Harpoon up on-line and fed it the target information. It took only a few seconds before he called out, "Weapon ready."

Foster ordered, "Shoot tube three."

The silvery aluminum Harpoon cannister in tube three was impulsed out to float up to the surface. As soon as the sensor probe on the front of the cannister sensed air, the lid on the front blew off. A rocket booster carried the little cruise missile fifteen hundred feet up into the air above the Med before it burned out and fell away. The turbojet engine ignited and shoved the missile forward. Its radar sensor energized, looking for any target in its path. It almost immediately detected the fast patrol craft on the bearing that it had been provided. The missile dropped down until it was only a few feet above the water and raced off in that direction. It slammed into the side of the boat, penetrating almost to the engine room. Only then did its 220-kilogram warhead explode. The remaining fuel in the missile detonated in a massive secondary explosion. The gunboat was gutted, nothing but a burning hulk, its remains slowly sinking below the surface.

Foster watched the gunboat explode and disappear. She also now knew the Libyan patrol boat had struck the fishing boat with its last salvo. She ordered, "Let's get over to the fishing boat and search for survivors before the Second Regency sends out another welcome committee. Steer course one-eight-zero, ahead one third. Prepare to surface."

Eric Householder looked hard at her.

She answered his unasked question. "XO, there are folks up there who may be injured. We ain't got time to wait until dark. Get the COB and the man-overboard party ready to go topside. Have Doc set up to handle multiple casualties."

Householder nodded and replied, "Yes, ma'am!"

Ψ

It took almost half an hour to search the area and pull the SEAL party and their young fisherman host out of the water. Billy Joe Hurt carefully handed Jim Ward's inert body up to Jesus Cortez, imploring, "He's hurt bad, COB. Take care of him."

Doc Halliday escorted the unconscious SEAL and the men carrying him down to the wardroom. The space was already set up as a combination emergency room/operating room, complete with operating room lights in the overhead, the wardroom table converted to an operating table, and the buffet loaded with instruments and monitoring equipment.

Halliday did an immediate assessment of Jim Ward and quickly determined that he was in over his head. He did not have the training or experience to do much for the badly injured Ward, not even the equipment to figure out how badly injured he was. All he could do was stabilize his patient for now. For the SEAL team leader to have the best chance to survive, he needed immediate care from a major trauma center. The nearest one was in Alexandria, Egypt, almost two hundred nautical miles away.

Foster pointed the *Gato* toward Alexandria and rang up "Ahead Flank." Then she called Jerry Baudsley on the *Harold A. Stanton*. He was a hundred nautical miles away and still towing the damaged submarine toward Alexandria. The destroyer's MH-60R helo was airborne, with the ship's corpsman, within fifteen minutes. With a maximum speed of 180 knots, the bird was overhead of the *Gato* in just less than an hour.

The sun was settling in the west as Jim Ward was wheeled into the trauma center operating theater of the Egyptian Armed Forces Medical Complex.

EPILOGUE

Jim Ward struggled to try to sit up enough to get a look out the window. He only wanted to catch a glimpse of bright blue sky and maybe some green grass. It had been a long time since he had seen green grass. It still hurt mightily when he sought to move, though. Then again, it hurt like hell not to move.

Truth was it just hurt.

A passenger jet, probably heading into Reagan National Airport, was coursing across the very top of what made up his limited view out the window. Other than that, all he could make out was the sky and a few scudding clouds. It looked like it would be a great day for a run. Or a swim. But from his hospital bed eight floors up in Walter Reed National Military Medical Center, he was much too high to see anything else.

Anyway, the wounded SEAL had been awake enough already—since he arrived here and before, on the long, torturous journey from Egypt—to know that he had been badly injured. And that all the tubes and wires connecting him to the blinking machines and IV bags above his head would make any movement next to impossible.

As it was, the slight movement just to try to check out the view from the window had triggered some alarm somewhere. The light above the open door out to the ICU desk was blinking rapidly and electronic bells were bleating somewhere out there.

Jesus, he thought, *hope I didn't break anything they'll make me pay for!*

The large glass door slid noiselessly back as the head ICU nurse trotted into Ward's room, a concerned look on her face. Then she saw the wounded, bandaged SEAL sitting up in bed with just the hint of a wry smile on his face, a pair of leads dangling uselessly from where they had become detached from the sensors stuck to his shaved chest.

"Damn it, Commander!" she remonstrated, but was unable to suppress a smile. "How many times do I have to tell you? You want something, push the call button. And we'll help you move, if that's what you want. You pull a probe or sensor, all hell breaks loose and we figure you're dying in here. You SEALs! Thinking you're invincible!"

"Well, of course we are and—" Ward started, but the nurse cut him off with an upheld hand.

"If you aren't careful, you'll be back in surgery again. But the docs are running out of places where they can sew you up. You're mostly surgical glue and scar tissue right now." She helped Ward settle back amid his stack of pillows and then said, "By the way, you up for company? You got some visitors been waiting outside to see your miserable ass, for some reason."

"Can you get me some water," he croaked, "and then send them in?"

He knew who those visitors likely were, and he was way beyond ready to see them. He was gratefully sipping water through a straw when most of the Ward family paraded in. His mother, Ellen Ward, pushed his dad, Jon, in his wheelchair. With his gunshot wound still healing, Walter Reed would only allow Admiral Ward to leave his room by that means of mobility.

Li Min was only a step behind, her smile adding to the room's bright light. She moved to kiss Jim innocently, chastely, on the forehead. Jim tried to reach out for her, to pull her closer, but that damned alarm immediately started to bleat again. And he started to ache in places he had not yet felt pain. He smiled sheepishly and dropped his hand just as the nurse returned to scowl at him, reattach the probe, and then turn to go reset the noisemaker. Li Min cautiously settled down on the bed next to him, took his hand, and clearly had no intentions of letting it go.

"How you feeling, son?" Jon Ward asked.

"Like I got hit by a bus and then run over by a bulldozer just before the fire ants attacked," Jim Ward answered. "From what the docs tell me, though, I guess I'm lucky to be above room temperature."

"Yeah. You know you were swimming mighty close to exploding ordnance," Jon Ward replied. "Didn't they teach you guys to duck at BUD/S training?"

"Guess I was absent that day. But how are you?"

"Fine as frog hair, if these women would quit fussing at me every time I move."

"I know the feeling," Jim replied. "I burp and it sets off alarms all over the state of Maryland. Don't guess you can tell me how you really came to get yourself shot, huh?"

"You know I can't. We're sticking to the street crime story 'til Gabriel blows his horn."

Ellen Ward turned the conversation serious. "Doctors are telling us that you will be in here for several months before we can take you home, Jim. Then you'll be having a lot of physical therapy and rehabilitation before you are anywhere near back to normal."

"Yeah, Mom," Jim Ward said. "Been down that path a couple of times already, you know. Remember that incident when—"

Li Min cut him short this time. "But this is different. You have a family to worry about. I want you around to help raise that son of ours. Mom and I have been talking."

Ellen Ward looked at her son, the concern obvious in her eyes. "Jim, the doctor cornered us just before we came in. He wanted us to promise not to talk to you about this just yet, but I wouldn't. Li Min and your dad agreed we discuss it right now. You need to know straight up that the medical staff is recommending a medical retirement from the Navy with full disability." She paused and swallowed hard. "The lead doc says their prognosis is that you might not be able to walk again." Ellen worked to keep her composure as she went on. "Even if you do, it's going to take a lot of effort and a long time."

Jim Ward hesitated only a few seconds. "I can do that. And I will walk again. Run and swim, too. Young Tom and I got some wrestling to do. You all know that, right?"

"That's why we wanted you to know what you're facing now," Li Min told him. Ellen and Jon nodded. "So you know you don't have to rush to get back to work saving the world. So you know what's ahead of you. So you'll know we're here for you all the way, regardless."

"But know that your SEAL duty is over and done with," Ellen said. "Dad had to face reality the day he left submarines. You've known since you left home for the Academy that the day would come when you would have to step down. We think it's time that both the Ward men retired from active duty and tried to live life more like normal people do."

"Let me think about it, Mom, Li Min," Jim Ward replied. "I probably don't have any choice. But understand, people like Dad and I are not normal people."

"No, we're not," Jon Ward added. "No, we're certainly not."

Ψ

President Sandra Dosetti rose from behind the Resolute Desk and stepped over to greet Secretary of Defense John Dingham and Vice President Sebastien Aldo as they entered the Oval Office. She waved them toward the couch and settee that sat facing the fireplace at the office's north end. She need not have bothered. Each man knew his place. Portraits of five former Presidents looked down on them from above the mantle, observing the proceedings.

"Gentlemen, I called you here to discuss the end game in the Libyan matter," Dosetti said as she sat in one of the leather wingback chairs. "As you know, we turned Ali Hakim Sherif over to the International Criminal Court with charges of crimes against humanity along with a bushel of evidence thanks to a very valuable source."

"But we aren't a signatory nation to the ICC," Aldo said. "How does that work?"

"Almost all of Europe is and Egypt just became a signatory," Dosetti answered. "They are actually bringing the charges. We just turned him over to

ICC custody. We may get involved in sending people to testify in the proceedings, but we won't be a party. Our folks say just ordering the seizure of the oil field and workers and shooting down all those Egyptian aircraft is enough to put this self-declared emperor away. And Egypt has stature and plenty of motivation to bring criminal charges if the ICC fails to do the right thing."

"That's smooth," Aldo agreed. "They should lock him up for a very long time. Out of our hair, for sure. What about that Chinese diplomat that Ward brought back?"

"I spoke with Tan Yong this morning," President Dosetti answered. "He agrees that Li Chung Sheng's actions in Libya were way beyond normal diplomatic mandate. To avoid further embarrassment for the People's Republic, and to keep quiet a lot of the details about the submarines and other toys he sent to Libya, he has agreed to remove all Chinese military aid to the country as of today."

"Yeah, read that as 'embarrassment to Tan Yong' rather than China," Dingham said with a snort. "That snake really needs to save face now that this whole mess went sideways on him. I'm betting that this Li Chung Sheng character goes back to China and disappears, never to be heard from again."

Aldo asked, "Is that a bad thing?"

"Not really," the SecDef answered bluntly. "He won't be helping anybody take aim and shoot at American boys and girls anymore."

"Well, the UN is sending in a peace-keeping force, with the backing of NATO, to maintain order in Libya until they can schedule something close to legitimate elections," Dosetti went on. "I never did trust those blue helmets to do much of anything, but it's not our fight. We're going to sit back and let the Mediterranean nations solve their own problem on this one. That's a whole lot easier now that the Egyptians have pushed back to their original borders and have enough oil to pay for everything."

"I had forgotten about all that oil," Secretary Dingham said. "Bet Egypt and the rest of the region hasn't. That find, it's got to be the great equalizer in the Middle East. Egypt will have more skin in the game than anybody else. Competition is a great thing. Especially when the guy with all that black gold is a friend of ours."

"Friend for now, anyway. In this world, nothing is forever," the President said. She glanced up at the portraits of the former Chief Executives of the USA.

None of them were smiling. Dosetti almost imagined she had seen Abraham Lincoln nodding in agreement.

Ψ

Bill Langley kicked back in his chair and took a deep swig of his Sakara beer. He sighed contentedly as he watched the condensate trickle down the sides of the green and gold bottle. He glanced out the window of his office trailer to see a bustling hive of activity. Ever since they had hit oil with that first exploratory well, then survived the takeover from the Libyans, Langley's company had been struggling mightily to map the full extent of the find while also bringing production online. To say the pace was frenetic was an understatement, but the prospects of this being a record-breaker were now even more likely. Even so, the investors wanted more, and they wanted it sooner. More production, more discovery, more profits. Langley understood. Oil speculation was a risky business. He would work 24/7 to make them happy.

Langley's cell phone buzzed, interrupting his reverie. It had to be the piping contactor up in Abu Minqar with a new set of excuses, pleading for more time to fill a massive order.

Langley took another swallow of the golden brew before he answered the call.

"Mustapha, what's your excuse this time? You got what I need or don't you?"

There was only a slight hum on the line for a long moment, then, "That's hardly the way to speak with your principal investor, Bill." Magnus Rosenblatt's Bronx/Middle European accent was unmistakable.

"Sorry, sir. I've lost my patience with some of these suppliers is all."

"Well, Mr. Langley, if you are going to be the head of a major energy company, we need to work on your presentation and communication skills."

"Mr. Rosenblatt, I'm truly sorry," Langley stammered. "I was expecting a call about a late delivery of pipe and... Wait. What's that?"

Rosenblatt laughed. "Be that as it may, I need the CEO of the newly formed Rosenblatt-Langley Energy to be here in New York by Friday to meet with our shareholders. We've been looking over those ideas you sent over and we think we can structure this new company in a way that we can get moving on some of them right away. We need you to be in charge. I suggest you turn the day-to-day stuff over to the best man from your staff and catch the next flight over here."

Bill Langley gulped. Then he laughed. "Just one suggestion, Mr. Rosenblatt."

"Sure. But you can call me Magnus. All my partners do."

"Okay...Magnus. I like the ring of Langley-Rosenblatt Energy better."

Ψ

It was a crisp December morning. A light breeze rippled the chilly waters of the Severn River and chased the last of the oak leaves across Radford Terrace. The VIP parking area in front of Dahlgren Hall was filled with official cars, most of them bearing little stickers with multiple stars indicating high military rank. There had been so many positive responses to the invitations to the day's events that the US Naval Academy parking lots were all full. Those in charge had resorted to opening satellite parking at the Navy-Marine Memorial Stadium parking lot with buses shuttling in attendees. Clearly, a sizeable contingent from the US Navy was gathering to say goodbye and thank you to a pair of its leaders.

The Ward family sat waiting in a roped-off space on the second-deck gallery of Dahlgren Hall, the old Academy armory. The Ward ladies were dressed as if they were attending an afternoon tea, complete with white gloves. The two Ward men were in dress uniforms with medals attached and swords at their sides.

Ellen Ward turned to Jon and asked, "You ready for this?"

Jon answered, "It's time. Guess I'd better be ready."

Carefully balancing himself with the walking cane that his doctor had prescribed, the elder Ward walked with Ellen and Li Min down to the main level. Then he stood with the official party at the back of the huge open room while the ladies were escorted to their seats up front.

Jim Ward, restricted to a wheelchair, used the elevator to go down and join the official party.

Vice President Sebastien Aldo pulled the two Ward men aside before they all progressed up to the stage. "Jon, Jim, President Dosetti asked me to pass on to you her highest appreciation and thank you for what you have done for your country. She wanted you to know she would be here herself, but she didn't want to draw unwarranted attention on what should be your day of celebration. But she does want to discuss possible new positions for both of you. She feels strongly that the nation can use men with your talents, experience, and sources. Take some time off, rest, and get healthy. We'll give you a call to set up for you to come over to the White House when you're ready." He shook each Ward's hand and said a sincere, "Thank you for your service."

A brass quintet from the US Navy Band began to play patriotic tunes and marches. It was a signal that the ceremonies had officially begun.

The proceedings offered all the pomp and circumstance, gun salutes, ruffles and flourishes, and "side boys" that tradition demanded for the occasion. Well-rehearsed orators stood at the podium and recited "Old Glory" and "The Watch." Bouquets of flowers were presented to Ellen and Li Min for their roles as Navy Wives. The guest speakers lauded both Wards' years of valuable service to their country and wished them "Fair winds and following seas."

Jim and Jon Ward looked out over the large audience, finding friends and family seated among the many guests. Admiral Tom Donnegan, "Papa Tom" to the family, sat next to Ellen. Bill Beaman was there, too, just up from his Bahamas bar and likely wearing a suit—and socks and shoes—for the first time in at least a decade. TJ Dillon winked at the younger Ward and gave him a thumbs-up. Commander Henrietta Foster, seated next to her XO on the *Gato*, smiled the entire time. And then there was row after row of former wardroom and crew and assistants from the Wards' submarine, SEAL, and Pentagon days. Many were retired. Some were still on active duty.

Jon Ward subtly nudged his son and whispered, "This a retirement ceremony or a funeral?"

"Not sure, Admiral. Not sure," Jim replied with a grin.

When it came time for each of them to speak, they primarily directed their comments to the midshipmen and junior officers seated in front of them, the men and women whose Navy voyage was only beginning.

Finally, it was time for a longstanding naval tradition, for the sailors to be "piped ashore" for the last time. Jon Ward, as the more senior, was the first to go "ashore." At the words "Admiral, United States Navy, retired, departing," and the shrill call of the bosun's pipe, Ward, with his cane rhythmically tapping the hard wood floor, marched between the ranks of the eight side boys. Joe Glass and Brian Edwards were the last two in line.

It was all SEALs who lined up to render the honors for Jim Ward. He sat up as straight as he could manage in his wheelchair as he waited. "Commander, United States Navy, retired, departing," the master of ceremonies announced and, again, the bosun's pipe called out.

Ward started to wheel himself down between the waiting side boys. But then he stopped and firmly said, loud enough for everyone in the hall to hear, "To hell with this! I walked into this man's Navy and I sure as hell intend to walk ashore."

The crowd was standing already, watching him, but now many of them were forced to hold back the tears as the injured SEAL, calling upon pure force of will, painfully pushed himself to his feet and somehow found his balance.

Those nearby could see his face go pale. The look on his face said that he was in agony. Li Min gasped. Ellen Ward put one hand over her mouth and gripped her daughter-in-law's hand with the other.

Then Jim's right hand went to his brow in a rigid salute. He took an unsteady step forward. Then more, all on his own. Six of them, as everyone in the packed auditorium watched and pulled for him. Though it took him a while, those six slow steps eventually carried him past the SEAL side boys who were standing there to honor him.

Senior Chief Billy Joe Hurt was the last SEAL in the left-hand line. When Ward managed that final step past him, Hurt grabbed his CO's arm.

"Skipper," Hurt said quietly. "I got ya. Always."

Argentia Station
The Tides of War Book 1

On the eve of WWII, a group of submariners brace against the tides of the gathering storm.

In the spring of 1939, four young, untested Ensigns emerge from the unforgiving halls of Annapolis and the US Navy's Submarine School, ready to enter the Silent Service. Alistair, the privileged son and playboy; Fred, the underestimated athlete; Stan, the farm boy with big dreams; and Brad, the admiral's wayward child. Drawn from vastly different worlds, they forge a bond stronger than steel as they prepare for the dangerous battles ahead.

Stationed in the cold, unforgiving waters of the North Atlantic at the secret Argentia base in Newfoundland, Canada, the men are tasked with a prewar mission few will ever know: supporting Britain's struggle against the German U-boats. With outdated equipment, overly cautious commanders, and whispers of sabotage, they navigate the treacherous ocean and freezing conditions to hunt an enemy beneath the waves.

And as the shadow of war stretches closer, and a German plot to dramatically disrupt the course of the approaching conflict comes to light, they begin to suspect that their mission is far more risky—and much more pivotal—any of them could ever have imagined.

ABOUT GEORGE WALLACE

Commander George Wallace retired to the civilian business world in 1995, after twenty-two years of service on nuclear submarines. He served on two of Admiral Rickover's famous "Forty One for Freedom", the USS John Adams SSBN 620 and the USS Woodrow Wilson SSBN 624, during which time he made nine one-hundred-day deterrent patrols through the height of the Cold War.

Commander Wallace served as Executive Officer on the Sturgeon class nuclear attack submarine USS Spadefish, SSN 668. Spadefish and all her sisters were decommissioned during the downsizings that occurred in the 1990's. The passing of that great ship served as the inspiration for "Final Bearing."

Commander Wallace commanded the Los Angeles class nuclear attack submarine USS Houston, SSN 713 from February 1990 to August 1992. During this tour of duty that he worked extensively with the SEAL community developing SEAL/submarine tactics. Under Commander Wallace, the Houston was awarded the CIA Meritorious Unit Citation.

Commander Wallace lives with his wife, Penny, in Alexandria, Virginia.

Sign up for Wallace and Keith's newsletter at
severnriverbooks.com

ABOUT DON KEITH

Don Keith is a native Alabamian and attended the University of Alabama where he received his degree in broadcast and film. He has received awards from the Associated Press and United Press International for newswriting and reporting. He is also the only person to be named Billboard Magazine "Radio Personality of the Year" in two formats, country and contemporary. Keith was a broadcast personality for over twenty years, owned his own consultancy, co-owned a Mobile, Alabama, radio station, and hosted and produced several nationally syndicated radio shows.

His first novel, "The Forever Season." received the Alabama Library Association's "Fiction of the Year" award. Keith has written extensively on historical subjects including World War II, submarine warfare, and fiction, biographies, and non-fiction works on a variety of subjects. He has published more than forty books, two of which—HUNTER KILLER and COLORS OF CHARACTER—have been adapted for the screen.

Mr. Keith lives with his wife, Charlene, in Indian Springs Village, Alabama.

Sign up for Wallace and Keith's newsletter at
severnriverbooks.com

ABOUT DON KEITH

Sign up for Don Keith's author newsletter at
severnriverbooks.com

Printed in the United States
by Baker & Taylor Publisher Services